MODEL ACTRESS WHATEVER

KIM NEWMAN

TITAN BOOKS

Model Actress Whatever
Print edition ISBN: 9781803366678
E-book edition ISBN: 9781803366685

Published by Titan Books
A division of Titan Publishing Group Ltd
144 Southwark Street, London SE1 0UP
www.titanbooks.com

First edition: May 2026
10 9 8 7 6 5 4 3 2 1

This is a work of fiction. All of the characters, organizations, and events portrayed in this novel are either products of the author's imagination or are used fictitiously. Any resemblance to actual persons, living or dead (except for satirical purposes), is entirely coincidental.

A CIP catalogue record for this title is available from the British Library.

EU RP (for authorities only)
eucomply OÜ, Pärnu mnt. 139b-14, 11317 Tallinn, Estonia
hello@eucompliancepartner.com, +3375690241

Designed and typeset in Arno Pro by Richard Mason.

Printed and bound by CPI Group (UK) Ltd, Croydon, CR0 4YY.

'John Lennon, George Harrison, Paul McCartney and Ringo Starr are mutants. Evolutionary agents sent by gods, endowed with mysterious powers to create a new human species.'

– Timothy Leary

'A Guide is honest, reliable and can be trusted.
A Guide is helpful and uses her time and abilities wisely.
A Guide faces challenges and learns from her experiences.
A Guide is a good friend and sister to all Guides.
A Guide is polite and considerate.
A Guide respects all living things and takes care of the world around her.'

– The Guide Law

'Look! Up in the sky...'

– Allen Ducovny and Robert Joffe Maxwell

For Yung

'With most music – songs, singles, LPs, symphonies, whatever – the question is "what did you feel when you first heard...?" or "where and when did you first hear...?" *With Never Mind* – strictly, it's called *Never Mind The Beatles* – the question is "what *happened* when you first heard...?" The answer is "everything."'

– DAEVE POPE,
NEVER MIND: THE MOMENT

'Did we know what we were doing? Of course not. Who could have known? Not you, pal, that's for certain. Maybe Arthur C. Clarke or T. Lobsang Rampa. But I have me doubts.'

– JOHN LENNON

'That noise when the needle settled in the groove. The omni-chord. THWANNNGGG! Made everything in the room rattle. I swear the girl in the poster on the wall winked. It was a resounding THWANNNGGG. I don't believe the chord ever ends. That room's still all a-judder and they knocked down those flats twenty years ago. It was all about the THWANNNGGG. I couldn't tell you what else was on *Never Mind* after that. But I can tell you *what it did...*'

– PROFESSOR CHRISTINA TEMPLE

'Our Deanie went up to her room to put the record on the Dansette – we were watching the wrestling in the front room so the big gramophone was off-limits – and came back down again a half hour later... *enlightened*. Scorched the wallpaper. Then Deanie opened a door we hadn't known was there – behind the Welsh dresser or in the Welsh dresser, it wasn't clear – and invited her friends through... into the house, into Market Harborough as a whole. Her friends who never left. Deanie was the first *enlightened* in our street. We didn't know what to make of her. But she had an idea about what to make us. We went up to her room in ones and twos... and listened to *Never Mind*. Some got *enlightened*, some not, some went halfway. A school pen in my top pocket has never run out. If I write something with it in an exercise book it comes true... though I learned quick to be careful. I'm not enlightened but my pen is. Deanie and Her Friends turned out all right. Except for the Squirrel, and I scribbled something to fix that perisher. They all live in the Forest of Birmingham now, the City As Was.'

– BRENDA COLFORTH, DUCHESS OF LATIMER CRESCENT

'We never had them before that bloody record. Not here. Not in England. What do you want to call them? Cloaks and cutthroats. Heroes and villains? Enlightened, my Aunt Fanny. Show-offs, if you ask me. Not heroes like we had in the War. Which war? Any war. If the blighters are so high and mighty, why do so many wear masks? Devil's Dyke's too good for 'em. Shoot 'em down, lock 'em up and good riddance!'

– DANIEL KEOUGH

ACT ONE:
'INTRODUCING THE ALL-NEW LADY SHADE'

CHRISTINE ON CALL

'IF I'D WANTED TO SLAP SMILES ON DEAD FACES,' Loulee told her, 'I'd have become a mortuary maid. Or set up shop in Highgate Village.'

Chrissie protested that she hadn't been up all hours again.

Loulee didn't believe her. Chrissie knew she wouldn't but had to give it a go. The Cattle Car was almost deffo wired for sound.

'Well, I *was* awake,' Chrissie admitted. 'But not on the Circuit. Except for Vidar's Thing and a look-in at Fakers. Honest, I hopped straight on the night bus. I had homework. I've scads of verbal this week. Feeding Nelly the "story so far". Besides you know I don't sleep.'

'Not so much at night,' said Loulee, working around Chrissie's eyes with a soft brush. 'But you nodded off in the chair. You've dribbled on the bib. I took a click on my Vone. Popped it on Peophole. Surge of eyes on your fizzog, girl.'

Panic clutched. Chrissie sat upright.

'You did not!'

'No, obviously. Though you'd have deserved it.'

Loulee was larking... but one grot click could prang a person before you could say 'Next Tuesday'. Snappers had been done over for leaking unflattering images.

She was at Loulee's mercy in the Cattle Car, Rediffusion-Televersion's make-up and wardrobe van for Supporting Regulars. Designed to be as space efficient as a moon lander, but now more cramped than cosy. Practical Effects Pete kept smuggling mystery boxes aboard. They were always under Loulee's feet or in the way of something she needed.

In comparison, Eleanor Wynter – leading lady of *Letsby Avenue* – took her ease in the Wynter Palace. Boxes delivered to that mansion on wheels were most likely gifts from Red-Tel management to keep the Empress of Early Evening sweet. Or from her adoring fans. Nelly's Nutters were a Spoke of the Wheel. To be worked around, like fog and writers' nervous breakdowns. The show must go out. Three nights a week, plus holiday specials and the annual panto.

The SR van was parked under a skyway flyover in Poplar while helper elves secured the location, a slow-flowing stretch of the Limehouse Cut. Passersby were told an advert for support socks was being filmed. Otherwise, civs would loiter and be a nuisance. Civs could be lied to, shooed away or shoved in a canal. Anything to get the day's pages crossed off.

Nelly rated tactful treatment and cossetting. She was a bright light, a banner client. Chrissie was lower down the ladder, a MAW.

Model Actress Whatever.

'The chair's so comfy,' said Chrissie, stretching. 'Did I really snooze?'

'You did. You make lovely tiny breathy snores.'

'I can't sleep when it's dark,' Chrissie admitted. 'It's new. Relatively. Ever since Mum and Dad set sail. I get a night-buzz. I don't need jabs, like Chell or Dr Crockery. Not even a late-evening mug of chee. In the dark, my skin pricks and I've ergs to burn. But I'm fagged out after sun-up.'

'*Peut-être* you're a vampire. Should *you* move to Highgate Village?'

'Can't afford it, Louls. Besides my canines are rounded. I can barely chomp the celery.'

She opened her mouth. Loulee was close enough to get a visual of her tonsils.

'Ugh, Chrissie, give a girl warning will you?'

She shut her gob.

Chrissie had a fractious relationship with celery. It was all Dr Zenf let her eat. The dietician was retained by the Schilling Agency. He insisted celery and distilled water – every three hours, day and night – was the optimal regimen for her body type. If she deviated by so much as a salted peanut, her figure would fill out. Not advantageous. So she nibbled like a rabbit to stay below the weight agreed in her contract. An ounce extra and she wouldn't even prang. She'd just be Gone. MAW no more.

No one wants to be Gone. Not on your eleanor they didn't.

Chrissie *had* been up all night. Not just learning her lines.

The Circuit was homework too. Chrissie had to do it at least as many nights a week as *Letsby* was on. Ideally, she needed to be seen at two parties, three clubs and a Thing. At least fifteen clicks and four clips. Clicks were still photos. Clips were moving pics. They fed the tabs, the swanks, Peophole and the Personals. Garnet Graill, her s.o., handled the visuals. Garn said s.o. stood for Significant Other but Chrissie told Loulee he really meant Sort Of. As a snapper, he was the business. Knew when to catch her spark. Chrissie didn't recognise herself as the gorgeous night creature in Garn's best clicks. That was someone else entirely. Daytime Chrissie, nodding off and dribbling, was the secret identity of the after-dark lovely.

She was a girl of many faces. Chrissie by night, Chrissie by day, Chrissie in a police hat, Chrissie on a treadmill (at Sunny Gym but generally too), Chrissie asleep, Chrissie on top of everything, Chrissie Chrissie Chrissie.

Loulee knew Chrissie's schedule as well as she did and wouldn't let her out in public unless she had a face on. If Loulee couldn't be there personally, she'd paint the inside of a gel mask which Chrissie could self-apply, let set, and peel off to turn grot to hot, switch dark for spark.

Christine Chambers and Louise Ling had been best friends since Introductory Assembly at Astelia Draycott's Academy for Young Ladies of Merit. Loulee – Chinese father, French mother, South-East London verbals – was a spark at seven. Chrissie – survivor of ill-advised elocution lessons which made her talk like a posh weasel – was more a light-under-a-bushel girl, if the bushel were in a windowless basement where the power was out. They came through the flames together when the Academy burned down thanks to Eunice Uglow, a prematurely enlightened young lady of merit. Pyro Pixie got sent to Devil's Dyke Secure Hospital, kept away from dry kindling. The Academy reopened when Conjure Man imported an unsinged version of the building from Parallel Pimlico but the halls whiffed of firelighter for ever after.

Nine years later...

Chrissie decided to spend her gap year as a MAW. Loulee signed on as helper elf. Besides maintaining Chrissie's face, Loulee advised on clothes. Even the hopeless blue serge sack she wore on *Letsby*. Loulee nipped, tucked and fidgeted with the uniform to make it almost acceptable. She had a magic touch.

They were seventeen months into that gap year. So it was a gap maybe two-or-three years. Chrissie was clickable and clippable. She was in the tabs and on the telly. Loulee, who Knew Things, said Chrissie would be a bright light. For now, she was a face but not a name.

And she was tired in the day but awake at night.

Loulee was always good with facework but her other talents came and went. She could be extraordinarily skilled at something – flower-arranging, rock-climbing, mental gymnastics – for a week or so, then move on and be exceptionally good at something else for an equally limited engagement. It was a mystery.

'Lips or not?'

Lips would be good for Chrissie. Her own were so pale some clicks made her look mouthless. WPC 'Perky' Purkiss, her character on the serial, was supposed to be chirpy-chirpy not cheep-cheep.

'Go on then,' said Chrissie, as Loulee selected a rose petal stick. 'But not so much Nelly kicks off.'

No one within a hundred feet of Eleanor Wynter could Look Like Anything – or else there'd be Issues. The bright light had been delighted with her previous WPC, a Muslim who wore full veil. Then fan natters on the Personals started rhapsodising about 'Sparkling Eyes' and there were Issues. One week, Sparkling Eyes had to wear cataract glasses. Next, she was Gone.

Loulee got close again, applying the light touch of an artist.

Chrissie's spark was one-fifth nature, one fifth agonising diet/health regime and the rest Loulee. If it weren't for the magic brushes, Chrissie wouldn't be rising on the Wheel. A fan natter had sprung up but it was called 'Pervs for Perky'.

'You've got glit on you,' said Loulee. 'Not from last night. Three-day old glit.'

Loulee made deductions from layers of make-up the way a police surgeon could tell how long someone'd been dead by the size of the maggots in the wounds. The glit was from Saturday Last, when Chrissie did the Full Circuit. Garn tailed her, of course, clicking and clipping. The Coterie were out in force. Polly O, Vidar, Chell, Dr Crockery, Hereward, Symon, the All-Powerful Jupiter Boy and Monica Maude.

The glit was from The Sparkler, who inhabited a micro-climate of the stuff. The cloak latched onto the Coterie at an Airship-Naming Ceremony on the Marble Arch Mound. Things escalated at the Spot Hot, where there was a takeover by Shock Jock and the Cuckoo – who got through most of their set before armed resistance swept them from the decks. The Sparkler took the credit for that counter-coup. There were clips to prove it. Shock Jock and the Cuckoo were bound over to keep the peace, which wouldn't stop them reoffending at Fakers or Marzipam next weekend.

'I'm going to need special equipment to hoover your cracks and crevasses,' Loulee said.

'It was The Sparkler.'

Loulee made a face.

'The Sparkler is barely a cloak,' she said. 'He's not enlightened. His Dad bought him the glittergun from Bernini's Outfitters. He's verps.'

She got Loulee's drift. Verps. Very Rich Parents.

Her friend always had the goss.

Helper elves keep the Wheel turning. A girl needed face-witches, dressers, publicists, drivers, minders, shoppers, accountants and legal aid. Who swapped gen in the Support Staff natter on Whispers. That was always an educational peep. Not just for the goss on who was up or down on the Wheel and what they got up to when they thought no one had eyes on them. Bright lights should learn to treat elves kindly. Sabotage was always a possibility. The cause of many a prang.

'The sparkle will wear off The Sparkler by Next Tuesday but his bleedin' glit is going to be turning up after he's good and Gone.'

Next Tuesday was what a MAW dreaded. When your number came up.

It wasn't literally next Tuesday. For many, it was sooner.

Chrissie shuddered for the many. Names everyone forgot or deliberately got wrong. The Gone no longer came up on the Hawkshaw Information Retrieval Service. Were they behind a counter at a Lyons Cyber House? Or rivet-punching in a bootworks in Barnsley? No one cared to know.

The Gone were just not on the Circuit anymore.

Roman gladiators had longer term career prospects than a MAW. But you had to not believe that.

Chrissie certainly didn't. She was here for a goodly spell.

Way past Next Tuesday. Well into Next Week.

The Wheel lifted her up. She would be a bright light.

Loulee said so.

Chrissie's hair didn't need much work. When cast in *Letsby*, she had two-foot braids. Then Loulee devised 'the Perky Crop'. The Powers That Be at Red-Tel and the Schilling Agency hoped the cut would catch on. Clicks were leaked to high street hairdressers in the expectation many young women would demand a Perky Crop. They'd be more effective moving adverts for the serial than a platoon of sandwich-board men on unicycles.

The crop took some getting used to. Chrissie had a version of the phantom pain amputees feel in missing limbs. When she took a pew, she couldn't not do a ridiculous shuffle to avoid sitting on hair she no longer had. A trim every three days maintained the visual.

Initial response was positive. Then word came down via Anju the Assistant Director that Perky should keep her police hat on. A gentle note from the Schilling Agency suggested Chrissie wear headscarves when out and about. The paranoid might suspect measures were being taken to stop a person from Looking Like Anything within a hundred yards of Eleanor Wynter. Bods who'd enthused that the Perky Crop was majorly gear, happening and the next coiffure craze made sour faces if the subject came up. Loulee shaved a patch above Chrissie's right ear to differentiate the Chrissie Crop from the copyrighted Perky Crop so at least appearing hatless in public wasn't a contract violation. If flak got too thick, she'd find a wig.

Runner Ralf rapped on the van. Chrissie was wanted on set.

'We'll have her in support socks in no time at all,' Loulee told him.

Runner Ralf didn't bother to laugh. The hours Red-Tel had him on, he wouldn't have time to laugh till three months after his breakdown. When he started laughing, he wouldn't stop till they gave him a happy jab.

Letsby Avenue went out three evenings a week on Red-Tel One, between *Fun News* and *Real News*. Against Limited Interest Sport on the Other Side and a Clever Lecture on the Serious Channel. It was usually the most watched programme in its slot, unless a breaking story kept the Other Side's *Nova News* on after six. Red-Tel lacked the access to breaking stories the Other Side had through their tie-up with the Nova Newspaper Group. Mostly, that wasn't a concern. The Major League and the Splendid Six, the leading cloak groups of the US and UK, didn't join forces to battle the jet janissaries of GEIST in the sky over Bristol Spaceport every month. Even when that sort of scrap was on, loyal viewers saved the news clips for catch-up and watched *Letsby* live.

The serial had been running since 1985. It used to be called *Dosson of Dark Green* but the title changed after the theatrical knight who played kindly Sergeant Bert Dosson in the early years was caught fiddling his taxes and scarpered to Spain. Of the original cast, only Canteen Cathy and Viv the Spiv were still regulars. They'd lived whole careers on the programme.

Everyone on the Wheel had an early or late *Letsby* credit. It was a ritual to be hauled into the interview room of Dark Green Nick – a tiny standing set at Red-Tel's Cardinal Wolsey Street Studios on the Isle of Dogs – to help plods with their enquiries. You couldn't win a BAFTA unless you'd once stolen underpants from a washing line or had your prize racing pigeon nobbled on *Letsby*. Every pop singer Chrissie and Loulee fancied when they were eleven showed up one week for an identity parade.

The format was settled. Crime on Monday. Investigation on Wednesday. Solution on Friday. Often, not a very serious crime, not a very thorough investigation and a fudge of a solution by an incoming writer replacing an off-in-a-huff scribbler who'd left behind no notes on how the case was supposed to wrap up.

Most of the fan mail was viewers poking holes in the stories. The rest was requests for shorter uniform skirts. Loulee kept sending those in under made-up names. She was no fan of blue serge.

Chrissie had been on the serial five months. At first, WPC Purkiss was just supposed to look pretty, be cheerful and ask silly questions. Everyone liked a fresh face who wasn't too much bother so she was promoted to picking up the prop phone and relaying plot points to WDS Jill di Ferrante – the role tailored for the tsarina of six-to-six-thirty three days a week.

On a Monday, Perky typically had a bit to say. On Wednesdays, she popped in to summarise the day before for viewers who'd missed an episode. On Fridays, she was a background blur when di Ferrante brought the culprit to book or – if it was one of the soppy scripts – let them off because they didn't mean it. So far, the writers hadn't thought to give Purkiss a first name. 'Perky' was the note in the script beside her first line ('wotcher, guv?') in her debut episode.

Today was Monday. Actually, it was Tuesday but on the schedule as Monday (Out of Studio). The location day for episodes due to go out the week after next. No one liked to say 'This Tuesday' since it was close to the dreaded Next Tuesday. 'Monday (Out of Studio)' caught on and became the term for Tuesdays. Yesterday, Calendar Monday, was 'Monday (In Studio)' – a long shift in Cardinal Wolsey Street, taping all the studio scenes for the Next Monday But One episode. *Letsby* was stingy about location work. A day's filming spread across a week's story. Crime scene, a chase if necessary, and one of di Ferrante's poignant wanders through the implosion zone where her husband and boyfriend evaporised last year when the writers lost track of their storyline and threw in a Q Bomb to clear the clutter.

WPC Purkiss mostly sat at a desk to answer the prop phone. Whispers natterers joked that she might be a robot below the waist. So Chrissie had to wear minidresses on the Circuit. Every few days, the tabs ran 'yes, Perky *does* have legs' clicks of her freezing on a red carpet. Because most of her scenes were on the Dark Green Nick set, she was rarely on call for Monday (Out of Studio). This week was unusual. WDS Jill needed someone to find a dead body in a canal. Perky got the gig. It was going to be the seventh identical corpse of the late DI Trinidad di Ferrante. The post-implosion story was on its fourth writer with no solution in sight. Perky was to be queasy so WDS Jill could be understanding. Chrissie had not yet worked out how to be cheerful and queasy at the same time.

Loulee did something miraculous with Chrissie's eyelashes.

'There,' said Loulee, taking away the bib. 'Peach.'

Chrissie looked at herself in the big mirror.

The girl who smiled back wasn't a bright light.

Yet.

But she was a Spark.

Things were happening clip by clip, click by click. She was rising on the Wheel.

'Here's your hat,' said Loulee.

Perky's WPC cap had the proper chessboard band and V-II-R badge.

'Do you need the zappy clapper?' Loulee asked.

Practical Effects Pete had cadged a real stunglove for the prop armoury. Police surplus. It didn't hold much of a charge.

'Mr Hands isn't directing this week. It's Captain Floppy.'

Loulee gave her the prop stunglove instead of the real one.

A reminder flared on Chrissie's Vone. Without comment, Loulee opened the little fridge where she'd stashed Chrissie's baby bottle of distilled water and twist-tied polythene bag of diced celery. Also in the fridge was Loulee's bacon sandwich with extra bacon and extra bread. Chrissie knew which she'd prefer for breakfast, lunch or supper. It wasn't the celery. Grimly, she nibbled.

By the time Ralf ran back for her, she'd finished her three-hourly no-gain nutrition intake.

She climbed out of the Cattle Car.

'Show your spark,' said Loulee.

Chrissie made a lightning-casting gesture and giggled.

RICHARD JEPERSON

'GEIST WERE AN AXIS THINK TANK IN WORLD WAR Two. YUREI in Japan. OMBRE in Vichy France. A clearing house for crackpot visionaries, occult cranks, unworkable science. Unworkable, then. Perhaps later, not. After the War, the survivors found new sponsors. Established an international network of loosely connected, self-contained satrapies. Our side hired them as often as the other fellows did. The original mad profs and masterminds died years ago. None of their projects panned out. A hollow earth. Flying Swastikas. Undersea robot armies. Brains in Think Boxes. But the *idea* of GEIST persisted. Straggling satrapies stayed in business, pursuing diabolical stratagems with dwindling bands of expendable minions. They never really went away. Evil doesn't give up, it goes quiet.

'After the moment of *Never Mind,* so much was overturned. Miracles and wonders all around. So why do things still go wrong? GEIST, of course. A new generation. Spiritual heirs to the court magicians of the dictator states, brainstorming fresh threats for an age of enlightenment. A malign international conspiracy. A coalition of criminality. Sleeper agents in government and business. Gangs of power goons bred in jungle refuges. In plain sight on the front pages. But you have to read between the lines to make the connections, to see it's all one big threat.

'They are out to get you. To bring you low.

'GEIST sets nations at each other's throats, unleashes foot-and-mouth, sabotages industries, ruins crops, sours milk, wrecks marriages. It's global in scale and dedicated to spoiling your favourite things. The warlord who plans to wipe a country off the map. The boy in the lending library telling you who did it in the mystery you've just taken out. Agents of GEIST. The new owner of the football club you support who sells the centre forward to the Hotspurs and the efficiency expert advising a firm to discontinue the sandwich spread you like. GEIST. Anything goes wrong – blame GEIST. Frustrated – take the war to them, look for a scrap. Root out a satrapy disguised as the local stamp club. Easy, isn't it? Easier than understanding how much more complex the world becomes every year. Much easier, Dear Brutus, to see fault in the stars than in our selves.'

CHRISTINE ON SET

GREEN-YELLOW FOG ROLLED ALONG THE CANAL, NOT much above knee-height. The London Smudge was a pest on location days. It was forecast to thicken this evening. The shoot couldn't overrun.

As Ralf walked Chrissie along the towpath, she muttered her lines.

'It's another doppeldeader, guv. Fair makes the stomach turn.'

She was just about confident when Anju the AD gave her pink pages.

'New sides,' said Anju.

Anjulie Glas was a Power Behind the Throne by dint of hard labour and willingness to carry out instructions without hesitation. On set, Ass. Dir. was pronounced Arse Dur, as in Hard Bottom. Apt, since she was known for her hourglass figure and wasp waist. Anju's black swan wing bangs had dramatic dyed-in white streaks. Tinted Lennon Spex covered what being awake for sixty-two hours at a time across shooting days did to her eyes.

New sides meant more for Chrissie to learn. Eleanor Wynter hated names, places and dates important to the story. Muffing them meant pricey retakes. The solution was to offload such gubbins onto WPC Purkiss. If worst came to the worst, Chrissie could flip her notebook and read out plot points like a speak-your-weight machine.

Chrissie couldn't see any Perky lines on the pink pages.

This had happened before. Suddenly, despite doing the homework, she had nothing to say. The camera would be on Jill di Ferrante, looking at a corpse. The bright light was famous for running through her four expressions in succession.

Loulee's facework would be out of focus in long shots.

Anju got out of Chrissie's way but Practical Effects Pete held her up. He lugged a contraption which resembled a Hoover turned inside-out and fitted with a firehose nozzle.

A stretch of the Limehouse Cut had been taken over. Prop police tape marked the staged area by the canal. Location tape further back made an outer rim. Two divers in squeaky wetsuits sat on packing cases. Chrissie didn't know whether they were guest cast or safety providers.

The grass verge crackled with frost.

It was January, so the effect might have been real first thing. Hours after sunrise, it was spray-on and extended halfway up the wall.

Practical Effects Pete raised his contraption and splurged Chrissie's midriff with spun sugar. If any got in her mouth, months of celery and distilled water would go to waste.

'I'm not scenery,' she protested.

Pete and Anju looked at each other. Chrissie was suddenly queasier than the pre-pink pages demanded.

Anju held up a board with a multicoloured, annotated master script clipped to it. The AD was the only one on the production team with the whole equation of *Letsby* in her head.

'No, Perky, you're a prop,' she said.

Everyone called Chrissie by her character name on set. The credits rolled so quickly few learned who Christine Chambers was. Three out of four times, the tabs tagged her as 'Perky' in clicks. It was not the dream but whingeing was no earthly use.

Loulee jogged up with her portable kit. Ready for an argument.

'Anything sprayed on Chrissie and I'm doing the spraying,' she said.

'It's effects not make-up,' said Pete.

He had a bad case on Loulee. The only courtship display he was up to involved being contradictory while not looking her in the eye. And taking up van space with mystery boxes.

'My girl is talent,' said Loulee.

'Not on the pink sheets, she isn't.'

Anju showed Loulee the script.

'Ah,' said Loulee, not happy.

'What is it?' Chrissie asked.

She scanned the pink pages again and couldn't see any Perky lines. It was just Jill looking at...

... *not* a doppeldeader of her late husband.

The corpse of WPC Sandra Purkiss.

Sandra. Finally, a first name! Really finally.

Perky was to be killed. No, *had been* killed.

Case closed. Or, rather, case opened. Solution on Friday.

Loulee said things in Mandarin and French. Tone of voice made her meaning clear. She expressed a strong opinion. Ralf and Pete – helper elves themselves, essentially – couldn't publicly agree. Backchatter on Whispers would be less inhibited.

Chrissie couldn't complain. It was in her contract that she not complain. She wanted to be sick. How was that for acting? Perky was queasy.

Adrian Jah, aka Captain Floppy, was ten yards away, nodding as Eleanor Wynter talked up at him. The bright light stood on one of her Nelly Boxes but the director was still taller by four inches. For supposed asthma, Nelly wore a fog-mask with tinted goggles. A loudspeaker grille amplified her voice. She looked and sounded like an insect totem cutthroat. Lady Locust. Queen Wasp.

Jah saw Chrissie out of the corner of his eye and covered his face. He was not happy. He couldn't deal with complications while the afternoon evaporised. His purpose in life was that *Letsby* go out three times a week. This was the last location of a short day and they'd lose the light before teatime. Brutes were not in the budget.

Eleanor saw Chrissie approaching.

'She doesn't look dead enough,' said the bright light. 'Make her deader. She's been shot in the face with an icicle gun.'

Pete raised his sprayer. Loulee put her hand over the nozzle.

'Don't you dare,' she said.

Chrissie was already frozen inside.

This was the end. The prang of all prangs.

It was Sparkling Eyes all over again. Chrissie gloomily supposed the discontinued actress – whose name was lost to memory and Hawkshaw – would be glad of the company. Chrissie had shed no tears for her predecessor. Some other eager spark would answer the prop phone – unless Nelly had script input and decided a telepathic pot plant or a self-aware Squawk Box could do the job just as well.

Pete Two, Pete's assistant, was using an industrial size spun-sugar splurger to create a frosty nest between a jetty and a barge.

'Dial your agent,' said Loulee.

Yes, she should. But her arms hung limp.

'No dialling on set,' said Captain Floppy. 'Perky, if you please...'

He indicated the frost cradle. She was supposed to lie in it.

Eleanor made a gun gesture. Pete gave Chrissie fair warning to shut her mouth and eyes then sprayed her in the face. Spun sugar went up her nose. Ghost sweetness prickled the back of her throat.

Loulee punched Pete in the arm. He'd have a bruise.

'Perky, you've been frapped,' said the director. 'Could we have a fixed expression of shock and surprise, with a glint of recognition? Frozen cheerful. Never forget the perkiness. You knew your killer. That's an important beat for Friday's episode.'

Chrissie knew who her killer was all right.

Eleanor looked this way and that, unsatisfied. Perky still wasn't dead enough. Her head was on the right-way round. The neck should be broken so Chrissie would be chest up/face down. Captain Floppy cough-harrumphed. He understood how long it would take make-up and practical effects to fix a head-twisting.

Eleanor took off her fog mask and folded it away. The bright light didn't wear blue serge. Her outfits were Stán originals. She rated three costume changes every twenty-five minute episode. WDS Jill di Ferrante had been known to switch visuals in the middle of a chase. For this crime scene, she wore an arctic foxfur jumpsuit cinched with a silverlink belt and matching cap. Her visual was Yeti's Trophy Girlfriend.

Chrissie allowed herself to be arranged inside the corpse outline. Once she was in place more spun-sugar was applied.

Loulee shoved Pete aside.

'Let's give you big blue lips,' she whispered. 'No one can argue with a frapped face having frosty sparkles.'

Loulee found tears in the corners of her friend's eyes and removed them with a wet-wipe.

'Don't let it show,' she whispered.

Chrissie was in frapped mode now – face stiff, limbs set.

'Yes, that's the ticket,' said Jah. 'Those frozen eyes. They'll haunt viewers.'

'I wouldn't recommend a close-up,' said Eleanor. 'Not at quarter past six. Put people off their steak and kidney pudding. I can sell it with a look of anguish.'

She pulled her Number Two Expression. More smug triumph than anguish.

Captain Floppy nodded agreement but made a secret sign to Camera Clare. Chrissie saw the lens iris as CC stole a close-up. Eleanor seldom sat in on the edit so Perky might get a final shot without Nelly in the way. One for the clip reel.

Eleanor hopped off her box and played the scene.

WDS di Ferrante had a long verbal. Eleanor tongue-tripped in the same place three times before an acceptable take was in the can. The frogmen did noddies but it was a Jill scene. Nelly made deductions and vowed vengeance. Every plod at Dark Green was on duty until the scrote responsible was nicked.

'Poor Peaky,' said Eleanor. 'We owe it to her to do all we can and seventy five per cent more.'

She then denied she'd got it wrong, even when it was played back – and wouldn't say the line again.

It got colder and dimmer. Chill seeped up from the canal. Chrissie's fibreglass float felt like real ice. Fog got in her eyes and stung. Even after Captain Floppy was satisfied, Eleanor wanted more 'moments' – to-camera close-up looks. Nelly's Nutters loved those. Fans spliced hours and hours of 'moments' into medleys, edited to spacey beat tracks.

Chrissie fell asleep. If the corpse snored, too bad.

Eleanor Wynter

'It's always about what's best for the story. That's the real bright light of *Letsby Avenue* – the story, what happens, what comes next. No one character or actor is more important. Right now the story is Jill di Ferrante. Who she is, what she wants, who she cares for, what she'll find out. I'm as keen as any viewer to learn the answers. I tear through scripts when they come in from our supremely talented writing staff – even if they're late, or have pink, yellow, purple and white on black pages.

'I'm on a journey with Jill.

'When we began, we couldn't have known where it would lead. The implosion shook us all. Me most of all. Not a week goes by when I don't miss my telly husband and telly boyfriend and the others lost along the road. Or in a canal. I've so many more sides to learn now. It's a challenge.

'I am consulted about future developments but Red-Tel have the final say. They've been extremely understanding and often seek my input, which is super of them but also clever. I can't claim to have written a line of *Letsby* but I have rephrased a few. It's the mystery of Jill. Now there's this thing with Peaky. Iced to death, poor thing. She'll be missed. But that's the story, isn't it? It rolls on... a savage beast, which must be tamed. It's all in the Turning of the Wheel.'

CHRISTINE AND THE CROCKS

SHE WOKE UP IN THE DARK. SHE WAS COLD AND WET, lying in foul-tasting fog.

'Uck,' she said.

Chrissie unkinked herself and stood. Crusts of sugar frost fell away.

The taping had moved on. WDS Jill was finding clues scene of the crime experts had missed. The way the writers had it, Dark Green scene of the crime experts wouldn't notice a confession written in neon on the side of a barge. That left it to Nelly to work out the week's solution with an 'ah-hah!' and a gaze to camera.

Only Pete Two was left to guard Chrissie's frapped body.

Her glower dissuaded the lad from expressing an opinion.

She was going home.

She wasn't on the Circuit tonight. It was Wednesday (In Studio) tomorrow and she would be on call.

Except she wouldn't.

If there was an autopsy, they could tape it with a mannequin.

When DI di Ferrante and Toy Boy Terry imploded, the credits ran without music over slowmo clips of the characters in livelier days. Perky wouldn't rate that. She was another statistic. A MAW with the A kicked out of her. A MW. Maybe just a W. Thanks to Nelly the Serial Killer.

Chrissie scraped rinds of fake frost from her tunic. She was about to lick her fingers when her Vone flared.

Her celery stash was in the Cattle Car.

A lick of sugar wouldn't hurt. Who'd know?

She was already off *Letsby*.

Loulee had told her to dial her agent. Eleanor Wynter was a Schilling Banner Client so Chrissie knew how that conversation would go.

If she kept quiet, she might be placated with another gig.

She'd be lucky to get an actual support socks advert.

Throwing herself in the canal seemed an option. Her first screen role had been 'Drowning Girl' in a public information film. That would be flagged in her obits.

The fog was up to her waist now. Thick around her feet, so she had to be careful not to step off the towpath but gauzy above that. She heard the slow flow of the canal.

She wasn't frozen anymore. Measured anger and despair gave her a core of warmth. She wasn't tired either. Playing dead had given her a chance at an afternoon nap. She had the beginnings of a night-buzz. Was Garn dosing her celery? Or was it phases of the moon? She couldn't be a werewolf. Loulee would do her nut if she had to brush Chrissie's face fur and blot her wet snout three nights a month.

Someone small ran out of the fog and smacked into her.

A little face looked up and cried tears of relief.

'A police,' said the child, who wore a white parka and hat. 'We're saved.'

'Hold on,' Chrissie began.

But she was hugged tightly around her blue serge hips.

Her nightsight improved. She'd noticed that lately too. She could even see through London Smudge.

Up ahead, under a bridge, people gathered around another little girl in a white outfit – miniature of the clobber Nelly was sporting in the afternoon's shoot. The child couldn't run. Someone taller held her shoulders. The kid-grabber had a knobbly silhouette head. Other shapes in the shadows wore oversize hats. Spouts stuck out of some foreheads.

Crocks.

It started with avoidables barred from a Lyons Cyber House

for antisocial behaviour. The voids hung about on the pavement outside the caff wearing tea-cosies, petitioning to be let back in categorised as crockery rather than customers. Cosies gave way to soft felt teapots with handles, spouts and googley eyes. Crock girls teased beehive hairdos into cup-shapes and had braided handles stuck out the side. When crocks stepped up the antisocial, the swanks stopped running features on crock fashions and the tabs started tagging them as a problem gangcult.

Marcus Milner of the Coterie called himself Dr Crockery. He was one of several style pioneers who claimed to be the original Crock. Chrissie and Loulee gave him a hard time when the first reports of crock scraps came in. For Marcus, it was all about clips and clicks. He didn't even go to Lyons – which he said were refuges for urchins who couldn't afford a Vone. But he cashed telly fees for appearances on *Scene Machine* as spokesman for the lifestyle and wouldn't condemn crockery violence. He wore the biggest, stupidest foam rubber teapots. They had to be squashed when he went through revolving doors.

Marcus Milner, was, in fact, a void.

But Dr Crockery was multiple layers removed from street crocks. He was in green rooms handing out contact details, not under bridges robbing schoolgirls.

The tall crock stepped out from a shadow, shuffling the other little girl before him. His hat was shaped like Battersea Power Station. His face was painted like red velvet cake, eyes and mouth outlined in strawberry icing.

'They took our Vones,' said the girl hugging Chrissie. 'And won't give them back.'

The painted cake smiled. His eyes glistened.

The crockpot was on jabs. They made your eyeballs drool.

And bestowed limited abilities. Mostly, the jabbed were strong and didn't much feel it when punched in the face. Not who you wanted to get into a scrap with. Especially if they were vicious voids in the first place.

'We have clicks of Nelly on our Vones,' the girl went on. 'We were watching the taping.'

The little girls – nine or ten – were Nelly Nutters. Poor mites.

'We don't care about the Vones,' said the captive girl. 'They're only cheap ones. We just want the Nelly clicks. I'd like my purse back. There's no money in it but it's a nice one Nana gave me for Christmas.'

'I'd like my purse back *and* the money in it,' said Chrissie's girl, as if talking to Santa. 'And my Vone with the Nelly clicks.'

'Oh no, it's a police,' said a crock with a lemon drizzle face. His tone was mocking. 'A V2R vera... a rozzette... Fiona the Filth. I'm so, so afraid. Please Missy Pretty Policey, tell me the time and cuff me round the ear...'

Chrissie held up her hand. She still wore the prop stunglove.

... which could have been the real one if she'd asked Loulee for it.

She might be able to bluff this out. If the crocks were too jabbed not to spot a prop and not jabbed enough not to care about a stunning.

'Are you going to arrest them and put them in Devil's Dyke and make them give us back our Vones?' asked her new friend.

'No, she isn't,' said Battersea Teapot.

'But she is. She's a police.'

'No she's not. Are you, *Perky*?'

Just her grot luck to run into a crock who was a *Letsby* viewer.

The girl stopped hugging her and stood away. She looked up at Chrissie, puzzling out that the face she saw out of focus through tears was the same one she saw out of focus behind her favourite bright light three nights a week.

It was a toss-up whether the kid was disappointed Chrissie wasn't a real police or ecstatic to meet someone only one remove from Nelly herself.

'We'll be having your Vone and pocket money too, Perky.'

This was an aces end to an aces day.

Motes glinted in the fog around her. She was puzzled but didn't have more than a moment to think about it.

Her prop stunglove crackled like the real thing. Had Practical Effects Pete rigged it? A violet flash sharply defined the cake-painted faces of six crocks. Lemon Drizzle, Rum Baba, Fondant Fancy, Custard Slice. A crock girl got up as a cake stand.

The crockpot's head snapped back as if he'd been slapped.

Blood, richer than strawberry jam, poured out of his nose.

Chrissie felt ergs building up in her – that night-buzz! – and had to get rid of it.

Her ungloved hand crackled and darkness came out of it in a blurt – like ink spilled on a picture, blotting everything out.

Lemon Drizzle came at her with a nunchuck of oversize teaspoons. Violet lightning struck his chain. He jumped into the canal like a galvanised frog. He splashed and glugged, disturbing surface mist.

When the *Letsby* gig came up, Chrissie had booked a self-defence class at Sunny Gym, anticipating scenes in which Perky wrestled jabbed crims or rugby-tackled gangcult operants wearing bomb-weskits. In the class, she was repeatedly slammed onto a sweaty mat. The instructor was working off grudges. If there were an entrance exam for the School of Hard Knocks, she failed. Then again, the only close combat Perky got to do was with the prop telephone cord.

So why was Chrissie winning this scrap?

Purple lightning struck, again. She moved swiftly and hit hard.

When she came out of it, there was broken crockery on the ground.

One of the little girls had her Vone back and was pointing its camera at her.

Jasmine and Richard at Devil's Dyke

JASMINE WORE BLACK AND RICHARD WORE WHITE. SHE sat while he stood.

'The GEIST hypothesis is such a satisfying delusion a true paranoid would suspect it was engineered,' he reasoned. 'It's believable. It explains much. Makes sense of a baffling world. If there really were an all-powerful cabal of dreadful people out to wreck everything, we'd have someone to blame. We'd have a road map to solving the world's worries. Smash GEIST and utopia ensues. That's why it's hard to give up the delusion... to see things as they really are. Complicated. Difficult. Inconclusive.'

'But GEIST are real,' she said. 'You know that.'

'*Were* real. Yes, of course. I've seen the files. Including the horror comics MI5 and MI6 won't show each other. The top secret gen. But they're not real *now*. The last satrapy was broken up years ago. We only have a ghost of GEIST, a bogeyman for the feeble-minded. Like me.'

She did not sigh – no matter how much she wanted to.

She and Richard had been doing this dance for years. His delusion would be dispelled but return in altered form. No argument stood against it. No evidence overturned it. As he said, the best delusions were satisfying. They met needs and gave answers. They gave comfort.

He named his own syndrome. The GEIST Delusion Delusion.

In his poor misled mind, he believed they were not out to get him.

Which they were. They were out to get everyone. GEIST had been more active than ever these last few years. A satrapy in Weston-Super-Mare opened a portal to the Purple last Boxing Day and unleashed a wave of Magenta Meanies on the Mendips. It took the British Lions and the Reddleman working fractiously together to shut that nightmare down.

The name of Richard Jeperson was high on the GEIST list of People to be Got.

It was possible they *had* got Richard. Look where he was.

Though her understanding was that, after all he'd seen and done, he'd got himself. It became all too much.

She felt that too. One day, they might change places.

She'd be the patient and he'd be the head-shrinker.

Really, it was his place to sit. He preferred to walk and talk, pacing his room, wrestling phantoms.

She got off the couch.

No more Wagon Wheels on the plate. Had Richard eaten even one?

'We'll revisit this,' she said.

He smiled, comfortable in his conviction that he was cured.

But wrong. He needed his paranoia back.

Richard Jeperson was a national hero. But not a cloak.

He was only slightly enlightened. His empathic, intuitive abilities – always latent – became more acute after *Never Mind*. He couldn't read minds but knew how people felt. A useful facility for a therapist, if the turnabout happened. He'd never been famous like Magic Ian or Poltergirl. He didn't have a tradename. He didn't wear a mask, except at certain parties. His exploits were recorded in sealed archives. He'd earned medals he couldn't wear in public.

After three days' scrap, with half the Splendid Six lost to injury, Richard Jeperson had won the Battle of Battersea single-handed. He'd commandeered Jasmine's autogiro and flown it through the Eye of the Octopiranha. He'd tagged Sir Hector Harrap, the Mole of the Mall, minutes before the traitor could deliver schematics of the Channel Defence Dinghies to the GEIST satrap on Sark. In coronation year, Richard thwarted three separate regicide plots. Queen Vee offered him a knighthood. He declined the K with respect.

He had dismantled successive GEIST regimes, taking them off the board satrapy by satrapy... only to find the enemy regrouped. GEIST never ran short of bad ideas and worse people.

The absurd, Sisyphean struggle eventually told.

Now Richard believed his whole career in public service a delusion.

His room was on the White Corridor, the Most Secure wing of the Secure Hospital.

Jasmine wouldn't resign from Devil's Dyke so long as Richard was here.

They'd been close once. Now, when he looked at her, he only saw Dr Chambers. In his delusion, he'd blanked her other face. It was easy to forget the mask. The last time she wore it – and night-coat, boots and britches – was here. An attempt to shock Richard into his senses. He was just puzzled. Since then, she'd tendered her resignation to the Shadow Cabinet, folded her uniform, retired her trade-name and mothballed the autogiro.

Exit Lady Shade. A cloak no more.

She could still be of public service.

Richard's room was white. Walls, floor tiles, ceiling, plastic chairs, sheets. In place of a window was a white lighting panel. Patients on the White Corridor wore white hooded robes, loose white trousers and white elastic-sided shoes. Richard listened to atonal minimalism on white vinyl and read books with white slip-covers. He watched black and white films on the telly.

Colour was too painful.

In her black tailored scrubs, Jasmine was a scarecrow in this milky limbo. She was concerned the visual was too close to her cloak costume. Some patients had negative associations with Lady Shade. She'd put cutthroats in here.

The monochromia was Sewell Head's idea. She wasn't convinced of its therapeutic value.

The director had to consider control before cure. Devil's Dyke's brief was to be more Secure than Hospital. Considering the White Corridor roll-call, it was the best policy. But Jasmine couldn't think of herself as a zoo-keeper. She had to hope she was helping.

In private practice, her specialism was treating those who lived through the moment of *Never Mind* – as she had, at ten years old – and found it hard to keep the world before and the world after connected in their internal narrative. Minds got blown to bits and put back together in new configurations. Most benefited but a few really didn't. Half a century on, it was a much-studied field.

Some believed they'd wake up one morning and the mess of miracles would be back in its box. The fifty-plus-year trip had really lasted only as long as an album side. It'd still be 1972. The record would finish, needle ticking in the groove beyond the unlisted mantra after the last track. They'd be in their childhood bedroom or at a school disco or in the park with a transistor radio. It was a dream, put in their heads by the bloody Beatles. A blunter, more common syndrome than Richard's personalised method of tuning out reality. Sufferers believed they alone knew the truth. Group therapy was risky. Individual delusion threatened to become a movement. She monitored Peophole Purviews and Personals Presences to keep an eye on that. If it suited them, people could disbelieve anything.

There were intricate, complicated, overlapping fantasies of what the real world was like outside the *Never Mind* effect. Few appealed to Jasmine, but her circumstances were special. Like Richard with his latent psychic radar, she wasn't completely unprepared for the changes. She had a family tradition. Her grandparents, Kentish Glory and the original Dr Shade, wore night-masks and worked under trade-names decades before music from another plane splashed tins of psychoactive psychedelic paint over everything. Thanks to them, Jasmine was born prematurely enlightened.

Richard turned on the telly and got absorbed by a black and white play made in the 1960s. People in kitchens arguing, in factories working, in wars carrying-on. No cutthroat mindmaster scheming to boil the Archguru of Canterbury's brain by focusing on a meteor crystal like in real life. Jasmine was semi-addicted to that channel too, though the grey world of her primary school years was as remote a memory as old money. She'd grown up under dayglo skies, even if her own path wound into the dark.

She checked Richard's charts. He was in perfect physical health. For a pensioner, he was a miracle. An extended prime of life was a common benefit of the New Victorian Era. A gift of *Never Mind* few wanted to return in the January sales. She didn't look her calendar age either.

He had no after-effects from his many injuries. Not physically. The enlightened were generally hardy as oak trees.

She gave his hand a squeeze and left him to his programme.

CHRISTINE AFTER THE SCRAP

BAILEY AND LENKA SAID PERKY WAS THEIR NEW co-favourite on *Letsby*. The girls learned her real name and dialled in to her Peophole Purview for Clicks and Clips. They said they'd keep up with her on the Personals.

Chrissie knew better than to tell them what was happening to Perky the week after next. She also dodged questions about Eleanor Wynter. Some Lights shone so Bright they got away with foibles which would prang a lesser spark. Nelly was protected by the Powers That Be. So much was invested in her that inconveniences were taken care of. Grot clicks evaporised... Misspoken quips deleted... Supporting Regulars with nascent fan clubs discontinued.

Chrissie had other things on her mind. Like... *violet lightning*!

She'd never have believed that on the day of her discontinuance, her date with Next Tuesday was not top story on her front page. Perky's death ran below the fold, between the Smudge Warning and today's lottery numbers.

Headline of the day was What Happened Under the Bridge.

She hadn't killed anyone – which for a horrid moment she thought she might have. The crocks weren't going to be good for much for weeks, though. Not that being good for anything was part of the crock lifestyle.

The Cakestand was least injured but didn't take the opportunity to vanish in the fog. She stuck around to look after her moaning gangmates – while giving them a hard time about their poor showing in the scrap.

Chrissie posed for clicks with Bailey and Lenka. She let Bailey wear her WPC hat.

The Cakestand, receiver of swag, handed back purses. Lenka wanted to kick foam-rubber teapot heads for larfs. Chrissie persuaded her that wasn't the dream.

So she was a role model now. Miss No Excessive Violence.

The Cakestand was about Chrissie's own age. The crock girl was embarrassed to look her in the eye, as if they vaguely knew each other from Draycott's or Sgt Pepper Night at Fakers but couldn't remember whether they got on. Considering her choice of gangcult, they probbo didn't.

With Lenka's Vone, Chrissie dialled 999. The real police said they'd be round sharpish. An unskippable survey delayed the hang-up. She stabbed random numbers to give ratings on how satisfied or unsatisfied she was with the service rendered by the Metropolitan Police. A civ hiding under the sofa while burglars ransacked their house would have been highly unsatisfied at being forced to fill in a survey when they had much else on their mind. The survey shut down cheerfully with – what else? – an up-tempo version of the *Letsby Avenue* theme.

Chrissie should slip away before the constabulary wanted an explanation. Her Perky hat didn't give her a licence to clout crims. No matter what the girls said, she was liable to be accused of affray. Impersonating a police officer was a serious offence. Being a bogus bogey with violet lightning might go down less well than just being a robbing crock. They were regular voids, not unusual individuals.

Was she unusual? Enlightened, even.

She didn't know. She still felt a night-buzz.

Everyone wonders whether they'll grow up enlightened. Chrissie and Loulee were mad about it when they were Bailey and Lenka's age. They spun fantasies about abilities they'd develop, costumes they'd wear and trade-names they'd take as a cloak-companion team. They settled on Glamour Girl and Sparky, then had a three-day row about who was who. Eunice Uglow's example made them rethink. Pyro Pixie had to take her O Levels in a Secure Hospital. Deffo not the dream. They hung up imaginary cloaks. The Circuit seemed safer and required no abilities beyond putting on a happy face and keeping a trim figure.

Did Chrissie generate electricity like Shock Jock? Away from the bridge, she tried to conjure lightning. She rubbed her fingers together in the air.

Nothing happened.

She felt no different.

She looked at the canal. Did she feel a pull of the water?

Crumps, what if her enlightenment involved an animal totem? A common circumstance. Look at Flat Cat or the Cuckoo.

She could not bear to be Electric Eel Girl.

She imagined a green wetsuit, glistening and form-fitting – with a jagged bolt across the chest. Twenty minutes to get out of it if she needed a wee. Bug-eye goggles. Fins down the back. Unenviable and unfanciable – not even companion material. She'd get stuck with being the Goofy One in a Kid Kloak Krewe like the Double Deckers. She'd prefer to be a civ, ta very much.

She didn't feel voltage now. Only her usual night-buzz.

In the scrap, Chrissie had known instinctively where to hit. She hadn't learned that from one wretched morning being duffed up at Sunny Gym.

Had Chrissie been temporarily possessed? Puppeteered?

She hadn't seemed like herself.

Though she didn't sense anyone else string-pulling. She didn't think she was an operant.

Was she bonded to Bailey and Lenka, liable to be pulled across space and time whenever they were in a pretty pickle? She had a feeling the girls – who must have bunked off school to spend the afternoon pestering the *Letsby* shoot – were often in trouble. She didn't want to be the rescue resource whenever they hadn't done their homework or got teased by big boys in the playground.

She got to the Cattle Car. Someone had spray-painted 'Justice for Jesmond' on it.

No one was minding the shop so it was locked. Loulee had let Chrissie in on the trick of opening the van with three taps and a kick. She gained entry and took off her blue serge sack for the last time. Not a thing she'd miss but her eyes went wet. She changed into civ clobber – oversized hooded windbreaker from Präno, linen trousers from Rags, Bull Boots.

She hung up the WPC cap then decided to keep it and popped it into a Briteway Stores bag. With job prospects circling the plughole, she might put it on Going for a Song and hope someone in Pervs for Perky had deep pockets.

Loulee Ling – Ghost Lantern Girl

SHE WAS ON THE BOOKS AS GENERAL SLAP-AND-DEFRUMP merchant, not Christine Chambers' personal beauty elf. But she supposed killing off Perky meant she'd get her cards too. Still, she had to work out the shift.

She kept her head down for the last half-hour of filming – which, as flaming usual, took an hour and a half. Eleanor Wynter made a meal of moody looks to camera when the red light was on and complained when it wasn't. Having swallowed a live mouse, she had a jab-buzz and wanted many, many takes.

During not-much-happening spells, Loulee found it hard to ignore the ghosts.

Today's uninvited guest was Ninurmahmeš, not one of the particularly useful spectres. The tall, thin woman stood by the canal, fog threading through her. If she took it into what was left of her mind, she could walk on the scummy water. Many ghosts were wary of showing off. They were rebels, rogues and harpies in life but stick out a Keep Off the Grass sign and they bee-well kept off the grass.

Ninurmahmeš had lived between circa 1355 and circa 1326 BC in Beth Shemesh, near Jerusalem. Loulee got the dates from Hawkshaw. The ghost wore a green dress and a circlet of what looked like coins. Her hands were a different shade of brown to her face. Her name meant 'Lady of the Lions' but her party piece wasn't wild beast-related. In life, she had perfected a process for tanning hides. Ninurmahmeš, poor love, talked a lot about hides. It was more or less her only topic.

Loulee thought of it as monversation, an extended sub-audial 'how-to' on the ins and outs of skinning, flensing and tanning. Dog muck was a key ingredient. The lecture was soothing, almost lulling. Only cold and fog-sting kept her awake.

The Smudge made Nelly's eyes water too.

Loulee was needed for touch-ups. She tuned Ninurmahmeš out and hopped to.

Adrian Jah told Loulee to trace a single tear track on the bright light's cheek. Jill di Ferrante was deeply affected by whatever her name was getting frosticled. It was Eleanor Wynter's fault her character had no one to open up to. She'd had WDS Jill's family, lovers and companions written out. Soon, there'd only be Canteen Cathy left.

Loulee hesitated before doing anything to Nelly's face.

The bright light had her own dedicated staff. Demarcation was a big thing in telly. Channels went off the air over disputes about whether a quiz show light-up scoreboard was a prop or an effect. Loulee sought clarification but Captain Floppy frowned a 'get on with it' look at her. They were losing visibility.

Loulee approached Nelly. Alarums did not sound. Stungloves were not clapped on her shoulders. A powdered cheek was presented.

Was this a trick? Touching the sacred fizzog might give Red-Tel grounds for getting shot of Loulee. Equally, hesitation or refusal might trigger no-redundancy-pay dismissal.

Following orders was the least risky option.

And – secret weapon! – she didn't want the job anyway. Not after they'd pranged Chrissie. If they didn't sack her, she'd split.

Loulee thought of writing 'Evil Witch' on Eleanor Wynter's forehead but made do with turning the tear-track into a rude ideograph. *Năiniú,* ie: cow. Even Chinese viewers wouldn't make it out. But it was a gesture.

Chrissie must be fuming. This was knockback of the year. And it was only January.

Her friend had bet her purse on the MAW number. This

could be the end of the gap year-and-quite-a-few-months.

It was time to tell Chrissie about the Ghost Lantern.

Loulee had held back because Chrissie had so much on her metaphorical plate (what with the Coterie, the Circuit and *Letsby*) and so little on her actual plate (what with the flaming celery) that letting her in on the spook sitch seemed like giving her extra grief she didn't need. There were precedents. Chrissie hadn't told Loulee about Garn till they'd been sort-ofs for three months. Sometimes, news went over better if saved up for a spell. Excitement built. If an item cooled or went bust before it was shared, no harm was done.

The Ghost Lantern was above the fold news, though.

It had taken up most of Loulee's spare time in the last five months. She'd opened a cupboard in her flat and found a Chinese lantern. It cast thin light with no apparent flame. When she turned around, she was not alone. Her first ghost was Yvyra, a Guarani who lived in the late 1500s in a jungle which was now part of Paraguay. She had climbed trees and thrown poison-tipped darts at Jesuits and conquistadors.

Loulee tossed a saucepan through the ghost's head to no effect. She noticed Yvyra's large, flexible feet. Her own toes twitched in her slippers as if they'd become prehensile. The only climbable thing in the flat was a wardrobe. She scrambled up it with an ease pre-Lantern Loulee couldn't have matched.

When Yvyra was with her, Loulee could climb walls which seemed to offer no hand-holds. She knew which flowers and moulds mixed to make poison. Anyone out to colonise Holloway Road would get a shock. Conquistadors might swarm off the Overground at Highbury & Islington but their advance would be checked by darts from above.

When a ghost was about, Loulee was good at whatever the woman had been good at in life. Her ghosts were all women. With proper knives – and poo from a particular breed of North African cur fed on a diet of dates and olives – Loulee could take Eleanor Wynter's face off and fashion it into a tanned mask.

That might not strictly be called for.

When a ghost's party piece was something now considered immoral or illegal, Loulee had qualms. Being a whizz at sums like Eupraxia Leonides was handy. Even being mistress of the cavalry sabre like Oghulqaimish had helped once or twice. Too many ghosts were good at things with limited contemporary application. Or would get her in trouble. If Dolly Filch manifested, Loulee's fingers itched to steal. The Filcher qualified for the Lantern because of her unparalleled skill at picking pockets. In 1803, aged eight, she was hanged outside Newgate Prison. Dying young made stronger ghosts. After fighting off Dolly's fluence, Loulee had to return small items she'd snaffled.

With the final moody look in the can, Anjulie Glas crossed off the last pink page and announced that the day was done. Happy grumbles from the crew.

Loulee took out her Vone to dial Chrissie.

'Who's that dreadful woman in fancy dress?' demanded Eleanor Wynter. 'With the tiara of chocolate pennies. She kept getting in my eyeline. Set security ought to be higher priority. I've had stalkers, you know. Flan-flingers, even.'

Unpopular names often took a flan to the face. Popular ones too.

Anjulie hadn't seen the woman Nelly meant.

'She was right there. Dressed for a Nativity play.'

The bright light pointed at a swirling absence in the fog.

Ninurmahmeš wasn't there – but had been.

Had Eleanor Wynter seen the ghost?

Until now, only Loulee saw her Lantern visitors. Early on, she'd mistaken one or two of the more anonymously dressed spirits for women who happened to be standing around. Were the ghosts – or just Ninurmahmeš – becoming apparent to other people? Nelly being sensitive to *anything* would rate a headline.

Another development. Hard to keep up with it all.

This must have been how everyone felt in the 1970s, after *Never Mind*. Every day, some new marvel.

Eleanor retired to the Wynter Palace. Loulee sort of hoped Nelly's personal paint-stripper recognised a cow ideograph when they saw one.

When the bright light was gone, Ninurmahmeš reappeared.

So she knew she'd been seen and had taken steps not to be.

Loulee's understanding of the Ghost Lantern was fuzzy. She wished there'd been a book of instructions in the cupboard.

Best policy – she decided – was to stay away from Eleanor Wynter.

Which shouldn't be difficult and wasn't any sort of sacrifice.

Nelly could find her own lantern if she wanted ghosts – which, from what she said, she didn't.

The *Letsby* crew choked in fog. As they packed up equipment, there was hacking and complaining. Another day had run long. Loulee and Chrissie usually went for an after-work wine-and-whine together. Today they'd need an overnight session. It wasn't as if Chrissie had to be up early any more days this week. Or next.

She dialled Chrissie and got a recorded message. She sent a blurt.

Maybe Chrissie was back at the Cattle Car. Or beetled off home. She should not be alone.

These days Loulee was never alone. Which put a crimp in her love life. It was hard to flirt while ignoring the indecent advice of Madame Wilcox, a *grande horizontale* reckoned the most devastating seductress of Paris in the 1870s. Ghost lectures were on a channel only Loulee was tuned to. It could be turned down but not off.

Fresher ghosts were more engaged and engaging. She could have back-and-forth with the best-defined of them. Even the strongest presences faded over the years, to become recorded messages. Some felt themselves dwindling. Ni Tien, a calligrapher from the seventeenth century, said she wasn't leaking away like tea spilled in sand but funnelling from one place to another. Sobbing Sybil, who predicted everything accurately in life, had a darker view of where the dead fetch up and how they were treated there. Her wick burned so low she was barely a flicker.

Ghosts had many theories. Loulee had imagined they'd know answers but no such luck. They knew things they'd learned in life. How to squeeze venom from toad warts or where the secret coin pocket was in Beau Brummell's best waistcoat. They were vague about what happened after they were killed. Pretty much all the ghosts had been killed rather than just died.

When her darts ran out, Yvyra was converted to Christianity. She drowned in the Paraná trying to escape forced baptism. Oghulqaimish – whose name meant 'Next Time a Boy', suggesting the value twelfth century Mongols put on girl children – took an arrow in the back of the neck from the next-born boy. Her jealous brother wanted the family sabre, which he lost after getting drunk on fermented yak piddle at the funeral. Ninurmahmeš, accused of witchcraft by the exclusively male tanners' guild of Beth Shemesh, was executed by public stoning.

Loulee's dream was not to get killed (next week or month or round the corner), preferring to succumb to old age in a distant future when she was ancient. Forty or something.

Loulee did a quick check of her portable touch-up kit. Everything went back into its place. She was running low on tears. You couldn't just use water because it didn't show on film so she mixed her own with gelatine. Perfectly safe to drip in people's eyes. She could register the recipe but Red-Tel might own anything she came up with while on their payroll. She was pleased with the tears, though. It was satisfying to do something well, even in a field so tiny she could brag to few about her tricks. Make-up was her party piece.

The Lantern ghosts were all women with party pieces. They were very good at something requiring talent, practice and patience. Loulee hadn't registered how good she was at what she did until she understood the Lantern rated her on a level with the artists, craftswomen, athletes, warriors and saints who fuelled its flame. It was as if she'd won a BAFTA she didn't know she'd been nominated for.

Being chosen by the Lantern wasn't a wholly wonderful thing.

It hadn't skipped Loulee's notice that many of her visitors were turned into ghosts by men who took their talents as personal affronts. Even more depressing was the list of those killed because other women were put out that some clever clogs of a girl or nuisance of an aunt was very good at something. Madame Wilcox was stabbed with a steel hatpin by a wife whose husband she couldn't even remember seducing. The hubbub – the fractious communion of Lantern ghosts – understood Eleanor Wynter. If spooks could vote, Nelly's Peophole and Personals scores would plummet. She reminded the ghosts of people they'd known when they were alive – often people they'd known at the *end* of their lives.

Still, this was the twenty-first century. Killing make-up

artists wasn't common. Today's evil harpies got you sacked and blacklisted.

Loulee zipped up her case and said her goodbyes.

Practical Effects Pete lingered at the edge of her circle of comfort. He knew this was a bad time to chat her up but his imp of the perverse compelled him. Loulee was not in the mood to let him down gently.

Ninurmahmeš made stone-throwing gestures at the effects man.

'Loulee,' said Anjulie, pushing in front of Pete, 'could you hang on a mo?'

Here come the cards!

She looked over Anjulie's shoulder. Pete shrank into the fog.

'Go on, Anju. What's the latest grief?'

'Sorry to ask... but could you sign this?'

A clipboard was presented. Loulee scanned text. Her eyes watered. She regretted not wearing fog-goggles.

It was a non-disclosure agreement with her name on it.

She was to pledge to Rediffusion-Televersion on pain of discontinuance, fine and imprisonment not to divulge information which might cast a poor light on *Letsby Avenue,* Red-Tel or any of the company's employees or assets, the television industry in general, and Eleanor Wynter in particular. She was not to say, do or think anything – or agree, concur, disseminate, or chortle sayings, doings or thoughts of any other person – which could be construed as critical of *Letsby Avenue,* Red-Tel or any of the company's employees or assets, etc. The agreement was backdated to the dawn of time and valid throughout this (or any other) universe until the stars burned out.

Even before she signed the NDA, she'd violated it with the cow character.

'I'd prefer not to,' she said.

'It's just a formality.'

'I'm not really formal.'

'No, it's verit just a formality. You already signed by inference when you cashed your first wages. You did read the back of the cheque.'

Loulee had known that would haunt her. Enyedi Boglárka, a nineteenth century Hungarian lawyer, had told her as much.

Boglárka was killed by an unethical client. Assuming a woman lawyer must be a total incompetent, he'd hired her to represent him in a case he needed for complicated reasons to lose. She won. He refused to pay her. She challenged him to a duel. He bribed the referee to give her a pistol with a plugged barrel. She died when it exploded. Happily, she'd made a contingency plan. The pastries brought to the duelling field to celebrate her murderer's victory were poisoned. The referee, the seconds and the litigant expired in agony, leaving a mystery.

She'd known Boglárka was right about the small print on the back of the cheque but needed the money before her Access card bill came due.

She took a pen from Anjulie and wrote 'Bù kāixīn de xiǎo jīnglíng' above her typed name. She looked at it.

'That's a lot of characters for "Louise Ling".'

She shrugged.

'What does it really say?'

'"Unhappy elf."'

'It's a formality. You're still bound.'

'Now what?'

'Congratulations. You've been promoted. You're the new personal make-up artist for Miss Eleanor Wynter.'

That was worse than being fired.

'I quit,' she said.

'Withdrawing labour requires you give thirty weeks' notice. It's industry standard.'

Enyedi Boglárka might have had something to say about that. Ninurmahmeš – who hadn't come up with a convincing argument that a mob of envious tanners shouldn't bung rocks her way – had nothing useful. You often didn't get the ghost you needed.

'This is a Turn of the Wheel, Loulee,' said Anjulie. 'Not a punishment. It's more money. An onscreen credit. Privileges and facilities. Nelly isn't stupid. Why do you think she's a name? She's seen Chrissie Chambers without a Loulee Ling face on and Chrissie Chambers with a Loulee Ling face on and knows the difference. She wants that for herself. And what Nelly wants...'

'... Loulee does, I get it.'

Though it felt more like being got.

CHRISTINE GOES HOME

SHE TOOK THREE CROWDED BUSES TO FOREST HILL. None of her fellow passengers had just pranged. They looked through the *London Scam* for clubs and films and happenings, read tell-alls and mysteries on Vooks and Vones, listened to tickertracks on Earvones, gossed with seatmates... or sat/stood/dreamed, minding their own business, day's work done or ditched, heading home to supper or out for evening excitement.

Good for them.

Not a lot of help to her.

She hopped off the Routemaster at the Horniman Museum stop and walked to Mum and Dad's house.

25 Ewelme Road. Where she'd grown up.

The street light six doors down was on the blink so she had to pass through a pool of foggy dark between oases of illumination. Every night, she had a moment's quease. As far back as she could remember, the lamp was unreliable – buzzing/flickering or out of order. She'd imagined something grey and gruesome lived in its stretch of gloom and fed on little girls' brains. Even now, the shaved patch above her ear prickled when she was six doors from Number 25. She used to cross the road to escape the Grey Gruesome's long tongue. Loulee shamed her out of it by performing a rite of exorcism she happened to know – so Chrissie put up with fear sweat two or more times a day.

Tonight was different. As she walked under it, the broken bulb cast light.

She looked up. A fog-wreathed violet fireball burned atop the post. Blacklight, like a negative image of a candle flame.

She knew she was doing it. She made the fireball pulse.

The dark pool was abolished. The Grey Gruesome was gone – turned tail and run. Not because Loulee laid into it with inky thread and Balinese bells but because Christine Chambers burned with a night-light it could not bear.

A curtain twitched. Nigel Timperley peered out from his front room. The retired maths teacher ran the Whispers natter for Ewelme Road, Woodcombe Crescent and the Fieldings. He took it on himself to put up professionally engraved if unenforceable 'it is forbidden to...' signs. In a mystery serial, he'd be murdered in episode one and it would take twenty-six weeks to sort through the suspects.

Cutthroat crime was a Nosy Nige hobby horse. It was forbidden to fly, telekinate, pyromance or stretch like an elastic band in Ewelme Road, Woodcombe Crescent and the Fieldings. The mildest talent lumped a person in with Adam Tussaud or the Go-Go Golem in his book. Nige wasn't even keen on card tricks or being double-jointed. In Battersea during the Battle, he'd cut off three of his toes with a spade while the Octopiranha sing-screamed inside his brain. Chrissie had to admit that would put anyone off the enlightened.

Violet fireballs weren't yet a specific no-no but Nige would be down the engravers if one caught his attention. He'd wonder about her purplish penumbra. She waved cheerily and hoped he didn't see phantom flame from his window. Maybe the lamp was finally fixed.

She walked on.

She was more puzzled than elated by the outcome of her scrap with the crocks. People had got hurt and she hadn't meant that. Okay, pretty grot people but still... Evaporising the Grey Gruesome was a buzz of a different magnitude. If growing up meant crossing off the terrors of childhood, she'd taken a significant step.

She needed to tell Loulee about new developments. It was a priority. She'd dial her as soon as she'd seen to the plants.

She let herself into Number 25. Three storeys of rooms with too many things in them but a surprising foyer and a good run of back garden. The atrium had a stained-glass cupola. It gave a grander impression than the pokey sitting room, dining room and kitchen or the low-ceilinged bedrooms upstairs. It was as if whoever built the house spent so much on the foyer they couldn't afford to make the rest of the place to its scale.

Set off by the opening door, Dad's pre-recorded voice piped up to remind her which plants to water and which to leave alone. The audio was on a cycle. She'd thought about deactivating it, only she'd miss the company and kill the plants.

Mum and Dad were on an unbelievable world tour. They'd won a competition in the *Sunday Supernova*. She was surprised they'd entered. Her parents were crossword-filling, War-on-Want-donating, why-can't-people-be-sensible *Spectrum* readers.

The once-in-a-lifetime trip on the *QVII* seemed as stretch-outable as her gap year. Postcards arrived regularly, eight to ten days after clips showed up on her Vook.

Mum and Dad had swum with dolphins over Christmas. This week, they were exploring an active volcano wearing Michelin Man magma-resistant suits. Dad had airmailed seeds from Sumatra she was supposed to plant in pots in the atrium in spring. She was strictly warned not to overfeed the Strange Orchids.

She put on wistful/sad music – Mellon Chollie's *Drizzle* LP – and saw to the plants.

Jasmine on the White Corridor

The patient in secure cell 15 troubled her. She hoped Richard Jeperson would overcome his delusion and leave Devil's Dyke. She wanted William Wax to stay where he was until they wheeled him out for cremation.

Jasmine looked through the magic eye. Wax was twisted impossibly at the waist, hands up as if warding off invisible bats. A shield of featureless papier-mâché covered his face. Dr Head let him have his mask. What was underneath upset even experienced blackcoats. She disagreed with the director. Staff should always see who Wax was. *What* Wax was.

He'd called himself 'Adam Tussaud', Master of the Chamber of Horrors. He wasn't even affiliated with GEIST. There was no agenda any could discern to his crimes.

It just popped into his mind to have a Reign of Terror.

New victims were found at the sites of famous murders. Rillington Place, Ratcliff Highway, Miller's Court. Witnesses identified long-dead culprits. Puppeteered waxworks, moving stiffly but panther-quick if cornered.

Jasmine felt all the healed breaks in her bones. One night in 1988, the Crippen figure pounced on her. She believed the real Crippen shouldn't have been convicted and hanged. He was guilty at most of contributing to his wife's death by overprescription. The Crippen figure was something else, fully the murdering fiend of popular imagination. Steel armature skeleton, mask of extraordinary plasticity. Lucky she had a small blowtorch in her medical bag. Not lucky. *Prepared.* When the pasty face melted, the metal skull grinned. She had to burn through its jelly eyes to loosen the grip on her throat.

She didn't miss that side of the glamorous nightlife.

She checked Wax's medication. She couldn't justify dulling him further. Subtler understanding of dosages had developed since Cora Crippen's autopsy in 1910.

Jasmine resisted suggestions that Wax be reassigned to the Abstract Chaos Corridor with the catatonics. Dr Head agreed with her. The director had a perfect record of no escapes since he took up the post and wasn't taking chances on breaking that duck.

Adam Tussaud had been performing in captivity for over thirty years, contorting for hours into poses a normal person would find agony to hold for half a minute. Even under constant monitoring, no one saw him shift. Dying Swan with Broken Wing one moment, Rodin's Thinker With Head on Backwards the next. He wasn't in a sit-down coma. He was playing silly beggars.

Was Wax the worst of them?

Perhaps. Or only the one who'd most nearly killed her.

The White Corridor was for prize pupils. Top cutthroats. Some from before her time, some from long after. Anthony Jago. The Jibbenainosay. Guy the Gorilla. Derek Leech. Persephone Gill. The Inner Voice. Roger Duroc. Scary Mary. Robert Hackwill. Not all her collars – or Richard's – but the second tier of dreadful. The first tier, of course, were the ones who never got caught – like Jun Zero, the world's greatest thief. No one knew whether he, she, it or they really existed. Some said Jun Zero was a myth fostered by the Red Rope so the rich would shell out for high-end security services.

League Division Two of Evil was appalling enough. Derek Leech, trade-name The Dealer, had run a casino where the House always won and players lost more than their chips. Robert Hackwill, trade-name Bad Mouth Bob, was a fluencer. For a price, he talked law-abiding dupes into murder. He was responsible for killing people, businesses, style trends, whole communities.

None of the prize pupils would see the outside world again.

They merited special diets, particular accommodations, and tailored restraints.

This was a hospital. They were getting treatment. For their own good, though she never forgot what they'd done and would do again given a chance. What was wrong with them probably couldn't be cured but could be managed. Each had a drug regimen. Most were on courses of therapy – not so much talking cures as holding patterns, to keep them calm. Those that could, plotted and planned. That even helped. Better they pass time trying to pick unpickable locks than making problems for the blackcoats.

Should Richard be on the White Corridor? Possibly not. He was here for what he knew rather than what he was, even if he currently didn't believe what he knew. Because he thought his career a fantasy, authorities worried he might spill beans. GEIST would want him on some mind robber's couch pouring out volumes of Top Secret gen. That earned him accommodation in Her Majesty's Cutthroat Collection. Jasmine argued his case with Dr Head, who was sympathetic but still a civil servant. An alternative would have to be found but progress was slow.

She went through procedures at the turnstile.

Her face was her own, not a wax cast worn by someone else (yes, that had been tried). So were her eyes and distinctive heartbeat. She collected the items she'd had to surrender before setting foot on the White Corridor – Vone, keys, coin purse, three-pack of Penguin biscuits, today's morning edition of the *Spectrum*. Letting the latest news onto the White Corridor was potentially as dangerous as giving the inmates flick-knives. If Guy found out the Hotspurs were facing relegation, he'd break his bed and stage another dirty protest. No one wanted that.

Geordie Jed was on the stile. Ex-copper, married to a rugby prop forward. He did the patter songs in the Devil's Dyke Gilbert & Sullivan Society.

'Hey, Jas, isn't your niece on the telly?'

'Christine? Yes. On that police soap.'

'This her?'

Jed showed her a clip on his Vook.

A scrap. Not well-staged, poorly filmed. Standards of television drama were slipping.

Her niece was in police uniform, making a fist with a stunglove. Crocks were flying. Jasmine was professionally wary of phrases like 'want their head examined' but anyone who willingly wore a foam rubber teapot hat was well on their way to the Polka Dot Corridor. Too silly to be a dire threat but barmy enough to need locking-up.

The penny dropped. This wasn't acting. This was verit.

She supposed it had to happen.

Jed chuckled as a crock went arse over tit into a canal.

'Nice one, Cyril,' he said.

Jasmine passed through the stile.

She called in at the Dispensary – the Tuck Shop – and authorised Wax's medication. She put a Bounty and a Walnut Whip on tick. She tithed a hefty portion of her pay packet to the pick 'n' mix counter.

She sucked on a grape gob-stopper and thought of Christine.

Jennifer Dew glided towards the White Corridor, ready for the hand-over. The doctor was a vampire, so obviously suited to the night shift. Jasmine gave her the day's notations.

No extraordinary concerns. Percy Gill had finished her pony book and requested the next in the series. Jago and Leech had some sort of beef and were in separate sulks.

'What about Wax?'

'Bad news. He's still alive.'

Dr Dew polished a red apple on her black tunic. She took a large bite and chewed. Her teeth shone.

Jasmine had nothing against vampires.

... except Jennifer knew something was up. Which pricked her fangs.

Jasmine's mind was guarded enough – Scary Mary didn't faze her, much less a bored bully like Bad Mouth Bob – but Dr Dew scented a pressing concern the way a shark knew a swimmer had a small cut. Blood sharpened her eye-teeth but she was more a mind vampire than a vein vampire.

'Family stuff,' Jasmine said, shrugging. 'You know how it is.'

On her way out, Jasmine visited the Rec Room. Patients on the Lime Corridor had privileges. Enlightened but not too damaging or damaged. Whisk Kid – basically a high-speed pickpocket – played ping-pong with herself. Eunice Uglow watched the big telly. Flame-resistant pyjamas made her look like a balloon bent in half on the sofa. She was a pyromantic with a black mark on her record. Therapy damped her burning fury. She would have been released on probation years ago – only she could raze a building with her mind. Eunice was set off when Draycott's Academy banned eyeshadow for eleven year olds. That year's fad – inspired by Lovely Rita's spring personality – was peacock designs around the eyes, with elaborately teased lashes and brows. The tabs called her Pyro Pixie or the Little Match Girl. Giving young, confused enlighteneds trade-names was unhelpful.

Eunice was watching the same clip as Geordie Jed. On Red-Tel's *Fun News*.

'It's Chrissie,' she told Jasmine.

Eunice had been at school with Jasmine's niece – until she set it alight.

A woman in uniform spin-kicked a crock in his cakeface.

'Good gravy,' exclaimed Jasmine.

'Will she be coming here?' said Eunice

'I really hope not.'

The *Fun News* cut back to Zuleiman and Fanci in the studio, chortling. Goss was that they snorted laughing gas during the clips. Zuleiman kept sliding off the overinflated bouncy couch. He wore frictionless Shiny Shiny trousers. Fanci snorted chee out of her nose.

Next up was an announcement that the Anglo-American Jupiter Mission was delayed again. Expansion of the launchpad at Bristol Spaceport was halted by a wildlife preservation order. Ponds reported to be the last natural habitat of the South-West Fen Frog were in the way. Zuleiman and Fanci ribbited.

Leaving the Rec Room, Jasmine dialled Christine. She got a recorded message.

Her niece was looking after the house while Lawrence and Nahrein were off on their enviable world jaunt.

She'd have to run up to town.

CHRISTINE, 25 EWELME ROAD

The reminder sent her to the kitchen. Unchopped celery was piled on a sideboard.

Oh joy.

She looked at the stalks and at the knives on the magnetic strip.

She couldn't suddenly chop vegetables with her mind. She couldn't reach out a mentacle and do tricks with floating knives.

Two more abilities she hadn't developed. Her tally of gifts: violet lightning, weird black stuff, seeing in the dark, bursts of swiftness, unpredictable strength and an itchy night-buzz. Oh, and an unasked-for habit of hitting people where it hurt.

She pulled out her Vone to dismiss the reminder and saw a constellation of silent flash-pings. She'd disenabled sound to maintain set discipline and – what with one thing and another – forgotten to turn the functionality back on. Three hours without checking her messages. A personal record.

A dozen missed dials from Loulee – only slightly more than average for a Tuesday teatime. Three squirts and a blurt from Garn. A GBTM from her agent – probbo to sack her. And many pointas to Peophole and the Personals. All to the same clip.

She dialled her Peophole Purview and saw herself with the crocks. For the first time, she heard the grunts, gasps and swears she made while exerting herself. While exercising, she heard heroic go-go music in her head and imagined devastating elegance. Shot from a low angle – because the girl with the camera was nine – she looked like a cross-eyed crash test doll and sounded like a constipated hippo on the loo.

Ta very much, Bailey and Lenka! One of them must have picked up a crock's Vone and filmed the clip.

Next time, Chrissie would let crocks play badminton with little girls' purses. Nelly could rescue her own flipping fans.

The All-Powerful Jupiter Boy sent a blurt. YOU'RE ON TELLY!!!!

The clip had been taken up by the *Fun News* on Red-Tel and *Mid-Evening What's Up* on the Other Side. Even *Matters of Moment* on the Serious Channel ran it to illustrate an item on the wave of prejudice experienced by those who embraced the crockery lifestyle (especially if they terrorised and robbed children, the spokescrock didn't say).

A Dr Crockery squirt pinged a black throbbing skull. He accused her of lifestyle-bias bigotry and demanded her discontinuance from the Coterie. He copied Vidar, Chell and Monica Maude but not Hereward, Symon and the All-Powerful Jupiter Boy. That told Chrissie who he was feuding with this week. Marcus Milner was always wanting someone thrown out of the balloon basket. He was usually easy to ignore. This time, she worried he'd get the votes. A girl who was likely to strike folk with violet lightning might not be majorly larfs in a Club or at a Thing.

The Crockery Set popped ridiculous rewards – free chee at Lyons for a month, an off-peak return to Southsea – for anyone who spotted Perky in the wild and clipped themselves slapping her stupid face. Now she couldn't so much as pop down to Briteway Stores for a packet of Omo without worrying about being assaulted. This was why so many cloaks had secret identities. They wanted to sip the occasional Gin & It without some put-away cutthroat's last remaining minion beaning their perms with an ashtray.

Vidar and Chell private-squirted offering support. They almost deffo private-squirted Dr C offering him support too. That pair never saw a fence they didn't want to sit on.

Monica Maude blurted that Marcus was stung *Matters of Moment* booked someone who went to school with the producer to represent the crockery community. Not a proper crock, just an old chum wearing a sponge teapot from the wardrobe department. The Serious Channel was full of people who went to school with each other. They notably hadn't reached out to have Chrissie on the programme. Then again, she wasn't ready for cross-examination. Her agent cautioned against personal appearances which might skew negative with her target audience. No, she didn't know what that meant. Proper people? Who's to say who they were when they were at home.

The All-Powerful Jupiter Boy asked if there was a gig opening for a companion.

They all seemed sure Chrissie was a cloak. An enlightened, enabled bright light.

She had no secure squirt from Martin Masters offering to put her on the waiting list for the Splendid Six. Not a surprise. Even the Double Deckers hadn't dialled.

Nothing from Polly O. Naturally. Her full name was Polly Opal but the O stood for Nothing. You got nothing from Polly. Ever.

Hereward sent a private-squirt saying he'd make a way more wondrous companion than the APJB. He attached a click of himself posing in his Micros.

Why were folk eager to be companions? Was that now a desirable gig?

Things had changed since the time Loulee didn't speak to Chrissie for three days when they had a row over who would be high-flying cloak Glamour Girl and who plucky companion Sparky.

She *must* dial Loulee... only first she should check Peophole. Sure enough, the scrap was there too. These things got picked up quickly and forgotten as fast.

The *Nightly Nova* Purview had one of Garn's clicks from the weekend. The Coterie and the Sparkler, after the scrap at the Spot Hot, with her face circled. A headline asked, 'Is Mauve Mystery the Sparkler's New Companion?'

She hit her forehead with the heel of her hand.

She'd have to issue a denial about the Sparkling Tossoff. Many denials. What larfs!

The scrap played automatically and she couldn't remember how to disable it so she watched again. It had been given the works. Whoever processed the clip scrubbed the audio and laid in a peppy, poppy vibraphone track. Motion was smoothed and lighting enhanced. She looked a *little* elegant when she scythed Rum Baba's legs out from under him.

She looked back at the metastasising Personals Debunk natter.

Shock Jock challenged her to a rematch but was bumped below the fold by a tsunami of nemeses she'd never heard of. Sluggo De'Ath. The Throbbing Brian – he probbo meant the Throbbing Brain but autocorrect had defeated him before Chrissie could. The Thumpulator – who would, presumo, thump her later. Not an especially intimidating parade of cutthroats. No one really horrendous – the Cartoonist or Lady Godawful – had challenged her. To date, her only scrap had been with useless voids. She wasn't confident she'd do as well against the majorly malevolent. Or even an average nasty piece of work out to build a rep by ripping off a new bug's mask to decorate their secret rookery.

Not that she had a mask – or that one would be much use now.

Following pointas, she sampled variants of the clip – sped-up to Benny Hill music, slowed-down with Japanese subtitles, intercut with Perky answering the phone on *Letsby.*

Dr Crockery blurted a petition. The Cake and Crockery Alliance demanded that the hate criminal Christine Chambers be removed from *Letsby Avenue.* Giving broadcast time to someone so bigoted was tantamount to lifestyle evaporisation. People who said those things never got results would have a head-scratcher next week but one.

She cradled her Vone then remembered she hadn't dialled Loulee and switched it on again.

While it warmed up, she glumly chopped celery and put the bits on a plate.

Yum yum, she didn't think.

Her doorbell rang.

It would be Loulee or Garn. Both would want explanations she didn't have. Then she had a panic.

The silhouette on frosted glass wasn't any of those possibles. A tall woman.

Had the tabs sent snappers after her? That would come.

She opened the door.

Auntie Jas – Dr Jasmine Chambers – stood on the doorstep. She wore her long black medic coat.

At the kerb was a Rolls-Royce the length of a motorboat. Nosy Nige would be out with measuring tape. He had put up signs about non-resident parking. Chrissie knew the National Health paid well but – *crumps!* – there were tycoons who couldn't afford to drive such a dream machine. The Rolls was mint. A 1933 ShadowShark. She'd bought the Dinky toy when she and Loulee had their car craze.

'Christine,' said Auntie Jas, 'we need to talk.'

Chrissie raised a hand in welcome.

A spark ran from Auntie Jas's shoulder to Chrissie's hand.

'That'll happen,' said her aunt. 'I'd tell you you'll get used to it but I'd be lying.'

ELEANOR IN THE WYNTER PALACE

WHEN FILMING STOPPED, REAL WORK BEGAN.

Eleanor's personal assistants Alf and Bert – Alfred Iger and Roberta Pelm – helped her out of her last *Letsby* costume of the day then hovered as she chose evening wear. Five possibles, hot off the silk loom, had been express-delivered from Stán. The dress-up game was serious. She had to pick a gown for the Soiree of the Gods on Marius Stok's river yacht, the *Norwegian Would*. The bash was also a variety special, going out in peak viewing time. Downstairs – this week's Number One guitar group – were top of the bill so she'd need earplugs to match her earrings.

The first frock out of the packaging was splatted with wet red paint and had bleeding ragged edges. The second was a tent made of curtain rings and triangular wedges of cheese in silver paper. It was official: Stán was off his face and having a larf. He'd been this way for months. Eleanor didn't even look at the other dresses. She'd feel less like a raving nit wearing one of the cellophane shrouds the clothes came wrapped in. Technically, they were also Stán creations or at least sported his visible logo. Wearing the garment bag instead of the glad rag would meet her contractual obligation.

Bert sorted through bins to find a suitable belt for the semi-opaque shroud.

A big telly in the Wynter Palace showed the *Real News* on Red-Tel One. The box couldn't be switched over to other channels. This being one of the two week nights when *The Rubbish Quiz* filled the *Letsby* slot, there was no need to enable sound. There was a to-do in Texas involving flying saucers and cosmic rays. The clips were poor so the news cut in animations and diagrams. British cloaks were on standby in case the Major League needed rescuing. That wasn't bloody likely but Red-Tel had a national service remit. Flying the flag and all that.

She sat in her swivel chair, footsies dangling. She would have to wear her highest heels on the *Norwegian Would* and wanted a few pain-free moments before clamping on the torture boots.

Alf ran through the deck of face-cards with prompts on tonight's names. Frances Minto, the Deputy Prime Minister – much more happening than the poor old PM. Marius always had the people who'd be on top Next Tuesday. He didn't much bother with people who'd be off the Wheel by then. Prince Boys, the royal nephew. Heir to the throne – unless Q Vee II did something quick about getting married and/or popping out a future monarch. Martin Masters and whichever two of the Splendid Six were taking a turn as cloak Couple of the Quarter – probably Quackanapes and Silly Millie. Quackamillie would bear watching. They always had pranks up their puffy sleeves. Sir John of Scotland Yard, who'd arranged Metropolitan Police credentials for her. Eleanor was officially a serving Inspector and outranked WDS Jill. *Letsby* was favourite viewing with top plods. Good for recruitment and the public image.

From the other side of the aisle, Marius would have a cutthroat or two. Someone from the not-exactly illegal arm of GEIST like the Cutting Commentator. Court cases had determined that the CC didn't mean anything he said even if oiks who took him at his word were inspired to do deeds which landed them in Wormwood Scrubs. Marius could invite someone off the Most Wanted list – Veronica Gorse, Lord Adder – and get them a free pass for the evening, declaring his big toy boat neutral territory. Marius was forgiving to a fault.

Alf said Bert would be within springing distance from her elbow, ready to block the view if a lowly reptile aimed to snatch a click of Eleanor with anyone inappropriate. Crooks, decadents and politicians could be smiled at over fizz with few consequences but some faces would sink her rankings. A suppressed click showed Eleanor enjoying a frozen giggle with Modred Murda, a cutthroat who'd committed dozens of public crimes in the 1990s and early 2000s but returned to society after a spell in Devil's Dyke. Honestly, the mad mindmaster – an alarming individual whose head (and one arm) floated free of his body – wasn't the worst person Eleanor met at that bash. But there was a fuss. Dorothy Schilling had kittens.

Telly viewers would see acts miming to pre-records. Cutaways to the audience on the yacht would show a sparkling firmament of bright lights. Eleanor would be lucky to be glimpsed in three wide shots and a single close-up, nodding to music she couldn't hear and wouldn't like if she did. She'd bandy words with the tuxedo tossbag covering the red carpet and accept compliments on her cellophane shroud.

'The car to the jetty will be here at seven,' said Alf.

She knew little about Alf and Bert beyond their names. They were supplied by Dorothy Schilling. One was very thin and the other very not. They might be married to each other or brother and sister. Alf and Bert breathed only to serve her... which is to say, the name and the face Eleanor Wynter, WDS Jill di Ferrante, Nelly the National Treasure and the Number Nine Schilling Banner Client. Alf maintained her Peophole Purview and Personals Presence. Bert collected clippings in leatherbound books. If she asked, Alf and Bert could secure a discontinued flavour Milquik at four in the morning when all the shops were shut. They'd serve long jail sentences for her. Or for the *idea* of her.

Her nightmare was that some day she'd be a ghost – no longer Eleanor Wynter but a tattered wraith wailing in outer darkness while someone flesh and blood used her name and wore her face. The dream made her wake with the taste of a no-longer-manufactured Milquik flavour in the back of her throat, gripped by panic which only gallons of the stuff could quell. It didn't do to ask too many questions about how the show kept on the road. Eleanor suspected bodies were buried in multiple sites.

She could do with that flavour now. Oily Nut.

The taste of her childhood.

She looked in the mirror. If she swivelled her chair just so and sat straight, she could frame her face with the reflection of the box, putting herself in the picture. And on one of the *Rubbish Quiz* evenings. The naughtiness made her giggle. She should add a click to the Personals natter which said she should be on every night of the week. Her head blotted out a swirling vortex over Dallas.

A thing had been done today which wasn't pleasant but was advised.

She'd discontinued someone. Not in so many words. Her wish had been anticipated by others involved in the never-ending process of keeping her light bright. It was her idea but she hadn't thought of it yet. Now she wouldn't need to. People acted on her unexpressed wishes the way the Cutting Commentator's followers sprayed liquid fertiliser over traffic wardens. Without legally provable cause and effect. As a Schilling Banner Client, she rated a Room. Clever people had her ideas for her and put them into practice. Dorothy Schilling didn't have time to decide which shoes even a client as important as Eleanor Wynter should wear, so she trusted the Room to brainstorm details. At the sharp end, Alf and Bert were there to fetch and carry and execute and implement.

The Wheel could turn under her. If the Room decided Eleanor Wynter's life was too perfect, too enviable... that fans would love her more if she suffered a loss... adopted Bolivian earthquake orphans and live with the demanding brats for a whole series of *At Home With Nelly Off the Telly*... appeared in a raga rock musical *Saint Joan* with an all-Floppit supporting cast... be embedded on *Crew Selection: Jupiter Mission*, mocked for spewing in zero grav and not knowing which hose to connect to her spacesuit... be on the receiving end of flung flans whenever she stepped out in public.

Three *Letsby Avenues* a week and an omnibus on Sunday.

That was where she was on the Wheel.

Between six and six-thirty – with a single advert break – she was brightest light on the box.

Twenty-five minutes out of the day, three days a week (and catch-up on Sundays).

It wasn't enough. The Personals said that. She knew that. Dorothy Schilling knew that and had the Room working on it.

There were worlds to conquer. Peak viewing time.

Three years ago as a lass of twenty, she sparked in a *Monday Night Musical* on the Other Side. The natters spurred Red-Tel to mount a raid and snatch her before she could ink a long-term contract. She'd played Christine in *Chandelier!* with Staunton Gwyn, trade-name FlexiFace, as the Phantom of the Opera. In another recurring nightmare, she found herself back on that set with Flexi-Face swinging from ropes high above the studio floor. A chandelier dropped on the audience to persuade the management to replace ageing diva Carlotta with young hopeful Christine... only Eleanor was shouted at by the director and laughed at by the audience and forced to hop out of the way of belaying pins thrown by the Phantom. She was in the wrong costume, with the wrong lines learned. She wasn't Christine, billed after Flexi-Face... but Carlotta, listed below the comic impresario and the pointless police inspector.

Every Christine is terrified she's a breath away from being a Carlotta.

As she remembered the dream, she perspired.

Alf was there with a powder puff.

Alf!

Oh yes, the powder person was discontinued. Gone.

No offence but they were off the Wheel. They were Carlotta. This new person was Christine.

The new person was here. She came into the Wynter Palace.

Eleanor blinked, seeing double. The new person – Lulu – was not alone. Not in the mirror. She stood in front of someone, almost blocking them from view. Turning away from the mirror, Eleanor saw Lulu and nobody else.

Alf handed the new person the powder puff and pointed at Eleanor's face.

Lulu got to work. On her own.

Eleanor still thought another someone was in the Wynter Palace. Standing wherever she wasn't looking.

She didn't need to talk to Lulu. Any person brought to the Palace wouldn't have got this far if she had to be told what to do.

Lulu had a light touch. She wasn't easily satisfied. But knew when to stop.

The previous person had started doing too much.

Alf said the previous person made Eleanor look like Lovely Rita.

(Lovely Rita was the Carlotta di tutti Carlotti)

That was when Eleanor knew the person was going to be previous.

And Lulu was coming in. An adjustment had to be made to allow that. *Letsby* had writers to take care of the details.

('Here's your implosion bomb, Carlotta – take care of it, don't mind the ticking... have you met *Christine*?')

It wasn't even the girl's fizzog the Room reckoned would bother Eleanor. It was her name.

If the actress were called Georgine, Peaky wouldn't have been flash-frozen.

Something flicked at Eleanor's mind to make her think about a thing she'd usually let slide off unnoticed.

That woman who came in with Lulu was behind the door to the chill-out cave. In shadow where she couldn't be seen. The blind spot. Where lurk flan-flingers, fertiliser-squirters, flexi-phantoms and ghost persons with grudges.

Eleanor swivelled around to look, which made Lulu back off.

The loiterer was gone – nipped into the chill-out cave to hide under a heap of giant-size plushions? – but there was still something wrong with this picture. The farmer had a shoe on his head and two left hands. A chicken was mooing.

It was the telly. Showing something wrong.

On the box, Peaky – a Christine! – was in an unauthorised scrap.

Insurance wouldn't let Eleanor do scraps, though she was up for it.

Before *Phantom*, she'd played a secret agent in a leotard in a Milk Tray advert. She knew how to throw a stunt man off a parapet. WDS Jill needed to biff some crims. Moody looks to camera were fine and good so far as they went. A clip of her putting a felon on his arse and shouting 'you're nicked, Nobby' while her hair fell perfectly in place would clock repeat views on Peophole. She'd love to spend a Monday (Out of Studio) punching a crim in the fizz and booting scrotes into a canal. Another Milquik flavour that got her going – a touch of blood, salt and copper on the tongue.

Surely this scrap would end with Peaky getting face-froze to death?

But that wasn't what they'd filmed. Budget wouldn't stretch to a scrap. And it was *Rubbish Quiz* night.

This wasn't *Letsby*, this was *Real News*.

'Isn't that...?' Eleanor said, conscious that her brows were knitting.

'You what,' said Lulu. Her tone didn't best please Eleanor.

Lulu turned and saw the scrap on the box.

Peaky shot purple light out of her hands. A Fondant Fancy slammed into a wall. The crock fell away from a soot-burned human outline which was making a scaredy hands-up gesture.

Lulu was astonished. She dropped her powder puff and pulled out her Vone.

She said something in another language.

If Lulu was to continue as face maid, Alf or Bert would have to provide subtitles so Eleanor could be copied in.

'Recorded message,' said Lulu, listening to her Vone. 'I have to go.'

Wait, what?

Lulu was out the door.

Someone darted after her, quicker than Eleanor's eye.

Who *was* that extra woman? Eleanor recognised the loiterer with the head-dress. She'd been getting in her eyeline and on her wick all afternoon. If looked at directly, she hid behind people. She'd come into the Wynter Palace with Lulu, hung about not saying anything. She'd sprinted off after the make-up person like a demented fan.

Make-up persons did *not* have fans.

Eleanor was ready to give Alf and Bert what for. They shouldn't let a civ get close. Who knew what flans were concealed under that dress-robe affair?

Where was security?

Bert came back with three possible belts. Eleanor liked the one in the middle best but picked the one on the left. When presented with three choices, she knew not to pick the one in the middle. Picking the one in the middle came across as careless or indecisive. The one on the left or the one on the right. That was the way to go.

Picking a belt gave her a jolt – almost a buzz.

But not enough to make up for the gripes. Lulu's hanger-on could wait. Eleanor had an inkling that if she brought her up, she'd get blank looks. The *Real News* item was more pressing. It would have consequences.

She was gowned and belted by seven when the car came.

CHRISTINE AND JASMINE

CHRISSIE MADE CHEE FOR AUNTIE JAS.

In the kitchen was the wood table where the Chambers-Mirza family had Christmas dinners and birthday parties. Board games had been played to death or bankruptcy on this surface. One leg had two perfect-bound issues of the Ewelme Road Residents Newsletter stuck under it for balance.

Auntie Jas laid her hands on the table.

'You've beaten the wobble. Good for you.'

'It'll be back,' said Chrissie.

'I suppose. Wobbles always return.'

Dr Chambers was her father's older sister but looked younger than Dad. Impossibly younger, now Chrissie came to think of it. By twenty or thirty years. Loulee had to work for half an hour to give Chrissie a glow her aunt came by naturally. Her agelessness was a mystery. Loulee harped on that she could tell Jas didn't even dye her hair, which hung like a silk snood. Midnight black and full-bodied.

Auntie Jas opened her mouth to speak, then thought better and kept quiet.

She was thinking of ways to deliver good and bad news and not liking any of them.

'Now, Christine,' she said, at last.

Chrissie nibbled a celery chunk and interrupted.

'Before we go on, I have to ask... A *Rolls-Royce*! Don't you drive a Mini?'

'Yes. These days I do. I like a nippy car.'

'A Rolls-Royce ShadowShark isn't what you'd call nippy.'

'No. Not at all. It was my grandfather's, originally.'

'Granddad's Dad. I've seen clicks. Holiday snaps. He was a doctor, too. In the old days. Before the National Health. And anaesthetic.'

Auntie Jas smiled then looked serious.

'Jonathan Chambers was Dr Shade,' she explained. 'The original.'

That trade-name rang a bell.

'He was a cloak in the 1930s and through the War,' Auntie Jas continued. 'He used contraptions and gadgets. Struck fear into the hearts of wrong 'uns. He went after cutthroats and spies and wasn't too gentle about it. My grandmother played the night-game too. Her trade-name was Kentish Glory. She had moth-wings and antennae. Floated rather than flew. This was before *Never Mind* – when extraordinary really meant extraordinary. People forget there were cloaks and cutthroats before 1972. Not so many and not so magical but they were about. Men of Mystery. Mind Over Matter Maids.'

Chrissie wasn't well up on history but knew Dr Shade.

He was one of those cloaks who looked like cutthroats. Shadowy, spooky... like Urban Fox or Night Mist. Fedora and infrared-goggles. Long black coat. Not the sort who save children's cats from burning haystacks and stay for scones afterwards. The sort who make hooligans run screaming into alleys and knock themselves out slamming into brick walls.

'You've been going through changes lately,' said Auntie Jas.

Chrissie looked at her hands. No lightning. She wiggled her fingers.

'Yes, that...'

Chrissie popped a celery chunk into her mouth and swallowed it whole.

She'd been hungry for so long she'd learned to ignore her stomach.

After the day she'd had – and having an inkling how the next few days were going to go – she could eat a field of celery without washing dirt off the stalks.

'Dr Shade wasn't enlightened. He was clever and well-funded. He had a mask, the car, an autogiro...'

'A what?'

'A kind of mini-helicopter. Like a go-kart with rotor blades. I've one too. Not the same one. Rolls-Royce don't make autogiros so they don't hold up well enough to become heirloom vehicles.'

'Why do you have an autogiro?'

'Because I am – or was – Lady Shade.'

Auntie Jas paused, expecting a reaction.

'You were who?'

Auntie Jas laughed, not bitterly.

'That's your first lesson. It doesn't last. What is it you girls say? Next Tuesday. My Next Tuesday came a long time ago.'

'You were a legacy cloak?'

Like Spinning Jenny II or Son of the Beech. Chrissie wasn't an idiot. She could work it out. Dr Shade... Lady Shade. Was there a Shady Dog too?

'Mostly off the books. I'm not surprised you haven't heard of Lady Shade. I tried to stay mysterious. Be elusive. So I could get on with other work. I have a C.B.E., remember. For treating the *Never Mind* disorder, not the night-time shenanigans. The mask was only a part of my life.'

'You brought it, didn't you?'

Auntie Jas took something out of her Vautrill handbag – exclusive to Signor Fred of Knightsbridge (talk about well-funded – *Eleanor Wynter* couldn't afford Signor Fred!). She unrolled darkness over her forehead and cheeks. The mask was blue-black with a rigid noseguard and mirror glasses. It attached with tiny skinhooks and left her mouth and chin bare.

'I forgot the beauty mark,' she said.

Auntie Jas dabbed her chin with a forefinger and left a convincing mole.

'You look like you're wearing a mask,' said Chrissie.

'Few twigged the secret identity. I was a smidge disappointed. No one much seemed to care. They were just grateful to be saved.'

'You saved people?'

'All your questions sound like prompts. Yes, I saved people. I hit people too. Often. I struck them with lightning.'

'Shut the fridge.'

'Yes, Christine... it's hereditary. Kentish Glory had unusual abilities. Others in the family too. I did two terms of genetics and it wasn't my best subject so you'll have to find someone else to test for the cloak gene. I had it – have it. You'll have it too.'

'Crumps!'

'Double crumps, as we used to say.'

Chrissie looked at her hands. They seemed green and she wanted to eat her fingers.

'I know it's a lot to take in.'

Chrissie fidgeted with celery.

'Must you do that?' Auntie Jas sounded like Dad – which shouldn't surprise her.

'Do what?'

'Play with the bunny food.'

'What bunny?'

'Don't you have a rabbit? Bunsen?'

'Beaker. He was run over years ago.'

'Yes. Very sad. But why the celery?'

'The Schilling Agency has me on a strict regime. Celery and distilled water every three hours.'

Auntie Jas looked horrified.

Properly aghast. As if this was the most insane thing she'd heard all week – and her job was listening to mad people.

'You must be *starving*,' she said.

'That's the point. Have to keep a trim figure.'

Auntie Jas stood up and walked round the kitchen. The table was too big for the room, so she had to squeeze. Her form was admirable and elegant. Chrissie only now noticed how deft her aunt was, like a dancer or an acrobat. She ducked out of the way of hanging baskets and sidestepped the laundry basket.

She opened the pantry cupboard and saw more celery.

She looked back at Chrissie.

'I blame myself for not telling you sooner. I've known, ever since... well, always. You were a spark as a little girl. Even Lawrence said so and he's – sorry for saying this – the most blissfully, wilfully obtuse man. He saw me up close in the mask and didn't recognise me. Nahrein knew at once I was Lady Shade, by the way. Not fooled by the beauty spot at all. I can never get it in the same place twice.'

Chrissie couldn't look away from the pantry.

Auntie Jas sorted through celery, hoping to find something else. There was a small tin of Briteway's Own roll-mops at the back, well beyond its use-by date. She dropped it in the swing-bin.

'I'm not sure if you're going to want to kill me or kiss me,' she said. 'How long have you been on the celery diet?'

'About a year.'

'What did you have for Christmas dinner?'

'Celery.'

'What about clubs? I know you go to clubs because of Peophole. Remember Eunice Uglow? She's my patient. She's a devoted peeper of your Peophole Purview and highlights pointas to all the clicks. I see you with cocktails.'

'Holding, not drinking,' Chrissie admitted.

'You must sip *something*.'

'Distilled water with celery in.'

Auntie Jas looked up at the ceiling and spread her hands.

'Celery is just water and string,' she said. 'Even for an ordinary girl, this would be torture not a health regime.'

'It's not about being healthy, it's about being trim.'

'Thin. Trim means thin. Clinically undernourished. You're not normal, Christine.'

Now she wanted to cry. She'd been worried. In Chrissie's circle, eight days a week with pangs of privation was a given. Polly O said she lived on air and starlight. Monica Maude swore by ground nuts. Hereward climbed onto the Wheel with a pre-existing eating disorder. For him, a celery-and-water blowout was a scrumptious feast.

'Look at me,' said Auntie Jas, 'what do you think I had for lunch?'

Dr Chambers was enviably trim.

'Something light. Hummus and half a pitta bread?'

'Fish and chips. Three portions. Extra salt and vinegar. Apple pie and custard. Two pints of Graill Ale. And a Twix.'

The thought made Chrissie light-headed.

'That's to keep me ticking over at a low level. I'm not in

the night-game any more and my spark has dimmed. I'm not looking to scrap with Modred Murda and the Mannikin. So I'm not refuelling the way you ought to. Our bodies burn ten times more calories than the norm. It's the Shade legacy. Right now you're barely existing on rabbit food. Crumps, you should have been eating whole tubes of Rolos every half hour. This afternoon, under the bridge, the scrap with the crocks... was that the first time?'

'The first time like that. But I've been thinking. Lots of things have happened over the last year or so that make more sense now. Or might do. I lit a broken street lamp.'

'If you'd been eating properly, it'd have come on earlier.'

Auntie Jas peeled off her mask and looked at Chrissie.

'We have got to get grub into you. Stat.'

GARNET GRAILL

'WITHOUT PICCIES – CLICKS OR CLIPS, PREFERABLY clicks *and* clips – it didn't happen. Show didn't go on. Happy couple ain't legally wed. Flan weren't flung. That's the rule. With piccies, everyone knows it happened. Even if it didn't. Piccies can lie. Scrub that. Piccies do lie. All of 'em. Every representation is misrepresentation. Some gloomy duck goes round all week with a face like a haddock but flashes teeth for the micro-second you catch in a click... then the general public know Madame Misery as a cheery smiler. What they know is wrong but if they know it long and hard enough it really don't matter.

'I can name half a dozen notables you've got arse-about ideas of. What I say won't change your mind. You look at the piccies and know what you know. I snap 'em. Which clips and clicks you see isn't my shout. I only *contribute* to what you think you know. Bods I couldn't name at Peophole and the *Nightly Nova* look over what comes in – not exclusively from me, worse luck – and pore through contact sheets to find the pics *necessary* to the story already filed. If *Real News* wanted to lead off with an item about Lovely Rita putting kittens in a blender, illustrative material could be found from the files. Without even doing anything as crude – and, as it happens, illegal – as splicing a pic of, say, Lovely Rita spilling out of a low-cut frock with a pic of, say also, a kitten turning to ratatouille in a Robot-Chef. My mission is to provide the raw material. Which don't mean I can't exercise artistry. In fact, it's a priority. I want backroom bods to know a Garn Graill when they see one and pay extra for the privilege.

'Any herbert can point and click. It's about being where you need to be to point and click the good gravy. Tonight, it's this Soiree of the Gods shindig. Ton of faces from across the board. You need to click the upwardlies looking bright and the downwardlies looking shady or else the piccies don't sell. Once in a blue moon, counterintuitive is choice. Say, a right bastard like – well, like Rikki Bastard – looking innocent licking an ice lolly at Skeggy Fayre. Or Queen Mum Floella shoving an old dear out of her way to gazump a bargain at the Harrods Sale. Mostly it pays to play into ongoing narrative rather than spring a plot-twist. The Soiree of the Gods is a Marius Stok Thing. A-List only. The Red Rope is there in force to keep freelance snappers back but not turn us away. They call us reptiles but we're part of the game. Me and about twenty other solos and a couple of telly crews, a-jostle in case Quackanapes and the Cartoonist prance out of limos at the same time and start slinging exploding dead cats. Then you have to be careful too. You got to take risks but be mindful of crossfire. No use having that great click if the camera gets smashed – or your bonce broke. You got to take the piccy and walk away to turn it over to the platform which bids highest. I've a way past the Red Rope. Connections with connections.

'Thing about the stuff with the faces and names – openings, bashes, happenings, stunts, whatnot – is that you generally know a day or two beforehand where and when it's going to be. You do prep, secure access, scan guest-lists. Other clickable gubbins – crimes, disasters, rescues, scraps, miracles, *real* real news – is unscheduled. You got to work for it. Rewards are commensurate. Sky high in some cases. You need contacts in crisis-facing walks of life – cloaks, crims, emergency services, *psychics* – to give the heads-up. And a reliable means of transport to blimmin anywhere. Something nippy and easy to park. A bubble car with a bit of oomph or a motorbike. Most of all you need the Luck. If I were to develop a single enlightened ability,

I'd want the Luck – a sense of where to be when. To feel the pull of that quiet spot in the middle of nowhere where action is about to kick off.

'We can all dream, can't we?'

JASMINE RECALLED TO DUTY

A CYCLE MESSENGER FROM CATHAY OLÉ DELIVERED A Szechuan Tapas Fusion Feast. Seventy boxes of high-cal foodstuffs. To be washed down with honeyed chee. Jasmine had told the restaurant the order was for a family of eight. It might not be enough. Christine wasn't the only hungry Chambers at the table.

Jasmine had scoffed her last Penguin while driving through Haywards Heath. Pre-delusional Richard would have rebuked her for getting crumbs in the upholstery and choc smears on the dashboard.

Christine started gingerly, wielding chopsticks as if struggling against mesmeric deep conditioning. Jasmine wouldn't put it past Dorothy Schilling. Eyeclamps, negative reinforcement electro-shocks, and a Viennese-accented voice instilling prohibitions on any food but celery. The racket ought to be investigated. If her old arch-nemesis Modred Murda was behind the Schilling Agency, she'd not be surprised.

Murda must still have a grudge about what happened when she wrapped a noose of darkness around his neck. Transporting a slice of him to another dimension didn't appear to be inhibiting – except, perhaps, socially. But she tried not to repeat such drastic misuse of her dark ribbons. It might do Christine good to see the old cutthroat in his retirement rookery, to understand how casual exercise of her abilities in the heat of a scrap could have permanent effects.

Christine popped a small fried starfish into her mouth. At the taste of something not celery, she closed her eyes and had a long moment of impure joy.

She slapped the table and swallowed.

Lawyers didn't magically appear to prohibit contract-violating calory consumption. Christine tucked in. Jasmine barely snaffled some *churros con cajeta*. Once Christine got going, she couldn't stop. It was heartening. She ate skin, bones, wax paper, spicy peppers, bamboo leaves. She used chopsticks, spoon and fork, and her hands. She shovelled, chewed and savoured – and swallowed. Then ate more. Her violet penumbra sparkled. She was like a Vone in a charging cradle.

'This is Better Than,' she said, through a mouthful of something sweet and sour.

'Better than what?' Jasmine asked.

'Just Better Than.'

'Ah, I see.'

A young ones thing. Jasmine remembered Eunice saying Worse Than – meaning Lovely Rita's Viking Robot frock at the Royal Command Performance – and asking 'worse than what' and getting 'just Worse Than' as an answer. She'd have to hear the expression two or three more times before it didn't seem wrong. By then, Better/Worse Than would have expired and be something Lawrence might say. A young one in earshot would cringe. That was how the Wheel turned.

The Wheel wasn't a young or an old thing but a *Never Mind* thing.

That moment hung in the air a lifetime – well, for some people, a lifetime – after the needle settled in the groove.

'I prefer the Stones,' Lawrence said after Jasmine played *Never Mind* the first time. 'They shouldn't have broken up when Keith married Yuki-Onna.'

Jasmine's little brother was tone deaf to wonder. He didn't see the darklight pouring from her eyes as the music played or notice she was sitting in the lotus position six inches above the cushion.

Years on – bless him – Lawrence still didn't understand what the fuss was about.

Lawrence was the Dad who Disapproved – of pop music preferences, skirt lengths, diet, unsuitable friends (Loulee excepted, of course), non-sensible career options, cropped hair, etc. He held his tongue because his one clever habit was listening to Nahrein, who had a spark herself. His wife had been in the Commonwealth Games.

Christine crushed two fistfuls of fortune cookies and funnelled the bits into her mouth. She put the paper strips aside. She explained that Loulee would translate the Chinese for her. They often gave a different fortune than the English one. 'Keep Waiting for the Right Moment' was 'Your Boyfriend Sells Grot Clicks to the *Nightly Nova*'... though she admitted she took Loulee's word for the exact translation.

In her first year at uni, Jasmine slept for three days and woke up knowing languages. All of them.

Christine showed Jasmine the old fortune she'd saved to confront Garn with.

'That says "Keep Waiting for the Right Moment",' Jasmine said.

'What a ratbag,' Christine said, laughing. 'I gave Garn frost for weeks.'

She'd met Christine's photographer boyfriend, Garnet Graill. He'd snapped her on the sly. The clicks might be worth something if she were sued for malpractice or murdered by one of her patients. Jasmine worked with a vampire and thought tab snappers were more nakedly predatory. Garnet came from money. Beer Money, actually. His family owned the Graill Brewery. He had a nice smile, an expensive haircut and a half-decent eye. Jasmine drank Graill Ale, so she gave him some points. Worse boyfriend options were available.

She cautioned Christine about being snapped or clipped too often when exercising her abilities. An instinct to pose and smile or pose and pout had been inculcated by the Schilling Agency. Jasmine told her night-work wasn't like walking the red carpet. Christine should take things at her own pace.

Then she let the girl eat. Christine had much catching up to do.

A silent pulse radiated from her top pocket. Jasmine took out her Vone.

'No clicks,' said Christine, in a panic. She hid behind food boxes. 'If Schilling see this...'

'I have a blurt from work,' Jasmine explained.

A high-alert blurt. Three blinking red skull-and-boneses. Geordie Jed – with bad news.

'Dr Chambers, there's been an escape. From the White Corridor.'

The world slid sideways.

One of her shady tricks was limited second sight, more confusing than useful. Flash images. Dark red pooling on white linoleum. Someone tall and thin, reflected in the liquid mirror. An open cell door. Terrifying eyes. Dr Dew, hand pressed over a pulsing neck wound. Klaxon horn and emergency lights. Alarums and signal flares.

Dr Head's duck was broken.

'Not Wax,' said Jasmine.

'No, Doctor. Not him.'

She breathed again. It wasn't the worst she could imagine.

No – she shouldn't be relieved! Wax might be the worst *to her* but others – Scary Mary, the Jibbenainosay – were as much danger to the public. A White Corridor patient at large was a disaster.

Fifty weeks of the year, Persephone Gill was a county set young biddy of surpassing dimness. The other two, she went to sleep inside her head and a her from an alternate reality took over the rudder. Parallel Percy – Miss Kill – was a cutthroat nonpareil, a dark-enlightened assassin. There was no way of predicting when those two weeks would come. Which was why she was on the Corridor. If she still was...

'Who, Jed, who?'

'Jeperson.'

'*Richard*?'

Jasmine must have yelped the name. Christine looked at her.

This didn't add up.

'Richard got out?'

'*Was* got out. Dr Dew's been stabbed with wood. An alert's gone to the local nick, automatically. Devil's Dyke's on lockdown. The patient may still be on the grounds but I doubt it. They'll be well away with him.'

'They?'

'Two or three, at least. The security footage is blurry. They disrupted the tape like sound on vision.'

They. GEIST.

'I'm on my way.'

Jasmine hung up.

'A work emergency,' she told Christine. 'Sorry, we'll have to reconvene. There are things you need to know. My prescription – keep on eating, take regular vigorous exercise, don't let off lightning indoors and for the moment stay out of scraps. You could do someone an injury if you're not careful.'

'The emergency. Can I help?'

Jasmine was tempted. A lass who could punch like Christine might be useful.

But her niece had only just found out she was enlightened.

She wasn't ready for GEIST or the prize pupils. Few were.

'Hold fast for the moment. I'll dial you.'

Devil's Dyke had cloaks on retainer. Not anyone near as public the British Lions or Moonlight Flit. But experienced night-workers. Plain Jane and Hughbert Hound.

GEIST brought wood to pin the vampire. They were prepared.

'Auntie Jas,' she protested. 'I can tell it's serious.'

'Of course you can. And you want to pitch in. But it's one of my patients. You know who I work with.'

'You let things slip when you were on the elderflower wine at Christmas. Adam Tussaud.'

'Yes, him. Not a name I should mention. But you're sharp. You pick things up.'

'That's not what Loulee says.'

'She knows you're sharp too. But you pick things up from me especially. It's because our enlightenments are alike. Not the same, because they never are. But related, as we're related. You're a Shade.'

'Do I get a Rolls?'

'Not right now.'

'But sometime, maybe?'

'Maybe, sometime, yes. I don't know.'

Christine was happier at that than with the Fusion Feast.

Jasmine remembered Nahrein ordering specialty items from Hamley's when Christine was ten or eleven. She had a car craze. Collected models and zoomed them around an obstacle course in the back garden. Who knew how that got in her head? Dr Shade, her great-grandfather, was the auto enthusiast. It wasn't quite time to tell Christine that the ShadowShark was only one of a fleet of heirloom vehicles in the Lock-Up. No sense in dumping all her Christmases – and the keys to the Bentley, the Jaguar and the Hovercraft – on her at once. Now she came to think of it, car craze or no, Christine had failed her driving test and never got round to retaking. She'd have motivation to learn hand-signals properly now.

'I have to go.'

'Duty calls?'

'Since you put it like that, yes.'

'Duty as who? Dr Jasmine Chambers, Head Doctor or Lady Shade, cloak?'

'Both, I suppose. I'm not really a cloak anymore but you can't play the night-game for years without starting all sorts of business which takes forever to be done with. It's why I work where I do.'

Her heart raced. She was charging too.

At this moment, Richard might be having a nice cup of chee in what he thought was a Lyons Cyber House, telling a sympathetic soul the funny things which bobbed around in his head. A mature woman, glamorous and just a bit mumsy. That's who'd get results with him. GEIST would know that. He could disclose decades of secrets. Give away the hidden cards. Spill the codewords and black site locations. Identify the informants. When he was used up, they'd throw him away. They might not even kill him. That could safely be left to the Shadow Cabinet.

She hadn't told Christine about the Shadow Cabinet!

Time for that later.

Jasmine went out into the atrium. Yellow fog roiled over a stained-glass angel. She'd never puzzled out how this vaulted space fitted into Forest Hill. A touch of strange. She was glad of it. Everyone was owed a go on the mystery-go-round. Living here, Christine had the angel to look up to. It was as well her eyes be drawn to the sky.

Jasmine put on her mask again. There was a tingle, a whisper of cool against her face and the tiny pleasurable pricking of micro-hooks under her ears and along her hairline.

Twice in one night – after, what was it, months? Years.

Once for show, and once – for what, seriously? *Lady Shade Returns.*

She pulled open the front door and found herself mask to crash helmet with Loulee Ling.

'Hello, Loulee,' she said. 'Sorry to dash.'

She stepped past Chrissie's friend. Loulee's mouth hung open.

Jasmine twisted her signet ring and the ShadowShark's driver-side door hissed open. She slipped behind the wheel and took an emergency Twix from the glove box. Attuned to her S-ring's sub-audial harmonic, the engine auto-started. She took the wheel.

Curtains twitched as the Rolls-Royce purred down Ewelme Road.

CHRISTINE AND LOULEE

'WHY WAS YOUR AUNT WEARING A LADY SHADE MASK?' asked Loulee.

Loulee's Lambretta was outside. She'd cajoled an Honorary Residents Parking Permit out of Nigel Timperley, an impossible and never-again-bestowed privilege.

'You've *heard of* Lady Shade?'

Loulee looked at Chrissie as if she were gormless.

'*Of course* I've bleedin' heard of Lady Shade. You've heard of, I don't know, Admiral Nelson?

'Admiral Nelson the pub?'

Chrissie was trying to keep Loulee away from the kitchen.

'Admiral Nelson the Admiral. "Kiss me, Hardy." "I see no ships." Bloke on top of the column in Trafalgar Square, pooed on by pigeons...'

'Rings a bell.'

It was no use. Loulee was unstoppable...

... from the atrium, doors led to the lounge and the kitchen. To go upstairs, you had to go through the kitchen. For fifteen years, the routine was that on arrival at the house Loulee would go into the kitchen for chee and a nibble. Mum kept special Loulee nibbles in plastic pantry containers. That Mum was exploring a volcano on the other side of the world didn't throw Loulee off.

Chrissie trailed Loulee into the kitchen.

Loulee was, for once, astonished.

The remains of the Fusion Feast covered the table. Additional unopened boxes were piled on other surfaces. A chee-cauldron – unused since three Christmases ago when the Mirza cousins visited – was on the hob.

You'd swear a family of eight had tucked into this spread.

Her friend looked from the table to Chrissie and shook her head.

'Flaming Nora,' she said.

Chrissie realised she must be sticky.

Loulee picked up chopsticks and, as delicate with them as with eyebrow tweezers, unglued grains of rice from Chrissie's face and detached noodle-fragments from her hair.

'I've a bone to pick with you,' said Chrissie. 'You've been mistranslating cookie fortunes.'

'Every time I did that was to tell you something you needed to know but didn't want to hear.'

Looking back on it, that was true.

The *Scurrilous Rag* ran a click of Chrissie doing a teapot pose to make fun of Dr Crockery while he crashed a Justice for Jesmond vigil outside City Hall. Garn had been snapping that afternoon. Marcus deserved the lampoonery. He was there for a publicity op not the cause. He didn't even know who Jesmond was. After the click ran, Red-Tel sent Chrissie a curt memo enjoining her not to make controversial political statements. An upside to Perky being killed on *Letsby* was that she could now admit she wholeheartedly supported the RSPCA. Who knows, she might even get Justice for Jesmond – or use her new enlightenment to work out who Jesmond was and what flavour justice they deserved.

Garn rated an arm-thump at the least.

'Did you and her get through all... this?' Loulee asked.

Chrissie found a box of tempura prawns and offered Loulee some. She used fresh chopsticks. The Fusion Feast came with about fifty pairs.

'Um, Cathay Olé, lovely,' said Loulee.

'Auntie Jas ate some of it,' Chrissie said. 'Not much.'

Loulee looked in the pantry. Sad heaps of celery remained.

'Want to help me bin that vile veg?' Chrissie asked.

'Want to explain?'

'What? Auntie's mask? Easy. She *is* Lady Shade.'

Loulee choked on a prawn. Chrissie let her have a cough.

'Didn't you see the Rolls?'

'A ShadowShark,' said Loulee, not quite finished with her cough. She cleared her throat. 'Tasty motor,' she said.

'Jas took off the mask, Louls. Gave up her secret identity. That's not the order she did it. She put the mask on, then took it off. And said she was this Lady Shade.'

Loulee swallowed the last of the prawn.

'Respect,' she said, thumping her sternum. 'She caught Adam Tussaud.'

'I know about *him*. I saw the film with Gary Oldman.'

'And she broke up the Humphreys.'

'She didn't say she was a homewrecker.'

'The Humphreys were a gangcult. Thieves. They'd steal anything. The police had posters up... "Watch Out, There's a Humphrey About". They were a GEIST satrapy in the '90s. And Lady Shade totalled them. She scrapped with Modred Murda. You know this, Chrissie. There was a paperback and a TV series. She's a Very Important Cloak. Lamb Bear had her poster up in his bedroom.'

Lamb Bear – Lambert Ling – was Loulee's twin brother. He worked in London Zoo, which Loulee and Chrissie thought was hilarious. He was Assistant Curator of Reptiles and Amphibians.

'She was at the Battle of Battersea,' said Loulee.

'Auntie Jas?'

'Apparently, yes. Your Aunt Jasmine.'

'Auntie Jas who's useless at Cluedo? Who drives a P-Reg Mini Cooper with a wonky indicator light?'

'She has another car.'

'Which was news to me. She has an autospiro too.'

'An autogiro, you mean. A mini-helicopter.'

'That's the one. Though I'm not sure she needs it. Maybe she can fly by flapping her arms.'

Loulee sat. She finished the prawns and grazed. Outside of farthing-sized omelettes with bits of celery in, everything was a treat. She opened a box and found crispy seaweed, a particular Loulee nibble. Chrissie must have subconsciously left it for her.

'So that's the Auntie Jas bombshell, Chrissie. Now...'

With her left hand, Loulee took her Vone out and dialled the scrap clip. With her right, she dipped her sticks into crispy seaweed and fed her face.

The clip was followed by a sit-down interview with Bailey and Lenka, who now wore matching blue serge mini-size WPC uniforms and Perky caps. The girls had started a 'Punch Up Like Perky' campaign. Red-Tel would have something to say about that. Sandra 'Perky' Purkiss, her distinctive likeness and even her death were wholly owned and trademarked and copyrighted. Maybe they had already signed off and expected a share of the takings.

Nelly must be doing her nut.

'So Chrissie, what haven't you been telling me?'

LOULEE CATCHES UP

CHRISSIE DISHED OUT THE STORY SO FAR AS IF SHE were Perky summing up Monday's *Letsby* on a Wednesday. She'd found out she was enlightened. She had abilities but wasn't too sure what they were. So far, all she'd done with her shady tricks was scrap with voids and fix the Grey Gruesome's street lamp.

When she could get a word in, Loulee ought to tell Chrissie ghosts didn't like that patch of pavement any more than she did. Before that, though, she'd have to explain about the Ghost Lantern. Yet again, this didn't seem the moment to share her news. Chrissie had the conch and a lot to get through.

So... Chrissie's aunt arrived and unmasked herself as a semi-retired cloak. Then had to rush off again – in a Rolls-Royce ShadowShark! – to tackle a crisis. Calling All Cloaks. Maniacs at large. Oh, and the celery diet was majorly discontinued. What Chrissie needed was proper food in big helpings. Puzzling circumstances now made sense. Dr Chambers' sweet tooth was explained. The mystery of who ate all the chocs off the tree before Boxing Day was solved.

It even fit in with things Loulee had gathered from ghosts.

When Chrissie was around, the hubbub went quiet. Ghosts either showed respect or were wary. Some seemed a tad jealous. The Filcher hid. The Perky costume reminded her of Bow Street Runners. Oghulqaimish calculated how to beat Chrissie in a sabre scrap. Until now, Loulee reckoned her friend wouldn't know which end of a sabre to hold. If Chrissie could generate lightning, anyone who went after her with a sword should insulate the hilt with a rubber grip. Loulee felt herself nudged along that line of thought by paranoid, prickly ghosts. A concern. Sometimes she caught herself thinking more like them than herself. Oghulqaimish was confident she could parry lightning. Yvyra saw points where nerves intersected and dart-pricks would be fatal.

Ghosts needed to understand something.

It would never ever be Ghost Lantern Girl vs Christine Chambers. It would always be Loulee and Chrissie against Whatever Came Along.

Of course, the Whatever was now redefined. It wasn't Nelly blowing a fuse – Loulee needed to tell Chrissie about her 'promotion' too – or Dr Crockery being a snark, but real cutthroats. Devil's Dyke cases. Agents of GEIST. Lord Adder. The flaming Cartoonist!

Loulee sat while Chrissie prowled. Her aura – mauve with star-sparks – was like a wraparound toga. Chrissie had said she was more awake at night. Now it was obvious. She was more *everything* at night.

'Have you chosen a trade-name?'

Chrissie sat down and leaned in.

'I have our old list. It's not going to be Glamour Girl.'

'No,' Loulee agreed.

'That's an enlightened light trade-name. I suppose I'm enlightened dark. Dr Shade, Lady Shade. That's the lineage. There was a Kentish Glory too. I suppose she sounds quite Enlight-Light.'

'So, not teeth and smiles but pout and snarl. Mystery Maid.'

'That's the area. But not that, obviously.'

'Something simple, classic… the Shadow?'

'Taken. Protected trademark.'

'Miss Night?'

'There'd be jokes. Nightie jokes. Nightly jokes. Anything with "Miss" is asking for a ribbing. Remember when Eunice wanted her trade-name to be "Miss Fire" and didn't know why we laughed?'

'We stopped laughing when she pyromaniad the school.'

'That's another thing. Eunice is one of Auntie Jas's prisoners. Patients, they call them. Suppose she's the one who's escaped. Scorched her way out. She follows me on Peophole and the Personals. Fringe stalkery. Crumps, she must remember us laughing at "Miss Fire"! Louls, do you think she's going to be my... *arch-nemesis*?'

'That happens. Some cloak-and-cutthroat feuds start at school. They say on the Serious Channel that cloaks and cutthroats haven't really grown up. It's an infantile stage... Fancy dress costumes, taking a trade-name, getting into scraps.'

'You watch the Serious Channel?'

'If I watch telly at all. When you know how programmes are made you don't want to see them going out. When was the last time you actually watched *Letsby*?'

'The Q Bomb thing.'

'See. Years ago. Before you were on it.'

'I've fast-forwarded.'

'Back to trade-names, flibbertigibbet...'

'Maybe for a cutthroat – though Flibbertigibbet sounds like a cutthroat *companion*. Like the Cuckoo or – whatjumacallher? – Adam Tussaud's popsy.'

'The Mannikin. She wasn't a live woman. He puppeteered a wooden armature. A shag doll, basically.'

Chrissie made a sick face. She coughed out a blotch of darkness.

'Best not do that again,' said Loulee, wiping the ectoplasmy stuff up with a paper napkin. 'I wasn't suggesting Flibbertigibbet. I was calling you one.'

'Fair dos. I've a shedload of night-buzz. I think I'm a bit jabbed... without jabs. I'm burning ergs from the Fusion Feast.'

'I had noticed. You're racing ahead and hopping about. Handy in a scrap, irritating in a conversation. Trade-names. Is Lady Shade II going spare?'

Chrissie grimaced. 'I don't want to stress the legacy aspect.'

'Makes sense. Clean blackboard. No need to inherit your aunt's nemeses when you'll have your own queuing up.

Cutthroats keep Grudge Diaries and carry on feuds to the next generation.'

'I've had suggestions from the Personals. Ultra-Perky is out in front.'

'Red-Tel presumo own that. By association. They own a lot of you thanks to that contract the Schills made you sign in blood.'

'It was only a drop. And you made yourself clear at the time.'

Loulee had consulted a professional over Chrissie's contract. Enyedi Boglárka looked over the terms and recommended challenging Dorothy Schilling to a duel to settle the insult. Loulee reminded the ghost how that had worked out for her last time.

'They made you cut off all your hair because a focus group said Girl Punished by the Resistance for Flirting with the Occupation Forces was going to be the high street visual of the New Season.'

'... which it might have been if not for some bright light getting jelly.'

Chrissie dialled her Personals Presence on her Vone and read more possible trade-names.

'Violet Vision, the Mauve Marvelle, Night-Thwacker... lots of variations, from men who steam their specs at the thought of women hitting people and probbo have a kink about being hit by women. Punchin' Judy.'

'That's funny.'

'You'd stop laughing after a week and start hating it.'

'Verit. Besides, don't use a name from the Personals or Whispers. If you do, whoever popped it will get lawyers and want a tithe. In fact, dial off now and never connect again.'

Chrissie clasped her Vone to her chest and looked more upset than when she saw her character's death announced in the pink pages.

'Joking, obviously,' Loulee specified. 'But underline the rule. Never Take Advice. Except from me. I'm different.'

'Are you actually volunteering to be Shady Wotsit's companion?'

'Leave it out, ladybird. We're not having that barney again.'

Loulee already had a trade-name. Ghost Lantern Girl. She supposed ghosts counted as companions. Or a gangcult. She was less a cloak, more a fluencer.

'One suggestion was That Sad Moo,' said Chrissie. 'You could be Cow-Bag to go with that.'

'What bolus put that up?'

Chrissie looked at her Vone.

'DrtheoriginalfirstCrockery.'

'That's an extra wallop next time our paths cross.'

'Real wallops hurt more than play wallops. Giving them out, not just receiving...'

Chrissie showed Loulee scraped knuckles.

'Let me put ointment on that.'

She took the first-aid box out of her big bag and started working like a medical manicurist.

'Drop Ms Moo and Cow-Bag', she told Chrissie. 'Too niche. The leather and lactation community is fringe of the fringe. You should go mainstream.'

'I agree. But we need to fix on something before the tabs stick a trade-name on me and I'm forced to go along with it.'

Chrissie's hands were slightly electric. Loulee felt her hair rising, drawn towards Chrissie as if she had a Van de Graaff Generator for a heart.

'How about Dr Van de Graaff,' she suggested.

'Like the electricky metal orb? Too Serious Channel.'

'You could be Dr Dark... Or Dr Darkness.'

'They must have been used.'

'Must have.'

'... and I'm not going with "Doctor" Anything. Auntie Jas actually is a qualified quack and she doesn't. Her granddad was the original Dr Shade. He was a GP. Too many – Marcus Milner, for one – stick 'doctor' or 'professor' in their trade-names without any right to. Dr Robot isn't a doctor or a robot.'

'Madame Tenebra.'

'Don't like Madame. Sounds elderly.'

'Night Mary.'

'Too like Scary Mary. I don't want *her* for an arch-nemesis.'

'Night Woman.'

'Sounds like an office cleaner.'

'What's wrong with that?'

'Nothing. But it's not a trade-name.'

'*Năiniú* Girl.'

'Come again?'

'Awesome Girl.'

'Loulee... You're sneaking round to That Sad Moo again. *Năiniú* means cow. You first told me it meant awesome when I wanted a Chinese character tattooed on my shoulder.'

'Fair cop.'

'What about Awesome Girl, though?'

'Utterly generic. And presumptuous. Other people should say you're awesome, incredible, amazing, whatever. You can't call yourself something flattering. You can have preferred pronouns but not preferred adjectives.'

'What about the All-Powerful Jupiter Boy?'

'I rest my case. He's not a cloak, he's not enlightened, he's twenty-eight and he's a bolus.'

'Twilight Zoe.'

'Problematic. Everyone would get it wrong in print and you'd have to explain what you meant. I like it, though. Maybe stay away from the night theme. What else is dark or black or deep purple?'

'Insides of cupboards. Horses you don't expect to win – but Dark Horse would be another "asking for it" name. The tabs'd say you had a companion called Rank Outsider. Coal is black. So is tar. Or pitch. How about Susan Soot?'

'Leave off, Louls!'

'So, Mauve Mabel it is, then?'

Chrissie stabbed her with a used chopstick, which broke.

'Park the name for now,' said Loulee. 'What about the uniform?'

'Well,' said Chrissie, 'I have been thinking...'

CHRISTINE TRIES ON SOME THINGS

'FIRST OFF,' SAID CHRISSIE, 'I'M KEEPING THE BULLS. They're comfortable and don't let in water. When I kicked Lemon Drizzle in the goolies I didn't break my toes.'

Bull Boots were a given. She should start with brands she actually wore. She could get sponsorship. ClodHoppers weren't nearly as good at twice the price.

'You'll have to peel off that grotty transfer,' said Loulee. 'You don't want Justice for Jesmond anyway. Jesmond is guilty, you know.'

The sticker – reflective silver lettering on a shocking pink roundel – did catch the eye.

'I put it over the gluey fluff circle left by the price sticker.'

'I know a fix for when glue doesn't come off,' Loulee said. 'Fill a cur's drinking bowl with wine and olive oil and use its wee as a salve. It only smells for a day or so – and all the manky gum washes away.'

'You know this how?'

Loulee had one of her evasive looks. Elaborately innocent.

'Let's try vinegar first, shall we?' said Chrissie.

Loulee closed her eyes as if someone invisible were nagging her.

'That should be fine,' she said. 'Cur wee isn't essential.'

Chrissie stood in front of her full-length bedroom mirror in what she had so far for her uniform. Marks & Sparx underwear, InvisiStockingsocks and the Bulls.

Loulee knuckle-poked her in the tummy.

'What was that for?'

'Seeing if you're invulnerable.'

'What?'

'You're not. Look. Little bruises.'

Blue marks faded.

'It hurt too,' Chrissie said. 'Did I mention that being thumped hurts?'

'Best not to be thumped, then.'

'I scrapped with five or six crocks. Some of them hit me. I wasn't keen. I have scrapes and bruises. Had, rather. I heal fast, apparently.'

'Can this be your visual? Underwear Model. Some cloaks get away with a bathing costume and kinky boots. Brighton Belle. Weather Girl. You'd have snappers falling off buildings to get clicks.'

'Too obvious. Remember Nelly in the Milk Tray ad?'

'That was more leotard than swimwear. Do you still have your dance outfits? The leggings with two left feet?'

'Cheek.'

'You weren't exactly prima ballerina...'

'I was twelve, Louls. I'm more co-ordinated now. And grown-up. Leotards don't stretch that far.'

'You? Grown-up? Hah!'

Chrissie put on her Puffy Floppit dressing gown. She'd had that since she was twelve too – and it still fit. A wearable duvet, covered with appliqué felt Floppit faces. Nothing bad could happen to a girl in a Puffy Floppit dressing gown. It kept out gamma radiation and German measles.

'*Not* a visual to strike fear into the hearts of cutthroats and evil-doers,' commented Loulee.

'The Puffy's not for visuals – it's for me not freezing.'

'So, your uniform *isn't* boots, bra, knickers, dressing gown and WPC hat.'

'No.'

Now she thought of it, Chrissie wasn't feeling the cold. It

might be all the scoff she'd had. She burned ten times more fuel than the norm.

The Puffy was more about being comfortable and protected.

Loulee looked through the wardrobe in Chrissie's room.

'Haven't you got anything glammy from the Circuit?'

'That's mostly supplied by Schilling and has to go back. We get tithed if there's damage.'

'So no Stán?'

'I wish. He's Banner Clients Only. Nelly is exclusive to Stán…'

'She hates his clobber, though. Tonight she went out in a cellophane wrapper rather than wear what he sent over.'

That was insider information. Loulee had her sources but…

'First cur-wee, now Fashion Secrets from the Wynter Palace?'

'That's easy to explain, Chrissie. Red-Tel made me Nelly's personal make-up slave.'

'Treason!'

Chrissie felt stabbed but it wasn't Loulee's fault.

'I tried to quit but…'

Loulee held up her wrists in a handcuff gesture.

She went back to the costume issue. She raided every wardrobe in the house for options.

'This is what you've got,' said Loulee, laying out something like a shed snakeskin on the bed. 'Your Mum's figure-skating costume from the Commonwealth Games. Metallic tights and matching mini-dress. Armoured underweave to minimise injury if you fall and are scraped across twenty feet of ice. A desirable feature for the scrapper about town.'

'I'm hoping to avoid that side of cloakery.'

'Let's hope it avoids you. So far as I can see, all cloaks do is get into scraps.'

'I'm still not keen.'

'You do plan on being a cloak, though. You weren't thinking…'

Loulee sawed her hand across her throat.

'Crumps, no. Can you imagine…'

Loulee's eyes narrowed in thought.

'No,' said Chrissie, 'I *can't* imagine. I don't want to break things or steal things or hurt people. It's – what's the word? – *wrong*.'

Loulee hugged her and stayed hugging a bit too long. Chrissie suspected it wasn't her being hugged but the Puffy Floppit. In the end, Loulee let her go.

'Truth, justice and the Ewelme Road way,' said Loulee, saluting.

'Yes, but without being a bolus about it.'

'This is a bolus-free zone, aye aye.'

Chrissie took off the Bulls and Puffy. She put on the tights and Loulee helped her into the dress. The ensemble zipped up the back and was snug.

'Do some Floppit Hops,' Loulee ordered.

Chrissie jumped up and down.

'The magic's still there,' said Loulee, pinching Chrissie's cheek.

Chrissie threw punches at an imaginary Eleanor Wynter balloonface. She did a high kick, printing the Charging Bull treadmark on Not There Nelly's forehead. A phantom of That Trainer Guy from Sunny Gym went down after a one-two-three combination to the chin. How did he like the taste of his own sweaty mat, eh? Bring on the crockery crew too. She could take them.

Violet crackles lit the room. Loulee oohed at the sparks.

Chrissie stopped pretend scrapping.

The dress hadn't ripped. Seams didn't cut into her when she stretched or bent. The armour wasn't inhibiting or uncomfortable. Chrissie had watched clips of Mum skating at the Games. She'd have won Silver on her own but her partner wasn't up to her level. She didn't meet Chrissie's dad until after she retired from competitive skating. She went on to design light fittings for the company where Lawrence Chambers supervised after-purchase agreements.

The leggings tingled a bit. Metal against skin prompted minor electric crackle.

'What about a cloak?' she asked Loulee.

'Not many cloaks wear actual cloaks these days. Which might be a reason to go retro. I could do something with those curtains.'

'Best not. Mum and Dad will come home eventually.'

'You're sure about that?'

'Yes. And they'll want to find the wine undrunk and the curtains up.'

'Point. I saw something of your dad's.'

Loulee sorted through clothes heaps and came up with a black trenchcoat Chrissie had borrowed for a fancy-dress bash. She'd gone as Inspector Hawkshaw, the Information Retrieval Service mascot. Like other things Chrissie had borrowed, it wound up in her wardrobe – at the back, like the ruby earring under the eggs in a magpie's nest.

'Way too styley for your Dad.'

'I don't think he ever wore it.'

Loulee settled the coat on her shoulders like a cloak and swished a bit, swivelling her hips.

'A Christmas present from Aunt Jasmine,' said Chrissie. 'The cloak.'

'That makes sense,' said Loulee.

'It'd look great on her.'

'I think it did. It's part of the Lady Shade uniform. Perhaps she needed a last-minute present because she was too busy scrapping with Modred Murda to go shopping that year.'

Loulee gave Chrissie the coat, which settled nicely.

'Arms in or out?'

'Out for the moment, with the option on in.'

Chrissie looked at herself in the mirror. The coat was darker than night. With a velvet collar. The figure-skating outfit lacked pockets. The coat's pouches, pockets and toggles would do for gadgets and doodads.

'It's not too "legacy", is it?'

'You'll wear it differently. I'll take it in so it's a slimmer fit.'

Some weeks, Loulee was an expert seamstress. At other times, she got the thimble on inside-out and couldn't scissor a straight line to save puppies from an incinerator. Another talent which came and went.

Loulee cast a critical eye over the ensemble.

'You'll need to unpick the sponsor insignia from your Mum's dress. I doubt you'll want your cloak activities endorsed by Cheesy Wotsits.'

'I don't know... Smoky Bacon flavour is choice.'

Chrissie was still hungry. Auntie Jas had mentioned regular tubes of Rolos.

'I don't think there was a Shade logo as such,' said Loulee, dialling on her Vook. 'Dr Chambers tended not to stick around after scraps to be clicked. I can't find clear pics of her uniform.'

Loulee showed Chrissie some clicks.

The masked woman was hardly recognisable, which was the point of a secret identity. She only knew Lady Shade was Auntie Jas because of that beauty mark.

Should she ask Loulee to give her a black spot? As a tribute? Only obsessives would notice. As well to pander to the core fan base a smidge. Just not enough to put off the casual followers.

Loulee dialled again.

'The only images I can find of the original Dr Shade are artists' impressions. He was one of those see-a-camera-smash-a-camera types.'

'Is the mask the logo?' Chrissie asked.

'Could be. It's not a generic domino or a ski hood.'

Chrissie dialled back to the clicks of Lady Shade.

'I'm not wearing a mask,' she said.

'Why not?' asked Loulee. 'Less work for me if you cover two-thirds of your fizz. Imagine how much more I can do if I only have lips and chin to concentrate on. I'm thinking dark scarlet lippy.'

'I don't see the point. I reckon the secret identity option was scotched in the scrap with the crocks. I was identified too early to get away with a mask.'

'You've not spoken in public yet. You can deny it's you. No one will listen to grudge-holding teapotheads. There're only those two girls to argue with.'

'Bailey and Lenka. I reckon they'll be believed over me.'

'Agreed, reluctantly. So, the bad news is that cutthroats will know who you are and can hurt you by coming after your family...'

'Good luck with that. Mum and Dad are off the map and Auntie Jas duffed up *Gary Oldman...*'

'Adam Tussaud.'

'Yes, him. A Gary Oldman level arch-nemesis. Cutthroats who want to hurt me – and, yes, annoyingly they're out there already, three hours after my first scrap – will not want any of that. I'm more worried they'll go for *my friends.*'

Loulee's face went blank for a moment. Then she barked with laughter.

'No, Louls, I'm serious...'

Loulee kept laughing. She did this sometimes. As if she suddenly remembered the funniest joke in the world but couldn't convey the humour to mortals. What larfs.

'It's not just voids,' Chrissie insisted. 'There's someone who calls himself the Thumpulator. What would you do? Take the shine off his conk with talcum and spackle over his blackheads?'

Loulee got it under control.

'Don't worry, Chrissie. You won't have to avenge me. I'm set. Trying to get to you through me would be a poor lifestyle choice. Carry on cloaking with no concerns. I have resources.'

Chrissie understood. Worrying about Loulee was not a thing she needed to do.

'If not a mask, what about dark glasses?' Loulee suggested.

'At night? I'm a night-person, remember.'

'Pfui, half the Coterie wear Spex... mostly to hide the jab-tears but also because sunglasses after dark is a classic visual. The ultimate not-a-disguise disguise, for when you want to be seen to be unobtrusive. Stay away, leave me be, I want my privacy, take my picture, more clicks on page nine...'

Loulee was imitating Hereward – with whom she once had her official Worst Date of the Century. The mockery applied to all of the Coterie, not excluding Chrissie. Loulee was caustic about Hereward and fondly indulgent of Chrissie for roughly the same foibles.

Dark glasses prompted a thought.

'Schilling sent me a box of Spex. Night-vision goggles but stylish.'

'Haul 'em out.'

Chrissie dug the box out from under her bed. One set had wireless frames so you could dial a Vone by blinking. Another had sound effects balloons on the arms – SPLAT! POW! KRUNCH! She wasn't wearing those in this lifetime.

She put the CyberSpex on and looked at herself. Loulee pouted over her shoulder.

She looked through and over the Spex. And was satisfied.

Schilling would be happy if she wore client clobber.

'Your aunt wore a hat,' said Loulee. 'A slouch-brim fedora with a velvet band. So did Dr Shade.'

'I've got the Perky cap.'

'Uh-uh. Red-Tel IP, remember?'

'Point. I've a binful of hats I was ordered to wear to cover the crop. I don't like any of them. What about my hair?'

'What about it?'

'What about just my hair?'

Loulee pinched some of the crop and pulled.

'Ouch,' said Chrissie.

'That wasn't hard. Not half as hard as this Thumpulator chummie would yank.'

'Aunt Jas wears a ponytail which is easier to grab hold of than the quarter-inch bristles you've left me with. She's around cutthroats way worse than the Thumpulator. I reckon he's a bolus using a made-up name for his Personals Presence who has never thumped anyone.'

'Cut any closer and you might as well shave it all off,' said Loulee. 'I'm not sure you could get away with the Baldie Bonce visual. You might have a spotty scalp.'

'What do you call those form-fitting hoods? Like an armour balaclava?'

'Cowls. Also not you.'

'Fireman's helmet and gas mask.'

'Save me work but no. If you've not got a secret identity, you need to show your face. Or else there'll be natters claiming it's a stunt-person doing the scrapping. Remember the Street Sweeper? Turned out he only did photo ops. Had three masked stand-ins to scrap with hired hooligans. Some useless rupert he was. Since him, even cloaks who wear masks uncover enough so you know it's them.'

'So what's your solution?'

Loulee reached into her make-up case and pulled out a wig. Glossy black, with a fringe and sharp bangs. It made the wearer look like a 1920s film star. Loulee once tried to cut her hair to match the wig but – as with physicians who botched healing themselves – it hadn't come out well.

If Loulee wore the wig, she looked like Anna May Wong.

When Chrissie had it on, she looked like Louise Brooks.

They'd Hawkshawed 1920s film stars to learn the names. Loulee had even gone to the National Film Theatre to see Anna

May Wong in *Piccadilly*. If Louise Brooks or Anna May Wong were on the Circuit, pretty much everyone – Eleanor Wynter, Polly O, Brighton Belle, Lovely Rita – would have to retire to private life and seethe with envy. Louise and Anna May had the visual even without Vooks or Vones to spread the news.

Before the Chrissie Crop – née the Perky Crop – it had taken a half-pound of pins, a roll of tape and some cheating before Chrissie could get away with a wig. Now, she might as well be a polystyrene shop-window display head. A single strip of double-sided tape did the job. Loulee set the wig on her. The fringe shimmered. She angled her head this way and that.

She pointed just above her lip.

'Beauty spot here,' she said.

Loulee took a tiny pencil and stabbed there.

'It's a tracking microdot so I always know where you are and how much trouble you're in. I can set it to ping on my Vone.'

'Really?'

'No. It's a speck of powdered pencil lead. But the tracking feature would be a plus.'

Chrissie shrugged. She eyed herself critically. Did she look like she was in fancy-dress? Well, maybe – but so did everybody in this line of work. Urban Fox or Dr Robot could hardly pass for civs. Was the visual stunning and spectacular? Not for her to say but Loulee – highly critical and annoyingly honest at times – seemed pleased with this as a first try. Later, there'd be tweaks and touch-ups.

'So my visual is wig, dark glasses and a trenchcoat,' she said. 'I look like I'm incognito.'

'Indeed.'

'... but I'm also obviously me. I look like me trying not to look like me.'

'That's the idea.'

'Gear,' Chrissie said.

Jasmine and the To-Do at Devil's Dyke

Any other evening, turning up at work in a Rolls-Royce ShadowShark would have been an above-the-fold item. Now, it just caused hassle. Her Main Gate tag was on the Mini. She'd switched vehicles to convince Christine she wasn't making up the Shade legacy.

Devil's Dyke was on lockdown.

Jasmine took off her mask and showed her face to the camera. The steel mesh portcullis clanked up to let her drive into the courtyard.

She parked in her staff space. The Rolls footprint was considerably larger than the Mini. She took care not to scrape Dr Head's Vauxhall Viva. Tonight, her motor was the stunner of the parking area. It threw shade (hah) on Dr Dew's midnight blue Lotus Elan with eyelashed headlamp covers.

She got out of the car and set its defence system with the key-fob.

A duty guard used a doodad to check her thumbprint, cornea and heartbeat. Three dings confirmed matches with the facility's records.

It was always a relief to be told she was herself.

Considering everything, she sometimes wasn't sure.

The Secure Hospital was half mediaeval granite, half post-war prefab. Every time a new prize pupil was sentenced to the White Corridor, the government of the day increased funding. 'More locks for the Morlocks' was a popular campaign slogan with the law and order brigade. What that meant was 'bury the bastards deeper'. 75% of the budget went into putting guards on the guards, shockwire on the walls and fail-safes in the surveillance set-up. So far, bunging cash at the problem had done the job. From outside, the hospital looked like a black pyramid.

Now there was a crack in the wall. The duck was broken.

99.99% escape-proof was tantamount to come-and-go-as-you-like.

Dr Head was already here.

The Director saw Jasmine. He didn't comment on the Rolls.

Head wore a tailcoat and white tie. His evening was ruined too.

She offered him a Rolo and he accepted without joy. He had a sweet tooth like hers. Was he invisibly enlightened? His bald cranium was football shaped. He might have extra thinking room in there.

It struck her that his name might be a trade-name.

Sewell Head. Swellhead. The Head Doctor.

He swallowed without chewing. Not recommended by Rowntree as the way to relish the richness of a Rolo.

'I've opened the contingency packet,' he said. 'Three simple instructions.'

He showed her a single sheet of paper.

1: Locate and readmit inmate/patient.

2: Review security measures.

3: In the event Instruction One is not carried out within forty-eight hours, Director to tender resignation.

'A draft resignation letter is helpfully included,' he said.

'They can't mean it.'

'They don't say it'll be accepted, just that it should be tendered. It's a dance.'

Captain Rawlins, the Night Watch commander, reported the latest area determined not to be harbouring inmate/patient Jeperson, Richard. An escapee might be out of their cell but not off the premises. Unofficially, that was the presumption. The first response to the escape bell was a thorough search to determine whether an inmate/patient was hiding in some crack or cranny. Two Polka Dot cases and one Wavy Lines patient had got loose in the time Jasmine had been attached to Devil's Dyke. All swiftly found. None got over (or under or through) the wall. A mislaid White Corridor patient merited more urgent response – which was a worry.

Rawlins was short, thick-set, neckless. Compacted and toughened by tours of duty in simulated Jovian gravity with the Special Space Service. On Earth, he was as strong as three normal men. Pressure inside his head bulged his eyes.

Rawlins came to Devil's Dyke with a crew of aggrieved, five-foot, meat-muscled astro aces. To spread costs, NASA-BSDC partnered with DuMont (US) and Red-Tel (UK) to produce *Crew Selection: Jupiter Mission*. A public vote to determine who'd fill the seven seats on the Zeus Lander picked alternative comic Jonty McDribblefart as Captain. Rawlins – an experienced but anti-telegenic spacer – scored *nul points*. Astronauts who'd trained for seven years in orbit or a sea-bed dome went on strike. The McDribblefart Mission had still not taken off.

Captain Rawlins took security personally.

Jasmine reminded him that he was most likely looking for a hostage, not an escapee. It was hard to get through Rawlins' skull – reinforced with brass implants – that Prize Pupil status didn't make Richard a shoot-on-sight case. Contingencies set for a breakout by the Inner Voice or Miss Kill should not apply to...

'... your old boyfriend,' she could see Rawlins thinking.

Shutters were down in the Captain's head.

A pen-pusher concerned with national security might think killing Richard preferable to having him tell all to GEIST. Rawlins would follow that reasoning.

Which was why she had to be here.

Cloaks were on their way – other cloaks, non-retired cloaks. Hughbert Hound and Plain Jane were retained by Devil's Dyke. Hound was a finder, Jane a keeper. They were on top of Instruction One: Locate and Readmit. So far, they'd shared Dr Head's 100% rating without having to earn it. Jasmine noted she was here before them. She squelched any spark of pride. A GEIST strategist might have nobbled the finder-keeper team before moving on Richard.

Dr Head sent Rawlins to sweep another area and escorted Jasmine into the central keep. She was thumb-eye-heart-checked again. As was the Director.

'Dr Dew is out of danger,' Dr Head told her.

'... and out of the infirmary, by the looks of it.'

Dr Dew was ahead of them, walking towards the White Corridor. A star-shaped sticking plaster was moulded to her neck, tan against pale skin. Her fangs were sharp. Her eyes glinted crimson. Sometimes you could look at Jenny Dew and not know she was a vampire. This wasn't one of those times.

She swore in mediaeval French, sprinkled with archaic Magyar – which, of course, Jasmine understood. Dr Dew referred in colourful terms to the warts on the Devil's arse.

Geordie Jed was on the stile. His shift should have ended at midnight. Yvonne Ayres, the twelve-till-dawn keeper, was there too. They smushed together at post, trying to occupy the same space. Ayres was one of Rawlins' astro aces: short, wide and capable of holding her breath for three minutes in airless vacuum. Devil's Dyke staff were nurses not guards, though their union was a branch of the Prison Officers' Association.

'If they accept my resignation, Jasmine, I won't recommend you to succeed me,' said Dr Head. 'That would scotch your chances. You'll need to play politics. The Deputy Prime Minister will want to impose someone from outside. It'll seem resolute. Frances Minto won't want a Doctor. She'll push for a Guard. That'll be the end of this place as a hospital.'

Jasmine didn't want to be Director.

She also didn't want to be having an Instruction Three conversation. Instruction One was still on the agenda.

Locate and Readmit.

After another set of thumb-eye-heart checks, Jed took out the Black Vook and asked Dr Head, Jasmine and Dr Dew three questions each.

First, Fifth, Seventeenth and Forty-Third letter of Memorable Phrase.

Title of a film, book or LP with capital letters, lower-case letters, numbers and shift-keyed top row symbols.

A Thing About You Nobody Else Knows.

Jed dialled in their answers and an off-site Think Box

determined, from data on file that all three petitioners were who they said they were. There was a hiccough because Dr Dew meant *2001 – A Space Odyssey,* which passed the tests but Jed dialled in *2001: A Space Odyssey,* which didn't.

'No offence, pet,' said Geordie Jed.

More than three misdials and the whole system would cycle again.

The first thing Jasmine suggested she thought nobody knew about her was that she used a hairpin to probe Revels so she wouldn't be surprised by orange ones. Jed said he actually knew that... and Jenny Dew did too.

She struggled to think of a thing nobody else *really* knew as opposed to something they were too polite to mention they knew.

Not everybody could have four hundred years experience racking up things no one alive knew.

'I understand archaic Magyar,' she said.

'I did not know that,' said Dr Dew.

The doodad confirmed that Jasmine was Jasmine. Sharing secrets did something unique to brainwaves. The principle of the Third Question was not a favourite of anyone who had to answer it regularly.

Dr Head had three pebbles from Brighton Beach in a tobacco tin in his desk. Now he'd have to remember to add or subtract a pebble for the next time he was asked to come up with a Thing About Himself Nobody Else Knows.

This was part of the Lockdown Protocol.

It occurred to Jasmine that an excellent way of paralysing the institution was to initiate a how-d'you-do which required this ultra-secure rigmarole. Rawlins' astro nuts had to check each other's thumb-eye-heart readings every few minutes, which didn't help them get on with the search.

The stile finally buzzed open.

Halfway down the White Corridor was a vivid splash of scarlet on the wall.

Richard's door was shut.

The monitor showed an empty room. No disarray or disorder. Patient missing but all else in place. Bed made. White on white on nothing.

'Were they enlightened?' Dr Head asked Dr Dew. 'Cutthroats?'

Jenny Dew shrugged in a very French way. Technically, where she was born was the Duchy of Burgundy at the time.

'I don't know if they were a they,' said the vampire. 'If I shut my eyes and stuff cotton in my ears I still know where people are standing. Live people are warm, like stoves. I can usually sense presences.'

'Echolocation?' suggested Jasmine.

'Something like,' Dr Dew agreed. 'I've met invisible people and "see" them as well as I see you. Tonight, nothing. I felt the pencil go in my neck. As for anything else, they weren't just invisible... They were imperceptible.'

'We saw shadows on the surveillance clip,' said Jed.

'Shadows, yes.'

'Where did the pencil come from?' Jasmine asked.

Yvonne looked down. 'I was doing the *Spectrum* crossword.'

The next security review would insist on crayons across the institution. Then some malign intellect would find a way of murdering people with a crayon. Melt it down into...

Wax!

How could she not have thought of him?

'You've checked all the other cells?' Jasmine said.

Geordie Jed and Yvonne Ayres looked at each other.

'Locking and unlocking is automatically logged,' said Jed. 'None of the other doors opened or shut this shift.'

'That's a "no", then,' said Dr Head.

'Protocol is to search places inmates... patients can get into,' said Astro Ayres. 'Bathroom, broom cupboard, supplies...'

'Most likely first,' said Jed.

'If I were hiding, I'd choose least likely first,' said Dr Dew.

Geordie Jed and Yvonne Ayres looked at each other again.

'Get the digikeys,' said Dr Head.

Christine and Loulee Consider Their Fortunes

After midnight, the night-buzz got buzzier.

Chrissie wanted to experiment with her violet lightning – only she wasn't so buzzed she forgot Nosy Nige. One electrocuted squirrel and there'd be 'it is forbidden to' signs up.

With the lights off, she got juiced from the dark.

She wanted to ask Aunt Jas if she needed to discharge ergs. How long could she hold it in without burping electricity?

She stood in the kitchen – with Loulee sat on the stairs – and let herself feel the dark. It was bracingly cool. Tingle-making. Comforting. Confidence-boosting.

'I know where everything is, Louls.'

'Of course you do. You live here.'

She walked round the kitchen, not bumping into tables, chairs or hanging baskets. Aunt Jas had moved with similar ease and she didn't know the room as well. It wasn't only the familiar stuff. Chrissie knew where food cartons were and which ones weren't scraped clean. Edible scraps called out to her. She had X-ray mentacles.

'I can tell where walls, doors and windows are. I think I know where people are.'

Behind her back, Loulee silently crab-walked backwards up five stairs.

'You've gone up five steps,' Chrissie said.

'You looked.'

'No,' she said, turning. 'I didn't.'

Loulee slid back down into view. She had her Vone up.

'No clicks,' said Chrissie, hand over her face.

'Smiley-smile for the tabs, luv,' said Loulee, imitating Garn, 'then pouty-pout for the swanks.'

'He does *not* sound like that!'

'Some enhanced senses you have! He does so sound like that. Gor blimey strike a light and leave it aht, guv – wiv the benefit of elucidatin' lessons and a lick of the old silver spoon.'

At St Cuthbert's, Garn had learned not to sound like the Clever Channel. Like many poshos, he put on a barrow boy accent. It was expected of a society snapper who was due to inherit a brewery. If he used words there was no barrow boy equivalent for, his cut-glass voice came back.

Chrissie pouted and Loulee clicked her.

They turned the lights on and looked at the pics. Chrissie was really into the wig. She liked the straight lines framing her face. UnPerkylike – a plus. She half-expected a legal letter saying Red-Tel owned any facial expression she'd used on *Letsby Avenue*.

'You should tidy up this mess,' Loulee said. 'Can you telepath it all in the bins.'

'Telewhat?'

'I mean port not path. Mind over matter. Hey presto – litter begone!'

'I'm not a genie, Louls.'

Chrissie looked at the mess.

Loulee unrolled one of the scrunched cookie fortunes from the table.

'"Dark endeavours should not be entered into lightly."'

'You're still making them up.'

'No,' she said, showing the strip.

Chrissie accepted it.

Loulee looked at another. She did a take and looked at it again.

'Is your aunt funny?' she asked.

'With a few sherries in her, at times, yes. Why ask?'

'This has to be a wind-up – and with you, me, her and Cathay Olé as suspects, she springs out as most likely.'

'What does it say?'

'In English, it says "Those who respect their neighbours respect themselves".'

Chrissie and Loulee yawned in unison. That sounded like Nosy Nige. A roundabout way of saying 'do what I want or else'.

'In Chinese, it says "Your Aunt is in imminent danger at Devil's Dyke. She needs your help, Christine." That has to be a leg-pull, right?'

Loulee gave Chrissie the strip. The Chinese characters were Greek to her. And she sort of knew Greek – or at least the letters.

Chrissie had Loulee turn the lights off. She felt dark pour in.

Did she have a sense for imminent danger – to herself or loved ones or interested parties or strangers?

She felt a different sort of tingle, as if she'd been sitting on her ankle.

Thinking of it, Aunt Jas had rushed off to danger. Without hesitation. Part of the being-a-cloak brief.

Not a part Chrissie viewed with enthusiasm but not something which could be got round.

Maybe she wasn't a cloak. Nor a cutthroat. Just a Whatever.

'Even if it is a wind-up, we should go along with it,' she said.

'I agree. Your aunt might be testing you to see if you're worthy to inherit the mantle.'

'Mantle is just another word for cloak.'

'There's a fine difference. A cape is another thing too. But that's not the point. This could be a hoop you have to jump through.'

'You too.'

'How so?'

'I can't read Chinese. The message is for me but you had to read it.'

'Well, I'm not letting you plunge into danger alone.'

'You don't want to be left out, more like.'

'That too, *un petit peu*.'

'I couldn't leave you out if I wanted to,' said Chrissie. 'We can't get to Devil's Dyke with a Tube-Bus pass.'

Loulee saw what Chrissie meant.

'To the Lambretta,' she said.

Jasmine Takes a Head Count

Geordie Jed and Yvonne Ayres checked the other prize pupils. Dr Head had to authorise access and provide thumb-eye-heart authentication. Even then, cell doors wouldn't open without the digikey and an individual inmate/patient code.

Word had seeped through walls that one of the class had done a bunk. Most bad lads and ladies were awake and interested. Richard wasn't in their club so there was no mug-clanging of approval. Even outcasts cast out faces who didn't fit.

Jasmine reviewed the surveillance footage.

Jenny Dew was beset by flickers which could be optical distortion. She registered on video but no photographic process – chemical or digital – could be trusted with vampires. A flying pencil stabbed into her neck. Ayres stumped into view to help. Blood on the wall. No sign of Richard. The log recorded that his cell was unlocked for seventeen seconds. Cameras, triggered by movement, shifted to catch the action with Jenny and Ayres. The attack was to distract the surveillance. Canny. Very GEIST. The cell monitor blinked off when the door opened. Before: Richard, in bed. After: no Richard, bed made. A flourish. Seventeen seconds to abstract the patient/inmate and tidy up as if he'd never been there. So, not just GEIST.

Some bighead addicted to the pause for applause. Not a type in short supply round here.

The flickers didn't give anything away. Usually, there were no shadows on the White Corridor. That was slightly uncomfortable for Jasmine. Long shifts under striplights sapped her energy, no matter how many sweeties she ate. Vampire Jenny wore red spectacles. The lighting regime didn't suit her either.

Some cloaks – Phoebe Rays of the Major League, notably – were empowered by light the way Jasmine was invigorated by dark. But Phoebe Rays wouldn't take a zoo-keeper job. The thin sickly lighting here was calculated not to nourish bods who photosynthesised. The idea was to withhold stimuli.

After three rewatches, Jasmine was no wiser. She left to catch up with the head count.

Light panels in the cells dimmed at night but were never off. When a door was open, the patient was to stand in a designated area or be stungloved. Jed and Ayres took turns watching the inmate while the other searched their cell. Richard was man-sized so there was no need for the thorough turning-over of regular hunts for unauthorised books, home-made shivs or black market Vones. Most cells could be searched by looking in the single cupboard, checking the shower/loo and peering under the bed.

Guy the Gorilla and Derek Leech made the same joke.

'There are no monsters under the bed...'

... then a pause. Guy sold the punchline with eyebrow-wiggling but Leech had to spell it out... 'the monster is *over here*.'

Hackwill was eager for goss. He bombarded guards with questions. Standing orders were not to tell him anything. The less Bad Mouth Bob knew, the better.

The Inner Voice couldn't say anything. And drew a zero on the notepad he used to communicate with staff.

Percy Gill was one of the few prize pupils found snug in bed, asleep. She put on a dressing gown and fluffy slippers and trudged to her designated area with hair over her face, rubbing her eyes.

What did this continuum's Persephone Gill – *not* a deadly assassin – make of Devil's Dyke? Did she understand why everyone was afraid of her?

Richard wasn't in Percy's room. They let her get back to bed.

Roger Duroc would only comply with orders given in French by a man. Jed read the phrases off a card in a broad Newcastle accent. Duroc, a male supremacist, didn't enjoy having Yvonne Ayres threaten to glove him senseless. His party piece was percussive *savate* – dirty fighting with fireworks. He'd be packed off to *Île de Monstres* when the UK-Common Market extradition treaty was signed. Jasmine and Dr Dew would be glad to see the back of him.

Last for the count was William Wax.

The overhead light came on. Ayres opened the door. Jed flexed the glove.

Jasmine looked into the cell. Wax stood at attention in the designated area, mask front, arms by his sides. No silly pose, just compliance.

'No one hiding here,' reported Ayres.

Jed backed away.

Whenever Jasmine looked into Wax's cell, she sensed wrongness. Her skin prickled. Tonight, that went in spades. Was something more wrong than usual?

This was the first time Wax didn't have to be picked up – bent stiffly like a human liquorice bowtie – and carried to the designated area. She couldn't remember him ever standing straight.

Geordie Jed pushed the door shut. Jasmine wouldn't let him reengage the lock.

'We should look under the mask,' she said.

The guards froze. They weren't easily spooked or they'd not have been cleared for this duty but the idea went against instinct and standing orders.

'Really?' asked Jed, looking to Dr Head.

'Best be sure,' said the director.

The guards pulled the door open again.

Wax was there, under the light. Shade on his mask gave the impression of an expression changing. Growing sorrow.

Jed and Ayres checked their glove charges.

Dr Dew's teeth and nails elongated and sharpened.

Jasmine felt a pulse of dark energy in her chest. It wasn't too late to fetch the dart-gun from the guard station.

'Your turn, pet,' Jed said to Ayres.

She held her glove up ready to clutch-zap and reached for the mask with her other hand. When she touched papier mâche, it crumbled like an arrangement of old leaves. She stepped back, smartly.

The wrong face looked out. Not only wrong but not alive.

Jed laid a glove on Jenny Dew's shoulder and gripped. A crackle of shock and a sharp discharge of ozone and the doctor fell in a heap.

Jasmine looked from one face to the other.

The dead face behind the mask. The live face on Geordie Jed.

The same face.

'Lock the cell,' she shouted.

Ayres was nearest the door but didn't move. Was she under a fluence?

Dr Head made a dash. A glove-arc lashed out and tripped him.

Jasmine gathered a ball of dark energy – what little there was of it under these lights – and thrust it into the fake face. She dodged a glove-strike.

The Geordie Jed face melted but didn't come away. The features cracked and ran. False eyes plopped out of gunge.

Jasmine saw through the ruin to the face she would never forget.

Adam Tussaud.

He held the master digikey. He could disengage any lock in the hospital.

'Let's open doors, pet,' said Wax, still using Jed's voice. 'Let everyone join the jolly.'

CHRISTINE AND LOULEE: FOREST HILL, LONDON, TO DEVIL'S DYKE, SUSSEX

OUT OF LONDON, BEYOND THE LAND OF ORANGE street light, comforting dark pressed in. The trip was fifty or so miles. An hour and a half clinging to Loulee's back. Past midnight there was little other traffic. The Lambretta fairly whizzed along.

Night-sounds were sharp. Chrissie's attention constantly flitted. As she got used to her enlightenment – her *dark* enlightenment – she'd have to be careful not to get serially distracted. She could hear owls hooting three fields over but that didn't mean she had to pay attention. She mustn't become rapt with the kaleidoscope of night or she'd be awa' wi' the fae. She should ignore chaff and focus. That would take practice.

Here she was, haring off with few clues what she was doing. She must keep hold of herself, of Chrissie Chambers. Whatever trade-name she ended up with shouldn't supplant her self. She was verit. The other was a mask. She needed to talk with Auntie Jas about this split identity business.

They started seeing signs for Devil's Dyke Secure Hospital – not directing to but warning away from. Unauthorised visitors were forbidden. A freephone grass-up number was posted for ramblers who spotted anything suspicious.

Up ahead, a car from *Real News* was parked badly on a verge.

Uniformed guards – titches with bicep measurements bigger than Chrissie's waist – had practically dismantled the vehicle. Two snappers were bent over the bonnet as snarly dogs sniffed their bottoms. Credentials were sneered at.

A checkpoint to avoid.

Garn said when news was happening officialdom should be circumvented.

Loulee switched the Lambretta to silent mode and went offroad. When it got too bumpy to continue, they dismounted and wrestled the scooter behind a litter-bin. Shrubs of useful size were in short supply on the broad, flat, gently sloping grasslands.

A bell dinged regularly. That must mean something specific. Deffo not something reassuring.

Only now did Chrissie think about the Main Gate. Getting to it would be easier than getting through it. Messages delivered in fortune cookies wouldn't impress whoever had the door list. Britain's most dangerous loons – sorry, Auntie Jas, patients – lived here. Chrissie and Loulee would have to come up with something. Maybe Loulee had a hidden talent for this occasion.

The Secure Hospital was a big black presence, more tomb than castle.

It had a glow and a hum. At least, that's how Chrissie saw and heard it.

She saw and heard – and *felt* – things she didn't before. A particular excitement and anticipation. If she didn't know herself better, she'd think she was spoiling for a scrap.

Rushing into danger didn't seem a stupid idea.

Yes, she knew the Devil's Dyke cutthroats were far worse than voids in floppy hats. Minor offenders like Shock Jock or poseurs like the Throbbing Brian were small potatoes next to criminal lunatics like Adam Tussaud or the Jibbenainosay.

If the White Corridor Gang threw a party, Chrissie did *not* want to be invited.

Though here she was, ready to crash the bash.

Chrissie and Loulee circled away from the approach road to avoid checkpoints, then got back on course. There was only one way in.

'Can you hear that?' she asked Loulee.

'My teeth chattering?'

'No... That...'

They stopped still. Chrissie heard whispering, a sub-audial susurrus.

She had that just-before-a-storm thrill again.

'Hurry on, Louls,' she said.

'Your shout, Chrissie.'

A spotlight above the Main Gate was aimed down at a long car. Brown, low-slung, floppy-eared dogface on the bonnet. Driven by a children's entertainer? A kids' birthday party in the middle of the night at a facility for the criminally insane wasn't the maddest thing she'd come across lately.

'You there,' Chrissie shouted, hoping to sound more confident than she felt, 'what's the sit-rep?'

That was a frequent Jill di Ferrante line.

A slim, jowly fellow in a brown bodystocking turned round.

He wore a trilby with attached bloodhound ears and a weightlifter's belt with an HH logo buckle. Hughbert Hound. With him was a woman in fur-trim flying jacket and aviatrix helmet. Plain Jane. She was reasonably pretty. The trade-name must mean something else. The Biggles get-up suggested she might have started out as Plane Jane.

Hound shrugged.

'An hour ago, we'd have been some use,' he said.

'He's locate,' said Plain Jane. 'I'm readmit.'

'That's our brief. Locate and readmit.'

'Find 'em and bang 'em up. He's ruff, I'm tuff.'

'But the brew has boiled over. Finding 'em isn't an issue.'

Hound indicated the closed gates – a metal mesh curtain had fallen over them – and paused so everyone could hear muffled racket beyond. That bell went off again.

'Another one out,' said Plain Jane.

'Readmission is going to be a bugger. Good thing Rawlins' astro aces are in there. They're trained in riot control.'

'If the corridors are mingling, we'll need serious cloakage to put the lid back on.'

'Special Section,' said Hound, tapping his long nose.

Chrissie had never heard of Special Section. Which was presumo the point.

'Can we get in?' Chrissie asked.

'What are you?' exclaimed Hound. 'Mad?'

'This is a madhouse... Where else should we be?'

'They don't like to call it that,' Plain Jane told her. 'It's a hospital.'

This was a hoo-hah and a how-d'you-do.

'We have to go inside,' said Chrissie.

'Not without laminates,' said Hound.

He and Jane held up plasticised cards on lanyards.

The Coterie had been crashing bashes without laminates, wrist-stamps or invitations for yonks. Chrissie learned how to get past the Red Rope well before she sat her O Levels.

'Hand them over,' said Chrissie, imagining Captain Floppy saying 'with *confidence*... with *authority* and *assurance*'.

The cloaks peered at her with matching cross eyes.

'We'll take it from here,' said Loulee.

Hound's nose wrinkled. He could sniff a tall story.

'Who *are* you?' Plain Jane flat out asked.

'Special Section,' said Loulee.

'Identification?' demanded Hound.

'Hah,' said Loulee. 'Nice try. Special Section carry no ID.'

Hound and Jane looked at each other, then back at Chrissie and Loulee.

Then they took off their laminates and handed them over. Chrissie stuck Hound's laminate into a reader slot in a gatepost. A red light turned green. The chainmail curtain rolled up and the gates parted.

'Seriously,' said Chrissie, 'the most secure location in Britain shouldn't be as easy to get into as this.'

'I think the idea is that getting out should be harder,' said Loulee.

Eleanor at the Soiree of the Gods

The ballroom was at the prow of the *Norwegian Would*. A wall of reinforced glass afforded a view of swirling fog. Eleanor only knew they were past the Tri-Lion because the Burning Beacon cut through the Smudge.

Marius Stok could have paid Weather Girl to clear the air. She cast rainbows every other Saturday to launch her latest fragrance. When Bruno 'Back of the Net' Brookes, the sport reporter, married Ilona Ffoulkes, the Ladies Open winner, a July blizzard tore through the marquee. Bruno was WG's ex and under a cloud ever since their break-up. The wind-witch could easily dispel fog for an evening. General spendthrift Marius was reluctant to hire the enlightened for frivolous purposes. A quirk for such a big spoke of the Wheel.

Marius was not enlightened. But was so rich it didn't matter.

The host only briefly showed face at his own glitz blitz, with Frances Minto on his arm. Their matching green tuxes had a rippling wetlook effect. Their hair was styled with a swampwater sheen. The visual was an oblique acknowledgement of the charity which was to benefit from the evening – the Relocation of the South-West Fen Frog. Marius made a witty speech about endangered amphibia, complimented the Deputy Prime

Minister on her latest approval poll, and disappeared beyond the Reddest Rope.

There were levels of security and access.

Eleanor was Redder Rope (And No Further).

She needed to up her access. It was time to throw her weight around. Being a Schilling Banner Client and a Red-Tel Telly Treasure ought to come with more benefits.

'Bona frock,' said one of Lovely Rita's mouthpieces on behalf of Herself.

Rita had a platoon of alfs and berts in gymtights to relay comments. She'd stopped speaking in public after whatever she'd had done to her lips in Switzerland.

'It's a Stán,' Eleanor said. 'His Spring Look is see-through.'

If Lovely Rita turned up at the Chelsea Arts Ball in a sweetie wrapper, it would be down to Eleanor's fluence. Rita was doolally enough not to listen to sounder advice. The Fading Light drove fashion consultants potty.

Everyone laughed at Rita but her platoon were allowed beyond the Redder Rope.

Onstage, Sredni Vashtar played 'My Old Man Said Follow the Van' on electric sitar. This would go on for many minutes. To give telly viewers a chance to nip out for a pee or put the kettle on so they'd be back on the sofa in time for Downstairs or, more importantly, the adverts.

The Redder Zone was divided into people who wouldn't speak to her and people she wanted not to speak to. Faces needed to be seen in juxtaposition with other faces. Twos and threes formed as accredited snappers got clicks, then broke apart after release forms were thumb-stamped.

She took a mocktail from a waitress dressed as a sexy fen frog.

'Jilly,' boomed a voice, 'you're out of uniform.'

Sir John of Scotland Yard made the same joke whenever they met.

WDS di Ferrante never wore blue serge – yuck! Sir John had better things to do than watch *Letsby Avenue*. He'd been briefed on Eleanor by his own alf or bert when she attended the Metropolitan Police Gala. He had her mixed up with Jill di Ferrante, who was not a real person. She let it ride. Contradicting or correcting a blithering posho came across as petty and ill-humoured. Dorothy Schilling advised against even frowning quietly. Lines in her forehead would be expensive to smooth out in five years' time.

Eleanor showed Sir John happy teeth and raised her mocktail.

'Chin chin,' she said.

'What is that objectionable thing?' he asked.

The mocktail was full of grassy fronds and squashed berries.

'It's a Fen Frog Fancy,' she said.

Sir John pulled a face.

'I'm on Natterjack Daniels myself,' he said. 'Caught any good crooks lately?'

'More your line, Sir John.'

'You'd think so, wouldn't you? Sometimes it seems my lads just clean up mess. Cloak johnnies leave cutthroats lying around with bruised bonces and broken legs. Half the villains get off because the precious maskies don't show up in court to give evidence. Still, they takes their lumpses and learn their lessonses. And we'll always have traffic. Lots of traffic policing done the old-fashioned way. No enlightened wallah with a light-up forehead is going to call himself Belisha Bill and stand in Oxford Circus regulating rush hour flow, eh what ha ha ha?'

The Met had an Enlightened Patrol Group but kept them quiet. Whispers threads which vanished swiftly alleged the EPG did more than bruise bonces. Notorious cutthroats disappeared from the Most Wanted list and were never heard from again.

A Wristband – one of the Red Rope's messenger girls – approached with a folded note on a tray.

Was Eleanor being summoned to beyond the Reddest Rope? About time.

No, the note was for Sir John. He was requested into the presence.

Sredni Vashtar was hooked off and replaced by the dance troupe Crufts, three leggy girls in nodding dog head-masks, wagging tails attached to their furry shorts. They flung themselves about dramatically to 'How Much Is That Doggie in the Window (Ruff Ruff)'. Mercifully, the music was muted on the boat.

Eleanor looked around. A couple of civs – competition winners, the bane of any bash – homed in on her with Vones out. They wore garlands of drinks tickets.

She attached herself to Sir John's arm and wouldn't let go. They were escorted to a roped-off circular stairway.

The Wristband was doubtful but Eleanor gave her a determined-to-get-the-truth Jill di Ferrante look. Red bangles didn't give an officious alf or bert rank over a face.

'Hurry up, woman,' said Sir John.

Eleanor showed threatening teeth to the Wristband.

The Reddest Rope was lifted. Eleanor let Sir John think it was his own naughty notion to bring 'Jilly' with him to the party beyond the party.

The rope was lowered to bar the competition winners.

'What's up there, babby?' asked the civ bloke. He was a Brummie.

Eleanor was originally from the Forest of Birmingham. It took expensive hypno-therapy to get rid of the accent.

'Off limits, sir,' said the Wristband.

'We're Access All Areas,' said the winner. 'Our fen frog slogan won Special Merit.'

The Wristband laughed, not pleasantly. She explained that Access All Areas meant All Areas Between the Outer Perimeter and the Redder Zone. Strictly, they should be back behind another rope – ie: on the deck, enjoying the bracing fog and a singalong with the Sex Wurzels, who'd come second in Eurovision ten years ago.

The competition winners retreated, muttering about swizzes.

Eleanor followed Sir John up the staircase.

On the landing, a snapper who'd made it this far was being detained by a Wristband with *four* bangles. Eleanor hadn't known Red Rope bands could have four bangles, which possibly empowered the agent to heave civs over the side. Confiscation of private property was allowed. The reptile's camera cooked in a microwave. No use complaining. By stepping on the *Norwegian Would*, guests (and media) consented to abide by the owner's rules. If Marius Stok buried it in small print, he could harvest your organs and sell them at auction. If those competition winners had bothered to read the terms and conditions, they'd know they weren't in England and protected by the Queen any more.

The microwave pinged and the camera burst. The smoking

mess was handed back to the snapper, who was escorted along a walkway by two more Wristbands.

What was the point of a party without piccies?

Eleanor saw through a glass porthole in a cabin door and realised this wasn't a higher tier of social event but an inner circle of movers and shakers.

Marius Stok, Frances Minto, Martin Masters, Dr Robot and a few low-key intense alfs and berts gathered in front of a big telly. It showed an aerial view of a battle happening in realtime and not in Texas. A logline identified the location as Devil's Dyke Secure Hospital, Sussex. Explosions suggested the site wasn't as secure as advertised.

Sir John's face fell as he realised he wasn't being invited to a cosy nook for special drinkies and party games.

He was back on duty, no matter how many Natterjacks he'd had.

Eleanor clocked the seriousness of the sitch and knew from the hard stare she'd never get past Four Bangles.

She backed off – but Three Bangles had come up after her.

The competition winners were relegated to a Singalong in the Smudge. The snapper (who hadn't even got close enough to see what was up) had his press card punched. Three Bangles was after the salmon which had slipped through her hands.

Sir John went into the cabin without looking back. She could expect no help from him. After all, he didn't even know her name.

She couldn't get away with pretending to be thick. As her mam said, she was too sharp for her own good.

The Wristbands were in a pickle. They couldn't admit Eleanor to the War Room (or whatever the cabin was called) but couldn't let her go back to the Redder Zone either. A tap at the cabin door summoned a higher-up to make a decision.

Carter de Beers, Chief of the Red Rope Agency, wore a half-mask with a ceramic forehead plate. Enough crimson cord to do the Indian rope trick was wrapped about his midriff. The bouncer uniform was ceremonial. She doubted he'd manned a door and nutted hooligans lately.

'Eleanor Wynter,' he said.

'Cart,' she said, smiling but showing no teeth.

'We're going to need you to sign a non-disclosure agreement.'

The alternative was likely to be walking the plank. Lord knew what lurked in the Thames these days. She scribbled on a document and authorised her signature with a thumb-press.

A groan went up from inside the War Room.

On the box, static bursts broke up the live feed.

'Take Miss Wynter to a comfort cabin,' de Beers told Three Bangles.

She was firmly escorted along a walkway high above the ballroom.

A few souls peered up, presuming she was one of the Gods the soiree was about. She felt more like a relocated Fen Frog.

As Eleanor was guided into a corridor, her Vone was extracted from her purse. Three Bangles prised off the rotary dial then gave her back a brick. She was led to a door which opened with a swipe-card. Beyond was a small cabin with no porthole.

'This is a holding cell,' she said.

The Wristband shrugged.

The reptile whose camera had been fried was inside. She'd seen him at red carpets and click-walls but didn't know who he was. Some snappers were worth a face-card. Not this one. She tagged him as a nobody with a nice haircut. Locking her up with him must be a violation of her rights as a Banner Client.

'Cheer up, Nelly,' he said. 'There's a minibar.'

CHRISTINE AT DEVIL'S DYKE

FROM THE AIR, THE HOSPITAL MUST LOOK LIKE A black Polo Mint. A thick ring with a courtyard for a hole. Spotlights ranged across the open space. A bonfire was fed with the crushed debris of prefab huts. Sheets of burning paper became swarms of fireflies and ash flakes. The place smelled like Bonfire Night.

Mimes in buff dressing gowns passed along invisible buckets of water to be emptied on the blaze. The mime in white pyjamas at the head of the line improvised that the water turned to petrol. He staggered in slow motion as if blasted backwards. The bucket line caught his lead and wobbled in sync, falling over each other.

Chrissie remembered this gangcult. Silent Terror. Press releases described their daylight robberies as 'innovative disruptions'. They were shortlisted for the Turner Prize. Moonlight Flit caught them raiding Hatton Garden. Silent Terror were a *cludge*: individuals with a psychic link, enslaved by an enlightened fluencer called the Inner Voice (that fellow making a meal of pretending to be blown up). The mindwarping cutthroat leashed others ('operants') to his will and puppeteered the troupe like meat robots. A good thing he hadn't formed a political party.

Real flames drove the pretend firefighters back.

Doors which ought to have been triple-locked were wide open. People spilled out of the wards Auntie Jas called corridors. Patients were dressed in the colour and pattern of their corridor. White inmates – like the Inner Voice – were the ones to be most afraid of.

Chrissie tried to remember the other categories. She thought Lime Corridor was for mild cases. Polka Dot Corridor was dangerous antisocials. Wavy Lines Corridor was career cutthroats, who understood they were breaking the law but didn't much care. Wavies were here because Dartmoor or the Scrubs weren't equipped to hold dark enlightened convicts. Buff Corridor was the heft – minions, voids, operants. The ground was littered with dozing or groaning Buff bods.

Hectic Squiggle Corridor was for catatonics, though she guessed the two women in action painting night-dresses must have been shamming coma. They ran about like harpies – pushing a young woman in a lime onesie back and forth between them, slashing with claw-fingers. The victim had her arms over her head.

Guards with stungloves and truncheons tried to referee chaos. They were doing poorly.

Auntie Jas was here – or, at least, her car was. Several other vehicles were turned over or burning but the ShadowShark was inviolate. A ring of malcontents lay groaning or unconscious around the Rolls-Royce, electric burns on their hands. The motor could take care of itself. Unlike a groovy little Lotus three spots over. Its front end was smashed flat as if a Monty Python Sky-Foot had stamped on it.

Not that many loose patients were acting up – scrapping with guards, ranting and raving. Most stood around or huddled together. Some watched and waited for opportunities to do mischief. A few were so far gone they didn't know what was happening.

A searchlight exploded in a fireball. Splinters of hot glass pattered on concrete. Cheers sounded.

'Where do we start?' asked Loulee.

'We need to find the White Corridor. Jas will be there.'

'That's where the bad ones are?'

'Jas doesn't like terms like "bad". She doesn't find them helpful.'

'Ordinarily, I agree with her. At the mo, let's be extra leery of anyone in white.'

'So noted.'

Loulee picked up a guard's truncheon. Its prickleprod charge was gone but it was still a handy blunt instrument. She waved it like a Pirate Queen repelling boarders with her trusty cutlass.

'We can't all shoot lightning out of our fingers,' she said.

'I'm not sure I can either.'

'It might be a propitious time to find out.'

'"Propitious"?'

'Triple word score.'

A man in a wavy lines tabard crept up on Loulee and Chrissie from a blind spot.

Loulee sensed him coming. She spun, truncheon extended, and fetched his neck a mighty blow. If she'd been wielding an edged weapon, the bolus would have lost his head. As it was, she slammed him against a wall. His lights went out.

He had three forks stuck between his fingers. He was a hostage-taker

'Want to zap him, to make sure?' suggested Loulee.

'This isn't our scrap. We don't want to get caught up. We have to find Jas.'

'Not sure we get to pick and choose,'

A few predators gave them the evil eye. What Loulee did to Fork-Fist gave them pause. That would wear off.

An elderly Polka Dot person approached, insufficiently disguised by a guard's peaked cap. He held one of those thumb-eye-heart readers.

'Who might you be, new bees?'

Good gravy – the Rhymer! A blast from the past. A thorn before her mother was born. An obsessive-compulsive who painted himself into a corner with overly specialised rhyme crimes. He stole Keats' sheets, Poe's hoe and Shelley's belly (actually, Percy's dried heart). The Poet Laureate lured the Rhymer into a patch of sticky tar, so he came a cropper thanks to Betjeman's bitumen. More pun than rhyme. A proper punishment. Poetic justice. He must have languished here many a year. Gone to ground where he'd not be found. Wasting away while awaiting the day...

Loulee hit the Rhymer in the head – not killing him dead but putting him out without a doubt...

'Wakey-wakey,' Loulee said.

The Rhymer was a low-level psychic nuisance.

'I went all poetic,' Chrissie admitted.

'Something etic beginning with a p, I should say.'

Loulee did sabre dance moves with her truncheon.

It seemed Loulee had a new talent. She showed off a bit.

'*Minii iriig amtlaarai, muu sanaatan,*' she said.

'Come again?'

'"Taste my blade, villain!"'

'In what language?'

Loulee thought about it.

'Is "Mongolian" a language?'

'If you speak it, shouldn't you know?'

'You'd think.'

The Rhymer stirred and Loulee tapped his forehead.

'*Untakh, mölkhökh!* That's "go to sleep, creep!"'

The Rhymer was out cold before the language lesson could sink in.

'Loulee, we're going to have to talk about this.'

'I know... I've been meaning to but there's always some you-drama in the way.'

'Is that Mongolian too? Udrahma?'

'No, it's... you know what. Drama with you. Everything else pushed below the fold. Urgent, immediate, to be dealt with now.'

'You mean like in the middle of a prison riot?'

'Hospital riot.'

'With my aunt in dire danger?'

'I see your point. Let's table it, again.'

Loulee was being strange. Her privilege. Chrissie wouldn't have her be any other way. Still...

'I'm semi-possessed by the ghost of Oghulqaimish, a twelfth century sabre fighter. Happy, now?'

'Uh, okay, I suppose.'

'See. You have questions.'

'*So many* questions.'

'I found a lantern in a cupboard. Now I attract ghosts.'

'Now I have *more* questions.'

'I said we should table it. Look out, there are mimes about.'

Silent Terror had a new game. They joined hands and encircled Chrissie and Loulee. They picked up knees and feet exaggeratedly.

Chrissie sensed something a little like the poetry push she felt when the Rhymer was awake. She picked up a psychic hum but couldn't make out words. This was how the cludge worked.

The Inner Voice stayed back, fingertips against his temples in the show-of-mental-prowess pose proper telepaths scorned. He braincast directors' notes to his troupe. Loulee cracked a few heads. The Inner Voice didn't care when his operants got bopped, biffed or battered. He wasn't on a feedback circuit, worse luck.

The round-a-rosy ring closed. Silent Terror sped up their minatory morris dance.

Minatory – quintuple word score, at least!

Two steps forwards snarling and spitting, then all the way back – arms stretching – and hop hop hop... then two steps forwards again but closer this time.

They all had filed teeth. Chrissie saw how this was going.

'Time for your party piece,' prompted Loulee.

It built up inside her.

'Your eyes are glowing violet,' Loulee said. 'Through the Spex.'

Artifacts sparked in her vision. Her hair prickled under her wig.

Silent Terror pulled gargoyle faces – tongues out, ears flapping – as they stepped back and made piranha chomps when they came forwards.

Chrissie felt charge accumulating in her upper chest, neck and mouth as if she had an implanted battery. She harboured a rent in the fabric of the universe behind her collar bone. Blacklight from a dark star gathered to pour through. She saw dancing violet spots in the darkness, where people were. Varying degrees of brightness related to... what? Body heat, insanity, threat? It would have helped to have a crib sheet.

The charge burst out of her.

Violet lightning – not a broken toaster crackle but an untamed bolt of primal force – struck the Inner Voice.

Silent Terror all fell down without so much as an a-tishoo-a-tishoo.

Operants lay about Chrissie and Loulee, eyes like fish, mouths gaping. One or two stirred, free of the Voice in their heads. They might even be cured. Others were just unconscious.

The Inner Voice was on his knees – bright blue eyes open in a purple face, shoulders of his white jacket scorched and smoking. His mouth gaped to show a red cavity. Chrissie remembered he'd had his tongue surgically removed to amp up his talent. He pressed his hands to bleeding ears. He looked like the Munch painting. His next trade-name should be the Silent Scream.

'Congratulations,' said Loulee. 'You've won your first super-scrap.'

That was right. The Inner Voice – whose non trade-name Chrissie couldn't remember – was a White Corridor case. One of the worst. Silent Terror were a joke gangcult but their crime spree wasn't funny.

'Remember, I knocked out Fork-Fist and the Rhymer first.'

'I duffed up half a dozen crocks earlier. Your two were barely enlightened. The forks were plastic, Louls. And the Rhymer was an old-timer...'

'Watch it, he's coming round.'

Loulee tapped him again. Chrissie stood over the Inner Voice, who shrank away from her.

'Stay down, clown... ah, mime,' she said.

'We're impressed,' Loulee allowed.

'You and Oghulqaimish?'

'Me and the viewers at home,' she said, pointing up.

There were courtyard cameras on the towers. Fly-eyes in the sky. Chrissie saw red recording/transmission lights.

Not just a scrap won but a scrap publicly won.

The patients not locked into their own heads while out of their cells paid attention. They would be wary.

The bullies in the psychedelic sick-up bed-gowns stopped batting about the girl in lime and cast eyes across the courtyard.

Chrissie knew they'd make a move.

They were middle-aged, with whiskers daubed on their

cheeks and claw-slashes across their bibs. They held themselves like cats, tense but casual, confident in their sharpened fingernails. They had tails – no, they had *a* tail, an elasticated rope of flesh and bone which connected them.

First teeth. Now claws.

The cat women weren't two people but one. Separate bodies linked. Siamese twins. Siamese panthers.

They'd been sleeping – or pretending to sleep – and were now looking for mice.

Chrissie still wasn't sure how to do the lightning trick.

It might be automatic reflex. The difficulty might be turning it off rather than on. She felt spent and wanted another carton of *churros* to refuel on. She did not have the power of magically fetching snacks.

'You take the one on the right, Louls.'

'Your right or their right?'

'Never mind.'

The cat women were startled. The backs of their hospital gowns were on fire. They screeched and ran, stretching their tail. They snapped back together and knocked their skulls.

'Impressive,' said Loulee.

'That wasn't me,' said Chrissie. 'I think.'

'It wasn't me either. Or Oghulqaimish.'

The girl in lime uncurled from the ball she'd made of herself.

The cat women rolled on the ground, patting at each other's flames, screeching.

The girl in lime was Eunice Euglow. The Little Match Girl – grown up.

She pointed gunfingers at her tormentors, directing the fire up and down and round and around – then snapped her fingers and turned it off. The catty twins huddled, hair scorched, whimpering.

'Chrissie, Loulee,' said Eunice. 'It's been a while. Hello.'

ELEANOR AND GARNET

THE REPTILE WAS GARNET GRAILL.

If he were just a snapper, his name wouldn't stick in Eleanor's mind. But he was one of the Graill Ale Graills. Verps earned him a provisional face-card. With his cheekbones – and the wealthiest macrobrewery in the UK behind him – he was practically on the Wheel.

Minutes after they were locked in, Garnet reached into his mouth as if removing a dental plate. He pulled out a memory bean the size of a Smartie.

'Always back up,' he said.

He dried the bean with a hankie.

'What have you got? The Deputy PM stamping on an endangered fen frog?'

'No. Real News.'

'The thing at Devil's Dyke?'

He nodded, sharply. 'What did you see?'

'The name and random bang-bang shoot-shoot.'

'That's about all I clicked too but there's an unholy flap on. Look who's chewing their nails off... Stok, Minto, Sir John... *Dr Robot*. Could be another Battle of Battersea. Bigger than the Dallas saucer scare. Know who they keep at Devil's Dyke?'

'Us, if we stick our noses in.'

He cracked a smile. He was intense, earnest and just a bit wicked. There might be use in him. He was one for crossing lines. He'd gone off his patch at the whiff of a story. He talked to her as if extending a courtesy. A symptom of Posh Boy Syndrome. Anyone not PB, from the Queen down, wasn't on their level and didn't really matter. He was on a different Wheel, a better one you had to be verps and have a prick to sign up for. Or be a prick and have verps. He was only talking to her because he thought she didn't count and couldn't hurt him.

Which, if she shouted for a Wristband and told them about his hamster cheek-pocket contraband, she certainly could.

For now, she held off.

He was excited by the story – whatever it was – and looking to climb aboard the rocket.

She could be a footnote. Or she could be out in front on camera. Someone would have to show face in his clicks, giving human scale to turbulent action.

'There's a news blackout,' Garnet said. 'Which means an exclusive. We have a head start but can't use it because we're locked in.'

Eleanor took a miniature can of Vimto from the fridge and a sachet of sweetener from the tea trolley.

'Those don't go together,' said Garnet.

She sprinkled white powder on the lock and dribbled Vimto into the swipecard slot.

A fizz and some sparks. The door opened.

'It was on *Letsby Avenue*,' she explained. 'Red-Tel got complaints about "imitable criminal behaviour".'

He managed to push her out of the way without seeming a thug.

He was entitled to take the lead, so he did. After all, hadn't he just broken them out of the cosy cell?

Eleanor already remembered it that way. If she concentrated – going against standing instructions not to knit her brows – she knew her own wicky trick had sprung the lock. If she relaxed, she understood it was Garnet's idea all along. He had kindly waited for her to catch up.

The walkway outside was empty.

'Now we have to jump ship,' he said. 'My press credentials

aren't going to get us a motor launch... and you're only a face...'

He made a distinction between a face and a name. Then assumed he was neither but better.

She gave him a minute or so to come up with the idea. No joy.

She took out her Scotland Yard warrant card.

'This might be the ticket,' she said.

For an instant, he wanted to pity her.

'I don't think a prop police ID will be much help,' he said.

Then he focused and saw the card was real.

'... but this has possibilities. When asked, say I'm undercover. Deep undercover.'

There was something about Garnet Graill. Given the dullness of the bash and the low-level glums she'd felt since seeing Peaky in a super-scrap on the telly, she decided not to throw him to the Red Rope yet.

Someone had to take the clicks.

CHRISTINE AND THE SHADE BRIGADE

Eunice Euglow might be bonkers in the nut and a danger to the public. The long-term Lime Corridor patient hadn't grown out of setting fires.

Still, it was nice to see a friendly face.

'How've you been?' Chrissie asked.

'Peach,' said Eunice. 'I got a Distinction in A Level Chemistry. It's not so bad here. I get fan letters. Mostly skin-crawly but one or two nice. There's a Whispers natter called "Light My Fire" about me. You're doing well, WPC Perky. I saw you on the news. In a scrap with crocks.'

'More a scrape than a scrap,' said Chrissie. 'Compared with this racket and ruin.'

Something exploded on the other side of the courtyard.

Out of the corner of her eye, Chrissie saw into shadows where some inmates were hiding.

'What did you get?' Eunice asked.

'In my A Levels?'

'No. In...' She held up her hands and made flame fairies dance on her palms.

'Oh, that. Enlightened abilities. I don't have the full rundown yet. It's been sudden onset. Violet lightning. Strength and stamina. Night vision. These black ribbon things. A huge appetite for chocolate and chips...'

'Like your aunt? Dr Chambers.'

'Yes, it turns out to be a family tradition no one told me about.'

'Can you fly?'

'I don't think so.'

'I tell you now, first thing anyone asks when they find out you're, you know, enlightened... is "Can you fly?" They say Moonlight Flit was pecked by a radioactive starling.'

Instinctively, Chrissie looked up in the sky. When Moonlight Flit was mentioned, everybody did.

'You can read minds, turn invisible or lift an elephant over your head and people will still think you're a bolus if you can't fly,' said Eunice. 'It gets majorly boring. Some who can fly are useless at everything else.'

'Can *you* fly?'

Eunice shrugged. 'I've tried making hot air cushions and floating on them. Nothing doing.'

'Shame.'

'Yes. Though this place has rules about flying, obvs.'

'No one seems fussed about rules tonight.'

'It won't last,' said Eunice. 'Someone unlocked all the doors except the Main Gate.'

'That has to be deliberate,' said Chrissie.

Whoever set this off wanted inmates and guards where they were, rioting or cowering. They could have allowed a mass escape but chose not to. Something else is going on.

They had also let Chrissie and Loulee in. Oversight or part of the grand plan?

That flaming fortune cookie fortune said Aunt Jas was heading into a trap. Could it have been part of the trap itself? A piece of cheese set to lure Chrissie and Loulee under the same neck-snapping bar?

Trying to put herself into the mind of an unknown diabolical strategist was giving Chrissie a migraine. The ace detective side of being a cloak was deffo not her strong suit. She wasn't going to be Lady Hawkshaw.

There were skirmishes at the gateway. Stocky, disciplined guards fought off a rabble of patients. The staff had the advantages of armour, riot kit and shared purpose. The folk trying to break out were armed with broom handles and exercise gear. They got in each other's way. No evidence of a master plan there.

A grey-haired woman in polka dot overalls took a running jump – she had kangaroo thighs – and would have cleared the wall if a force shield hadn't knocked her back. She fell on her feet and whanged about the courtyard like a rubber ball, bowling guards and inmates over like skittles, then knocked herself out.

'That was Bouncing Betty,' said Eunice.

Chrissie and Loulee had never heard of her.

'BB used to be a smash-and-grab jewel thief. Not for the money but for the sparkles. Like a magpie.'

'Is she all right?' Loulee asked.

'She'll be fine. Rubber bones. BB often bee-beans herself when she does her party piece.'

Bouncing Betty was bruised but not bleeding.

'Are you Chrissie's companion?' Eunice asked Loulee.

'Not likely,' said Loulee. 'Glamour Girl here didn't get teleportation, so someone has to drive her cloakliness to scenes of high adventure. I have a scooter.'

'So you're... just you, Loulee?'

Eunice was trying to think of a nice way of saying 'non-E'.

'Loulee is possessed by a Mongolian sabre expert,' said Chrissie.

'Semi-possessed,' said Loulee, swirling her truncheon. 'I can do things she could when she was alive. It's not like demonic possession. No effing and blinding or sicking up. Oghulqaimish isn't my only ghost guide.'

'She isn't?' said Chrissie. 'That's news.'

'There hasn't been time to fill in picture captions, what with one thing and another,' Loulee told Eunice.

Chrissie had the idea Loulee was in a bit of a snit. She still didn't want to be 'faithful Sparky' and resented Eunice asking if she was a companion.

'We need to get to the White Corridor,' said Chrissie.

Eunice's fire-fairies puffed out. She looked alarmed.

'You don't want to go there.'

'Not want. Need. My aunt...'

'Oh, yes, Dr Chambers will be there. But so will... Well, so will people you'll want to stay away from.'

'See that fellow lying there, the Inner Voice...'

'Ian Vance.'

'That's his real name?'

'Possibly not. It's his inmate name, for roll-calls.'

'Anyway. The Inner Voice is from the White Corridor. I struck him with lightning. He doesn't look so dangerous now.'

Chrissie tried to sound confident.

The Inner Voice was out of it but drooling.

Doubts nagged. This was her first day as a cloak and she was rushing into scraps Dr Robot or Poltergirl would think twice about.

The White Corridor was the Chamber of Horrors and Rogues Gallery folded together. They kept Adam Tussaud there. Chrissie remembered disturbing things about him. She knew other famous trade-names: Bad Mouth Bob, Scary Mary, the Dealer. Fluencers, hobby murderers, master crooks. All your nightmares in a one basket.

'You're not un-dangerous yourself,' she told Eunice. 'You burned off the Kitticat Sisters.'

'They're horrid. When they're not asleep.'

'I'm sure.'

Eunice nibbled her lip, thinking. 'The White Corridor isn't easy to get to.'

A whooshing blew Chrissie's wig-bangs about. A slim girl of about twelve appeared like a genie from a lamp. Her lime jim-jams were too big for her so she'd folded and pinned sleeves and legs. She had her hair up in puffs and decorative scarification on her bare arms. Her party piece was moving faster than the eye could register. When she slowed, she could be seen. She hopped from foot to foot and shifted this way and that. Her body blurred even as her face was in focus,

'This is Ftatateeta Sha'arawi,' said Eunice. 'Whisk Kid.'

'Ldrsrpn,' Ftatateeta spat.

'E-nun-ci-ate,' said Eunice.

Ftatateeta took a breath and said, 'Allthedoorsareopen.'

'I should have thought of that,' said Eunice. 'All the doors are open. Including the five or six which are there to stop you getting to the White Corridor.'

'Orstoptheprizepupilsgettingout.'

'Yes, as she says, to stop the prize pupils.'

'It's all right,' said Loulee. 'We-can-follow-fast-talk.'

'Youcanfollowfasttalk?' said Ftatateeta.

'Yes-but-not-talk-it-properly.'

'*Jyid.*'

'All *jyid*,' said Loulee.

'Peach,' said Eunice.

'Gear,' said Chrissie.

Ftatateeta jumped up and down, disappearing and reappearing. Happy to be understood.

'Here'sahowd'yedo,' she said.

Was speed one of her new abilities? She'd been quick in her scrap under the bridge. She waved her hand in front of her face as fast as she could. It didn't disappear.

Scratch that off the list. She had good reflexes but nothing special.

'Is my Aunt Jasmine on the White Corridor now?'

Ftatateeta disappeared and reappeared, nodding.

'DrChambersisthereinoneofthecells.'

'You went there?' said Eunice.

'NoonesawmeIdidn'tstop.'

Chrissie wasn't sure the girl had been safe. Surely some White Corridor inmates had third eye abilities?

'Is she okay... *jyid*?,' she asked.

Ftatateeta had a microexpression of alarm. She could shift faster than the human eye but had no poker face at all. Whatever she thought, she showed.

Aunt Jasmine was not *jyid*.

'They'reoutoftheircells.'

'The prize pupils,' said Eunice. 'They're the...'

'I know,' said Chrissie. 'Dangerous, deadly and dire.'

Eunice looked down. At junior school, she'd been the most dangerous girl in year six. At Devil's Dyke, she was Lime Corridor. Lowest risk. Chrissie bet she knew how this place worked. You were ranked on the harm you'd done or still might do.

But Eunice was talented. So was her younger friend.

Chrissie looked at Loulee, Eunice and Ftatateeta.

'We have skill, fire and speed,' she said. 'And when I get my puff back, lightning. I'd bet on us.'

Ftatateeta flashed a double thumbs up. Loulee and Eunice were more doubtful.

'Happy to provide the skill,' said Loulee. 'I can also offer legal advice and tanning tips. But heft wouldn't go amiss.'

'Heft?'

Loulee made a punch gesture, putting her shoulder into it.

'Muscle, you know. All cloak Crews have a Muscle. For lifting and knocking down. Like Great Britannia in the British Lions.'

Great Britannia was a fifteen-foot-tall redhead with a helmet, shield and trident. She crashed through a lot of walls. Chrissie heard her granny was Welsh and she got her vim from eating special Scots oatcakes, though she was mostly from Hampshire. Her best friend was the Iron Norn, leading mystery maid of Northern Ireland. They had a pet neolithic lion named Manx Cat and were registered for tax purposes in the Channel Islands.

Loulee did a muscle pose. Everyone got the piccy.

'TonofBricks,' said Ftatateeta.

'Good shout,' said Eunice. 'We have your Muscle. If we can find where he's hiding. I know he's out and about.'

She pointed to the Lotus Elan with its bonnet – and engine! – squashed flat.

'Ton of Bricks did that,' Eunice explained.

Chrissie and Loulee hissed. Whatever this Ton of Bricks was in for, he ought to get ten years added to his stretch for such an atrocity.

Ftatateeta disappeared again and came back holding an unkempt fifteen-year-old boy. She dropped him and he sat down badly. His t-shirt rode up over his pale tummy. His lime jacket was turned inside out to show white, lint-flecked lining

'Is anyone fooled by this?' Loulee asked, pinching his jacket shoulder. 'Is your catch-phrase "kick me, I'm soft!"?'

'Tunno, show 'em,' said Eunice.

The boy looked uncomfortable and discombobulated.

Chrissie had an idea he'd never been alone with four girls before and was torn between not much liking being bossed around by them and very much liking the view from where he was.

'Putoutthefire.'

Ton of Bricks had weeping acne around his neck and chin.

He crossed his legs and arms, as if refusing to take part in a class activity.

Chrissie and Loulee looked at each other, unimpressed.

'Give him a mo,' said Eunice.

The lad held his breath. His pink face went red to match his spots. His eyes screwed shut. He shook a little.

Then he let go and exhaled.

An area of the fire in the courtyard was crushed. Burning furniture turned to a carpet of cinders. A bollard just outside the fire-line was hammered into the concrete.

'It's how he got his trade-name,' said Eunice. 'He makes these cubes of invisible weight, high up in the air, and drops them...'

'Like a ton of bricks?' said Chrissie.

'Aw, you guessed,' twitted Eunice.

Pyro Pixie was always an impertinent little minx, Chrissie remembered. Nine years on, she was the same but sly with it.

'Itdoesntworkonanythingalivelikepeopleoranimals,' Ftatateeta explained.

Chrissie could follow what Whisk Kid said but every time she spoke, the extra bit of concentration made her head hurt. She couldn't half do with a Kit-Kat.

'It works on cars, though,' said Tunno, looking up.

'We've a bone to pick with you,' said Loulee, pointing her truncheon at his nose. 'That's a 1965 Lotus Elan. Worth more than its weight in winegums. A beautiful machine.'

'It belongs to a bloodsucking monster,' he said, with disgust.

'Don't exaggerate, you spotty herbert,' said Loulee.

'He isn't, really,' said Eunice. 'Dr Dew is a... Well, I don't like to say.'

Eunice put her forefingers in front of her mouth like fangs.

Ton of Bricks crossed himself.

'Still, leave nice motors alone, Brick Boy,' said Loulee, sternly.

He looked up at her, eyes shining. Loulee kept her truncheon steady.

'What's your actual name?' Loulee asked.

He went red.

'It's Gerald Bone,' said Eunice.

'Gerald,' said Loulee, unimpressed. 'Let's stick with Tunno, shall we?'

He nodded, eagerly.

Flaming Cowflops, another one gone!

Everywhere Loulee went, men and boys – most likely male dogs, cats and goldfish too – were smitten. Love at first sight – or something soppily mindwarping which passed for it. She picked up a train of blindly deluded blokes. Operants, even. Had she got that from a ghost too? Some twelfth century Mongol Love Cult High Priestess? If she put her mind to it, she could be as powerful a fluencer as the Inner Voice. Her gangcult could be Loulee's Lonelyhearts.

'See that Rolls-Royce over there,' Chrissie said, pointing at the ShadowShark.

Tunno shut his eyes and hugged himself again. Loulee tapped him, very lightly, on the head and he stopped gathering force.

'Thank you, Louls... Less of that, Gerald. What I was going to say is that my aunt drives that car and she – I – *Loulee* – wouldn't want it flattened. Are you with me, Ton of Bricks?'

'Yes, miss.'

'I'm not a teacher,' she said. 'It's Christine. Chrissie, if you're not a bolus. This is Loulee.'

'Loulee,' he repeated, utterly gone (the clot).

Ftatateeta flashed a microexpression of jealousy then got over it.

Chrissie had a band, like the Splendid Six or the Double Deckers. She was Great Britannia in this British Lions. Group Captain.

What should they be called.

Chrissie's Chrewe? Uh-oh, no. She wasn't putting her name up front.

The Coterie? Taken – and she hadn't yet resolved how being enlightened squared with her existing affiliations. Dark, Deft, Swift, Hot and Heft? Nope – a novelty act they were not. Children of the Night – too 'Highgate'.

The Shade Brigade?

'We're going to the White Corridor to make sure my aunt's all right. *Jyid?*'

Jyid, they said back at her. Well *jyid*. Aces. Gear. And peach.

Jasmine and the Prize Pupils

On the White Corridor, the staff were in cells and the patients free to roam. The old story of the inmates taking over the asylum. Copyright Edgar Allan Poe.

Adam Tussaud had imposed an honour system.

Doors were not locked but they were told to stay put. Some prize pupils would look for any excuse to make examples. Not staying put would be an excuse. Others didn't need excuses. Jasmine hoped they were either grateful to or afraid of Wax and wouldn't double-cross him yet.

She was in Richard's cell. Sewell Head, Jenny Dew and Yvonne Ayres were in others. None were badly injured, though Dr Dew was having a grim night. The vampire hadn't completely recovered from being staked through the neck when she was stungloved.

Not all the prizes were out of their cells. The Jibbenainosay and Mary Yatman were here because Devil's Dyke didn't have a Whiter Than White Corridor. Even Wax wasn't enough of a fruit and nut case to open their doors. They wouldn't distinguish between white and black coats. Anyone who caught their eye would be red all over.

Derek Leech didn't want to be involved (Dealer's Choice?). He stayed put, playing patience with Tarot Cards, listening to the Stones on big headphones. He'd had 'Sympathy for the Devil' on replay for seven years. Everyone who spent time on the corridor found their skull thrumming the 'whoo whoo'.

She was doing it now. 'Whoo whoo'.

She sat in Richard's chair, spent. She'd snaffled a bag of Revels but Wax confiscated the tuck. Not out of spite. He just knew not to let her feed. He'd memorised more Shade Facts than the most devoted fan on the Personals.

What was this about?

As Geordie Jed, Wax had fooled the thumb-eye-heart monitor. Wearing Jed's face, he could have walked out of Devil's Dyke then carried on with whatever diabolical liberties he dreamed of all these years. But he stayed. This wasn't about escaping. Or not just about escaping.

It had the feel of a GEIST stratagem. Or one of Modred Murda's intricate games of gotcha! Richard had the knack of unpicking perfidious puzzles. Presented with random oddities, he made connections and saw where things were going. She hadn't the patience to think like that. And neither did Adam Tussaud. He went in for crimes which made no sense. Hard to predict, tricky to stop and impossible to treat. Locking him up and trying to understand him had made no difference...

... except to the people on the outside he hadn't been able to murder in the last thirty years. Little comfort to Jed's husband.

Wax could make up for lost time with a massacre before morning.

Thinking about it, Jasmine was surprised not to be dead.

Besides escape, there was always revenge. William Wax wasn't the only White Corridor patient with Lady Shade in their Grudge Diary. Were they playing potatoes to see who got the privilege of killing her?

If this were an ordinary prison riot, hostages would be held while negotiations took place and old scores settled. Devil's Dyke was an out-of-the-ordinary prison. This was more like a Happening. Through fly-eyes and internal security cameras, a Dark Whispers live feed could solicit viewer votes about who died next and how horribly. *Crew Selection: Morgue*. The overlap between cutthroatery and show business was notable. So many clowns, so few laughs.

Higher powers might also be glad of an excuse to make examples. All doors were open except the big one. Guy the Gorilla couldn't shift the main gate on his own but give him a crew of hefts from other corridors and they'd wrench it off its hinges. Rather than risk barbarian hordes rampaging through Brighton, the Government – which was to say Frances Minto – might prefer to drop a Q Bomb and close all the files. Get shot of a busload of voids in one go.

The implosion crater could be marked with a granite monument.

Cock-up was more likely than conspiracy. GEIST orchestrated campaigns to achieve stated aims. Adam Tussaud dropped matches into pools of spilled lamp-oil to see where the fire spread.

She got up from Richard's chair and went to the door. She couldn't see into the corridor but heard voices.

The prize pupils were mostly still here.

The Inner Voice had hared off to round up his Wavy Lines cludge. Without Silent Terror, he was barely a person, let alone a cutthroat. The other prizes scorned him as too reliant on operants.

For a while, she and Dr Dew held group therapy sessions on the White Corridor. Dr Head discontinued the programme. With few exceptions, these inmates didn't want to help themselves, let alone others they saw as rivals, obstacles or irritations. The Inner Voice, Rob Hackwill and Derek Leech were fluencers. Apart from Persephone Gill and Guy the Gorilla, the others were too mentally shielded to be got at. Guy, a backbreaker-to-order, had worked as heft for Little Madam, Top Dog and half a dozen boss villains. By now, he'd be fetching, carrying and battering for someone.

The White Corridor might now suffer from Too Many Chefs/Not Enough Waiters Syndrome. She strained to listen. Were the prizes getting on together?

After the group sessions, she and Jenny Dew discussed hierarchies and fault-lines. Hackwill was always playing 'let's you and him scrap' by fomenting trouble. On the outside, he was devastating. When the *Spectrum* ran a feature on 'the safest street in England', Bad Mouth Bob moved there and joined the community association. Within a month, neighbours had fought a dozen small wars, burned down houses and seeded prize-winning front gardens with salt so nothing would grow there again. In Devil's Dyke, Bad Mouth Bob tried his tricks on people clever enough to see through them and annoyed enough to give him lumps for impudence. Similarly, Duroc – tradename Le Haineux – had misjudged his abilities. He persecuted random women who 'didn't know their place', beginning with Personals jibes and escalating to vitriol splashes. When he wouldn't look Mary Yatman in the eye, she put him in the infirmary for six months.

Like Richard, Persephone Gill didn't really belong here. However, even the deadliest prizes didn't go after most-of-the-year Percy. They knew the trouble they'd be in if Miss Kill came to visit. Jasmine had only seen Parallel Percy once, for a few minutes of side-eye sizing-up before Placid Persephone was domme in her own brain again. Miss Kill set off Jasmine's darkest instincts. She'd drawn shadow into herself in the expectation of a scrap. Geordie Jed asked what was up with the lights. She brought her gloom to work that day.

How had Wax got to Jed? She'd probably never find out.

When was the elimination round? The prize pupils had common cause now but they'd be squabbling by dawn and scrapping by mid-day. Again, that could be the whole idea. No need to bring back hanging and pay an executioner when the necks you most wanted stretched were prepared to take the work off your hands.

William Wax was ostensibly the prime mover. Yet he'd never interacted with the others. He'd been playing statues all these years, not passing notes in bread pellets. Other criminals only interested him if he could recreate them in wax and clockwork. But he'd set this up and pulled it off. He must have had help.

She walked across the cell and sat on the bed, which moved on castors...

An arm flopped out. Someone had been under the bed all along—

That couldn't be. It had been checked.

By Geordie Jed. Who wasn't Jed but Wax.

Jasmine swore and pushed the bed further aside.

She looked down at Richard Jeperson, who had thumb marks

on his neck and open eyes. His mouth was slack. She didn't need to check for a pulse.

The light in the cell dimmed but did not go out. She was too weak for that. Or too old. Shadows did not give her strength.

The shock was profound, exhausting.

Suddenly, the list of Things About Her Nobody Else Knows was much longer. She had shared a lot with him and no one else.

She'd been to the Dark Side of the Moon with Richard Jeperson.

Eleanor and Garnet at the Gate

Her Scotland Yard ID got them a long way. Eleanor kept it in her purse in a fold-out wallet with her Access card, some Green Shield stamps, Schilling Banner Client gold key (a card, not a key) and the Freedom of the Forest of Birmingham (a slim badge).

A police launch ferried her and Garnet Graill from the *Norwegian Would* to a jetty where an unmarked Wolseley Fifty-Six waited. A WPC stood by to hand over the keys to anyone with authority. Would Sir John have issued quite so authentic an honorary warrant card if he'd had any idea it might be used for anything besides jumping theatre queues and drinking after closing time? Especially since the car was supposed to be at his disposal. Still and all, Eleanor could say she was on police business.

Surprisingly, Garnet wanted her to drive. She dialled the AA map on the dashboard Vone and fed a route into the Think Box. Her semi-opaque dress-cover steamed up and got sticky. It wasn't designed for wearing, let alone sitting down in. On the trip, the snapper sat in the passenger seat, fiddling with photographic gear retrieved from a locker at London Bridge Station.

Garnet looked at the clicks saved on the memory bean on the viewer of his Ensign Advocate. He couldn't make out anything new. He scanned wireless frequencies and skipped from through-the-night *raga* to the 24-hour-news channel. They were covering the aftermath of that flying saucer dust-up in Texas. No mention of anything closer to home.

'News blackout,' said Garnet.

She suggested using the car's two-way radio to eavesdrop on police chat. He said he was just about to and she believed him... despite the mental hiccough she had when telling herself it was his idea.

The nearer they got to Devil's Dyke, the more chat they heard. Mostly instructions to the East Sussex Constabulary to stand down while outside squads set up shop. Plods who knew their patch grumbled about townies cocking up. The situation at the secure hospital was not good news for anyone...

... except Garnet Graill, for whom bad news was good news.

Jill di Ferrante was always running into danger. Eleanor Wynter wasn't.

But this was better than being stuck in a cabin while the adults played. No matter how large her fan following and how valued a Schilling client she was, she was Light Ent – below the fold unless mired in scandal (she'd dodged several bullets, some of which she'd fired at her own foot). Until tonight, it hadn't occurred to her that she might have her own mobile dressing room and contractual say-so about what went out on *Letsby Avenue* three times a week but was still on the ground looking up at flying people, flying saucers, flying everything. Not allowed beyond the Reddest Rope.

Garnet Graill was a rope-cutter.

He annoyed her. On a brief acquaintance, she was already storing up complaints to lodge with her agent. He wouldn't be near the action without her but she wouldn't have hared off to Devil's Dyke if they hadn't been clapped in the same cabin.

This was, as Dorothy Schilling might say, a bold career move. Not advisable but interesting.

The road across the South Downs was a river of tail-lamps. Media vans and a few unlucky civ cars were shoved to the verge. Access-all-areas official vehicles trundled towards Devil's Dyke. Eleanor's warrant card kept them moving. The constable who checked it was a *Letsby* viewer and happy to wave them on if she signed an autograph and promised to remember him to Canteen Cathy, who'd opened his infants' school twenty years ago. She told him she would.

Garnet congratulated himself for thinking of that – and she agreed with him.

She must pop an aspirin when she had the opportunity. Her head was becoming something fierce.

Beyond a perimeter, they mixed with more police cars – mostly also Wolseleys – and armoured vehicles. Folk in and out of uniform stood around intensely, not doing much. Muffled conflict was heard from inside the sealed facility. Occasional starbursts above the high wall – objects disintegrating against a force shield. Someone had clamped the lid on the pressure cooker without judging the flame properly. Gas mark ten thousand.

They got out of the car. Garnet kept his camera under his Burberry like a hit-man walking through a crowd trying not to draw attention to an unholstered pistol. She went ahead to attract all eyes while he hid in her shadow. Being background while someone else showed their face was good for getting one over on the Red Rope. That really was his idea.

The Red Rope were here, of course. Were the Splendid Six or the British Lions on the way? Quelling riots was beyond their usual remit but she had a notion this was a call-the-engines situation. The gathering of high mucky-mucks on the *Norwegian Would* suggested a major incident.

At the gate were a couple of low-level enlighteneds...

'Hughbert Hound and Plain Jane,' said Garnet, who'd memorised multiple packs of face-cards.

'She doesn't look that plain to me,' said Eleanor.

'I think it means plain-speaking, not plain in appearance.'

'Poorly advised with the trade-name, then.'

He had nothing to say to that.

'... two young women from Special Section went in,' Plain Jane told a tall, wide man in camouflage gear. A globe like a football covered his whole head. 'They used our ID, which shouldn't have worked but did. The gate was locked and sealed before and since. Whoever has control wanted them inside.'

'You shouldn't worry about escapees, Striker,' said Hound. 'There are none. You should worry about casualties... staff and inmates. Those women.'

'We don't understand,' said Striker – or was it The Striker? – through a squeaky mouth-grille. 'You said these were agents from Special Section.'

'Yes. Two of them.'

'But *we're* Special Section. We're First on Scene. Did they show ID?'

'Hah,' said Plain Jane. 'Special Section carry no ID.'

Striker fished a laminate on a lanyard out of his camo jacket and held it up.

Eight toughs in matching camo with smaller football-head helmets did the same thing. Security beans embedded in the laminates winked.

'Of course we carry ID,' said Striker.

Hughbert Hound and Plain Jane looked at each other.

Eleanor felt a fingerprod in her shoulder. She turned. Garnet had his camera up. Clicks and clips would show her face full on with cloaks and Special Section personnel behind her.

She'd given Garnet the code-words and frequency for the Red-Tel newsroom. They had to hope whoever was manning the board in the small hours had the nous to patch the feed to the through-the-night channels. The wireless would take it out of desperation to fill the long dead spot between *Ovaltine Presents... the National Anthem* at midnight till *Wake Up with Bendy Wendy* at six-thirty. If there was a spark of enterprise in the room, this would go out on telly too.

'Hello, early risers,' she said to camera. 'This is Eleanor Wynter. You may know me as WDS di Ferrante on *Letsby Avenue*. I'm at Devil's Dyke Secure Hospital in Sussex. Behind me is unfolding a story more sensational, more frightening and scarcely less unbelievable than any you've seen on *Letsby*. Authorities have lost control. The nation's worst cutthroats are kept at Devil's Dyke where, in theory, they can do no harm. How much longer that theory will stand is a question we have to ask. Look out, Britain, the Monsters Are Coming!'

As she spoke, Striker jogged towards her, head bobbing.

This was where she learned what penalties came with breaking ranks on a news blackout.

Garnet backed away, preparing to vanish into the crowd with

his camera under his coat while she got arrested and given a right bollocking. Well, nackers to that!

'Mr Striker,' she said, turning to aim the directional mike at him, 'or is it *The* Striker?'

'It's The Striker, thank you,' he responded, croaking through the grille. 'Too many people get it wrong. It's a trade-name and a rank.'

'Thank you for clearing that up. We're with The Striker of Special Section, the elite force tasked with protection of the public in situations like this... which happen, how often would you say?'

'More than we'd like to admit, Jill.'

Eleanor mini-harrumphed but pressed on.

'Can you offer reassurances to viewers who might feel nervous?'

'Once we're inside, it'll be a matter of restoring order and subduing the ringleaders. We have enlightened individuals for any occasion on the squad.'

'Cloaks?'

'We don't call ourselves that.'

'As so often, the real heroes are modest, and want no thanks for their service.'

Garnet was getting all this.

'Now, when will Special Section go in?'

The grille sputtered and Eleanor knew the voice-box hadn't malfunctioned. The Striker had no answer he'd want on the record.

'Who let these reptiles through?' demanded a loud, unmuffled voice.

Carter de Beers wasn't happy to see her.

'We're joined by Carter de Beers, director of the private security firm Red Rope, who have recently weathered controversy about the mishandling of...'

'Less of that,' he said.

She knew he'd cut her off – had banked on it, because she'd need a researcher to tell her what the Red Rope had mishandled lately. She guessed several bungles would come to the director's mind. The gambit was a Jill di Ferrante scrote-questioning technique the writers overused. It apparently worked in real life.

'Are the Red Rope here in support of Special Section?'

'No comment. Shouldn't you be detained in a secure cabin?'

'This seems to be a night when the concept of security has been tested.'

'Very funny. You ought to be on the telly.'

'I am, Mr de Beers. So are you. Who has authority here? Special Section, an accredited arm of the British state, or the Red Rope, a private company most associated with the entertainment industry?'

Neither de Beers nor The Striker wanted to answer that.

'There you have it,' said Eleanor, to camera. 'We'll have to wait for a ruling on chain of command. Almost certainly from the Deputy Prime Minister.'

Red Rope personnel filtered into the scene. The Striker's ball-heads deferred to them.

De Beers and The Striker turned away to confer, under the common misapprehension that if their faces weren't on camera what they said to each other couldn't be recorded or broadcast. Eleanor didn't tell them different. Security specialists ought to know better.

'Communications with the prison?' asked de Beers.

'Hospital,' corrected The Striker. 'Down. No open channels.'

'Just the staff inside? Captain Rawlins' astro aces?'

'They're on site, at least the overnight shift. We presume they have limited control. They'll have sustained casualties. If you were a nutter let off your chain, who would you go for first? The Little Hitler who's too free with the stunglove at pat-downs?'

'We need to get our people in.'

'Two unknown agents were able to gain access.'

'Unknown?'

The Striker looked to Hughbert Hound and Plain Jane. De Beers aimed his shiny forehead at the third-stringers.

'Who were they?' De Beers asked.

'Cloaks,' said Plain Jane. 'One in a costume, of sorts. One in a mustard tracksuit and motorcycle jacket.'

'Did they give trade-names?'

Plain Jane shook her head. 'The girl in the Spex reminded me of a cloak from the '80s. Do you remember Lady Shade?'

CHRISTINE CHAMBERS – LADY SHADE II

'"JYID," I SAID. "GEAR". "ACES". AND "PEACH".

'Then I thought "this is how I get my friends killed."

'I was all for a mass charge-in, which was fair enough. I couldn't *not* try to save Aunt Jasmine. I had a powerful night-buzz. But did I have the right to take people with me? Into a scrap to end all scraps – and probbo end several people? I paid enough attention in history to know what happened to the Light Brigade. I'd honestly rather die than have to explain to Loulee's mum and dad that I got her hurt. I was iffy about looking after myself, even after shutting up the Inner Voice. I knew I might not be able to look after the others.

'Yes, Loulee had the skill of a Mongolian sabre champion. Know what she didn't have? A sabre. She was waving a stick. Not even a pointed stick.

'Whisk Kid was a pickpocket. Ton of Bricks a vandal. They were in the Junior School version of a gangcult called the Tufty Club. If they weren't enlightened, they'd have ASBOs and be picking up litter. Not in prison – now I'd seen Devil's Dyke, I knew calling it a hospital was flannel – with first division cutthroats.

'Eunice Euglow ought to have a handle on her firelighting. She'd had her party piece longer than the rest of us and more time – and professional help – to learn how to use it. But Devil's Dyke isn't about training the talented. Their focus was getting Eunice *not* to burn stuff. Which, to be fair, I completely understand. I wish they'd done more to stop that Tunno kid from flattening cars.

'We weren't the Splendid Six or the Whatever-Begins-with-an-F Five. The Shade Brigade was a non-starter because we hadn't worked up to it. Aunt Jasmine had years to get good at being Lady Shade. We'd just taken a plunge at the deep end.

'Know what I thought as we walked towards the White Corridor?

'And, yes... we absolutely did that stroll-in-the-park, breeze in our hair, ignore-the-screaming-maniacs, not-fussed-about-nearby-explosions strut down the hallways. We're kids, what do you expect? We were completely showing off. Eunice had the Brighton Belle slowmo hair-toss thing down pat. Shame Garn wasn't there to get clicks. There'd be Shade Brigade posters.

'Anyway, what was I thinking?

'Everything I'd read about cloaks and how they got started. First issue, with the free spinner or hair-grip. "This is the one, true believers," on the cover. Not the victory photo ops – Poltergirl halting the march of the Angry Ants in Shoreditch... Great Britannia holding a bendy bus above her head in that click on the cover of the official biography... Dr Robot bowing to Queen Vee as she stuck the magnetic Victoria Cross to his tin chest... Moonlight Flit crouched on top of the London Eye, risen above the Smudge, surveying a city under his protection.

'No, I thought of the paragraphs buried deep in the profiles. Bordered in black.

'Motivational losses. It seems every cloak has one. Benny Caroli, Quackanapes' comedy idol, was murdered by the Cartoonist, who left him on display in Piccadilly Circus as a starved skeleton on a tiny desert island with a single palm tree... Phoebe Rays' whole family was evaporised at Los Alamos in the unplanned nuclear physics event which bestowed near-unlimited abilities on her... Saintly Stanley, Night Mist's brother, was stabbed to death outside the Crown and Two Chairmen on Dean Street – still an unsolved, unavenged crime... Even the Street Sweeper's imaginary murdered grandad, an origin story cooked up by a focus group. The dead loom large in survivors' stories. A party piece isn't enough. A cloak needs a reason to do right by the world. As if doing good wasn't enough on its own.

'I wouldn't be like *those* cloaks. *Couldn't be.*

'If Loulee were killed, it wouldn't motivate me to carry on regardless. It'd scare me off the front line. I'd never forgive myself.

'Ftatateeta and Gerald – kids I'd just met – would haunt me. Eunice, maybe, not so much... but, crumpets, we were Draycott's girls together. Nothing would even the scales if any of them were harmed. Medals, swag, acclaim, Liza Doolittle in a Monday Night Musical, *nothing.*

'All this went through my mind – faster than Whisk Kid could run – and I tried to back-pedal.

'If I went and got killed on my own, I wouldn't feel bad.

'Unless Loulee brought my ghost out of her lantern to give me a hard time.

'I was so terrified about what might happen I broke up the group five minutes after we got together. How's that for a chart-topping run? Cancelled out of the gate. Posters straight to the remainder bins.

'I told the Shade Brigade to stand down and – after getting directions from Eunice – went on my own to the White Corridor.

'There was an easy-to-follow white line on the linoleum.

'Though I'd taken back getting my friends killed, I was still on the way to getting myself killed. I couldn't see any other option.

'Aunt Jasmine was in danger. I had to go.

'It didn't take a mysterious fortune cookie to tell me that.

'If I died, Loulee would work out what that was all about.

'On the way to the White Corridor, lights grew dim. Bulbs flared and popped. Sickly red emergency strips came on then faded out. I was doing that. As every shadow grew I got stronger – intoxicatingly so. I already knew enough to be wary. Dark was like food for me but more immediate. Spinach which got you stoned.

'I still reckoned I might be killed. *Would* be killed.

'Maybe my last *Letsby* would go out with silent end credits after all? I'd get a pull-out remembrance spread in the *Sunday Supernova*. Someone would have clicks of me in the Shady get-up. There were fly-eyes all over Devil's Dyke.

'Was my trick with the lights killing the hallway cameras? High-angle clips would show me walking unsteadily along the white line then cut to fuzzy static as my Spex flashed in the lens.

'More and more light-bulbs burst. There were no windows to let in natural light and the red strips were failing fast. The few people I met were scurrying away from where I was going. They went around me, keeping their distance.

'The secure gate to the White Corridor was open. Its scanners were on the fritz. As I approached, even the little power lights on the Think Box stacks went dim. Torches on low battery. Candles in the wind. But I could see in the dark.

'I went through the gate.

'I saw Aunt Jasmine's prize pupils. The New Chamber of Horrors. I knew most of the names. Recognised faces from true crime drama-docs. But I'd not expected the worst people in Britain to be mostly middle-aged men – and one gorilla – in white jim-jams. Without masks, costumes or armour, they were nondescript. It was the middle of the night. They had five o'clock shadow and bed-hair. Even Guy the Gorilla was grizzled around the gills.

'Only William Wax – dressed as a guard – was expecting me. I've no idea how Adam Tussaud even knew who I was.

'They turned to take a gander at the new girl, unimpressed. Some were nastily amused. A Frenchman with a stripey vest under his pyjama top shot hatebeams out of his eyes – metaphorical ones, fortunately. Guy beat the floor with a truncheon and bared aggressive teeth.

'"Whoo whoo," I hummed, not knowing where it came from.

'Jasmine was in one of the cells. Ftatateeta had told me that much.

'William Wax saw I'd come alone and congratulated me (in an unexpected Geordie accent) on thinking of others. He said he'd find my friends and murder them anyway. "Just to be on the safe side, pet."

'So that wasn't peach.

'"Who's this?" asked Robert Hackwill, aka Bad Mouth Bob. "Are they sending surrender demands via singing telegram girl now?"

'"This is Dr Chambers' niece," said Wax. "The All-New Lady Shade."

'I sensed laughter about to erupt...

'... which is when I turned *all* the lights out – and listened to the screams.'

LOULEE AND THE LUVVERS

SHE WISHED CHRISSIE WOULD MAKE UP HER MIND AND stick to it.

One moment, it was all about getting a group together. Hey Hey, all the way with the Shade Brigade!

Then it was a far, far better, nobler, sillier thing to rush off on her own.

Oghulqaimish could name several champions like that. Enemies sent back their heads as a reminder of how stupid they'd been.

Not only had Chrissie left Loulee behind. She'd put her in charge of Pyro Pixie and the New Two, Runsandtalksveryquick and the Car Squasher. Not in the sense of asking them to sit quietly and read a book. In the sense of making sure they weren't crippled by guards or goons.

There was still a riot going on.

So long, Shade Brigade! Meet Loulee and the Luvvers!

(Or Louise's Losers.)

Inside the fortress wall, Devil's Dyke looked (and smelled) like any other hospital, school or civil service building. The government must have taken up a special offer on soup-coloured linoleum since they used so much of it. Cork boards announced social events, fire regulations, cleaning rotas and film shows.

They were months behind the Odeon Holloway Road in the three-hour musicals which were all Elstree made these days. How did criminally insane audiences like *Gert Goes Gear*?

Lights were going out.

She took out her pencil-torch. It shone brightly then went out like a match.

Chrissie was doing this.

Enyedi Boglárka advised her to get the terms of their partnership in writing soon. If there was a soon.

'Icantseeandkeeprunningintowalls,' said Ftatateeta.

'Maybe this will help,' said Eunice.

Announcements pinned to a corkboard nearby caught fire. Flamelight was different. Chrissie didn't eat that, apparently.

Pieces of paper didn't burn long.

Loulee saw people looking at them. They were noticed.

Inmates who wanted to escape had gone outside. That was where the scrapping was. The ones indoors had less gumption. Or wanted the fun to come to them.

The Luvvers counted as fun.

A small gang felt their way down the hall towards them. Their leader could see in the dark. A thin woman with golden reptile eyes and greenish scales.

They were in no hurry.

Loulee was desperate to make use of the moments before they got got.

If they were Loulee's Luvvers, this new crew were the Haters... the sort of voids who'd spell it Haterzz.

Oghulqaimish knew how to fight blindfolded. The skill had taken many months' practice, with attendant scrapes and laughter from the other pupils in warrior school. She'd never made use of the training in her lifetime. All her battles had been fought with her eyes open in daylight.

'I could really do with a sword,' said Loulee.

'Put your truncheon down on the floor for a bit, miss,' said Ton of Bricks. 'Quick, before the fire burns out.'

Loulee went along with it.

Tunno's eyes went crossed and sweat popped from his pores.

The Haterzz held back. Those snake eyes were intrigued.

Most of Loulee's truncheon flattened, popping its hard

plastic sheath to show a steel core. Tunno left about six inches of handle but pressed the rest into a crude blade – not pointed but edged. She picked it up and saw the last of the firelight in the metal.

Oghulqaimish was impressed. If Gerald Bone timetripped to twelfth century Mongolia, he'd be onto a good thing.

When Oghulqaimish was killed by her brother, she was closer to Gerald's age than Loulee's. Many of Loulee's ghosts were death-frozen younger than her. It said something about historical life expectancies – also the dangers of being a girl and good at anything.

The golden eyes were close now. A forked tongue flicked.

Loulee remembered who this was. Asmida binti Geoffrey Reynolds. Trade-name: the Naughty Naga. Wavy Lines pyjamas. Exotic booth-dancer by night, slither-through-a-window burglar by later at night. Sometime heft for the Little Madam Mob. Close friend of the odious Lord Adder.

Asmida had a pack of voids with her. Buff pyjamas jobs.

At a hissed command, the mob charged. Tunno, who couldn't use his bricks on living things, crouched and cringed. Ftatateeta hopped and skipped. Eunice scorched the lino. That (finally!) set off sprinklers. The flames were doused. Steam filled the hallway.

Asmida came at them, barbed fingers out. Others followed, trousers squelching.

Loulee fought in the dark, slashing at the Naughty Naga and six or seven voids. Her crude sword struck sparks off someone's steel-laced skin. Loulee let Oghulqaimish take over... but pulled back killing strokes. If she had to be in the night-game, she was one of those no-fatalities goody-goodies. She stuck to pokes, prods and slaps.

When she let the ghost guides have the controls, she earned quiet moments to herself. In the Lantern, which was also a cocoon.

She was sad for the girls who'd died.

She watched her body best a serious cutthroat. The Naughty Naga was heft, not a mastermind. She didn't rate white pyjamas. But she was a brand-name baddie. She'd been in the Scream Team. She rated a face-card in the Deck of Doom. She even had a sad story to explain her turn to crime – though no amount of being teased at school excused her behaviour. Asmida took breakdown and blackout as an opportunity to round up a gang of gits and pick on people.

Piloted by Oghulqaimish, Loulee made the Naga shut her golden eyes and roll into a ball.

Some of the others backed off. But not all.

The steel-skinned chap was Irn Bruce, a Glasgow debt collector also known as 'the Girder Murderer'. Someone had widened his mouth by cutting his cheeks. He had extra teeth implanted.

Eunice had to stand back to concentrate. It was hard to focus on a moving target when conjuring flame. When Irn Bruce went after Eunice, the fire went out. She couldn't pyromance if she was too frightened. An enlightened ability which conked out just exactly when it was needed wasn't the dream.

Ftatateeta stood next to Irn Bruce and rubbed his back...

... from the Lantern, Loulee could see quickness – not a trick of the eye but of the mind, processing images faster...

Irn Bruce's jacket shredded. Ftatateeta rubbed skin. Instead of tattoos and piercings, the inmate had patterns of rivets and solder.

Friction led to heat. Silvery pink glowed red and swole up, then burst in a gush of mercury blood.

The inmate's screech was high-pitch and he dropped.

With the Naughty Naga and the Girder Murderer down, the buffs thought of better things to do. Alphabetising their cigarette card collections. Writing apologies to victims in the hope of leniency when they were up for parole. Making sure they had clean underwear on for their next strip search.

Loulee was back in herself and Oghulqaimish in the Lantern.

She had broken a sweat and had venom stains on her jacket. The truncheon handle was slick and heavy in her aching hand.

'Ftatateeta, good show,' she said. 'Eunice, Gerald, well done.'

The others were puzzled. Why was she congratulating them. Was she a P.E. teacher now?

'For being alive,' she said.

JASMINE IN THE DARK

WHEN THE LIGHTS WENT OUT, JASMINE WAS KNEELING by the bed, forefinger pressed to Richard's neck.

He was warm but had no pulse.

This was the tableau Wax wanted. Richard Jeperson Dead. Lady Shade Defeated. A study in despair. She could see it roped off in an exhibition. The Triumphs of Adam Tussaud. Once he'd recreated wax crimes with real people. Now it was the other way round.

But where was he?

He wouldn't be satisfied unless he could watch.

The blackout wasn't planned. No point in an exhibit the punters couldn't see.

He didn't have her dark-adapted eyes.

On the White Corridor, people screamed.

Not sound effects.

Whoo whoo!

She stood, intending to investigate – her old cloak instinct to run into kerfuffles normal people would run away from. She'd self-diagnose a complex.

The cell door slid open.

Guy the Gorilla bounded in on all fours, trussed in ribbons of dark matter. He was trying to get away from something. The black snakes constricted, hobbling him like a rodeo steer. He fell heavily. His hip replacement gave way. Ribbons twisted into rope and pulled him back through the doorway. Guy tried to bite the floor to anchor himself. It didn't work. He scraped grooves in white lino as he was dragged into the corridor.

Jasmine knew from the black ribbons who had hold of Guy. Her niece was playing with dark matter. That had taken Jasmine months.

She'd told Christine to stay put. Her niece had no more obeyed than Jasmine would have at her age. Or any age. That complex again. She'd lost count of the times the Shadow Cabinet told her to stand down and she'd ignored orders. Richard knew better. He never told her not to do what she'd do anyway.

Jasmine followed Guy. She had an impulse to tickle him under the chin.

The White Corridor was littered with cutthroat casualties.

Hackwill had a broken shoulder. Pain distracted him from the wavering black holes in reality sliding across his face and chest. His Bad Mouth was shut. A sticky black X over his gob might be permanent, so it'd be drip-feed or nothing from now on.

Duroc was flat against a wall, eyes obsidian marbles. He'd been *sent away*, into the Purple. It had taken years for Jasmine to realise *sending away* was a thing she could do. A card not to be played in anger, especially after what happened when Modred Murda tried her patience one too many times. He was lucky most of him was still on this plane of reality – especially since his condition generated a certain official sympathy which earned him early release.

Going the whole hog with *sending away* involved too much risk. Her mind could be pulled after the sendee. One visit to the Purple was enough for her. If not for Richard, she'd still be there. Body on the Dark Side of the Moon. Spirit in another dimension.

She had a pang of worry for Christine.

Then Duroc's eyes came back. He was home in his head again but his vim was poured out. He slumped to the floor. No threat to anyone.

Her niece had managed this. Not in fury but with a cool

Jasmine envied. Christine was so new to this she didn't realise the scale of what she'd done...

... or rather, was doing.

This was still going on.

Christine summoned dark. Tendrils of black swirled around her. She wore a wig, Spex, trenchcoat, skating dress and sensible boots.

Jasmine saw her niece open a chasm under Anthony Jago, who could warp space and time if he put his mind to it. His abilities were off the scale. It had taken the Splendid Six of the '90s and the New Wave Ravers to bring him in and that had been a close thing. With the baffles removed, Jago was a Free-form Disaster. Christine wasn't anywhere near ready to dance in his disco. Yet he sank to his waist in the floor, which solidified around him. He gave up struggling.

'Christine,' Jasmine shouted. 'Where's Wax?'

Adam Tussaud wouldn't have left.

The ribbons shadow-shrouded Christine. As she drew in dark, emergency lighting undimmed. The White Corridor was redlit, as if floor and walls were covered in thin blood. There ought to be a siren.

William Wax was at the end of the concourse, fiddling with the digikey. Two final doors to be opened.

The Jibbenainosay and Scary Mary. He was letting the beasts out.

They'd probably kill him first. By now, he might not mind.

He'd been planning this bash for ages and hadn't seen Christine coming.

He must be *furious*. Meet the new Shade, same as the old...

Christine took hold of the red shadow Adam Tussaud cast on the floor and pulled it out from under his feet like a carpet. He lost the digikey.

The doors opened. The cells beyond were black.

Christine had shut down the most dangerous prizes where they were, behind locked doors. They'd be sitting in their own darkness, unable to stir.

Jasmine hadn't expected Christine to think ahead.

It wasn't like her niece. Not as she used to be – all of two days ago, clicked for Peophole in nightclubs, pretty face on silly telly, subsisting on celery and distilled water, fiddling with her Vone. The new Christine, the All-New Lady Shade, was as much elevated as enlightened.

She had let the dark think for her.

Jasmine remembered her training days, with Richard – *Richard!* – and others. Gurus and guides and veteran cloaks. Being enlightened can be like being possessed. You mustn't put the demon in charge... no matter the temptation. It can also be like grog, jabs or pep pills – a rush. Act on instinct, regret it when you came to.

Christine was a wonder. Jasmine hoped she was still the girl inside... model, actress... as well as the... as the *whatever.*

The doors slammed shut and locks engaged.

Wax was hauled along the floor on his bum.

Jasmine could make knives of shadow and kill him. No one would blame her. Few would even know.

She'd been in scraps before. Not everyone came through alive.

Every cloak knew the drill. You couldn't shove nemeses off a waterfall. You could stand aside and let their own impetus carry them over the brink. Then watch gravity finish the job.

If someone awful was standing too close when their deadly device malfunctioned, no one asked questions about their evaporisation. Blown-apart or dropped from a great height cutthroats had a habit of not dying... or only provisionally dying. Even if the crim croaked, the trade-name might be passed on. There were legacy cutthroats. Feuds were carried to the next generation. The merry-go-wrong never stopped.

She made the knives – six-inch blades, like ebony ice – but didn't use them.

She wanted Wax alive to know he'd failed. To rue it.

Everything Christine did now was his fault. He'd brought her out. Lady Shade II might have been a one-scrap wonder if he'd stuck to tying himself in knots. Christine came into her abilities on the night Wax took over the White Corridor. That coincidence should be questioned.

An issue Richard had with cloaks was that they were better at making a mess than tidying up. They liked to take a victory lap or pose for snappers. Richard wanted to know how the trouble started in the first place and what needed doing to make sure the embers didn't burst into more, bigger flames.

Wax couldn't have done all this on his own. Who helped him?

How had Christine got into Devil's Dyke?

Other doors opened and survivors came out of cells. Dr Head. Dr Dew. Ayres. Persephone Gill.

One made a run for it.

Not one Jasmine expected, though she should have.

Richard would have worked it out. Once, he would have foreseen it. He must know how Yvonne Ayres felt.

Christine stopped the guard before she could reach the dart gun. It had been used once this evening, of course – to shoot a pencil into Dr Dew's neck. Wax needed someone on staff. Jasmine had thought it might be Dr Head. She'd even considered Jenny might have stabbed herself. She remembered the security video. Ayres wasn't running to help the doctor but to check she'd aimed true.

The short, stubby guard barrelled at Christine. She had the muscle-mass to bowl her over. Jasmine knew from experience that a knack for cunning manipulation of elemental or extra-dimensional materials and a panoply of enlightened abilities didn't help much if you got the wind knocked out of you. Even first-division cloaks were too often bested by simply chucking a brick at their heads. It was why reinforced cowls were popular.

Christine stepped aside like a matador, trenchcoat flaring like a cape. She delivered an elegant thump to the back of Ayres' neck. The guard dropped.

'Yvonne, why?' asked Jasmine – though she knew the answer.

YVONNE AYRES, ASTRO ACE – AGENT OF GEIST

'THE VIEWERS DIDN'T PUT JONTY MCDRIBBLEFART ON the Jupiter mission because they thought he'd be a good Captain. No, they wanted him *off the planet* and hoped he'd spew in zero gravity. They voted for him to drink recycled wee for eight years. In the comments section, they said Ground Control shouldn't fuss themselves too much about bringing him back from outer space.

'The rest of us on *Crew Selection* weren't funny but we got laughed at.

'Before telly came in on the project, Rawlins was a cert for Captain of the Zeus Lander. I was in line for First Officer.

'Know what clever people said in the 1960s? "They should have sent poets". They missed that astronautspeak *was* poetry. "The eagle has landed". "One small step..." "Houston, we have a problem..." That wasn't what clever people wanted, though.

'I was the answer. Before the space programme, I was published in *Granta*. I was one of the Ten Under Twenty-Five. Poet first, then astronaut. A full decade with the British Space Development Company. A larf and a half. You meet the basic physical requirement of being a stocky shortarse, then they work on you. Exercise. Diet. Surgery. Endurance trials. Acclimatisation to extremes. Eighteen-month tours on the

Prospero, to habituate your body and brain to weightlessness. A year at the bottom of the Norwegian Trench, adapting to pressure and dark. Not conditions the human body is designed for. I've been drastically altered for two entirely different, non-terrestrial environments. A metal sheath hurtling through a vacuum and the moons of Jupiter. When you then spend the rest of your life in an environment fit for regular people, there are consequences.

'My eyes bulge. I can't buy clothes which fit. I keep snapping the heads off taps and handles off doors. I'm too short and wide to be served in busy pubs. Solid food feels wrong. I can't have children. A set of convictions – for instance, that I don't mind that I can't have children – have been instilled via post-hypnotic suggestion and can't be overridden though I *know* what I feel or believe was drummed into me for the convenience of the mission. I *mind* that I don't mind my barrenness. Not just in a reproductive sense. So many things were leeched out of me or put into me. I had to be rewired to accept them. I've filled my head with five PhD's worth of maths, astronomy, engineering, physiology. Actual rocket science. And published on schedule. Papers and poems, every month.

'But the viewers voted to send Jonty McDribblefart to Jupiter. Jonty's on the Moon, OK? Not OK. Not acceptable.

'And he *doesn't want to go*. The void will do anything to weasel out of it. On *Crew Selection*, he didn't even try to complete the tasks. He aimed for larfs and votes. I can't find anything funny. Something else I gave up – a sense of humour. It was squeezed out of me at human crush depth. But I didn't go in with GEIST for revenge. I think I did it because it was funny. People died but who cares, eh? *I* wanted the larfs this time.

'So what does it matter? What did all of it matter?

'Compared to the Zeus Lander, a *Prospero* class satellite or a Maracot Bell, a cell in Devil's Dyke is After-Eight-mint-on-the-pillow luxury. It's a controlled environment. Health and safety regs mean all patients are made as comfortable as possible. This is therapy, not punishment. Barometric pressure in my cell is adjusted to my body so my eyes don't look like poached eggs.

'The way it worked out, little changed. I'm just on the other side of the bars.'

CHRISTINE ON THE WHITE CORRIDOR

AUNT JAS WAS SAFE BUT NOT HERSELF.

A guard she knew and one of her patients had been murdered by Adam Tussaud. The cutthroat didn't look much like Gary Oldman. Now, he didn't look much like anyone. In the scrap, Chrissie had put him on the floor.

She had more of a sense of what happened on the White Corridor than with the crocks under the bridge. But it was like remembering something someone who wasn't quite her had done. Perky on *Letsby Avenue*. Or the silly goose who went swimming in a rubbish-filled reservoir in *Prohibited Pond*. Did all cloaks feel that way when they wore a costume – that they were not just (or not even) who they were the rest of the time?

Violet lightning was involved. And quantities of black stuff – dark matter? – which manifested as needed. Versatile as a weapon and fashion accessory. At Draycott's, Chrissie did a Music, Movement and Mime project on Ribbon Gymnastics, a form of dance popular as a competitive sport in China. The skill was transferable to the supple, strong, blacker-than-night lengths of darkstuff she could now conjure. From where? Under her wig? From any given shadow? She'd have to ask Aunt Jas. There was a Ribbon Gymnastics martial arts style. Chrissie supposed she was now the primary Western exponent of streamer fu.

Power came back. The prize pupils were locked in their cells by the vampire doctor and short, tough guards. Famous cutthroats went meekly or had to be carried. Most were hurt, dazed or in a coma. Chrissie didn't feel a jot guilty about that. She'd been attacked by a flipping gorilla! At least two old creeps had tried to talk inside her mind. Plus that horrible fellow with the thin moustache. She retained enough O Level French to get the drift of his chat-up lines. He deserved to choke on his beret.

The guard who'd helped Adam Tussaud was majorly unpopular. She was in thumbcuffs.

The egg-headed blackcoat in charge – funnily, his name was Dr Head – stood in front of an array of telly screens. When the lights came on and the pictures came back, a lot of folk looked sheepish, caught on camera at less than their best. The odd scrap continued but ergs were running low. More weary slappies than proper punch-ups. One telly showed the main gate, which opened as if with a fanfare. A heavy mob marched in. Red Rope Wristbands in sharp suits. A squad in spherical helmets and fatigues. Scrapping died down. Order was restored. The sun was up. It must be nearly nine.

She couldn't half do with a cooked breakfast.

Chrissie looked at the screens, trying to spot Loulee.

Her friend might be miffed. She'd understand when she found out what happened on the White Corridor. Chrissie was only thinking of keeping her safe.

It wasn't too late to reconvene the Shade Brigade.

Dr Head was on his Vone, asking questions and not getting answers he liked. Good news that the riot was nearly over didn't make up for the bad news that it happened at all. The original report was wrong. No one had escaped. The missing inmate was dead and hidden under a bed.

'We have to talk,' Aunt Jas said to her. 'Later.'

She was more upset than expected. Not for herself – and, thank the lucky stars, not about Chrissie being reckless. It was her dead patient. Richard Jeperson. The name didn't ring bells so he couldn't have been very terrible. Aunt Jas kept it together but Chrissie could tell she wanted to go somewhere dark and have a nice long cry. With chocolate.

She asked Aunt Jasmine how to get to the courtyard.

Jas hugged her, tighter than expected.

LOULEE IS VOX POPPED

THE IMPORTANT THING WAS NOT TO BE MISTAKEN for a rioter and kept at Devil's Dyke. She tossed her makeshift sabre down a stairwell.

On the way to the courtyard, a guard tried to clout Gerald with a truncheon. Eunice puffed a fireball at the thick-necked runt. It set light to Loulee's arm. Burning leather whiffed something awful. Ftatateeta sawed round the shoulder seam with deft fingers and unpeeled the singed sleeve. Now Loulee's jacket was lop-sided.

She was ticked off. She loved the jacket. It had been given to Lamb Bear before it turned out he was useless on a Lambretta. The lapels were studded with badges, vintage tiepins and novelty stick-ons. Each meant something. Some were totems for ghosts.

Outside the building, inmates were divided into pyjama groups like classes on open day. Loulee was left over. From her mustard sleeve, guards didn't know where to shove her. Which was handy. She was too fagged out to shove back.

In thin, cold morning light Loulee saw unexpected familiar faces.

Eleanor Wynter, whose make-up she'd put on yesterday evening, showed no sign of recognising her. Garnet Graill, who she'd not talked to in weeks, knew her straight off. He pretended not to be as surprised to find her here as she was to see him.

'Talk to that girl,' Garn told Nelly. 'Get a first-person account.'

Was the bright light playing On-the-Spot Reporter?

Red-Tel must be desperate for an increase in the *Real News* viewing figures.

Garn aimed a camera. Fly-eyes hovered in formation, slaved to his mixing bracelet. This might be live. Loulee took out a compact and checked her face in the little mirror. She had bumps and bruises and no time to conceal them. Her hair was fine, though. She'd do.

'The situation at Devil's Dyke remains perilous,' said Eleanor, to camera. 'A revolt of the deadliest cutthroats in Britain has been contained by the combined forces of the Red Rope and Special Section... but who knows what dangers are still posed?'

It was all over bar throwing a bucket of water over smouldering ashes. No one wanted to scrap any more. They'd been up all night. But by all means terrify early morning viewers with scaremongering over their Sugar Puffs.

Eleanor advanced on Loulee with a microphone.

'It's Nelly Off the Telly,' said a bloke in buff pyjamas.

A ripple of interest ran around the courtyard. Even mad people – strike that, *especially* mad people – followed *Letsby Avenue*. Eleanor showed one of WDS Jill's rarer expressions – sweetly humble but single-minded about cracking the case. Why was she here instead of some dimbleborough from *Spectrum* or the Serious Channel? With Garnet Graill, a snapper for the tabs. Were they doing a *Crew Selection* series about combat zone reporters?

'Could you tell us who you are,' Eleanor asked Loulee, 'what crime are you guilty of and what are your demands before you start executing hostages?'

Loulee laughed in astonishment.

'You know who I am. Your make-up artist. Not a criminal or a mental patient.'

Strictly, that was debatable. It was probbo against the law to sneak into Devil's Dyke impersonating an operative of Special Section. And anyone who did that ought to be detained at least for a thirty-day observation period.

Calculator wheels went round behind Eleanor's eyes.

'Lulu?' she said, unable to make the numbers add up.

'Close enough.'

Loulee even sympathised. She didn't know how they'd got from last night to this morning either.

'I have no demands and the show's over,' she said.

Inmates meekly grouped into corridor classes – Wavy Lines, Polka Dot, Lime, Buff. No White and few Weird Squiggle. Guards with clipboards and tally counters went round, taking the register. The Red Rope manned the gates. Special Section had little to do and formed their own line-up. The visual sold the story of danger passing.

'Louise,' said Garn, one of the vanishingly few people in the universe who called her that. 'Where's Christine?'

'Ah,' said Loulee, 'funny you should ask...'

CHRISTINE GIVES AN ENCORE

SHE WAS CRASHING. EVERYTHING WAS FURTHER AWAY than it should be. She trudged as if with handicap weights. Her eyes ached. She'd taken several good wallops. An ear-worm gave her brain-throb, *whoo whoo...*

Last night in the dark, she'd nutted a gorilla and won scraps no one would have expected her to survive. In the cold light of this morning, she'd fall over if someone chucked a floppy teapot at her.

She needed a fry-up and gallons of stewed chee. With chocolate digestives. Thanks to Dr Zenf, she hadn't eaten a CDB in two years. She trusted McVitie's hadn't changed the recipe since her farewell biccy – which she'd scoffed and sicked up in fear of being found out. She might experiment with Hobnobs. Her palate could have evolved while she was depriving herself. *Needlessly* depriving herself. Was Dr Zenf her arch-nemesis?

For a first night, Lady Shade II hadn't done shabbily. Chrissie's record so far – all fifteen hours of it – rated a gold star. A mouse-squeak of sense, sounding in her head like Loulee doing a cartoon voice, suggested this would be the clever time to quit. She was undeniably ahead of the night-game. Less risky options were on her table, even after being discontinued from *Letsby Avenue.*

When she woke up in three weeks' time, she *must* dial her agent.

First she needed to find Loulee (and her Lambretta) and make a getaway.

Red Rope Wristbands regulated the flow of felons to the courtyard. A mind glitch overlaid the scene with memories of coming up to doors of clubs. Only now Chrissie was not mixing with the Coterie but the criminally insane. She might have grievances against Dr Crockery but he hadn't tried to maim her yet.

Patients lined up for inspection. The shady get-up stuck out a mile in daylight. A White Corridor void had called her a singing telegram girl. A job she could get.

Her breath misted. It was parky. Frost on the tarmac.

She spotted a mustard tracksuit sleeve.

Loulee was by the main gate, talking with...

Good gravy – with Nightmare Nelly! And Garn.

The world shifted sideways again and struck another iceberg. Chrissie tried to put the pieces together. Had she already taken her three-week nap and woken up to an altered reality?

She hadn't realised Garn even knew Eleanor Wynter.

It made sort of sense. Garn was trying to climb above the fold. He often talked about it. That stroked Chrissie's fur the wrong way. He implied anything she put effort into was trivial nonsense next to the wars, strikes or collapsing buildings he'd prefer to snap. She didn't entirely disagree but was fed up with having her shallowness rubbed in every night of the week with a Sunday afternoon omnibus repeat.

But Nelly?

A Walking Curse. A verit nemesis. A malign spectre. When she manifested, pianos fell from the sky. Now Chrissie came to think of it, the Cartoonist played the dropped piano joke on a choir who were singing 'Squashed Tomatoes and Stew' to Silly Millie. Chrissie wasn't being fair to Eleanor. The bright light was dreadful but not cutthroat dreadful.

Eleanor marched across the courtyard, microphone aimed. She had on a belted see-through mac with an autopsy scar double zip and the Stán logo. Next week, Bailey and Lenka would be wearing cellophane knock-offs.

Garn followed with raised camera, a formation of fly-eyes hovering above. He was getting multiple angles of Chrissie looking a sight. Whispers natters would be brutal.

Loulee gave Chrissie the 'fake a fainting fit' signal but Chrissie was too tired for acting exercises.

Chrissie had one odd, tiny revelation-realisation.

Garn and Nelly didn't immediately recognise her. The costume, such as it was, fooled them. They couldn't take on board someone familiar showing up in a completely unexpected place.

This was her world now. She expected the unexpected. Anyone who didn't was a civ.

Should she do a voice? Low and husky as if she'd smoked a packet of snouts? Maybe an accent. The writers thought of making WPC Purkiss Welsh but changed their minds after they heard Chrissie's 'Blodwyn From Barry' routine.

Loulee was right. Chrissie should faint rather than speak.

'Here at Devil's Dyke,' Eleanor said, looking to one of the fly-eyes, 'order has been re-established and the possibility of mass break-out thwarted in no small measure due to the bravery of a hitherto-unknown cloak affiliated with the hush-hush Special Section. We've secured the first public interview with this extraordinary young woman. This is an exclusive for Red-Tel, brought to you by your reporter on the spot, Eleanor Wynter. You may know me best as WDS Jill...'

Nelly went on at such length telling viewers who she was – which they already knew – there wouldn't be time for more than a few words from the hitherto-unknown cloak. A mercy. Chrissie hadn't even settled on her trade-name yet. Lady Shade II was deffo just a place-holder.

'... di Ferrante in *Letsby Avenue*...'

The grey-haired, bulky woman Chrissie had seen earlier broke rank from the Polka Dot head count and ran at the gate. Eleanor was knocked out of the way. Garn kept his camera steady on the charging inmate. Fly-eyes auto-swivelled to catch the action. Peach. He'd have five angles of his bottom being kicked by a maniac to choose from. If Eleanor got a scrape where it showed, Red-Tel would find someone to sue. Chrissie could lose her parents' house and her aunt's car.

The inmate, more panicked than angry, inhaled mightily. She inflated, stretching her buttonholes. Her clothes were loose. The puffing up must be a natural effect the hospital took into account when issuing nightwear.

Chrissie couldn't remember how dangerous Polka Dot inmates were supposed to be.

The woman's neck disappeared. Her ponytail shifted into a topknot as her head expanded. Baggy pyjama bottoms became leggings.

'Watch out,' shouted a guard, 'Bouncing Betty's going to roll!'

BB stuck out Humpty Dumpty arms and cartwheeled. Guards and Wristbands scattered. Someone swore and threw a tally-counter away.

Even after the night she'd had, Chrissie was fazed.

BB ploughed through and over anyone in her way. Folk who'd thought the crisis over were peeved to have to shift sharpish so as not to be bounced on. She was big and soft like a huge beanbag.

This wasn't a rampage but a panic attack.

Chrissie sympathised but someone would get hurt soon.

The Red Rope had come prepared to put down an uprising by mad murderers. They wouldn't just have rubber bullets.

A blackcoat tried to talk to Bouncing Betty but she wasn't listening. Her ears were tiny flesh-flowers on the sides of her expanded head. They didn't get big with the rest of her. Neither did her eyes or fingernails.

BB slammed into a wall and bounced into the air, knocking out fly-eyes. She went from beach-ball to wrecking ball. She took the roof off a shed. A rat-person who'd been hiding in the eaves fell out. Chrissie heard rounds pumped into breeches, stuncannons power up, kill-orders issued.

It was a cloudy, gloomy morning – but the night was gone.

There was almost no shadow in the courtyard.

Chrissie didn't even know if she had abilities in sunlight. She might be a Cinderella cloak – crime-fighter by night, useless weed by day.

Bouncing Betty bounced harder. Someone's leg got broken.

As if in a click, she saw Eleanor – with a terrified, authentic expression never shown on *Letsby Avenue* – cringe against Garn, who struggled to keep his camera aimed. Shadow grew around them. An incoming human meteor.

She took hold of that shadow and raised it like a table tennis paddle.

Bouncing Betty struck a hard invisible plane three feet above Eleanor and Garn and bounced, higher than before. Chrissie hoped Eleanor and Garn would have the presence of mind to get out of the target area before BB slammed back down again with more force. The higher she bounced, the heavier she landed. Chrissie wasn't sure she could manage that trick twice. Eleanor and Garn froze in place like complete prawns. Drat. Chrissie would have to burst a blood vessel in her brain to save them. Or else they'd be paste on concrete.

Loulee took Eleanor's arm and pulled her away. Garn got the message and scrambled out from under. His camera clicked, clicked, clicked.

Quick-thinking, Ghost Lantern Girl!

Bouncing Betty hit concrete hard.

Idiots started firing at her. She was, of course, bulletproof. Folk in the trajectory of ricochets generally weren't.

The blackcoat issued orders to the Red Rope and the Soccer Heads not to shoot at the invulnerable woman. The rescue and recovery squads should have spent more time learning the stats on the back of the face-cards.

Everyone cowered, trying to be small. Some crawled under cars or pressed through doors to the main wards.

Chrissie stood square, trying to centre herself.

She tapped into her reservoir of darkness, which was almost dry.

Bouncing Betty came at her from a height and at speed.

Chrissie put up a hand, giving the halt signal. She saw BB's panicked eyes – startled little olives in a yard-wide face. The woman wanted to *stop*, to calm down, to go back to regular size.

She couldn't help herself so someone had to help her.

The human boulder halted in mid-air and was gently lowered.

She dwindled with a squeaky wheeze. A Montgolfier balloon with a slow leak.

Chrissie went to see if the poor woman was all right. Bouncing Betty fell at her feet, exhausted.

Clicks and whirrs.

Garn was getting piccies.

'To me, Chris,' said Garn. 'Look to me. Give us a smile.'

So he'd seen through the wig and Spex. That was always going to happen.

Unless she had chocolate in the next seven seconds, Chrissie wouldn't need to fake a faint. She held a pose.

Clicks and whirrs. All eyes on her.

THE SHADOW CABINET

MARIUS STOK: You've seen the footage from Devil's Dyke this morning.

JOSHUA UNWIN: It's the girl, of course. From the telly serial.

SIR FREDERICK REGENT: That's not confirmed. Jasmine hasn't reported yet. The girl is her niece.

LADY LEAVES: Always lax, that one.

JULIAN RATTRAY: Have a heart, Lady L. You know she and Jeperson were joined at the hip. She'll be devastated.

SIR FREDERICK REGENT: She isn't the only one. This country owes a great deal to Richard Jeperson.

LADY LEAVES: Duty comes first.

MARIUS STOK: I'm sure we appreciate that. I have issued a summons. We'll have a report from Dr Chambers. She's best placed to tell us what we'll need to know.

JOSHUA UNWIN: Then the girl?

MARIUS STOK: Yes, the girl. Christine Chambers...

LADY LEAVES: An "actress"!

JULIAN RATTRAY: Weren't you once a "dancer", Lady L?

MARIUS STOK: Please, concentrate. This is a crucial time. We must put up a concerted front. We'll have to see the girl.

SIR FREDERICK REGENT: Woman. She's twenty-one.

MARIUS STOK: You're right. Woman.

SIR FREDERICK REGENT: They like to be called actors now. Women who act.

LADY LEAVES: Do they really?

SIR FREDERICK REGENT: Did you call yourself a 'dancress'?

LADY LEAVES: [unintelligible]

MARIUS STOK: Whatever Christine Chambers has been until now, we have to accept that she's serious. Her showing at Devil's Dyke marks her as inheritor of the Shade legacy. It is imperative she be educated to understand her responsibilities.

LADY LEAVES: I agree. Children have no sense of responsibility.

JULIAN RATTRAY: Not like we did in our day, eh? Remember the Isle of Wight in '73, Lady L? You went undercover as 'the Groovy Groupie' to bust Blotch Casualty and the Acid Drop Kid. Not that much cover was involved - except that edible body paint.

LADY LEAVES: [unintelligible]

JOSHUA UNWIN: What can you tell us about Louise Ling? She wasn't even mentioned in the intelligence packet prepared on Christine Chambers last year.

SIR FREDERICK REGENT: Miss Ling is an odd one. Not enlightened, in the conventional sense... but you've seen the footage. We had Asmida Reynolds marked as a potential asset. A civ should not make short work of someone with the Naga's form. But Miss Ling did. She obviously has hidden talents.

JOSHUA UNWIN: Take her out of the picture? To be on the safe side.

MARIUS STOK: I don't think we're there yet. Mr Zero?

JUN ZERO: I concur.

JULIAN RATTRAY: I for one am excited. This new girl shows promise. It's been too long since we've had a proper Shade. Dr Chambers has been semi-retired for years.

MARIUS STOK: You can't force the dark. It has to bloom naturally.

CHRISTINE CHAMBERS

'No piccies, or it didn't happen. Here's how that worked out.

'That night, I scrapped with a Chamber of Horrors.

'Adam Tussaud. Guy the Gorilla. Roger Duroc. The Inner Voice. Robert Hackwill. Anthony Jago. I've Hawkshawed them all. I'm glad I didn't do that before I went onto the White Corridor. I had a general sense but not the gory details. If I think about it in the daytime, I'm terrified. That's not even counting Scary Mary and the Jibbenainosay, who I stopped without setting eyes on.

'Objectively, I was lucky to get off the White Corridor alive. That I bested the worst of the worst is a miracle. I still pinch myself.

'But that scrap didn't go out on the telly. Devil's Dyke internal security cameras are hardened against nuclear blast. Their clips have their own level of classified status. Aunt Jas won't even let me see frame captures.

'Me and Bouncing Betty – Elaine Hillier – were on the telly, though. Everyone and their cat saw that to-do.

'It wasn't even a scrap. I tried to defuse a sitch. Mrs Hillier isn't anyone's idea of a cutthroat, despite the jewel robberies. She's a nuisance, not a menace. She's genuinely at Devil's

Dyke for treatment rather than because she wants locking up. Thanks to Garn, no one knows that. Instead, the story is me and my Spex Appeal versus Polka Dot Peril. The visuals sell a fable of cloak and cutthroat. I saved Eleanor Wynter from a squashing – another turn-up I could have done without – and am now Official Favourite cloak of Nelly's Nutters.

'Garn told me to smile and – like a nit – I did. When I model, I'm not a smiler. I lick my lower lip and stick it out. My optimal expression. It's how my face works. I've been advised by well-paid consultants. But in all the clicks and clips, I've a smug, slap-my-face smirk on as I stand over a very ill woman who looks like she's been run down by a dustcart. That visual did the rounds. The tabs ran "It's a Knockout" headlines. I am a Victory Vixen.

'I see the click and it's me. But not me. Not *just* me. I see the shadow.

'It's the same with the clips of me and the crocks under the bridge. A Whispers natter claims UltraPerky and the Devil's Dyke Mystery Maid can't possibly be the same person. Though the main difference between them is one is wearing a WPC hat and the other has a Silent Movie Star wig.

'Boyd Waylo – you know, the Cutting Commentator – made a connection with Aunt Jas's clips, of which there are few of decent quality. A glimpse in the mêlée during the Battle of Battersea – which I'd seen a dozen times without recognising her. Clicks of Adam Tussaud under arrest, with Lady Shade gripping his arm. I don't see a resemblance but since Waylo pointed it out dozens of others do.

'So I'm Lady Shade. Not even Lady Shade II. I just get the name.

'And, as it turns out, a Rolls-Royce.

'So it's not all terrible news.

'Loulee's a little chilly about it but the Shade Brigade is on again. Eunice, Ftatateeta and Tunno got early release for not being complete voids during the crisis. My aunt pushed that through, though she's out of communication when I most need to talk with her. Which I fully understand. I know more about Richard Jeperson now.

'Perky stays dead. I've not even bothered checking the Soap Bubbles natter to find out who killed her. I already know. The

Coterie are rowing furiously about whether to big me up or chuck me out.

'I thought of sending Hereward, Chell and the celery-chompers clicks of all my meals. Schilling have asked me to play down the all-I-can-eat thing. Loulee argued against telling the Agency but it turns out to be a contractual obligation. Not informing them about any enlightened abilities I develop would get me thrown off the books and liable to a fine I can't possibly pay. I sent clips to my agent, identifying myself as Lady Shade. Maybe I could get stunt work if dark matter doesn't play merry hell with lighting rigs.

'An unknown number flashes on my Vone.

'It's Dorothy Schilling. I've been in a room with her but she's never spoken directly to me before. She exists five or six floors above my actual agent. My former actual agent. Yes, I'm now a Schilling Banner Client. In fact, I'm two clients. Lady Shade TBC is the Banner Client, while Christine Chambers is bumped up a tier or two but ticking over nicely. Call-Me-Dot feels a cloak should have a secret identity in case of emergencies. Even when everyone in the country knows who they are. She might have started that Whispers natter.

'"With great enlightenment," Dot says, "Comes great opportunity."

'So there's that.'

ACT TWO:
'STRICTLY
SUPER'

A Job Vacancy

[Cleared for Publication - MM.]

The retirement is announced of Urban Fox, a member of the Splendid Six for nearly twenty years. Initially a controversial addition to the cloak group, she won over early detractors and became an admired public figure.

Before joining the Splendids, Urban Fox was often miscategorised as a cutthroat. She began by prowling London's Hackney Marshes, conducting a one-woman war on night-crime. For a spell, she was listed as Most Wanted by the Metropolitan Police. It transpired that Councillor Rexwell Pitt, her most vocal critic, was the secret identity of gangcult boss Top Dog. When Pitt's empire of extortion, vice and illegal entertainment events toppled, all charges against Urban Fox were dropped. The former Top Dog was recently released from Wormwood Scrubs on compassionate grounds, seven years into three consecutive ninety-year sentences. Pitt is receiving care in Mother Mary's Hospice, Hackney.

Urban Fox made national headlines in the early 2000s, venturing beyond her postcode to conduct campaigns in the countryside. She teamed with Early Man to prevent the theft of Stonehenge by a GEIST satrapy. In 2006, Urban Fox was hand-picked by the Splendids' manager Martin Masters to fill in while Finnegan Drift (trade-name New Seeker) took a leave of absence which became permanent when he ascended to a higher plane. Commentators suggested Urban Fox was added to bring an edgier, less polite element to a group often seen as overly traditional. Urban Fox, a Splendid with claws, did much to dispel the staid visual of a greying line-up.

Reports circulated of Urban Fox's clashes over methods and tactics with then Group Captain Blackfist III, though the two were also rumoured to be a couple. She fought alongside the Splendids in the Which Wars and the Battle of Battersea, but never forgot her roots. When Top Dog was convicted, no new throat threat emerged to fill the power vacuum. After Rexwell Pitt, few wanted to pick a scrap with Urban Fox. Hackney Marshes is currently rated one of the safest districts in Greater London.

The Urban Fox uniform – rust-coloured bodystocking, sharp-nosed half-mask, red lipstick, flick-claws – was critiqued as basic but came to be accepted as classic. Her visual remained unaltered after her contemporaries ditched embarrassing ra-ra skirts, pouched bandoliers, inflated upper arms, dayglo headbands and teensy-tiny footsie boots. While other cloaks embraced corporate marketing opportunities, Urban Fox stayed street. She endorsed a minimum of merchandising through her Foxglove Foundation, which supports animal charities. She has no Peophole Purview or Personals

Presence and ignores Whispers Backchatter.

After three decades' active service, Urban Fox has unmasked.

As is traditional with cloaks who maintain secret identities, Urban Fox has confirmed her retirement by revealing her civilian name.

Meet Mimsy Mountmain, 53, proprietor of the Precious Pet Clinic in Cheering Lane, East Stratford.

Asked if she worries cutthroats might target her family or business, Ms Mountmain comments that few of her nemeses are in any condition to be pests. She was initially inspired to use her enlightened abilities – acute senses, heightened reflexes and agility, sympathy with animals (especially canines) – when she learned dogs from the refuge where she worked were kitted out with mechanical parts by Top Dog's Society for the Promotion of Cruel Sport and forced to compete and die in the arena.

Ms Mountmain ends speculation by revealing she is not involved with Julian Rattray, who retired as Blackfist III five years ago. Her longtime partner Karel Xhen briefly worked as Urban Fox's companion Beelzebrush but currently handles admin for Precious Pet and the Foxglove Foundation.

With the departure of Urban Fox, the Splendid Six line-up consists of Dr Robot (Group Captain), Quackanapes, Silly Millie, Blackfist IV and the Green Knight.

Which cloak will fill the sixth place on the roster?

The two-dimensional mystery woman Flat Cat is considered the bookies' favourite while long-term aspirant Brighton Belle – presumed to be a cert to join the Splendids two years ago, only to be edged aside by Quackanapes' companion Silly Millie – remains rank outsider. It is presumed Martin Masters will compile an all-woman shortlist. Unlike the Double Deckers, the Splendid Six do not have a constitutional commitment to gender parity – but have long since moved past the five-to-one fella-to-filly ratio of their earliest squads. Often criticised for lack of diversity, the Splendids might also seek a less white face – though Brixton Braden, inheritor of the Blackfist legacy, hotly takes issue with backchatter that he won his place through tokenism. Silly Millie, who maintains a secret identity under comedy make-up, has let slip that her family background is Anglo-Turkish. And no one is certain what colour the Green Knight is (except green).

Martin Masters states that, following the requirements of the Splendid Six founding charter, selection will be made on merit alone.

Further announcement can be expected from the Tri-Lion in due course.

CHRISTINE IN THE CLOCK TOWER

'BIG BEN IS THE BELL,' CHRISSIE SAID, IN THE SHADOW of the gothic rocketship. 'The building is called the Clock Tower.'

'I know,' said Loulee. 'I went to the same school you did. Visiting the Houses of Parliament was one of Draycott's Day Out wheezes. Eunice wore a Guy Fawkes hat and set off the sprinklers. It's a wonder she wasn't locked up then and there. For firelighter treason and plot.'

'Back then we weren't shown *this door.*'

Chrissie stepped over the do-not-step-over-this-chain chain and pressed weathered stone. The Clock Tower was late Victorian pretending to be mediaeval. The masonry began to crumble after fifty years and was in worse shape than proper olden times cathedrals and castles. Standards were always declining.

'What door?' said Loulee. 'Oh, I see, the *hidden* door. Do tell... and don't forget to walk us out through the gift shop. They sell big soft Palace of Westminster hats for the patriotic crock in your life.'

'No crocks in my life, ta very much.'

Loulee raised her hands in mock horror. 'That's *lifestyle prejudice,* Chrissie. You'll be blighted and barred.'

'Crocks will be long past Next Tuesday by the time they

sort that out and something just as stupid will have taken over. Marcus Milner is already claiming to be "post-crock". What comes after tea-time?'

'The Children's Hour?'

'I sometimes think we're in one long Children's Hour anyway. It's a wonder Muffin the Mule isn't Deputy Prime Minister.'

Chrissie ran her hands over rough stone.

'Are you feeling up a gargoyle?' asked Loulee.

'Just locating the catch.'

There was a trick to the door. Chrissie hadn't mastered it yet.

Poulton-Jones, watching from his perch, let her have three goes then took mercy and negated the magnetic lock from his end.

'Voy-ler,' said Chrissie.

Where there had been a wall, now there was an opening. A light went on like in the fridge.

'You amaze me,' said Loulee.

'It gets amazing-er from here.'

So much had gone on these last months – with the Shadow Cabinet, Dot Schilling and Shady Business, not to mention Loulee and her Lantern ghosts and the shake-up at Red-Tel. This was Chrissie's first chance to show her friend some of the bonus prizes which came with her legacy.

Loulee hadn't asked why Chrissie brought her to Westminster After Hours. Not much was going on. It was the half of the year when parliament sat in Hector's House, the purpose-built 1970s complex in Milton Keynes. The old chambers were under dust-sheets. Commons and Lords wouldn't be back till September, when tourists could again peer at peers and aim nuts at nuts from the visitors' gallery. That was tradition. On their visit, Draycott's girls competed to bounce cashews off Lord Archer's head. Loulee won by dinging Ann Widdecombe with a rebound.

Chrissie led Loulee into an old-fashioned lift cage.

With a clanking and rattle, they were pulled up.

'The shaft is on the blueprints as a counter-weight for the clock,' Chrissie explained.

'Remember when I told you that above the clock-faces was the nest of the Giant Swan of the Kingdom?' said Loulee. 'You wanted to know if it laid eggs.'

'You could be a horror, Louls.'

'And I've stopped?'

'Moderated. You spotted something, though. Space unaccounted for. It is a nest. If autogiros need nests. There've been Shades in the Clock Tower for generations. The original Dr Shade liked looking down on the government.'

The lift passed up through the clockworks. All four translucent faces were pale giant moons. The ticking took some getting used to.

'That's your excuse for forgetting the time gone,' said Loulee. 'Now you live in a clock.'

'Above a clock. I don't live here. It's a storage unit. A place to put extra clobber.'

'And somewhere you can spy on us from. Like the original Dr S…'

'Yes, that – though I don't do it personally.'

The cage rattled open into the surprisingly large pyramidal space. If the tower were a disguised rocketship, this would be the nose cone.

'Miss Christine,' said Poulton-Jones. 'All quiet tonight.'

Poulton-Jones wore an immaculate wing collar and overalls. If anyone asked, he was a maintenance engineer. He wasn't the Poulton-Jones who'd looked after Aunt Jasmine's autogiro because he was too young. Jas said the Shadow Cabinet – who were *not* to be confused with the Opposition Front Bench – retired Poulton-Joneses every so often and broke a new one out of a packet. There was continuity. Chrissie's first Poulton-Jones reminded her too much of a teacher. One minute, she was a grown-up with a secret identity scrapping with cutthroats. Next, she was being told off – by pursed lips and narrowed eyes, if not in words – for breaking rules she couldn't have known about.

'Hello Poulton-Jones, I'm Loulee Ling,' said Loulee, hand out.

Poulton-Jones showed her his oily gauntlet and Loulee took her hand back.

Loulee had no official Shady status and was still not up for being a companion. But it was understood that Chrissie needed to share privileged information with her friend. It being understood did not mean it being liked. Poulton-Jones looked at

Loulee as if she were a kitchen cabinet which didn't match the original features and would go back to Habitat after the bank holiday.

'Is that an aeolipile?' Loulee asked.

Poulton-Jones raised an eyebrow and stood aside from a large table-cum-stove which supported a copper globe. Kinked chimneys stuck out of the sphere, which revolved gently with a scented hiss. Chrissie had taken it for a souvenir of a past Shade exploit.

'Indeed it is, Miss Ling.'

'An independent power source? You're running the whole system on it, not the electricity grid.'

Poulton-Jones nodded.

'Immune to power cuts. Handy.'

Loulee looked around at the telly boxes and clock-dial panels Chrissie had taken for wired-together industrial sculpture and junk-shoppe surplus. She now realised the electric for the doodads was generated by the globe-with-crooked-chimneys. Poulton-Jones took a tray of chestnuts out of the stove and offered them round.

'Scuse fingers,' said Loulee, taking one.

'Is Fanny Widdershins still in parliament?' she asked, tossing the warm nut from hand to hand.

Loulee – who must have a ghost engineer sitting on her shoulder – was all over the aolithingy. Poulton-Jones happily showed it off – lifting grilles, opening little hatches. The copper gave the air a tang, like the blood from the root of a milk tooth.

'This runs on charcoal, water and clock-springs,' said Loulee. 'It's a marvel.'

'Indeed, Miss Ling.'

Chrissie was still waiting for her nut. It would have gone cold by the time Poulton-Jones remembered. Did Loulee even know she did this? It'd been going on since well before she found the Ghost Lantern. Was that why the Lantern worked for her? Dozens of other girls could stroll past the mystery cupboard and be ignored but when Loulee Ling hove in view its catch-handle waggled at her.

Poulton-Jones showed Loulee the autogiro, stowed with its blades removed. He let her climb into the plexiglass bubble –

which he'd told Chrissie not to do. Loulee didn't fiddle with the (very simple) controls but pointed to them and said what she thought they were for. She was always right. Getting full marks was easy with half the afterlife as a crib sheet, Chrissie thought but didn't say.

'We're visiting the Lock-Up later,' Chrissie said. 'To see the car collection.'

'The *famous* car collection,' said Loulee.

'It's maintained,' said Poulton-Jones. 'Kept in trust for when...'

He didn't need to say what needed to happen. Chrissie had now failed her driving test a second time. She'd intended to take extra lessons, then hadn't had free periods in her diary – what with *see above* the Shadow Cabinet etc. – to do more than a few hours on the road in her aunt's Mini. She'd been red carded by the adjudicator. The Mini wasn't available now Jas was on retreat. Getting a driving licence was one of Chrissie's important things to do. It kept being bumped further down the list.

Until her ticket was issued, she could only go to the Lock-Up in Vauxhall and ogle.

'Loulee has a ghost who was a rally driver before the Great War,' said Chrissie.

'Contessa Ercolina Medici d'Olivola,' said Loulee. 'Designed and built her own motor cars... Sabotaged in the Pyrenees and died of exposure.'

'Is Contessa Erco itching to get behind the wheel?' Chrissie asked.

'Yes, but she's not taking charge when I drive. I don't let ghosts elbow me out of the way when it's a thing I want to do on my own.'

Chrissie had been telling Loulee about the car collection in measured instalments, calculated to provoke eagerness and a smidge of envy. She dangled keys, knowing how potent the pull was. Next time there was a scrap out of town, she wanted an alternative to the back of a Lambretta. But if she asked Loulee to commit to driving her around (even in a tasty motor), there'd be another huff. Loulee was still testy about not wanting to be classed as companion. She hadn't opened a magic cupboard and become conduit to a wealth of supernatural skill just to be Lady Shade's chauffeur. Any future driving assistance had to be Loulee's idea. It would take more than a whiff of petrol to get her onside.

With all her newfound abilities, Chrissie was rubbish at cajoling friends into things. Deep down, she didn't want pushover friends like that. Garn got folk to have ideas which turned out to be to his benefit more than theirs – or stepped in as a thing was gathering momentum and about to happen, then made it seem it was his project and couldn't come off without him. People who'd done hard thinking and actual work would congratulate Garn on successes which came along – though they'd take the blame if whatever it was fizzled like a wet Catherine wheel.

Chrissie had not brought Garn to the Clock Tower. Or mentioned the Lock-Up.

He had done Official Lady Shade clicks for her. An obvious hire from the point of view of Schilling and Red-Tel. If anyone was a Shade companion, it was Garnet Graill. Camera Man. When he wasn't there, she grumbled – if only to herself – about the way he had a free ticket on her ride… but when he was, she relied on him. Now she was regularly quizzed on camera by Eleanor Wynter – the Woman With Permafrost Eyes – she needed to see Garn's supportive smile over Nelly's hairdo while trying to formulate answers which didn't make her seem a complete bolus. Garn could only do so much. She needed Loulee.

Bringing her friend to the Clock Tower was a start.

If she had to go back to school, she wanted someone to bunk off with, pass notes to and copy homework from.

She stood in shadow, feeling darkness course through her and seeing more detail in the vaulted space. Poulton-Jones showed Loulee pieces of kit Chrissie had thought were décor. Loulee – with a few prompts – persisted in understanding what every item was for.

What Loulee had did not come out of a packet. It was a gift.

It would be easy to doze off and wake up in a world where her best friend was the *new* new Lady Shade and she was in overalls and chauffeur's cap, happily a companion. Truly, really, she wouldn't mind.

Her months being better known as Perky than herself had turned her ideas about fame around. Doing the Circuit with the

Coterie felt increasingly like a chore – especially now she wasn't available so much and the others made more effort to get her along so they could be in clicks and clips with her.

She remembered listening hard-hearted as Polly O and Monica Maude complained about the pressures of being phantasmagorically beautiful in public. Now she had slivers of sympathy. Everywhere she went, people wanted something – if only a few moments of her time (which added up to *all* her time). Clicks, clips, scrawls (she was depressed to find out how much more her autograph would be worth on Going for a Song if she got killed), visits, meetings, endorsements. She was pitched business opportunities she mistook for chat-up lines and wasted ear-time on earnest men in suits who gave bullet point reasons why she should go out with them. Every other stranger wanted to get her on her own for nefarious purposes. That wasn't even counting flan-flingers (two near misses) and picketing crocks, plus Justice for Jesmond loons and the Bouncing Betty Appreciation Society (*everyon*e has a fan club, she'd found out). She'd imagined grateful caffs giving her chee on the house only to find she was expected to stand every round.

Being a cloak was like the car collection. A Christmas present she wasn't allowed to play with.

Only in shadow, unbothered, could she revisit the violet thrill.

It was there, more than ever. She sometimes wrapped herself in dark ribbons and went far away where the night was cool and her nerves thrilled with every tiny sound. Then she was above and beyond it all – running and racing ahead, *enjoying* her presents, finding time for fun and larfs.

Her Dark Vone pirriped.

She slid it out of the sheath on her arm. It was flexible, violet-black and a limited edition available only to Schilling Banner Clients.

A blurt from Dot.

Loulee and Poulton-Jones looked at her. Loulee bit her lip. Chrissie knew what they expected. Call to arms. City on fire. Cutthroats on the rampage. In other words, a scrap. She hadn't been in one, except for re-enactment poses, since Devil's Dyke. Putting the lights out for a flan-flinger didn't count.

Some nights, her charge was so great she wondered about going out 'on patrol' in dodgy districts – looking for crooks or crocks to clobber or foolish children to save from perilous ponds. But that wasn't her style. She'd only get waylaid by someone who wanted to put her face on an ice cream van.

'I'm in,' said Chrissie. 'It'll be announced tomorrow.'

'You're *in*?' said Loulee. 'The Splendid Six?'

'In the running for the Splendid Six,' said Chrissie. 'Not the same thing.'

'Running? You'll walk it. Look what you've got going for you. None of the others will have an autogiro, much less an aeolipile...'

An autogiro she couldn't fly and an aeolipile she couldn't pronounce.

'You know who "the others" will be, Loulee. Flat Cat, Brighton Belle, Soubrette, Poltergirl. Names and faces...'

'... from way back. Presently wrapping fish and chips.'

'I hope Flat Cat doesn't hear you saying that. You and your ghosts could wind up two-dimensional on a graffiti wall.'

Loulee's own Vone went off. Chrissie's Room would assemble at Red-Tel before the official announcement. Loulee wasn't just her make-up elf. She'd co-designed the Lady Shade uniform. She even owned the wig.

'You know what that'll be,' said Chrissie.

Loulee looked. Her eyes semi-goggled.

'Yes, I'm in too.'

'I couldn't run without you.'

'No, not in like that, not in your Room. I'm in *it*, Chrissie. I'm in *Crew Selection: The Splendid Sixth*.'

'You?'

'Well, not me – Loulee Ling. Me – Ghost Lantern Girl.'

Something crackled in the dark and everyone's hair stood on end.

ASHTON DAKIN – KUNG FU GRIP

THE MEET WAS CALLED AT AN OLD-TIME THROAT PUB. Like eight other places on Fleet Street, the Sweeney Todd claimed to be on the site of the famous barber shop. At the Wimpy next door, you couldn't raise a giggle by asking what went in the burgers. They'd heard it before and didn't laugh then. Fair dos.

Dakin didn't warm to folk who reckoned they were comics. Too many failed clowns turned to throatery. Giles Bateman, trade-name The Cartoonist, was a case in point. His murder tableaux were cleverer than funny. Boiling oil poured on carol singers. Exploding cigar as the last wish of a man condemned to the firing squad. No one got the woman deep-fried in the fish shop until Bateman went back and added a caption – Battered Wife. That was how Quackanapes caught him. Overly clever was indistinguishable from outright dim.

Dakin wasn't dim.

Though he'd been in some dim krewes. Top Dog gave his yobs hats with ears and stuck dog names on them. Dakin had been 'Sausage Dog' or 'Sausage', which was why he quit before Urban Fox took the Society for the Promotion of Cruel Sport personally and went to war with Wednesday Night Animal Antics. You never knew when a fiddle would tick off some cloak who'd have a mind to be disruptive. Then was the time to find another fiddle.

He glanced up and down the street. No rozzers. No fly-eyes. No cloaks.

He approached Todd's by the side-door. He held up his metal right hand. More of an identifying feature than his face. An eyestalk above the lintel winked. He was Known.

Downstairs, Todd's was a dump. They used to serve pints of whelks and plates of eels jellied in what looked like sweaty nitroglycerine. Now it was chicken in a basket and comical crisp flavours. Tourists sheltered from the rain, buying pisswater at inflated prices. They didn't know this was one London drinkery where you could guarantee not to have your watch lifted. As a haunt of crooks, it was a crime-free zone.

Thieves didn't tolerate being thieved from. Couldn't see the funny side. Murderers didn't much love being murdered, either – but for the most part complained less. Not a hard-and-fast rule. Some murders didn't take. When murderees came back with blood in their eyes there was generally argy-bargy.

In Todd's, Bouffant Lil was behind the bar. Her hair was five times the size of the rest of her head. Mice lived in it. She gave Dakin a wave. He slipped up the stairs.

No bother with passwords or funny handshakes.

He was expected on the first floor. If they put up blue plaques for all the blags plotted around the big table, there wouldn't be wall-space for the Royal Family pictures management were fond of.

This was a Serious Room. Firms were put together here.

Dakin had his red lines in place. They could stick whatever trade-name they wanted on him but he wasn't wearing a bloody hat. He had no appetite to join another Clown Show.

His metal hand made a fist.

At the head of the table ought to be a boss throat with a cigar and plans to a secret vault of the Midland Bank on Praed Street. Instead, the seat was filled by a cove in a shiny suit and rainbow-reflecting New Wave Spex. If there was a crime in the room, it was the price he'd paid for his haircut.

Dakin had seen chummie before – in the company of Martin Masters, manager of the Splendid Six, at a press conference about the retirement (about bloody time) of that terror in tights,

Urban Fox. He was something in the cloak business. Which was not Dakin's line.

But – hold on – the Splendids were for when Scorpions from Saturn invaded or the hoody-doody brigade opened a manhole to Hell in Pudding Lane. They didn't concern themselves with your average blag, except for Urban Fox and the cruelty to animals bee in her bonnet. If Top Dog put bees in bonnets, Urban Fox would have been frisky about it.

'Come in, sit down,' said a face Dakin knew – Major Wood.

The Major wore a cylindrical red coat with frogging and medals. His moustache was waxed to deadly points. His wood-effect domino had attached eyebrows. His usual mob were the Toy Soldiers. The Yellow Sub-Mariner had marched them up to the top of Primrose Hill and marched them down again until they were hors de combat. Major Wood hadn't been a serious throat in a while.

'Let's have a look at your hand,' said X-Ray Spex.

'Are you telling or asking?'

'Requesting, with respect.'

'Acceptable.'

Dakin pulled back his cuff and his metal hand swelled. The configuration of his fingers and thumb shifted.

'Very nice,' said X-Ray. 'Trade-name "Kung Fu Grip"?'

Dakin wondered if he were going to be asked to snap an iron bar or crush a marble bust. It was his party piece and he was too often invited to that party.

'Put it away, there's a love,' said chummie. 'I'm Don Loki Baird. They call me the Vision Controller.'

'Do they now?'

'It's more job description than trade-name. I'm Red-Tel.'

'You're with Rediffusion-Televersion?'

'I *am* Rediffusion-Televersion.'

The frames of the Spex were telly-shaped. White snow flickered across the lenses. If Baird fell asleep, would the snow dwindle to dots in the middle of the screens then wink out?

This was Baird's meeting. Dakin's metal hand went back to being a regular hand only silver-skinned.

He took an empty chair. He judged that there were two distinct factions at the table.

Along with Baird was a woman Dakin recognised from some telly serial and a bloke who didn't look throat-affiliated. His braces were blue but Dakin pegged him for a red-braces type.

'Eleanor Wynter, you know,' said the Vision Controller, presuming. 'And this is Adrian Jah.'

Jah stuck out a paw to be shook then remembered Dakin's Meccano mitt and withdrew the offer.

'The rest of the krewe will, I suspect, be old friends...'

That was one way of putting it.

The second faction at the table were throats. Dakin was lumped in with them.

The blue-eyed six-foot-six blonde glamourpuss was Cyndi Dolan. She was wearing her Summer Surprise Hail Fellow Yellow outfit – egg-yolk crop top, off-white hot pants, banana go-go boots and lemon lollipop deely boppers. Cyndi had lasted about three minutes with a bow in her hair as 'French Poodle' in the Top Dog krewe then worked for Little Madam. She had a nemesis thing going with Flat Cat for a while. Fed up with gags about her dimness, she buckled down during a layover in Holloway and took an Open University degree in organic chemistry. The tabs ran jokes about her Peophole Purview being half make-up tips and half death threats. She was on the crazy paving cusp – not quite mad enough to be as feared as the Cartoonist or Adam Tussaud but too cracked for a regular firm.

The shrimp with the bandoliers, pouches, camo kit and head-band was Johnnie Seven. Dakin had worked with him before, in an iteration of the Toy Soldiers distinct from Major Wood's regiment. Wood was all swords and muskets but these Toy Soldiers were an up-to-the-moment army... rocket-launchers and commando knives and plastic grenades. At any given time, Johnnie had seven different ways of killing you – though, so far as Dakin knew, he'd only ever inflicted flesh wounds on post office staff and bank clerks. He'd shot at a lot of ceilings – not always a clever thing to do. On their last job together, he'd brought down some strip lights and started a fire which melted his mask to his face. Some sections of plastic were still there, painted over with jungle green stripes. How tropical slap was supposed to blend into Fleet Street in the rush hour was a mystery.

The tubby, green-haired human plushion with staring eyes

and outsize hands was Upside-Down Gonk. It would be a mistake not to take the flabby oinker seriously. He'd done damage and given kiddywinks nightmares. The ted with neon tubes in his chest and a speaker grille for a mouth was Juke Box Jerry, survivor of the Fruit Machines – a South Coast mob Brighton Belle shut down ten years back. The pink-haired old gent in the customized stripy blazer and revolving swirl mask was Mr Swizzle, whose peculiarities made Dakin's metal mitten look normal. He had four arms, though only two at a time were in use. For hands he had nasty-minded homunculi who wore prosthetic extensions which turned them into a clown clutching a cudgel, a ghoul wife with her head split open, a constable with a spiked truncheon, and a saw-toothed snouty crocodile. He was a children's entertainer, until parents complained – then he went to the bad. Mr Swizzle raised his clown hand and waggled the club.

'Hell-ohh Little Boy,' squeaked out of his Punch hand.

The voice put everyone's teeth on edge. You needed someone in every firm to terrify the punters so you could go about the business without any have-a-go-heroes having a go and heroing you up proper.

This was a rum lot, though. Dakin wasn't sure he appreciated the invitation.

Why was Red-Tel putting a krewe together? This had better not be one of those hidden camera programmes. *Britain's Barmiest Baddies*.

'You'll have questions,' said Baird – not unperspicacious, then.

They did. But no one liked to be first to pipe up.

'Here are some answers,' said Baird, opening a satchel. 'Pass the parcels, will you.'

He handed out what looked like family-size bathroom sponges wrapped in brown paper. The civs – Wynter and Jah – got no goodies but there were pressies for everyone else.

'For me?' said Cyndi, in her high-pitched little girl voice. 'You shouldn't have.'

Dakin gave his sponge a squeeze with his flesh-and-bone hand. The package wasn't quite as resistant as a bathroom accessory but there was give in it.

The string was knotted with a bow.

He pinched the end between his metal finger and thumb – no one watching knew how much more difficult that was than ripping a telephone book in half – and undid the bow.

He wasn't the first to get to the prize.

'What a lot of lovely lolly,' said Mr Swizzle's Punch hand.

'That's what I want,' sang Juke Box Jerry – who also burped a guitar chord.

Johnnie riffled the wad of notes as if he could count them by ear.

'A grand apiece for being here,' said Baird. 'Nine more packages as a signing fee. Then you'll be on a salary commensurate with your abilities... for at least six weeks. Red-Tel will cover your National Insurance. Take you right up to your hols with a nest egg to get away to the sun.'

No one got up and left with the thou.

'Excellent. I see bright lights in this room. Names and faces. We're going to have you on the telly. Has anyone watched *Crew Selection*?'

A crocodile-snout hand went up. Shyly, everyone followed suit.

'I voted for that stumpy bit who went mental at Devil's Dyke,' said Dakin. 'You have to take a trip to Jupiter seriously.'

'I'm glad you said that. Because this is serious too.'

'You're not wanting one of *us* to be the Splendid Sixth?'

'No, Kung Fu Grip, I am not. No offence but you're not good casting for that.'

A flame that had never lit died in Dakin's heart. Urban Fox was a throat for a tiny mo before she went cloak. Others had gone that route – Night Mist, Soubrette – or the other way – Coffin Dodger, Gay Icon. Turning cloak wasn't for Ashton Dakin. He'd never cross the street. He was a superior sort of spiv, but a yob's yob and no regrets.

'Then what?' asked Cyndi.

'I'll let Adrian explain,' said Baird.

'As you probably know,' said Jah, trying not to look at Mr Four Arms, 'the next series of *Crew Selection* is prompted by the vacancy in the Splendid Six. The show will be about how it gets filled. The viewers will have their vote, along with Martin Masters and the five standing members. We've an exciting line-up of possibles. They'll go through rigorous testing. What does a cloak want above all other things?'

'Mad skills?' suggested Johnnie.

'A strong visual,' said Cyndi.

'Their head examined,' put in Eleanor Wynter, quietly.

'Most amusing,' said Baird, not amused.

'What cloaks want above all other things,' Jah ploughed on, 'is a chance to show their mettle. I imagine – and when I say imagine, I mean know because our researchers have dug up everything about you – your experience with the cloak community has not been positive. By definition, cutthroats and cloaks are at each other's, ah, throats like nobody's business. You are the anvils on which heroic legends are forged...'

'... you've all been bashed over your heads,' said Wynter.

Dakin felt that. He had scratches from Urban Fox, a persistent cough from Night Mist and wet weather twinges from where the last Blackfist but one punched him in the ribs when he was seventeen on his first look-out job as the Tufty Club stripped lead from a church roof.

'Candidates must be tested and tried,' said Jah. 'Obviously, all but one must in some sense be tested and beaten.'

'That's the way to do it,' said Mr Swizzle's clown hand, waving a cudgel.

The pictures on the walls shook.

'*Crew Selection: The Splendid Sixth* will present the candidates in competition,' said Jah. 'And in collaboration, because you can't be on a team without teamwork. There'll be a B-side, a second card on the bill. That's where you come in. You'll have our support and we'll make suggestions but it'll be on you – as a krewe – to formulate plans and put them into action. It's a condition of your employment that no one gets badly hurt. But we can live with a certain amount of property damage. And you can keep what you steal and get away with. Red-Tel will sort it out. Nothing on camera will be admissible in court. That's part of the deal. You can be nabbed, though. I'm not saying the cloak contestants won't get rough on you. As you'll be required to be rough on them.'

'Define "badly"?' said Johnnie.

'Pardon. Oh yes. As in "badly hurt". That's flexible, I suppose.'

'Somebody's gonna get their head kicked in tonight,' sang JBJ.

'Major Wood has leadership experience,' said Jah. 'Unless there are challenges... good show, dicey moment there, eh? – he'll be top dog, as it were...'

'Though not in the sense of the lamentable Rexwell Pitt,' added Baird.

Wood's moustaches went up and down like railway signals.

'Kung Fu Grip,' he said. 'You're Sergeant.'

Dakin nodded. He expected that. Better him than Nut Case Johnnie.

'Seven,' said Wood. 'NCO.'

Johnnie saluted. A flick knife flew out of his sleeve and poked him in the eye. Lucky it wasn't blade-out. The great steaming nit would have a purple bruise to add to the green and black patchwork of his face.

Were they really the best the telly could find?

Or was the point not to lob properly dangerous, uncontrollable throats at a bunch of rookie cloaks? If so, those famous researchers had turned over a couple of stuck-together pages and missed some information about Cyndi. Not to mention Mr Swizzle and his end of the pier nightmare show in Blackpool that summer. A proper definition of 'badly hurt' ought to consider that physical damage wasn't the only kind.

'What are we?' asked Upside-Down Gonk.

He was another proposition altogether – if they ever pinned him down, he was a cert for Devil's Dyke.

'You mean your branding,' said Baird. 'I'm glad you asked. We focus-grouped and field-tested and decided the best thing to do – what with so many fresh personalities on the programme – was not to offer up another novelty. So we've purchased a vacant franchise. A long-established cutthroat brand. We're excited to bring it back. Look around and shake each others' hands. Meet the New Broken Dolls.'

Dakin stuck out his metal hand and Cyndi tickled its palm.

He looked at the packet in front of him and hoped this wasn't going to be another big mistake.

CHRISTINE HONOURS THE GIRL GUIDES OF GREAT BRITAIN

A GUIDE IS HONEST, RELIABLE AND CAN BE TRUSTED, was the first pledge.

Chrissie was at a Banger Breakfast sponsored by Sid's Sausages in the grounds of Olave House in Hampstead. The feast was in honour of Girl Guide Achievements in picking up litter (like the wrappers from Sid's Sausage Rolls) or adopting one of the Regent's Park marmosets (without being eaten by one of the Regent's Park lions). Lady Shade was a night-cloak but Schilling insisted she show her face after sun-up to quash Whispers backchatter that she was a Highgate Vampire. She worried that her visual wouldn't hold up in daylight.

Did other candidates for the Splendid Sixth go around in outfits thrown together by rummaging in their parents' wardrobes? Chrissie looked like someone who didn't realise the party was fancy dress until half an hour before the cab pick up. An outfit suited to a chilly January night wasn't appropriate – or comfortable – for a simmering May morning. The grubby private eye coat was a dry-cleaner's despair. Mum's figure-skating skirt had a gold water lily on waves motif. Not a symbol to strike fear into the hearts of cowardly cutthroats and superstitious so-and-sos. Unpicking the emblem of Bangladesh might bring down the wrath of Mirza women. Scrapping with

Adam Tussaud again would be preferable to a dust-up with the Gran Clan.

She was stuck with the visual the way she was stuck with 'Lady Shade'. The trade-name still didn't feel right. She cringed when her matey overdraft manager said 'call me Ollie – Mr Edwards-Thistle is my dad' but recognised the principle. Lady Shade was Aunt Jasmine. Chrissie needed to be someone else.

A Guide is helpful and uses her time and abilities wisely.

The girls were lovely and fun – big smiles, no two caps worn the same way, catapults tucked down waistbands of dark blue skirts. The grown-ups were bewildering and a chore, even with Tish from Schilling to give prompts and keep away the worst opportunists.

Chrissie relied more and more on Tish, a small woman with a cyber eye – a steel ball-bearing with a red lens. One of Polly O's appropriated sayings was 'champagne for my real friends, real pain for my sham friends' – as if Polly O were anyone's real friend. Tish was at least honest about being a sham friend. She was in Chrissie's Room because she'd been put there. She took a moment to think what was best for Schilling – the red lens flashed, as her eye synced with a satellite – before doing anything to assist, protect or comfort the client. She was not Loulee.

A Guide is a good friend and sister to all Guides.

Chrissie missed Loulee.

One of them must break down and dial the other.

Chrissie thought it should be Loulee. She was the one being funny.

The *Crew Selection* scenario might be contrived to keep Loulee out of Chrissie's Room. It felt like a plot fomented by one of the many enemies Chrissie had managed to make without half trying or had inherited from her aunt and a whole line of Shades. The Sergeant Shade of the 1950s – a great-great uncle – was a right walloper, remembered unfondly by the grandkids of crims who'd got in his bad books. He was the only Shade to wear out three Poulton-Joneses.

Sun bore down on the lawns of Olave House. None of the Guides fainted during the speeches. They must have had practice. Chrissie could taste sausages through several walls. The sizzle pricked her sensitive tongue. She was, as usual, starving.

The rounds of toast and jam she'd had in her own kitchen before Tish picked her up in Schilling's Hillman Imp were but a distant memory. In raincoat, wig and Spex, she probbo looked hung-over. With no shadow, she was at her weakest. If one of those enemies wanted a scrap now, she'd be done for. She kept reminding herself she'd bested the worst at Devil's Dyke but that was five or six news cycles ago. Who'd she plastered lately? If some Inner Voice type fluencer puppeteered masses of Guides to rush her, Lady Shade would take a public fall. She'd be dropped from *Crew Selection* as a one-scrap wonder.

Which would, she had to remind herself, be bad.

Though there would be upsides. Like being able to dial Loulee.

A Guide faces challenges and learns from her experiences.

She wasn't required to make a speech – just hand over medals and be clicked with recipients. The smallest girls got the biggest prizes. This was so routine Garn hadn't got out of bed to join the snapper pack. He was in Chrissie's Room but Red-Tel had him slaved to Eleanor Wynter for general *Crew Selection* pics. Good luck to him. He'd done well for himself out of Devil's Dyke. Though he now knew Christine Chambers and Lady Shade (billing not final) were the same person, he treated her like two different people, a charity case and a headliner.

She sat at a long trestle table with the Guides as they tucked into bangers and mash. Someone in the flack pack thought it'd be larfs if Lady S had the biggest heap on her plate. Chrissie enthusiastically agreed. Tish reminded her that scoffing children's tuck in front of them would make a poor visual. Anti-Perky natters would crow over any click of her with a pork product near her mouth. Noshing a banger would be tantamount to flinging a flan in her own face.

A Guide is polite and considerate.

Tish slipped her a non-brand energy bar, which she chewed slowly. She was advised not to eat identifiable sweets while negotiations were in process in rooms well beyond (and above) her own. Cadbury and Nestlé were competing for her endorsement. She'd seen club loiterers passing out jabs and pep pills – and taking back rolled-up fivers – with the practiced move Tish had for providing between-meals snacks from her little blue bag. The bars, developed for the Jupiter Mission, were dry and tasteless.

The Guide who'd adopted a marmoset wanted to know if she'd met Flat Cat, her favourite cloak.

Chrissie admitted she hadn't. Flat Cat was more of a mystery woman – not gettable for gigs like this.

The shy Guide who'd picked up most litter went red and stuttered. Chrissie wanted to hug her and tell her it was all right – she wasn't obliged to talk unless she wanted to. But she worried she'd lose her mind thanks to the scent of Bisto and eat the child whole. Garn would be sorry not to get *that* click.

A Guide respects all living things and takes care of the world around her.

She wished she were a better Guide. The principles were simple and inspiring. She fell a long way short. If she couldn't live by Guide pledges, how could she fill the Splendid Sixth slot? She respected most living things, possibly because she could eventually eat them. She didn't judge herself to be a good friend and sister to all. She preferred to duck challenges, thus avoiding experiences she'd have to learn from. She shuddered at how unwisely she used her time and abilities.

The Guides gave her an honorary badge – there wasn't an official one for ending a prison riot – which she pinned to her lapel. It was the first element of her uniform she felt she should live up to rather than hide behind.

The plates were cleared away. Some ungrateful chits had barely touched their grub. Leftovers would now go to over-privileged pigs on a city farm. A band marched out of Olave House and played 'Octopus's Garden'.

Chrissie didn't know about being under the sea but would quite like to be in the shade.

JASMINE TO MIMSY

Dear Mimsy
Sorry to write out of the blue, especially with the way we left things at Richard's funeral. I have to ask a favour. You don't owe me anything but I know you were always one for duty. If only to animals. My niece Christine is in the running for your spot in the SS. I'm not sure it would be good for her to get it. Truthfully, I'm not sure it was good for you. It really doesn't matter, though. She's better equipped than either of us for that side of the night-work.

She needs someone to talk to about the rest of the business. She's extraordinary, of course. You know what she did at Devil's Dyke. Extraordinariness has pluses and minuses. She already knows that but could do with a voice of experience.

Since Richard, I'm a mess. I'm in Yorkshire at the Safe House. Yes, I'm chanting and contemplating and letting go. Sometimes screaming. Walking up mountains. Anything to stop me drifting into the dark and not coming back. I know you understand. Christine doesn't. She'll need to. Before everything becomes overwhelming.

I'm attaching her Vone number and details. She's with Schilling, so you'll need that vulpine stealth to get round Dottie to her. I know you've not retired from foxiness.

Please, Mimsy, please. Richard would approve (yes, I know that's blackmail). Once you get past the sparkle, you'll love Christine. Don't give her fashion tips, though. Or involve her with Hunt Sabs.

Love, as ever, Jasmine.

PS: my best to Karel and all the Beasts of Field and Stream.

CHRISTINE HAS ELEVENSES

CHRISSIE HAD A RESERVATION AT DERRY & TOM'S roof gardens. Elevenses with Vidar and Chell. She'd had to haggle for openings in her schedule to see friends, conceding that snappers could be admitted. This was an official engagement.

With *Crew Selection* gearing up, she needed Coterie support. Not because any pro-her statements they might make would have weight. Polly O had mastered the trick of being positive in such an affectless tone it didn't register. But Anti-Chrissie goss dished by coterites would get disproportionate play. Especially with clicks or clips to illustrate.

Her status shift from 'which one is she?' to 'face of tomorrow' had not gone down well. Some might settle for standing next to her but all – even, in her chilly way, Polly O – would prefer to *be* her. They ached to be enlightened, felt they deserved it more than some legacy parading about in her aunt's cloak. Who wouldn't want to be this year's most clicked and clocked?

The snappers were on the roof early, cadging buns. Chrissie and Tish arrived at ten past eleven. Tish took up an observer's post near the doors. Chrissie sat at the reserved table. Vidar would be hiding behind a phone box surveilling the entrance so he could hustle onto the roof in a powdery fluster minutes later. Persistent tardiness was Polly O's way of impressing on other people that her time was much more important on the cosmic scale than theirs. Vidar aspired to such airy presumption but couldn't break a punctuality habit drummed into him at St Cuthbert's. He'd been caught behind phone boxes several times. What larks.

Chell was adrift from her own appointment diary. She wore a broken Longines le Classique. She'd smashed it with a hammer to make a point – presumo that she could afford to ruin a grand and a half watch. She got sponsorship for the symbolic gesture and an all-expenses paid trip to Switzerland. It was a wonder B&Q didn't give her free hammers for life.

Tish allowed that Chrissie could order chee and a cream slice but was not to be clicked guzzling or scoffing. The public did not want a demonstration of her necessary calorie intake.

Twenty past eleven. No Vidar and Chell. A few snappers took solo clicks and left for a product launch. Chrissie heard the name Viper Strike. Did that do wonders for your kitchen floor or rid your garden of slugs? She suspected it was a male enhancement pill.

Chrissie had bargained hard for elevenses. Now she was stood up. She should have seen it coming.

Wait till she told Loulee. Her friend would have vengeance tips.

Oh, she remembered. Loulee had to dial her first.

'Champagne for my real friends,' she thought, 'real pain for my sham friends.'

Loulee had Hawkshawed it. The line was from *Jorrocks' Thoughts and Jollities* (1838) by R.S. Surtees.

A shadow fell. She looked up and saw a sham friend.

Vidar sat and drained her chee in one go. No one clicked him guzzling.

'Sols, Chrissie,' he said. 'Double booking. Apols from Chell. We tossed for it and she... lost and went to Hereward's Viper Strike launch. I'm there remotely while I'm here sincerely, see.'

Vidar's Vook was hooked to rings in his shoulder pads. He angled the device to share a view from Chell's unsmashed Spex. A caption identified Woolwich Arsenal Proving Ground. A gargantuabot was scrapping with spider-tanks rigged to explode in puffs of flame when zapped or punched.

The bothead had Hereward's face – disproportionately large, carved from blastproof glassteel. Its telly screen eyes showed his real face, wearing Spex which showed the same image, opening a wormhole to an infinity of diminishing Herewards.

She was right. Viper Strike *was* a male enhancement pill.

A yowling guitar sample blared out of a speaker grille in the gargantuabot's belly. Someone strangulated sang 'Vyy – purrr – *strakk*!' A pose went with the riff. Brake fluid leaked from the joints. It looked as if the robot had wet itself.

'He's been working on this for yonks,' Vidar said. 'Well before you, ah, became Mrs Enlightened. Bonfires of research and development coin. Courtesy of the verps. Personals natters say he's the next Dr Robot. Did you miss your invite? Only it's funny you chose this morning for elevenses with the Viper Strike launch happening at the same time. Or was it deliberate? You know you can be a scheming minx like that. Chell is waving, see.'

An animated egg with arms in the corner of the Vook was waving. Chrissie tapped it with her forefinger and Vidar giggled.

'Is Hereward inside the mecha?'

'Lord no, it's a box kite. He's tucked up safe in a bed-pod working things with one-fifth of his mind. Automatic Completion does most of the punching and zapping, though there's a manual override for when things get hairy. Bet you wish you'd had Viper Strike to take the lead when Bouncing Betty led you on that merry dance.'

Chrissie would have taken that bet.

Viper Strike towered over burning tanks. Hereward's carnival-scale bighead cracked a smile. The eyes lit up and confetti rained. That already-old 'Vyy – purrr – *strakk*!' riff sounded. The gargantuabot had textured metal abs. The crotch pouch was probbo more declarative than functional – though she wouldn't put it past Hereward to pack a rocket in there.

'Enough of that,' said Vidar, dispelling the Woolwich link. 'How are *you*?'

Chrissie took a moment to think. She really wanted to talk about Loulee but needed to phrase it carefully.

'I'm in a ghastly tizz about Monica Maude,' Vidar rattled on. 'It's the absolute finissimo now...'

Eleanor Leaves the Wynter Palace

The rack where Jill di Ferrante's costumes for the week hung in order of appearance was bare except for one (non-Stán) hospital gown. Soon there'd be a row of sharp-shouldered Mr Alan of Mayfair suits, signature visual of the not-so-late DI Trinidad di Ferrante. For now, Eleanor had to give up the Wynter Palace. Ivan Cornish, returning bright light of *Letsby Avenue,* was moving in.

For *Crew Selection,* Don Loki Baird wanted her based in his Control Room, close to the beating heart of the action. He needed key personnel within shouting distance. Garnet Graill was excited by the opportunity. However, he wasn't giving up a status vehicle – hard-won in a contract negotiation – to secure his spot. He wasn't on hiatus from a serial which bestowed national telly treasure status either.

But this was a good move for her, potentially.

At some point, Eleanor Wynter had to become a bigger name – Nelly Off the Telly – than WDS Jill di Ferrante. Continuing successes were traps. Only a lorry-sized dressing room separated Eleanor Wynter from Canteen Cathy, who'd given up on her original name (and personality?) to be billed as 'Canteen Cathy' in the credits. Better wear a pinny and hairnet from wardrobe and dish out spray-painted prop chips under studio lights than wash plates in a real Chauncey Chee until her hands fell off.

The tabs had got wind of the return of Trinidad di Ferrante. *Letsby* news ran below the fold all week. There was a lot of story to get through.

DI di hadn't died in that implosion with Toy Boy Terry after all. The DNA scraps came from the first of the duplicates strewn throughout the not-going-away doppeldeader story. Competing writers were roughing out rival solutions to be tested over the next few months.

At the end of last Wednesday's episode, Jill di Ferrante was felled by a needle-thin laserblast from the revolving restaurant at the top of the Post Office Tower. On Friday, she was in critical condition in Quarmby Road Hospital (from the afternoon bedpan serial *VIP Ward*). This was more about reusing a standing set than attracting a crossover ear-trumpet and stairlift audience. The original script had Jill laserblasted in the head. Eleanor insisted on shifting the injury to her shoulder. Characters on serials which did coma storylines had been recast with someone cheaper when the bandages came off. Eleanor spent a studio day lying in bed with no lines. Theoretically, Red-Tel could oblige her to lie next to a breathing machine in *VIP Ward* for the rest of anyone's life.

At the end of Friday's episode – as if Jill being shot was a minor build-up to the real 'tune in next week' cliffhanger – DI di Ferrante appeared, wearing one of Cornish's famous disguises. Unmasking at his wife's bedside, he vowed to bring the sniping scrote to justice. The identity of the laserblaster wasn't settled. Another mystery to be spun out. In the script, credits rolled over Jill's face with beeping life support in place of theme music. As broadcast, the episode cut from Quarmby Road to Dark Green Nick. Canteen Cathy served Trinidad di Ferrante a mug of spiced chee with a 'good to have you back' and a full-orchestral triumphant version of the theme – usually only heard on Christmas Specials – over a freeze frame of Cornish's gap-toothed grin. The continuity announcer sounded as if she'd peed her knickers as she promised more 'DI di' next week and in weeks to come.

Eleanor wouldn't look at Whispers or the Personals. Natters might lament the (temporary?) loss of WDS Jill but backchatter would be cockahoop a bloke was back on the beat. Whenever a woman was in charge of anything in a serial, battalions of moan-and-groan merchants complained till the cows came home.

What would the Wynter Palace be renamed? The I-Van?

Most of the gear stored here – even signed photos of bright lights of days gone by – was Red-Tel property. The van had been stripped while she was under starched sheets for eight hours as Cornish came up with twenty or so ways of taking off a false nose. Mr Hands dutifully pretended to film them all, even after getting a usable take on the third go.

Eleanor collected the few items which actually belonged to her. A half-read Green Penguin – *The Cadaver in the Credenza* by Carleton Knowles – lay on the bare make-up table. She'd been using WDS Jill's warrant card as a bookmark. Thorough elves had taken away the prop. She'd lost her place.

And needed to find a new one.

Crew Selection: The Splendid Sixth meant a bump in salary. More importantly, she didn't have to pretend to be anyone but herself. With so many junior cloaks competing, not to mention the odd lot of supporting artists she'd met in Fleet Street, she was positioned to become face of the series. It didn't matter who won the contest – Baird admitted it could be fixed, if necessary. Eleanor Wynter would be the big winner of the programme. If Quarmby Road Hospital were real and Eleanor broke her ankle dodging a flan-flinger, she'd rate a bed in the VIP Ward.

Trails for *The Splendid Sixth* had gone out with question marks for the competing cloaks. The line-up wasn't set yet and speculation was encouraged. Eleanor was front and centre in the new range of jackets created for her. Red-Tel upped the couture fee so Stán laid off the sewed-together-used-teabags waistcoats and fish-and-chip-paper skirts and sent over wearable clothes. The jackets came in a variety of vibrant colours, reflective piping ran around the seams like lightning. The line was called LaserBlazers. In the trails, Eleanor was only seen from the waist up. Stán hadn't yet designed trousers or skirts to go with the jackets. She bet he was holding out for another pay hike.

She snapped a cardboard Stán tag from her jacket pocket and stuck it in *The Cadaver in the Credenza* about two-thirds of the way through.

If it wasn't her original place, she'd make do with her new place.

A better place. Brighter, luckier, shinier, sparklier.

If she squeezed a button, the lightning piping crackled. She'd already been told off for playing with the doodad. Save it for when the red camera light is on.

Garn had taken clicks of her in a dark room, lit only by her lapels. She was recognisable as an outline.

One of those clicks was on a poster on the sides of buses and at selected Tube stations.

'She will put them to the test... You will decide who wears the cloak.'

'This makes me look like a cutthroat,' she told Baird.

He said that wasn't a bad thing. She would be someone's arch-nemesis.

Dot Schilling said the Vision Controller personally requested Eleanor for *The Splendid Sixth*. She was included in production decisions – even in matters which struck her as dodgy, like recruiting the New Broken Dolls. *Crew Selection* had more writers than a soap but Baird shaped content. He got poetic about the way a story could be told (and sold) in public. This, he said, was the telly of tomorrow. One big crossover soap. 'Whisper it,' he said, 'but the News is a spin-off from us. Everything feeds in, crime, business, politics, glamour, goss. It's puppet theatre and the real winner is the fellah who holds the strings.'

Since meeting that end-of-the-pier cutthroat with four arms, Eleanor was leery of puppets, dolls and clowns. A tingle of terror was a key ingredient, she was told. So long as it kept away from her, she thought. Her lapels lit up and crackled though she could swear she hadn't touched the button.

She was alone in the empty trailer. Normally, helper elves were about – fussing over costume or make-up. The dresses and the pancake were gone. Ivan Cornish's big box of false noses and stick-on whiskers would arrive soon.

Red-Tel had never fixed the blind spot behind the door to the chill-out cave. Eleanor wouldn't be sorry to leave that shadow behind. Where she was going, she'd have measures in place to ward away lurkers.

Broken Dolls.

Flan-flingers.

Laserblasters.

Naysayers.

Christines.

Assurances were given. She would have protection.

Fear bubbled. She was on her own in the Wynter Palace. No alf or bert or make-up minion or whining director. They'd all moved on. But she didn't feel alone. Or comfortable. She'd shut the door to the chill-out cave, she was certain. It hung open now, with shadow beyond.

Could she really leave behind the lurker in the blind spot?

CHRISTINE AND MIMSY IN HYDE PARK

THIRTY YEARS BEFORE CHRISSIE WAS BORN, THE first major cutthroat-and-cloak scrap of the *Never Mind* Age happened in Hyde Park.

The LP was on every turntable. Change was all around. Folk got carried away. Mistakes were made. Hazel Garland, a crank who took the trade-name Green Fingers, was inspired by the enchantment which transformed a hundred-mile-wide ribbon of the Midlands into wild woodland. Wearing a glitter-splashed pointy hat, Green Fingers sat on the rim of the Serpentine and taught the grass in the park to take root in anything – earth, stone, wood, steel, flesh, water – and swarm over the city. The enlightened adept Magic Ian, Wizard of Elgin Crescent, drew on the collective fantasies of generations of children and brought the Hyde Park statues of Peter Pan and Rima to life. The Boy who Never Grew Up and the Bird Girl from Green Mansions overpowered Hazel Garland before her tidal wave of lethal lawn overspilled the park.

Green Fingers could tap into primal forces but was otherwise an ordinary woman. Aunt Jas had warned Chrissie that enlightened folk tended to forget that being able to fly, practise thought transference or set a land-speed record without a car didn't mean they couldn't be run over at a zebra crossing, sent home from school with measles, or knocked cold by living statues. Magic Ian solved the problem in the showiest way imaginable. It was his debut, after all. He could as easily have tiptoed up behind the wood witch and beaned her with the lead pipe from Cluedo.

Decades on, the original mad growth remained. A quilt of grasses and herbs next to the round pond had an electric verdance unlike anything in nature. It glowed at night. The green demesne resisted weed killer and flamethrowers.

Chrissie had arranged to meet Mimsy Mountmain on the bench by the Magic Ian monument. The wizard sat in a lotus position on an oval dais, third eye open, hand raised. Stone, but not a statue.

In 1988, Magic Ian passed his ankh amulet and tesseract topper to his disciple, Magic Iona, and transformed into his own monument. He didn't get planning permission. Years of legal back-and-forth hadn't settled whether his presence constituted trespassing, vandalism or illegal disposal of human remains. Popular opinion was happy to have Magic Ian where he was, within hailing distance of Peter and Rima. So here he stayed. Next to a bench.

The wizard had promised to stir from his plinth if London needed him again. Since 1988, the city had coped with half a dozen large-scale menaces – the Octopiranha came to mind – but Magic Ian stayed put. Iona's hat-heir Magic Trixie pitched in at the Battle of Battersea so the legacy was secure.

Chrissie had a self-doubt twinge. The Magics managed a game of generational pass-it-on with no missteps. She worried she'd shame the Chambers line by besmirching the Shade mantle. Before this, she'd never have thought a sentence using any variable of the verb 'besmirch'. She recognised changes in her mindset and hoped she didn't sound too much of a prawn when they leaked through to her everyday speech.

Tish from Schilling was nervous about this rendezvous.

Aunt Jas sent a postcard from her retreat to encourage the meeting. Squinted at from a Schilling point of view, clicks of the rising face with the retiring name could be a coup. It might put into viewers' minds that the new Lady Shade was the natural successor to Urban Fox. The outcome her management wanted.

But Chrissie hadn't looped in Schilling and just sprung it on Tish – after casual walkabout clicks in Regent Street – that she was meeting Mimsy. She asked Tish not to report until later but that red eye was flashing.

Reading people was part of Chrissie's package of abilities. Tish desperately wanted further instructions. Her cyber eye clicked and glowed. Chrissie bought Strawberry Mivvis from a stall and gave the woman one. She sat on the bench but Tish didn't.

Tish wore Susan Small dresses and carried a shoulder bag with a capacity to rival the Magics hat. She scoped the perimeter, like a Red Rope Wristband scouting a public space for assassination sightlines before a royal visit. Two years younger than Chrissie, Tish was an unsalaried intern. Sir Jolyon Lough-Luff paid Schilling so his daughter Laeticia could get a start in the entertainment industry. Chrissie was never sure whether Tish was supposed to be her impatient governess, stalwart batman, little sister or the agency's snitch. Whatever Schilling needed, Tish would be. Fair enough. Chrissie couldn't decide whether she was grateful or annoyed. Should she feel sorry for leading the verp twerp in and out the easel? Or could she take wicked delight in giving her living ankle monitor hourly panic attacks?

She fed Tish lollies – which she was addicted to – on an equally regular basis. Strawberry Mivvis were a shared favourite. On duty, the helper elf was not to think of herself but only (officially) of the Client, which of course meant only (actually) of the Schilling Agency. Tish needed lollies or she'd keel over. Was Sir Jolyon getting his money's worth? In ten years' time, Tish might be running the Agency or babbling on a Kaleidoscope Explosion corridor in a secure hospital.

When Mimsy Mountmain stepped out of the bushes, Tish jumped.

Despite her eye-sensor, she hadn't twigged that the former cloak was near. That was to be expected. Urban Fox was known for creeping up and pouncing.

'Now you see why I wore a mask with a sharpened snout-guard,' said Mimsy.

Mimsy had a long nose. Her heroic hooter gave her a distinctive profile. Chrissie could believe Urban Fox had a canine sense of smell.

Like everyone famous, Mimsy Mountmain was shorter than expected.

A dark, compact woman. Red-tinged grey-black hair done up in bunches. Out of uniform, she wore plimsolls, dungarees with an explosion of cause-supporting ribbons sewn to one shoulder, fingerless knitted gloves and a flat tweed cap.

Because of the warmth of the day, Chrissie had given Tish the trenchcoat to stuff in her bag. She now felt a plonkette for parading in a 1990s skating costume and 1920s film-star wig. In contrast, Mimsy blended into any background.

'Miss Mountmain,' said Chrissie.

'Mimsy is fine, Christine.'

'Chrissie?'

'Makes sense.'

'This is Tish,' said Chrissie.

'Not Tishy,' said Mimsy.

'Uck, no,' said Tish.

Mimsy looked at the helper elf intensely. Her neon blue eyes contrasted with her tan face. Then, she turned to Chrissie as if they were alone. Tish's steel eye glinted.

'Your aunt asked me to see you,' said Mimsy.

'Yes. I'm not sure why...'

'I can tell you. She's ninety per cent a wreck after the love of her life was killed. The ten per cent left over is concern for you.'

Chrissie gathered that, though he was on the White Corridor, Richard Jeperson was not a cutthroat. He was more or less a cloak, operating at a deep level of secrecy. It was news to Chrissie that her aunt was in love with him. She'd never heard his name before Devil's Dyke. He wasn't one of the three men she knew Jasmine had been involved with.

'She can't tell you things you need to be told and has picked me as supply teacher. I warn you – Jasmine and I don't see eye to eye on much. What I say may well be not what she'd say. Do you follow?'

'I do.'

'Sharp girl. You'll go far. If you watch yourself.'

She was uncomfortable around Mimsy Mountmain. Her fixed gaze suggested she knew all the ways Chrissie fell short of the Girl Guide Pledges. Urban Fox had years of cloak experience.

She'd walked away from the Splendid Six. Come through a hundred and one scraps.

She wasn't an exemplar. If she lived by rules, it was because she'd independently worked them out. By sticking to private principles, she probbo made other cloaks feel foolish or inauthentic. She had that effect on Chrissie. By extension, she must terrify Tish.

'Do you know you're doing that?' Mimsy asked.

Chrissie was winding ribbons of dark around her fingers, wrists and forearms. Her fingertips, knuckles, the meat of her hands and sections of her arms looked disconnected from each other and her body. The darkstuff wasn't a substance but an absence. Through rifts, she saw points of violet and turquoise. Mimsy picked up a lolly stick and probed a ribbon across Chrissie's palm. It slipped in and Chrissie didn't feel anything. Mimsy flicked the stick into the void and it disappeared. That was one way to get rid of litter. Chrissie felt the stick ought to be inside her but it wasn't – it had gone somewhere else.

'It didn't have to be a stick,' Mimsy said. 'It would work with bullets. Think about that.'

Chrissie snapped her fingers and the dark went away. She didn't find a mucky lolly stick stuck through her arm. She wrung out her hands. The weird thing was that they *didn't* feel funny. She could crack the universe and not notice. That might well be what Aunt Jas thought she needed to be talked to about.

Following Mimsy's formulation, she was 90% grateful that older, wiser souls took an interest and offered guidance, advice and helpful information – and 10% fed up that grown-ups treated her like an infant and, no matter how it was dressed up, wanted to tell her what to do.

It wasn't just Aunt Jasmine and Urban Fox. Dot Schilling, the Shadow Cabinet, the Coterie, Garn, Red-Tel, Poulton-Jones. Even Loulee. All more sophisticated versions of Nosy Nige and his Keep Ewelme Road Tidy notices. Those things you can do, that you might be *really good at*... don't do them without adult supervision. Don't pull the communication cord – penalty £25.00. Don't turn out the lights.

Dark ribbons reformed and she made them go away.

'Sorry,' said Chrissie.

'I can't help you with that oojamaflip,' said Mimsy. 'My party pieces aren't like yours. You'll have to wait till Jas gets her head screwed on properly for hot tips on how not to bring down a curtain of eternal night. I just have to worry about going rabid and ripping through hen houses.'

A curtain of eternal night sounded extreme. And alarmist.

Everyone in this line of work exaggerated.

'Tomorrow Never Knows' drifted across from the bandstand. Every Thursday afternoon an orchestra got together to cover the eight records Magic Ian picked for *Desert Island Discs*. Guest celebrities read from his chosen book – Edward Lear's *The Quangle-Wangle's Hat* – along with the Bible and Shakespeare. All comers were invited to take a turn on the wizard's luxury item, a trampoline. Saving the city from witchweed fifty years ago earned him a weekly memorial.

No one could calculate what Chrissie saved the country from by preventing the escape of the White Corridor inmates. That earned her a wine and cheese do at Scotland Yard where she was clicked next to old men in suits. The reception was only because of Bouncing Betty, the least of anyone's worries. That win – clicked, clipped and broadcast – outweighed a dozen off-the-record victories over A-list cutthroats.

A drawback to being a Shade. You did your best work in lowest light.

Mimsy sat on the bench and took out a tobacco tin. She made a thin roll-up ciggie.

'Jas wants me to talk you out of being a Splendid,' Mimsy said.

Tish's ears pricked up at that. Mimsy lit up.

'She thinks it's silly, trivial, a waste of talent,' said Mimsy. 'A distraction from duty. She's not wrong but...'

'I'm not going to be the Sixth,' Chrissie said, as she always did (not meaning it but not jinxing her chances with presumption). 'I've nowhere near the qualifications you had. Look who I'm up against... Flat Cat...'

'She won't do it.'

'Weather Girl...'

'A nitwit.'

'Brighton Belle.'

'Come on, listen to yourself. This isn't a competition.'

'In that case, Rediffusion-Televersion are spending a lot of money for nothing.'

'It's a *pretend* competition, Chrissie. A distraction. You've been noticed. The right people are excited. The wrong people are afraid. It's not about qualification or experience. It's about enlightened abilities. And what you do with them. If you could change the weather by thinking about it, would you rain on your ex's wedding or write perfume slogans in clouds? Or would you irrigate deserts, restore forests, calm volcanoes and hold back tsunamis – all the while considering the geopolitical, economic and cultural effects of your actions?'

'I'd like to think it'd be the second one... but, look at me, I'm a model...'

'... actor... whatever.'

'Yes. If I can help, fine. But I'm not going to get into anything with – as you have obviously worked out – catastrophic consequences if I mess up. Think about it. If Weather Girl bungles a prank on her ex, it's minor goss in the *Scurrilous Rag*. That Cloak Bloke will make fun of her on his Peophole Purview. If she floods the Sahara, drowns nomads and starts a Middle East war, it won't be on the *Fun News*. She wouldn't be considered a cloak. She'd be in Devil's Dyke. I've been there...'

'So have I. Polka Dot Corridor. I escaped. It was hushed up.'

'Then you know. Being irresponsible in a small way is less damaging than being responsible on a global scale. Especially if it's me doing the doing. I've failed my driving test twice. Imagine me as the Splendid Sixth fumbling a catch and letting GEIST take over the country.'

'GEIST aren't what the Splendids are for. They're what your aunt and her fancy man dealt with. The Splendid Six are something else.'

'You were one of them.'

Having met Mimsy, that now seemed weird and unlikely. Chrissie remembered she was a controversial pick in the beginning. Too street for the Splendids. Didn't smile enough for the snappers and when she did the clicks got scotched as too disturbing. She seemed to have invisible feathers in her teeth.

'Yes... and you should be too.'

So this was where Aunt Jas and Mimsy disagreed.

'Being the Sixth will keep you safe,' said Mimsy.

'It seems like wearing a target to me. Right now, I worry about flan-flingers. As a Splendid, I'd have to be on guard against who knows what. Another giant demon squid? I surprised people – including myself – at Devil's Dyke. That won't happen again. As soon as the first clip – the silly scrap with crocks under a bridge – was out there, Whispers natters started about the best way to kill me. After Devil's Dyke, it wasn't just crackpot voids who spend too much time on their Vones. It was Cutthroat Rooms... GEIST think-tanks... strategists, scientists and professional soldiers. Getting pointy little heads together to pitch Clout Chrissie stratagems. I'd rather be a silly diversion and lose *Crew Selection* to someone like Flat Cat. Or you. They were lucky to have you.'

Mimsy stubbed out the scrap of her roll-up on the arm of the bench.

'If Dr Robot or the Green Knight can't cope with a threat by themselves, there really isn't much use for a woman with sharp ears and a long nose. Think about it. When a mystic lance blessed by the Lady of the Lake isn't enough to put a cutthroat down, why would you send in someone to scratch their eyes out?'

She held up her hands. She had long, sharp nails and a tracery of healed scars.

'You can mind-control animals, though,' said Chrissie. 'Summon a flock of gulls to peck an army.'

'Mammals. Not animals. Common mistake. Birds are off the menu.'

Urban Fox licked her lips. Birds. Menu. Mmm.

'Bats, then. Dogs, cats...'

'Those aren't the mammals I do best with. Here's what you didn't read about me in the tabs...'

Mimsy shut her eyes briefly.

Tish jumped, as if on the luxury trampoline. She bounced up in the air, accompanied by *raga* from the bandstand. Blissful, relaxed, cute-funny. Little Laeticia, happy again. She even let go of her shoulder bag. Chrissie had wondered whether she turned back into her goblin form if physically parted from the thing.

Mimsy blinked. Tish stopped jumping. She picked up her bag but showed no sign of remembering ten seconds ago.

Chrissie thought back to what she'd read and seen about Urban Fox.

Stories about loyal dogs summoned to the rescue... Cats dancing at community parties... Foxes suddenly ingenious enough to evade automatic hounds. Nothing about *people* being made to do anything.

'Mind control,' said Mimsy. 'The fluence, as wielded by fluencers. One of the major abilities. Like flying, healing, extra strength and looking twenty years younger than fifty-faffing-three. But it's not a cloak ability, is it? How would you feel about having your mind controlled? You're enlightened, so it'd be more of a fuss than giving Tishy a break from fretting... but I could make an operant of you. A person puppet. It's why Masters put me in the band. We kept it quiet. One or two hacks tumbled but knew what made a good story might not be good for them – or anyone – in the long run. Sharp claws, remember.'

Chrissie looked at the woman, who was rolling another thin ciggy.

'Now you're thinking of stratagems too. Manage Mimsy.'

Chrissie didn't deny it – and hoped she had some as yet untested ability to ward off mind control. She wasn't an aces bluffer and knew Urban Fox saw through her. Mind-controlling must be closely related to mind-reading.

'Here's the thing about the fluence,' said Mimsy. 'Using it on people is *wrong*. Even with the best intentions, it's a rotten road to take. What I did to Tishy is a violation. I will lose sleep over it. I'm not joking.'

Mimsy smiled sweetly and hunched her shoulders, looking mischievous and a teeny bit crackers. She lit up. Smoke plumed from her nostrils. Chrissie was unreassured.

'What I can do is nothing next to you, Miss Darkness Everlasting. Masters wanted me as a surprise injury time match-winner. He wants you because you can end a scrap before it starts. You can put out the lights and close the show. Your aunt is *terrified* by the Legacy and wears mental corsets so as not to go the way of the shadier Shades. It's why there's a Shadow Cabinet. To keep you from spoiling the party. Jasmine thinks you're as enlightened in your first months as she is after decades of meditation, psychic self-defence courses and holiday breaks on the Yorkshire Dales. You're going to be face of the year. If those Rooms working on the You Problem don't get their hits in first.'

'So I should become the Splendid Sixth to hide in the open.'

'No, you should sign up with Martin Masters and put on a big glammy smile with your chest out and hands on hips *as a disguise*. I got away with a secret identity. You don't have that option. Lady Shade will be your alter ego. Out there where all eyes are on you. The you they're worried about will be the real you. Damsel of Darkness. Princess of the Purple Twilight. Whatever. The Girl Who Can Change the World. You get that? If the civs understood, they wouldn't call you a cloak. You wouldn't even be something as trivial as a cutthroat. You'd be a monster. In Japan, a *daikaiju*. A city-smasher. If they had even a hint of what you can really do, a cry would go up... all cloaks on deck, to shoot you down.'

Chrissie realised Mimsy was still at least partly mind-controlling Tish. If the elf could hear this conversation, she'd be on her Vone to Schilling in panic.

Mimsy gestured with her ciggy.

'Know why I spent years in tights and a mask, up on a podium with Blackfists and comedy acts and parfait gentle champions? Because if I wasn't the Splendid Sixth, I'd be a scruffy werewolf from Hackney who could make you jump off a bridge with her mind. Silver bullets are surprisingly easy to come by. You be Lady Shade, above the fold, pin-up, bright light... face, name, cloak. Or else you're a living conduit to All Consuming Darkness and Everlasting Night. Which won't win you any popularity contests.'

DAKIN AT THE BROKEN DOLL SHOP

MAJOR WOOD TOOK DAKIN ALONG AS HEFT. MORE FOR show than need, though you never knew with Regency Gates – trade-name the Estate Agent. Some reckoned Gates the worst throat in the city, though his business was mostly legal.

The Estate Agent didn't personally show them round the Human Figure Works. He sent over a trouser suit samurai who introduced herself as Property Close. She wasn't put off her stroke by the Red-Tel fly-eyes. Gates had rubber-stamped a release form. Being on telly, even peripherally, was free advertising.

The New Broken Dolls were in the market for a rookery.

Red-Tel couldn't blatantly give seed capital to a criminal enterprise. Johnnie Seven suggested a post office raid to bring in readies. Whenever there was a lull in conversation, Johnnie suggested raiding a post office. When nobody turned up for his tenth birthday party, his old man told him the invitations he hadn't sent had got lost in the post. Even then, Johnnie must have known it was a porkie – but he still took it out on the Royal Mail. He always cleared out the stamps as well as the cash tills.

The Major ruled out a raid to fund the rookery. The krewe would be in it if they got nabbed by a passing cloak before their debut as Nemesis Central on *Crew Selection*.

Suitcases full of not-too-grubby notes were found and viewings set up.

The Human Figure Works was in Cowcross Street, Farringdon. Until recently, it was let to a manufacturer of dressmakers' dummies and shop-window mannequins. Battered figures – some headless – in cobwebby tableaux gave the space that abandoned, slightly creepy air popularly associated with rookeries. Big throats had glass and steel offices these days. They'd have the heft chuck tat like face-cracked dummies in the nearest skip. The Estate Agent knew the New Broken Dolls wanted the classic visual. Telly viewers would expect it.

On the top floor, offices were converted into one- or two-bed gaffs. If this was a live-in job, there was space for each Broken Doll to have their own lair. The factory floor was roomy enough for meetings and special projects.

Farringdon was full of post-industrial sites like this. Most went for luxury drums or pricey caffs. But the Estate Agent had cornered the rookery market. Close pointed out desirable features for a cutthroat lair. Secret exits. Reinforced shutters. Closed-circuit telly screens covering all areas of the building and the surrounding pavements.

They walked back to the street and stood outside the building. Dakin looked up at the sky. The Red-Tel fly-eyes were still there.

Major Wood gave Dakin the nod and he handed over the suitcases.

Sometimes, his metal hand wouldn't obey orders and relax the Kung Fu Grip. He concentrated and let go of both cases with equal ease. Close picked them up, nodding as if counting notes by weight. The down payment went in the boot of her Jowett Javelin. She had a priority parking sticker on her rear window.

It was a pleasant mid-morning.

Cyndi and Johnnie were across the road in a Chauncey Chee. Cyndi was in her Runaway Heiress Avoiding the Tabs outfit – Rorschach blot head-scarf, peppermint lollipop shades, velvet macintosh, laddered stockings and fast getaway plimsolls. Upside-Down Gonk and Mr Swizzle were in a bread van parked round the corner. Juke Box Jerry was window shopping outside a Susan Small Bengali Boutique. What he thought a sari would do for him was beyond Dakin.

Major Wood touched his moustache in an all-clear signal but didn't complete the gesture. He twigged first – a wake-up call for Dakin, who was supposed to be look-out as well as heft.

Something plunged out of the sky.

Johnnie tried to draw three guns with two hands. Cyndi threw her mac over him to prevent disaster. Property Close double-locked the reinforced boot of the Javelin.

JBJ gave a blast of 'Look Out – There's a Monster Coming!'

A great clanking robot landed in the road, cracking tarmac. More lights than were strictly necessary went on in its chest. A blaring fanfare drowned Jerry's thwanggg of 'Help!'

'Vyy – purrr – *strakk*!'

Was there someone inside? Or was it an unmanned box kite?

Dakin made a big metal fist. He doubted giving the thing a thump would do much good – but had to give it a go.

Though, come to think of it, renting a building wasn't illegal. The New Broken Dolls might be a criminal krewe but so far they'd been remarkably non-offensive.

That didn't wash with Metal Mandy. Viper Strike – if that was a trade-name not a catch-phrase – bristled with deadly features and endorsement logos. It was like a Christmas tree where all the relations added their own decorations until the trunk broke and it fell over in the lounge.

The robot raised its arm and made a fist. Four individual missile-heads poked out of knuckle-holes. Rockets whizzed across the street and exploded against the shutters of the Human Figure Works. Crowds panicked. Johnnie got out from under Cyndi's mac and popped shots which spanged off the robot's carapace. A face showed on a lenticular screen. It shifted to new expressions – a few seconds out-of-sync.

The robot levelled its other arm-gun at the tables outside Chauncey Chee.

Johnnie was in the firing line. Cyndi was under the table. Other chee-drinkers – a knot of crocks with spongy helmets and a Farmer Giles with a smock and a straw hat – were fear-frozen. If Frankenclanker set off another barrage, the krewe would be down a couple of founder members – but Farringdon would lose a caff and there'd be collateral casualties. Pound Shop Dr Robot was that bloody stupid. Even right nutter cloaks like Jack Pariah knew better than to light the blue touch paper with civs in the blast radius. Was this a runaway mad science toy? If so, Kung Fu Grip was about to make a debut as an honest-to-Blackfist cloak.

Major Wood gave him a different nod. Violence was approved.

Dakin led with his fist and charged across the street – but didn't connect.

Some sort of shock rattled his fillings. He fell down, jittering. But he'd distracted Iron Idiot from spitting missiles at Johnnie.

'You are warned,' crackled a voice from the robot. 'Beware the wrath of...'

That horrible guitar riff broke out again.

'Vyy – purrr – *strakk*!'

It aimed but the missiles were duds or the safety was locked. It tried again but no joy. A mercy for Farringdon.

'Vyy – purrr – *strakk*!'

Fire and smoke burst out of the robot's ankles and it lifted off, ascending through a swarm of fly-eyes. A barney like this attracted interest. The bit of road where it had stood was melted. A water main gushed. Good thing it wasn't gas.

'What was that all about?' asked Property Close.

Dakin looked to Major Wood. He was flattened on the pavement, chest on fire.

Maybe calling themselves Broken Dolls was asking for aggravation.

CHRISTINE AND HER ROOM

TWO DAYS AFTER HER BRUSH WITH URBAN FOX IN HYDE Park, Chrissie was in Cardinal Wolsey Street submitting to make-up and wardrobe tests. She was still turning over what Mimsy Mountmain had said.

She had to be a cloak. Otherwise she'd be a monster.

Cloaks were feted at galas and gave prizes to Girl Guides. Monsters were hunted by mobs with pitchforks.

Monsters had it worse than cutthroats.

She did not *feel* like a monster. But she didn't feel like the old Chrissie – whoever she'd been – either.

She wished she could talk with Loulee but that was off the table.

She also wished Loulee were here. Without her friend's light touch, Chrissie was at the mercy of torturers. Her face, hair, nails and visible non-face skin were worked over. In this chair, she was less a person than a racing car. Her wheels, engine and oil were changed in a rush while Tish tutted over a stopwatch.

It wasn't even a chair but an upright armature with crossbars. Fondly known as the Rack. Chrissie was stretched on it.

Loulee might be on another Rack in this same studio complex. As a contestant, she rated her own Room. Another reason to regret the chill. They could be enjoying a good old moan together.

Each procedure was more ridiculous than the last. Was this deliberate? The secret point of the programme might be to see how much aspirant cloaks would put up with before they walked out with what little dignity they had left. The joke might be on whoever lasted longest and was subjected to most humiliation. Jonty McDribblefart would tear through a paper wall and present the loser-winner with a wooden spoon and an economy-size can of empty larfs.

Studio 9 was draped with green fabric so the Colour Separation Overlay process could put newsreaders in crisis zones. Red-Tel and the unions were debating whether pre-production on *Crew Selection* counted as before the cameras or behind the scenes. Since fly-eye candid footage was a feature of the programme, Red-Tel hired actors to play staff. Accredited make-up artists suggested what to do to Chrissie but the chief torturer was Nina Ninian, an actress. She'd huddled with Adrian Jah to work out her fictional character. They decided Make-Up Mavis had a secret well of anger. Guess who she'd take it out on?

When Nina's pupils contracted Chrissie recognised her. Make-Up Mavis was the former 'Sparkling Eyes', discontinued to appease Nelly and make room for Perky Purkiss. Unveiled, thin-lipped, and wielding needle-nose tweezers on the woman who'd replaced her on *Letsby*. Peach.

The make-up crew went off-shift and Nina stood down. Next came a band of sharp-tongued wardrobe elves who treated Chrissie as a dress-up doll. They'd nixed having a Nina-type onscreen avatar and competed to catch the eyestalks while holding swatches against her face. They might have secret wells of anger too and kept pricking her with pins.

The launch of *Crew Selection: The Splendid Sixth* was imminent. A live event to reveal the contestant line-up would go out on Red-Tel One as the first episode. Nothing was settled, least of all what Chrissie was supposed to *do* on the series. The original brief from the Vision Controller was 'be yourself'. Every time anyone spoke to her, caveats, clarifications, footnotes and contradictions were added.

Being yourself was only possible once you'd decided – or someone had decided for you – who you were.

Christine Chambers. Chrissie.

Lady Shade. Lady Shade II.

Model Actress She Knew the Drill.

She was close to adopting The Whatever as her trade-name.

Today, make-up shades were tested on her – ranging from vampire pallor to golden syrup. After applications with paintbrushes and removals with vinegar, she clocked that Jah was having Camera Clare play with filters and brightness levels to experiment with even more shades of Shade. It was enough to make her consider an all-over-the-face mask like Poltergirl's.

Then came the costume. Schilling had secured a sponsorship deal from Bull Boots so multiples were available. Chrissie automatically sent Loulee a boast blurt about that swag blag. She got a received ping but not response pong. Labels bid to supply the trenchcoat. Fresh-in-a-box samples arrived from Burberry, Susan Small and Präno. None, somehow, sat as well on her as the manky old Dad hand-me-down.

The big row was about the skating dress, which everyone said had to go. Too '90s, not British, too contoured, too 'practical' (which meant not enough cleavage). Someone at Red-Tel who wanted an OBE got excited about tweaking the Shade Legacy to turn Chrissie into a patriotic cloak like Great Britannia or George Cross. It was suggested she wear a vinyl union jack bikini under the trenchcoat. She would take off the coat before scraps and show she meant business by flying the colours. A trade-name could be Union Jackie. Cutthroats would, of course, stand politely while she found a coat-hook and not zap her senseless when her back was turned.

Chrissie imagined Loulee asking whether Schilling really wanted the client to look like a stripper at a NaNa rally. There was already a wretched wealth of Lady Shade porn in the Smut Hutch. The Coterie delighted in forwarding pointas to the vilest examples. She didn't want to encourage any more of that, ta very much.

Several cloaks (and cutthroats) were mentioned who showed skin – Brighton Belle, the Slapper, Lady Godawful. The tabs leaped on any excuse to run 'battling beauty' clicks. According to Hawkshaw, these women all had some form of invulnerability. Chrissie wasn't blessed with bulletproof epidermis, impenetrable force-field or living marble musculature. What was proposed *might* look saucy, glammy or even healthy (if well-lit and posed) in a Sunday swank layout. After even a light scuffle, she'd be a mass of bruises. The row went up to Dot Schilling's desk. Miraculously, Dot saw it Chrissie's way. The board member's dreams of a trip to the Palace were squashed. Seamstresses worked up a lightweight armour-plate version of – yes – a 1990s figure-skating outfit. Dot even agreed to the water lily motif.

Chrissie was always surrounded by her Room. She had more ground crew than the Jupiter Mission.

Master of all was Don Loki Baird, the Vision Controller. Chrissie found his TV static Spex alarming but he always had sweet words (and sweets) for her. Though she'd never heard of Baird before, he turned out to have as much pull as Marius Stok or the Deputy PM. He wasn't on the Red-Tel Board of Directors but told them what to do.

Adrian Jah, less floppy on this project, was directing. Anjulie Glas, no longer Anju the AD but now Anju the AP, ran between participating Rooms. Her new ghost hood tracksuit was tailored to show off her wasp waist. Her plimsolls had a discreet '6' motif. Her tinted Lennon Spex had gold frames. Now she had to stay awake for a hundred and twenty hours on the trot – a full week's shooting. She had a prescription for something stronger than pep pills which had to be treated with gamma radiation to limit side effects.

Tish split her time and loyalties between Schilling's interests (ie: Chrissie) and Red-Tel's (ie: the series). She had feelers out for snitches who might relay gen about the other contestants. Their elves would play the same game, so vetting was underway to root out moles in Chrissie's entourage. GEIST satrapies weren't as devious as *Crew Selection* contestant Rooms.

The Shadow Cabinet approved her participation, somewhat to her surprise.

The show was already shooting. Fly-eyes buzzed about getting B-roll while Camera Clare hefted a shoulder-mounted Big Eye to record hi-def video. Garn was everywhere, clicking like a bark-beetle. He animated pics into pixellated clips, capturing Chrissie in many moods. Fifty shades of uncomfortable and irritated – frowning, sulking, in pain, falling asleep from boredom, terrified, annoyed... and all of the above but smiling because she'd been reminded she was in public and shouldn't look a fright.

She saw Garn more now *Crew Selection* was up and running but talked with him less. They'd given up on anything extracurricular until the series was done... and still hadn't had a long talk about her enlightenment. She also didn't know what was going on with Garn and Eleanor Wynter. They'd turned up at Devil's Dyke in tandem. Nelly was on *Crew Selection* as hostess, commentator and the viewers' friend. DS Jill was in a coma on *Letsby Avenue*. Chrissie wasn't fast-forwarding the serial any more but kept up through Personals natters. The return of DI di Ferrante had gone down well. Ratings were up.

Eleanor swanned into Studio 9 with her own crew, Camera Kenny and Mike Mick. She ignored Nina Ninian, not appreciating that she might be risking death by tweezer attack, and gave Chrissie a once-over. Meet Lady Shade – masked with face-cream and wrapped in blue-black tacky, trying not to scowl or smile. For a panic moment, Chrissie thought Nelly was looking into her mind. Surely, she wasn't enlightened? Then she scratched her nose. She'd not been thinking anything. To Eleanor Wynter, other people were props or scenery. She remained a person to be wary of. Cutthroats with serious previous had challenged Chrissie to scrap but Eleanor gave her heebier jeebies.

Garn aimed his camera away from Chrissie and at Nelly. Clickiticlickclick.

She bowed, simpered and posed – knowingly ridiculous but adorable. Nelly's Nutters loved that visual.

Eleanor Wynter must know who Chrissie was up against. More names were floated by press-pub wonks every day. Obvious choices, non-obvious choices, ridiculous choices. Flat Cat, Weather Girl, the Cuckoo, Sergeant Peppa. Even Bouncing Betty. Researchers monitored natters. Higher-ups made shouts. Elves paid attention to streams, alert for the tell-tales of manipulation. Brighton Belle actively campaigned, nudging her fan club to raise her profile. The Iron Norn vowed she'd never break up the union so often everyone reckoned she'd already said yes and was preparing to split from the British Lions and become a Splendid.

Something spooked Eleanor. She turned around several times and covered her face with her hands so she wouldn't be clicked grimacing. Backing out of the studio, she forced Camera Kenny and Mike Mick through the door with bumping and clattering. Then she was gone.

'What was that about?' Chrissie asked.

Garn shrugged as if he didn't know.

'Nelly doesn't like Studio 9,' said Nina Ninian. 'She thinks green ninjas are stalking her. Standing against the curtains with their eyes closed so they're invisible. Green ninjas dress all in green and have green make-up across the slice of their face which peeps out of the mask.'

Garn looked down.

Everyone looked at Nina, a bit shocked.

'What?' she said. 'It's true. She told me so herself.'

Now everyone looked for green ninjas which weren't there.

Tish signalled to Adrian Jah, who ordered everyone back to work. This session was all about Chrissie's visual, not ninja hunting.

Tish kept several Vones on her person – including Chrissie's – and held the Room together. She talked with Red-Tel, Poulton-Jones, the Coterie if she had to, helper elves whose names she learned without face-cards, and Chrissie. A constant flow of gen went through her steel eye to the Big Rack Think Box at Schilling.

A rival who wanted Chrissie out of the competition should kidnap Tish.

That thought prompted Chrissie to reason that every other competitor would have a Tish. Thinking like a winner, she should have the espionage network Schilling maintained for the benefit of banner clients identify these human linchpins. Then, those persons could be bopped on their noggins and wake up in cargo containers on the way to the Galapagos Islands. With, of course, a supply of food and drink, reading material, and a chemical toilet. Winning might be important but common humanity shouldn't be entirely set aside. Not this early in the series.

The worst thing was that Chrissie thought this through without a prompt. It was not in the spirit of the Girl Guide Pledges. *Crew Selection* had barely started and was already affecting her social life – Loulee in exile, Garn ever-present but beyond reach, the Coterie seething and snapping – and warping her mind. Mimsy said she'd end up not knowing herself. She wanted to get on, of course – but not like that. Not like a monster.

Mimsy said being Miss All Consuming Darkness and Everlasting Night would not win her any popularity contests.

So here she was – in a popularity contest.

Peach. Just peach.

LOULEE AT THE TRI-LION

APART FROM EVERY BLOODY THING ELSE, THE GHOSTS were giving her sustained grief.

Enyedi Boglárka was disgusted that Loulee had signed a standard Red-Tel contract without challenging half a dozen clauses. The dead lawyer didn't understand the television industry (not invented in her day) or accept that dim bulbs at Loulee's level didn't get to query clauses. Loulee's guess was that bright lights at Eleanor Wynter's level didn't either. The game was rigged.

Oghulqaimish was appalled Loulee wanted not to scrap with her best friend. In her day, no ties of blood or love were more important than going all out to win every battle. Oghulqaimish had a sneaking admiration for the brother who shot an arrow through her neck. He didn't let family feeling get in the way of victory.

And Contessa Erco wanted to take the wheel, figuratively (handlebars, literally) and *drive*. Lambretta scooters came after her time but she was smitten with the aerodynamics. If Loulee let the Contessa flex her thumbs while they were on the road, she'd be stuck with more speeding tickets.

So here she was, well under the limit – on the way to the launch event for *The Splendid Sixth*.

Loulee didn't have a uniform and wouldn't categorise herself as enlightened. She'd only opened a cupboard. She enabled feats of derring-do and cleaned up after the ghosts. She paid their fines. In the Shady circle, the person she was most like was Poulton-Jones. She was driving her own body around with the hubbub as passengers.

She steered the Lambretta towards the forecourt of the Tri-Lion.

This evening, the contestants would be revealed in a ceremony carried live on Red-Tel One. There'd be a massive media presence. The tabs had run endless speculation. Rumours flew around Whispers and the Personals. Even the Serious Channel was forced to schedule an after-party tut-tut with pundits lamenting the sorry state of cloakery between whatever duff clips Red-Tel chose to license to competitors.

Also invited were retired cloaks, banner-holding fan clubs, folk dressed as Floppits for no reason Loulee understood, the inevitable competition winners and a hard core of two-pounds-an-hour-back-row-seat-fillers who'd go through a buffet like Hamelin rats before the hacks could snaffle so much as a vol-au-vent.

Carnaby Stoke, the Cloak Bloke, was spieling at his personal fly-eye, showing off a Backstage Access laminate which he had to unstick from a sweat-patch on his vintage New Wave Ravers sweatshirt. He was a big voice. He'd exposed the Street Sweeper fraud, went out with (or been clicked standing next to) the Cuckoo, survived being kidnapped by Poly Pam, and claimed to be honorary companion of every cloak he'd interviewed on his *Secret Identity* Purview. Loulee didn't imagine he'd be handy in a scrap, unless someone wanted to throw him at Bouncing Betty.

Progress into the building was slow.

Peophole peepers, Personals natterers and Whispers whisperers were out in force, challenging each other like chimps. Vones, Vooks and Vatevers were brandished like flick-knives. Each faction had different colour laminates.

A Punch and Judy booth performed a particularly violent show to a section of a queue which wasn't moving fast enough. Loulee didn't like the look of the snapping crocodile.

No one knew who Loulee was (yet) so she couldn't get close to the entrance.

She dialled Anjulie and got directions to the Talent Door. Backing the Lambretta out of the crowd was a performance in itself.

She didn't let the Contessa execute a three-point turn. The ghost considered people to be soft obstacles and believed skidding in spilled blood a legitimate driving tactic. She was *exhausting*.

The Talent Door was round the side of the Tri-Lion, disguised as the exterior wall of a boiler room. The Splendids must sneak out this way if they needed to bypass stage-door johnnies and hurry to a crisis. Loulee imagined Dr Robot, Quackanapes and co creeping out on tiptoes.

Anjulie was waiting. Her Lennon Spex flashed green.

'Just need to check you're you,' she said. 'Thumb, eye, heart, please.'

Lynne Lythgoe, Anjulie's assistant, waved a doodad. It dinged three times. Loulee had passed. She was her.

Lynne – a country-fresh demigoddess with scarlet hair – sheathed the doodad in a toolbelt which matched her electric blue jumpsuit.

For Anjulie, *Crew Selection* was a promotion. Today, she'd swapped plimsolls for pumps. Anju now had Lynne to do the legwork. Her clipboard was replaced by a Vook Verity. She clipped scrawled-on papers to it with hair-grips. Old habits.

'Go on through,' said Anju.

Loulee trundled the Lambretta into a vaulted garage and parked next to a stanchion.

Most of the cars were civ models but she spotted the Green Knight's Trusty Steed – a Jaguar with an emerald chess knight on the bonnet – and Dr Robot's Widget Wagon. A black Bentley must be from the Shade Collection. It didn't have an L plate. She hoped Chrissie was taking her lessons in something less likely to depreciate if its big end crumpled against a bollard. Poulton-Jones must have driven her here.

She couldn't entirely blame Chrissie for being in a sulk but could partly blame her for not appreciating that Loulee had been bounced into what felt to them both like betrayal.

She hadn't put herself forward for *Crew Selection*.

She'd tried to get out of it. No dice.

First off, someone at Red-Tel saw clips from Devil's Dyke – specifically, Loulee's scrap with the Naughty Naga. They didn't know about the Ghost Lantern and she was not about to tell. The takeaway was that Loulee had an enlightened skill with edged weapons. Trade-name suggestions included Sabre Babe and Girly Dervish, both of which she made sick-faces at.

Her contract with Red-Tel meant she could be assigned to whatever position they chose on whatever programme they were making. She'd been taken off Chrissie and slaved to Eleanor. Now she was switched to a different job on a series which was not *Letsby Avenue*. It wasn't even unusual. An actor who won a BAFTA as lead in a Monday Night Musical still had to pop out of a door on the *Johnny Rotten Band Show* and take a flan in the face for larfs.

Loulee's choice was: appear on *Crew Selection* as a contestant, or be a) discontinued, b) prosecuted and c) blacklisted. Chrissie knew this but was still in a bate.

The thing was neither of them expected – or even wanted – to win.

How long would Chrissie or Loulee have lasted at the Battle of Battersea? A minute would be pushing it. In a rematch with the Devil's Dyke cutthroats, could they repeat their fluke victories? Not likely.

But Loulee had to show up at the Tri-Lion and take her lumps.

An elf in the garage beckoned her to a service lift.

'Ling, Louise?' he asked.

'That's me, yes,' she said.

'Is this what you're wearing?'

Sleeveless leather jacket (thank you, Wavy Lines Corridor) and burgundy bell-bottoms. Before things went skew-whiff, Chrissie suggested Loulee put a Hallowe'en spook sticker – floating sheet with big eyeholes – on her crash helmet to make a token attempt at a Ghost Lantern Girl brand. Loulee hadn't got round to it.

'I suppose it could work,' said the elf. 'It's street.'

They went up in the lift. The Tri-Lion had many levels.

The Sunday supplements had run cutaway diagrams. The Splendids operated a vertical take-off jet from the roof. They had laboratories, lounges and their own cyclotron. One whole wing was a Think Box. And, of course, they convened at the Star Table in the Hallowed Hall.

Ground level was an open-to-the-public museum she and Chrissie had visited on another Draycott's day-out. There were individual exhibits for the forty-plus cloaks who'd been in the Six since Splendiffery began. It'd be up to over fifty by now.

Perhaps with prophetic instinct, Chrissie and Loulee's favourites were the Splendids who didn't last long – who joined to fill a gap, then proved surplus to requirements on days their speciality wasn't needed and got relegated back to rank and file cloaking. They were both fans of the generally mocked swimming marvel Mark Shark ('wet, he was a wonder... dry, he was a drip').

The elf handed her off at the landing to a PA who walked and talked with her.

'Arsinoë,' said the p.a.

'Bless you,' said Loulee.

'It's your trade-name,' the PA explained. 'Arsinoë... younger—'

'—sister of Cleopatra, made Julius Caesar swim for his life, executed by Marc Antony.'

'Good, you're up on her. They considered other female warriors of antiquity.'

Arsinoë wasn't one of the ghosts, though she fit the requirements: woman with talent, more competent than men were comfortable with, done to death to appease a jealous relative. When she took command of the armies of Egypt, Arsinoë was fifteen.

'You know what "Arsinoë" will be abbreviated to?'

'"Noë", rhymes with Zoë?'

'I wish. More like "Arse", rhymes with farce.'

'I shouldn't worry. They know what they're doing.'

Loulee didn't know who they were but doubted the PA was right.

She was about to be named Arse Woman in front of the press and viewing public. It would be on the Personals and Whispers in seconds. Lamb Bear would pee himself. If they ever spoke again, Chrissie would never let her forget it.

Loulee considered letting Yvyra take the controls for an hour or so.

Maybe she'd come to surrounded by annoying people with poison darts stuck in them. Then she'd be packed off to Devil's Dyke and not have to be on this ridiculous programme. She and Chrissie had got giggly on Babycham watching the final heat of *Crew Selection: Jupiter Mission* and dialled in many votes for Jonty McDribblefart. This was punishment for that.

The PA shoved her into a hexagonal Green Room, which might have been designed so six people who didn't want to talk to each other had niches for their own cliques.

On a big screen, Eleanor Wynter was hosting the show from a stage somewhere in the building. She was with Martin Masters and Dr Robot, looking on while Crufts performed a 'Fox on the Run' routine. Clicks of Urban Fox over the years were projected behind them. This was the tribute section, establishing what big pawprints the series' winner had to fill. Mimsy Mountmain wasn't present.

Chrissie was in the Green Room, with Poulton-Jones, a girl with a cyber eye, and an older woman Loulee knew to be Dot Schilling. Chrissie wore the outfit they'd put together. She smiled to see Loulee then remembered they were quarrelling and scowled.

The argy-bargy with Chrissie was so all-consuming Loulee hadn't bothered about who else might be in the running. For the reason it seemed obvious without actually making sense, she'd presumed *The Splendid Sixth* would feature six candidates. It turned out the Vision Controller thought that way too.

Six will stand up. One will be invited.

Every contestant clocked who they were up against. Loulee was no different. She looked round while trying not to seem concerned one way or the other.

The woman with ironed blonde hair was Alexandra Beach, trade-name Weather Girl. Her bodystocking changed colour according to moisture, temperature and atmospheric pressure. Three young men with horn-rim glasses, short-sleeve shirts and egg-yolk ties were her helper elves. Weather Girl was often in the swanks with products, endorsements and good works – and always in the tabs for poor relationship choices (no condemnation from Loulee for that) and hissy fits involving sudden precipitation. Possibly, her thunder and Chrissie's lightning were set to clash.

Every article Loulee had read put Weather Girl on the list for the Splendid Sixth.

The other three were surprises, ranging across the board.

Mr Worst Date of the Century was here. Hereward Jackson-Walker was not, so far as Loulee knew, enlightened. His only talent was looking expensively thick. He huddled with some of Chrissie's Coterie chums, wearing a skinsuit studded with humming doodads and flashing thingumajigs. The verps' verp. Mummy and Daddy – Petronella Varish Jackson, the Minister for Equalities and Opportunity and Wallace Worcester Walker, CEO of British RoboDynamics – had bought Hereward in and out of everything since posh infants' school. Chrissie said they paid Polly O a stipend to let their idiot son into the Coterie. He'd be out on his perfectly sculpted ear if the cheques stopped clearing. So now the verps had bought him a cloak identity.

Buttered flaming crumpets.

Hereward made a fist with a metal gauntlet and punched the sky.

Horrible feedback sounded. Someone amplified yelled *Vyyy Purse Trike*!

Everyone looked, then looked away.

What happened to the All-Woman shortlist?

'Loulee,' cooed someone friendly.

It was Eunice Euglow, in a fireproof skin-tight boiler suit. She was with Ftatateeta and Tunno. They wore matching ankle-monitors because they were on probation. Eunice made a smoke heart in the air. Loulee imagined the pitch – ex-convict redeemed by heroic action. Urban Fox had been misunderstood as a cutthroat before she won respect as a Splendid. Pyro Pixie fit that narrative.

Eunice and Ftatateeta air-hugged Loulee – Tunno held back, hopping from foot to foot. Loulee felt a rush of warmth. She hoped Eunice's self-control was improving. Or else there'd be unfortunate fiery episodes. Good telly, some might say.

Over Eunice's shoulder, Loulee saw the real bad news.

Asmida binti Geoffrey Reynolds hissed and stuck out a forked tongue.

She was the who-the-Hell-let-this-happen? selection. Mischief goosed viewing figures like nobody's business.

Loulee was never signing anything again unless Enyedi Boglárka gave the all-clear.

The Naughty Naga's face was the vivid green of a freshly shelled pea. She'd shed her skin since Devil's Dyke but Loulee doubted she'd changed her spots. Which didn't parse zoologically but made an awful sort of sense. If Asmida had a shot at being Splendid, all bets were off. She wore an oversized white laboratory coat with snake eye motifs on the pockets. Instead of an ankle-tag, she made a statement with her parole monitor. It was the lock on a fetish dog collar which emphasised her six extra inches of flexible neck.

'It's a Big Welcome to the Big *Arssssse,*' said Asmida, hissing and cackling at the same time.

So that was out. Loulee would forever be the Arse.

She glanced over at Chrissie, who was staring at Loulee eyelocking with the Naughty Naga but looked away as if she hadn't been.

No quarter from that quarter, then.

It was tempting to let Yvyra or Oghulqaimish loose. There must be throwable or hackwithable items within reach.

If everyone wanted Girly Dervish...

DAKIN AT THE TRI-LION

HE'D BEEN AT THE DOLL HOSPITAL WHERE OFF-THE-books quacks were putting Major Wood back together when his Vone pirriped. A robotic squawk told him he'd won a competition. The prize was two tickets to the launch of *The Splendid Sixth*. He hadn't entered a competition. A mystery blurt suggested he not ignore his good fortune. He took the hint and dialled the redemption code.

Until now, mystery blurts from the patron of the New Broken Dolls went to the OIC Major Wood wouldn't be marching up or down hills for the foreseeable. Dakin got a battlefield promotion.

After the attack in Farringdon, the NBDs were on high alert. They didn't move into the Human Figure Works and took evasive measures... using codes, living out of the bread van. Dakin had been through this before when the British Lions hunted down Lord Adder ('The Great British Snake-Off', the tabs called that series of scraps). Usually, throats had fiddles on the go and cloaks reacted to foil them. Once in a blue moon, some masked big bonce got tired of playing catch-up and went on a tear. Then things got dicey. Generations of cutthroats remembered Sergeant Bloody Shade and Corporal Punishment.

The Splendid Six, for all the bells and whistles, were

form-filling, regulation-bound plods. But even they had their nutters. Urban Fox was a specimen of that breed.

Dakin missed the days of fiddles and fancies.

Viper Strike was all over the news. Farringdon wasn't its only outing. It had fired on a disused warehouse in Docklands and an abandoned funfair in Mile End, scattering throats who were using the venues to pirate videos of kids' programmes and stage lethal games of *It's a Knockout*. The gargantuabot was a box kite – remote-controlled by a son of privilege named Hereward Jackson-Walker. He'd been giving it mouth on telly and in the tabs. Dakin wouldn't trust an obvious prat like this Jackson-Walker with a Flymo but someone had sunk serious coin into a battle mech and given him the keys. A *Viper Strikings* Purview hosted blurry Vone clips of the box kite whizzing like a low-flying missile and making that bloody racket.

There was little sense that Jackson-Walker was targeting the NBDs more than anyone else. He'd gone for three separate krewes and done no follow-up. He hadn't even dialled the bizzies. For all the burned-down rookeries and toasted tossers, the strikings hadn't lead to arrests. Dakin reckoned someone fed the twit a location and he pressed a flipping button to send in the gargantuabot. He didn't need to get out of bed to make a nuisance of himself.

Jackson-Walker wasn't really on their trail. If Viper Strike came for the NBDs again, it would be when they showed up in public. Which they were required to do, as per their arrangement with the Vision Controller. They were in business to make *visible* trouble.

The point of this evening was to stick glims on the enemy.

Though her head stuck up above any crowd, Cyndi was his obvious choice for plus one. He didn't trust Johnnie in mixed company. Upside-Down Gonk, Juke-Box Jerry and Mr Swizzle couldn't pass for civs. Dakin only had to wear a glove and he was just a bloke with bleary eyes. Mr Swizzle volunteered – well, his Mr Punch hand did – to set up outside the Tri-Lion and entertain the queue. Dakin let him get on with it. Give any pickpockets in the crowd a break.

Cyndi was in her Actress With a Broken Foot Attending the Opening Night of the Hit Show Which Makes the Understudy the Toast of Shaftesbury Avenue outfit: sparkly mini-frock that showed off her stems, a mile-and-a-half mink shaped into a loose noose, daffodil hair-bow to match her daisy sunglasses, plaster boot with concealed pistol compartment. She was under orders not to assassinate anyone. The short fellow sat behind her in the auditorium squirmed. He was one of a row of assorted clots wearing Flat Cat tee-shirts and kitten-ear cricket caps. Dakin hoped Cyndi didn't notice the fan club. She had a short fuse on the subject. Flat Cat once plastered her to the side of a Tube train.

The Tri-Lion was enemy territory. Cloak Central. Its Burning Beacon could be seen from three postcodes away, reminding evil-livers that they were on notice. Normally, Dakin wouldn't come within a mile of the place.

On the stage, Eleanor Wynter was MC.

She gave out guff about the Splendid Six, all those who'd served, feats feated, fiends defeated, etc. etc. Dakin didn't know what to make of Eleanor Wynter. She wasn't a civ, that was certain. At Todd's she'd been all business, cards close to her chest. On stage she was different: a cheeky barmaid who knew when you needed a grog to settle the nerves... Not lording it about but clever enough to do the *Spectrum* crossword in ten minutes... Relaxed and smiley, with a hint of teeth which suggested she could fly off the handle and chuck a cleaver across the kitchen if you spoke ill of her tiramisu. Up there, she was a bright light.

At the back of the stage sat quiet, important folk – Martin Masters, Dr Robot, the Lord Mayor. Not the Vision Controller. He'd be in a room full of screens, twiddling with the horizontal and the vertical. This was his game. He was the ultimate source of mystery blurts. A woman in a mask turned up with Briteway bags full of readies to keep the krewe afloat. She used the trade-name the Green Ninja and said it was a private joke. Johnnie thought she was Eleanor Wynter in a head-sock but Johnnie was thick as mince. So long as she kept up the cash-flow Dakin didn't care about her secret identity. Maybe she was someone with bad hair and spots.

'... now the moment you've been waiting for,' said Eleanor.

A curtain went up and showed a darkened stage with six evenly spaced pedestals. Spotlights went on.

'*Vyy – purr – Strahkkk*!'

The gargantuabot was on a reinforced pedestal. Hereward Jackson-Walker, on site for a change, stood between its metal legs, motion-capture wetsuit carbuncled with lit-up ping-pong balls. He punched the air and the box kite matched the gesture. Coloured smoke squirted from its knuckles. Dakin hoped its rocket-pods weren't loaded.

Dakin and Cyndi joined in the applause.

Viper Strike loomed large but the other contestants posed and smiled. To get the gargantuabot's head in clicks, snappers had to pull back so the rest of the runners – all women – looked small.

The row behind them wasn't clapping.

'Where's Flat Cat?' they said.

'... and who the herbert is *she*?' directed at multiple fresh faces.

'May I present the Splendid Sixths on Approval?' Eleanor asked.

The crowd (mostly) boomed approval.

'Sandii Beach... Weather Girl!'

Dakin knew who she was. A warm breeze riffled through the auditorium.

'Eunice Uglow... Pyro Pixie!'

A titchy girl in an asbestos one-piece threw fire out of her hands and grinned. She'd be the lightweight. Everyone's friend until they decided to backstab her out of the contest. There was one on every series of *Crew Selection*.

'Hereward Jackson-Walker and...'

Another robot muscle pose and a jarring '*Vyy – purr – Strahkkk*!'

Voices joined in the sting, suspiciously evenly placed around the auditorium like a hi-fi nut's showoff speakers. Viper Strike had papered the house with paid fans. Flat Cat wouldn't have had to do that.

'Christine Chambers... Lady Shady!'

A girl in a black pageboy wig made a karate motion. She tore a violet-edged rent in the air, beyond which darkness raged – then zipped it up again and took a bow. Dakin wasn't sure what that party piece was. A conjuring trick, probably.

'I think she got the name wrong,' said Cyndi. 'It should be Lady Shade.'

Dakin knew Eleanor had got the name wrong but didn't think she'd made a mistake. It was a dig. So the wig witch was a Shade. Just what the world needed. Another of those characters. Grandad hobbled to the end of his days from the kicking Sergeant Shade gave him after an armoured car raid in 1957. Some other woman in a fedora and Spex had gone about casting shadow since the 1990s. Throats told their brats the Shades would get them if they didn't file the serial numbers off anything they nicked. They were bogeymen but you had to believe in them. Ask Grandad.

'Louisa Ling... *Arsinicola*!'

A sulky sister in a leather jacket clashed a couple of swords. She got unrehearsed hoots and cheers. Dakin had never heard of her. She was alone in her spotlight but maybe not alone on her pedestal. They'd need gen on this one. If she was here, she couldn't just be top of the class at sabre dancing. She'd have the enlightened ability to slice steel plates like stale Hovis or shift faster than Roger Bannister with a rocket up his bum.

'... and Asssssmida G. Reynolds... Garter *Ssssssnake*!'

Good gravy with onions, it was the Nasty Naga!

She had worse previous than most of the NBDs. What was she doing here? Dakin remembered when she was Lord Adder's squeeze – not that she stayed in that krewe long. Or any krewe. She slithered solo. For larfs, she added herself to the card of a Society for the Promotion of Cruel Sport open scrap evening and beat all comers. Including Minnie the Mongoose, who hadn't been seen down the shops since. When spivs warned each other off a bird because she was poison, they didn't usually mean it literally. Cut in a cab queue before the Nasty Naga and you'd be black-faced and coughing foam two minutes after she bit you.

Asmida ripped off her long white coat and threw it away.

She wore a Union Jack boob tube and matching slit-high-on-the-hip football shorts, red-white-and-blue against her forty-shades-of-green skin. Hosannahs and rattles from the patriots in the audience.

Applause went on and on.

Asmida made a curvy-wrist snake gesture which ended with a salute. Crowds went wild. The betty with the blades looked put out that she'd been the favourite for all of fifteen seconds before Garter Snake peeled her coat off.

The Naga wore an actual garter with '*honi soit qui mal y pense*' embroidered on it. A motto with an implied challenge. 'Shamed be whoever thinks ill of it'. Meaning if you've got a problem, take a slapping, wretch. It implied a seal of royal approval since the same words were on Queen Vee's shield.

It would take Upside-Down Gonk to work this out.

'Six have stood up...' said Eleanor.

The row behind was already empty. The Flat Cat fan club had quit the auditorium, swearing to get up a petition.

'... One will be called.'

'*Vyy – purr...*'

The recorded message choked off. Ice on the speaker grille.

So it had started early. Competition.

If it were up to Dakin, he wouldn't even take his glove off. A few nudges and this mob would do the job for them. They'd cripple each other before they could make inroads on crime. That wasn't the brief from the Vision Controller. The NBDs had to mix it in. So be it.

Since Hereward the Bolthead was one of 'em, they were more or less obliged to give as much aggro as possible.

'I've worked out how to kill two of six,' said Cyndi.

'Slow for you.'

'Only because I've never heard of half of them. We'll need gen on the unknowns but from these seats I can't say I'm impressed.'

Dakin would be inclined to agree but was cautious. He also distinctly didn't recall the Vision Controller authorising murder.

'We'll get blurts later.'

The Green Ninja had promised gen on the targets.

Six or seven mechanics gathered around the gargantuabot and argued about how to defrost the grille. They ignored any suggestions Jackson-Walker made. So he was out of the loop on his own box kite. Good to know.

Dakin reckoned Weather Girl had taken an early lead in the sneaky tricks department.

At the back of his mind, Dakin had supposed they'd be up against top of the range cloaks like Poltergirl or Night Mist. But, of course, the Vision Controller hadn't picked contestants for actual suitability for a slot on the Splendids – but as types who fit a series of *Crew Selection*. That ought to make the krewe's job easier but required a rethink.

Hereward was the knob who got on everyone's nerves but stayed in till the end to keep up the drama. Another regular type. The Boring Bosun from *Crew Selection: Royal Yacht* wound up so famously unpopular he got a gig reading the late-night shipping forecast on Red-Tel Radio. He was a broadcasting fixture, while the winners of that series languished in obscurity. They certainly weren't crewing the *Victoria II*.

Sandii Beach might be a joke cloak but was more experienced than the schoolgirls. She ought to have changed her name to something with Woman in it a while back. The Shade Maid, Matchbox Minnie and Sword Swallower Suzy would have to show grown-up railcards to get a half of mild in any boozer in town.

Which left – gawd help us – Asmida binti Geoffrey Reynolds.

Your herpetophobe's nightmare in a flag.

Eleanor Wynter read from the autocue. Blah about women in the workplace, strides for equality in a line-up of five to one, etc. She didn't mention that all the contestants were young and – depending on whether you were prejudiced against scales – pretty. No way would *Crew Selection* put the Wart-Hag on telly. Possibly, any cloak who'd been in the night-game for more than a season knew better than to get onboard this carnival float.

Dakin's Vone pirriped. Multiple blurts received.

'Here we go.'

'Three,' said Cyndi. 'I know how to kill three of them.'

'That's excessive, Cynd. We're only cleared for mischief.'

Then he remembered Major Wood. That was more than mischief.

'Read between the lines, Kung Fu Grip. "Six have stood up... All will get knocked down." That's a Saying of Cyndi.'

CHRISTINE ON A PEDESTAL

WHERE HAD SHE FOUND THE TRICK OF OPENING A RIP in reality as if stretching a cats' cradle? The darkness beyond swirled. Resisting the temptation to tear a bigger hole wasn't easy. After sealing the breach, she was spacey. All the lights in the auditorium – bulbs popping, Vones shining, arcs aimed – were dizzying. She could use a Walnut Whip and a cold compress. This was going out live. A close-up of her perspiring face was on tellies in homes throughout the UK. She tried to smile as if she were thinking of something pleasant.

To her left, Hereward held up his arms as if a tailor were measuring his chest, as his support crew examined the malfunctioning underarm grilles of the Viper Strike box kite. Hereward tried to hold the pose naturally, but a muscle in his cheek twitched. That tic was magnified by the face-screen on the robot's head. Surely the verps would scratch the project and turn off the money tap? A gargantuabot must be a bigger outlay than paying for damages in nightclubs and settling ridiculous boutique bills.

To her right, Loulee was looking away from her. Possibly because she was looking farther away from Hereward.

Chrissie saw Camera Clare in the wings, aiming a camera like a rocket launcher. Schilling were releasing clips on their recently launched *Shady Side of the Street* Purview to complement and – if necessary – contradict Chrissie's showing on *Crew Selection*. An attempt to get control of the narrative away from Red-Tel. Her Purview hadn't signed as many peepers as Weather Girl's long-established *Meteorology Maid* or even Hereward's *Viper Strikings*. But numbers were climbing and engagement – eyes per day – was up.

Ten minutes after the announcement, Chrissie was exhausted.

She'd had several extra breakfasts but was flagging. Lights sapped ergs. Sadly, you couldn't be on telly without lights. If this programme were on the wireless, she'd win easily.

She'd fretted so much about Loulee she'd not considered who else she might be up against. Obviously, her friend wasn't her only competition. As Eleanor went down the line with a roving mike, Chrissie reckoned both she and Loulee were fill-ins at best.

Everyone already knew Weather Girl.

Viper Strike had made a splash.

Everyone was about to know Garter Snake.

The Draycott's old girls – Chrissie, Loulee, Eunice – made up the numbers.

That Red-Tel suit's OBE hopes were rekindled. His suggestion had connected in the snake woman's Room. *Honi soit*, indeed. Who'd vote against Miss Queen, Country, Fish and Chips and Football? Even if she hissed and had gold-green eyes.

First to be interviewed was Weather Girl. Alexandra Beach talked earnestly about her admiration for the Splendid Six. She didn't mention any of her products. She'd done enough adverts to be princess of hard-sell but played *Crew Selection* differently. She had the biggest Room and had been at this longest. She'd be exceptionally well advised. She was with Marquiss Management, the company Dot Schilling left to found her Agency. MM handled half the Splendid Six and would be eager to collect the set.

'I have to bring this up, Sandii…' said Eleanor.

Weather Girl smiled and puffed her hair out of her eyes – a tell impressionists loved. She knew what was coming. A light breeze.

'I think I know where you're going. I'd like it on the record that there's no choppy water between me and Bruno. I hope he and Ilona are blissful together. I wish them nothing but sunshine...'

'... and *rainbows*?'

'Who doesn't like rainbows, Eleanor?'

Chrissie was so used to Nelly the bright light she didn't often ponder her place on the Wheel. Unenlightened, temperamental, replaceable. Next to Weather Girl, Eleanor was a minnow. Alexandra didn't need to flash Union Jack undies. She was a British institution by default. What did the country love more than talking about the weather?

Eleanor moved on to Hereward.

He was stuck in Fifth Position (the *bras en couronne* oval). The mechanics had plates off and found snow packed in around wires and circuits. That would teach him to step on Weather Girl's applause. Viper Strike was done for the day but Hereward still had to come up with a few words for the viewers at home.

'Mr Jackson-Walker, how does it feel to be the only boy in the girls' club?'

Hereward must have been briefed but was frozen. Neural feedback from the mo-cap balaclava was a big issue with box kite robots.

Chrissie tried not to giggle.

'You've earned a reputation for being tough on crime and tough on the *houses* of crime?'

Fixed smile. Tiny trickle of sweat on the forehead – a rivulet on the big face screen.

'Strong and silent, eh?' said Eleanor. 'Chill and frosty.'

Little lines appeared between Hereward's plucked eyebrows.

'Ohhhh Hereee-waaard,' said Loulee in her Polly O imitation voice.

Hereward's eyes shifted.

'You've got a blob of brake fluid on your nose,' said Loulee. 'Looks like yellow snot.'

Without thinking, Hereward broke the pose and wiped his nose.

Viper Strike punched itself in the face, cracking the screen.

The gargantuabot fell like a sawn-through mighty oak. Hereward was wrenched backwards, pulled off his pedestal.

The fall dislodged ice chunks. The speakers hooted.

'*Vyy – purr – Strahkkk!*'

The hall filled with laughter. Hereward wriggled and scraped his thighs, desperate for an off button. The gargantuabot thumped the stage like a toddler having a tantrum. Eleanor stepped out of clouting range.

Chrissie's podium wobbled.

Loulee took a bow and got cheers and whoops.

She'd brought down Viper Strike without supernatural or enlightened assistance. No ghosts necessary. Just a snark attack. If she stuck to this, she could win.

'Ladies, ladies,' protested Eleanor, with a smile, 'is this seemly?'

Chrissie had the giggles now. She looked at Loulee and set her off.

Eunice joined in.

'What you might not know but will have guessed is that these three went to the same school,' Eleanor told the audience. 'It was so good it was *approved*.'

Chrissie tried to strike a cloak pose, hands on hips. Loulee began to put her arms up in the ballet oval but was laughing too hard.

'Steady on, Louls,' said Chrissie. 'We're on the telly you know.'

Loulee stuck her tongue out at Chrissie.

It was going to be all right. They leaned off their pedestals and bumped heads, then steadied with a Floppit hug.

'I've missed you,' Chrissie told Loulee, off-mike.

'Me too.'

'We can get through this.'

'Crumpets, I hope so.'

They tried to stand straight.

At the far end, the snake woman hissed.

'For more madness,' Eleanor said to camera, 'come back after the break... and hope we have the ladies calmed down. I'm Eleanor Wynter and don't forget to natter on the Personals, backchatter on Whispers, and shout from the hillside. Tell us what you think of the show so far... and, please, be merciful. It will get more professional, I promise. Oh, and evildoers... *tremble!*'

The gargantuabot farted flame and Hereward's bodystocking shorted out.

'What idiot did that?' said one of his maintenance crew.

Loulee and Chrissie laughed all through the adverts.

CARNABY STOKE – THE CLOAK BLOKE

'THE HEADLINES ARE ALL VARIATIONS ON "CREW *Selection: The Splendid Sixth*: A Disappointing Line-Up?" Which I get. The absence of hot-tipped names is telling. No Flat Cat, fellas. Moonlight Flit in eclipse.

'I've seen a lot of "Anyone Who'd Enter the Contest Shouldn't Win It" blurts, known in the trade as McDribblefart Syndrome. At the end of this series of a light entertainment programme, someone will join the Splendid Six. They're not Britain's Major League, cloaktailers. The Major League are the Yanks' Splendid Six. Our brass band has been around twice as long as their beat group. If it's for larfs, I'm not chortling. Whoever sits at the Star Table plonks their bum on a seat occupied by legends. They should be Britain's best and brightest. This can't be a giggle. No, you, at the back, stop it. This is serious stuff.

'So, here's where we are, a day after the premiere episode...

'Sandii Beach promises a change in the weather. No more showers. She's soft-peddling sponsorships and offering sunny smiles. In a wide-open field, she's the bookies' favourite for the sole reason people have heard of Weather Girl. Not everything they've heard is good. Me, I've always liked her. After the Wet Wedding, I was Stand-with-Sandii not Bowled-over-by-Bruno. I use her Splash of Salt on my sensitive chin. She's talked down because, as she admits, the tabs make a soap serial out of her private life and she goes along with it... but she has serious abilities. When it counts, she's there. She kept civs dry during the Farnborough Floods. If it's about replacing that fox person, Weather Girl is the Stoke Selection.

'When the curtain went up at the Tri-Lion, the instant favourite was Viper Strike – a remote-controlled gunbus slaved to the son of a government mucky-muck and a captain of industry. The gargantuabot's been in the news, going after cutthroats up and down the land. Viper Strike has impressed pundits who shoulda knowed better. We've all had squirts and blurts with pointas to the *Viper Strikings* Purview which runs clips of the box kite in action. Not the clip which comes up first on Hawkshaw, though. That, of course, is the clanking clod bashing itself in its face and taking a stage dive which would shame an Italian centre forward giving his Dying Swan in the goal area at Wembley. "What idiot did that?" indeed. From front-runner to dead last in half a trice. I'm almost impressed and happy I didn't pay attention to Noddy the Numbers and put heavy coin on Viper Strike before the players were even announced. Cloaks have come back from worse but not lately. This sort of balls-up can turn a first-timer from cloak to cutthroat. Which is why I'm not going along with fair-weather tipsters and scratching Jackson-Wotsit completely. If I were him, and you can imagine how grateful I am not to be, the thing uppermost in my mind now would be revenge. Look at Viper Strike's backup. A pile of money. A team who learn from mistakes. Connections with clout. Unlimited wham-bam-blammo ammo. You heard it first here but I'm not ruling out "Viper Strikes Back".

'If that doesn't happen, there's no doubt Garter Snake has a segment of the vote sewn up. Pervs. You might not spend digi doughnuts at the Smut Hutch, which has Garter Snake out in front by a mile, but a whole lot of folk – mostly vicars and schoolboys – are dedicated smut-slobberers. As soon as the programme went out, the most popular information retrieval parameter on Hawkshaw was "Garter Snake Nude". In a certain light, I see it. Golden eyes, green thighs. I can also look up "Asmida G. Reynolds" and learn about her previous career as the Naughty, Nasty or Noisome Naga. There's a clip of Reynolds in her cutthroat days – about four months ago! – in a scrap with one of the other contestants during a riot at Devil's Dyke. Yes, Gertie Garter was a patient in a secure hospital. As was, incidentally, that sweet little Eunice Uglow – who once lived out the dreams of half the kids in Britain by burning down her school. I'm not sure that should be held against her. She's a firework. We all like redemption stories, and throat-to-cloak sagas aren't new. Soubrette has one, as she revealed when we did a *Secret Identity* on her journey from cutthroat companion to theatreland sleuth. But we also remember when Lady Godawful turned over a new leaf and ran for Lord Mayor as part of a fiddle which landed her back in Holloway.

'Then there's Lady Shade and Arsinicola, both competing in the change-that-trade-name handicap. It's supposed to be Arsinoë, apparently. Younger sister of Cleopatra. Hawkshaw her for details. I can't see the connection but our Arsinoë is a lovely little mover with a scimitar. Allegedly she has other talents. I can't help but think Red-Tel have been lazy in net-casting. No fewer than four of the Sixers popped up on our screens during the Devil's Dyke imbroglio back in January. As *Secret Identity* trusties know, that was an almighty put-up job. I reckon this is the payoff. Whose face was front in news reports of the "riots"? Eleanor Wynter. She happened to be handily on the scene when the balloon went up. I should cocoa. Who's fronting this series of *Crew Selection*? Why, it's Nelly Off the Telly. See how it fits together?

'Christine Chambers – model and actress, controversial for her views on the crockery community – and Louise Ling – beautician and fashion consultant, which doesn't explain her jacket – were mixed up in the pseudoscrap for reasons no one ever explained. That clip of Lady Shade and Bouncing Betty dancing around each other pretending to be mixing it up has been dialled almost as often as Ling thrashing Garter Snake. If you can judge anyone by ten seconds of scrap, they qualify in their weight class – but we know little about these dillydally dollies. Lady Shade has the Schilling Agency in her corner and you wouldn't want to underestimate Dottie's Hotties. Chambers is, so we're told, heir to the storied Shade Legacy – which goes back even beyond the moment of *Never Mind. Secret Identity: Shady Start*, on the Original Dr Shade, will give you gen on where Chambers is coming from. We'll hear more about the mystery package in the coming weeks, though I have my doubts there's anything much inside. I am on the record as crock-supportive. The Splendids should give no platform to lifestyle bigotry in any shape or form – so there's that. I also hate that silly syrup she wears. But it's seldom clever to bet against a legacy.

'My instinct was to rank Ling dead last... until she brought Viper Strike down a peg or fifty with a sly suggestion. Maybe she should bin the swords and call herself Miss Mouth. Now I've had a chance to review clicks and clips a dozen times, I'm convinced Ling is your actual dark horse. The whispers I've heard about her haven't hit Whispers yet – but keep an eye on Arsenal Sal.

'So that's where it stands for the moment, cloaktailers. Check in as the programme continues...'

CHRISTINE ON CREW SELECTION

THE CARDINAL WOLSEY STREET STUDIOS DIDN'T HAVE facilities to give all six contestants their own suites for make-up, wardrobe, training and downtime. Making Rooms mingle was part of the format. Cameras and microphones were positioned to catch telegenic clashes. Elves monitored feeds for catty remarks, acts of sabotage, hissy fits and other broadcastable bad behaviour.

Chrissie had half-thought the Sixths would scrap gladiator-style for the prize. It was worse than that. For the next episode, they had to collaborate. Part of what the Splendids looked for in a Sixth was an ability to work alongside other enlightened, unpredictable cloaks. Which wasn't necessarily what Red-Tel and the viewers at home wanted.

Every series had a Ruthless Nasty One and a Boring Nice One. The programme got higher BARB scores with plotting, treachery and back-biting than co-operation, amity and achievement. A feud on *Crew Selection: Windmill Girls* led to an almighty public scrap in the French Pub which landed rival revudebelles in the dock for GBH Audience research rated *Windmill Girls* as peak *Crew Selection. Jupiter Mission* was less watched. The Vision Controller demanded improvement.

The production team were under orders to make this the comeback series or else the parade was over. Great news, chums!

Crew Selection will take a well-earned rest next year and forever after. Enjoy repeats of previous series on Red-Tel Gold and tune in to the *Crew Selection* slot for your new favourite, *Mellon Chollie's Happy Hour.*

Anju the AP and Lynne the AAP waylaid Chrissie outside Studio 9. The white streaks in Anju's hair weren't dyed any more. The strain of promotion gave her natural frosting.

'There've been questions, Chrissie,' said Anju. 'Not many, what with everything else but it's as well to get ahead of the story before it breaks.'

'What now? Has someone dressed up as me and frightened children?'

'Children were most likely to notice,' said Lynne, holding up Anju's Vook Verity. 'Also most likely to be ignored when they did. You've seen Episode One?'

'Can I not answer that?'

Anju and Lynne groaned and looked up and down.

'I looked at clips on Peophole...'

The groans were more pronounced.

'It was a live broadcast and I was on it, so of course I didn't see it going out. Dad's fussy about who sets the video so I didn't record it either. I'll try to catch the repeat the night before Episode Two.'

She knew she was bleating.

'You're not the only one to skip the homework,' Anju admitted. 'We'd be happy to lay on a screening for you.'

'Might I get too self-conscious?'

'None of you could get *more* self-conscious,' said the AP.

'Here's what the questions are about,' said Lynne, dialling a clip on the Verity.

It was going to be Chrissie and Loulee making twits of themselves laughing at Hereward.

No, it wasn't...

Nelly introduced her with 'Christine Chambers... Lady Shady!'

'She meant to get that wrong,' said Chrissie.

Chrissie was centre screen, slicing air with her hand. Lynne slow motioned through Chrissie's demonstration of her dark enlightenment.

The tear in reality registered on video as a blackish buzz, like interference from a hair-dryer or a pigeon flying into the aerial.

'That's what was broadcast,' said Anju. 'Live. We have fly-eye coverage too. And Clare got you from the wings.'

Lynne fiddled the dial and showed the party piece from other angles.

The void was different in each version – a searing supernova, a mass of pixels, an open wound bleeding black, a nothing at all.

'I've only been enlightened a few months,' Chrissie said. 'I'm still learning what I can do... and what this all is.'

'Some children claim they saw red eyes in the rip,' said Anju. 'Only when it was live. They've dialled the clip since and say we changed it.'

'Some people see purple eyes,' said Lynne. 'And hands with long fingers.'

Chrissie was hungry. She worried dark matter was seeping from under her nails.

'It's been thoroughly debunked on the Personals,' said Anju. 'It's optical effects and you have no abilities whatsoever. You're an actress not a cloak, which isn't exactly not true. Or you're Hereward's girlfriend and nagged him so much he got you a gig on his show.'

'Ruddy cheek,' Chrissie exclaimed. 'That has to be libel!'

'Welcome to the Sue Queue. Know how many threats of legal action we've had since the programme went out?'

'A big number?'

'More than. One lawyer wants us to re-edit the programme to take out the gargantuabot malfunction, claiming it's prejudicial to the business interests of the manufacturers. Who are British RoboDynamics, part of the Jackson-Walker group of companies. Who are...?'

'Verps.'

Anju nodded. 'Valued verps. Bane of our existence. Rich people and their lawyers. Good thing Red-Tel are as rich and have nastier lawyers. We keep this quiet, so contestants don't worry their pretty little heads overmuch. The crockery crackpots are still trying to get you off the show.'

'I haven't said anything about them!'

'You don't need to. Flash the red-purple eyes and scratchy claws from Planet X.'

'I'm not the contestant with venom sacs.'

'Everyone loves Garter Snake,' said Anju.

'Everyone hasn't met her.'

'It's come down from the Vision Controller that he'd like you to be careful. You're his personal pick, you know. Not only because you're already under contract to Red-Tel. He's respectful of the Shade Legacy. He wants you to be too.'

Anju was, as usual, speaking for someone else. Don Loki Baird was an unseen presence at Cardinal Wolsey Street. The Vision Controller – and, apparently, some random bloody kids who shouldn't have been up past their bedtime – could peep into her personal darkness.

She remembered Mimsy Mountmain.

Smile more, swish the cloak, don't be a monster.

'I promise to be mindful,' said Chrissie.

'You'll have to be,' said Anju. 'Surprises are coming. Don't be caught unprepared.'

Don't push Nelly into a bottomless well of darkness, she meant.

In Studio 9, Chrissie found Nina Ninian and Loulee talking about what to do with Chrissie's face. Tish looked on with pursed lips. She was a diehard about collaboration with other contestants. Viewing any overture with dire suspicion, she kept stepping in. Tish was sure Loulee and Nina were scheming to write something appalling on Chrissie's forehead in letters which would show up on-screen. A vote-loser like 'I Block Crocks' or 'Jesmond is Guilty'. Chrissie decided not to share with Tish what Anju had told her about some colour-blind children with overactive imaginations – or disturbingly accurate intuitions she'd be a fool to ignore.

Tish needed to calm down. She'd been noticed in the debut episode. A Peophole peeper edited a montage of her anxious expressions set to 'Yer Blues'. The public tagged her 'Worried Winifred', which Schilling quietly registered as a trade-name. Chrissie wasn't sure Lady Whatever needed a comedy companion but kept schtumm. Let Schilling and the Shadow Cabinet squabble about that.

Keeping up with backchatter gave Tish exponentially more to worry about. Not that anyone else on the programme had it easier. Only the Vision Controller could hold the big picture in his head and stay calm.

Other peripheral characters were getting attention. Hyperactive Ftatateeta and placid Tunno were noticed huddling with Eunice at the Tri-Lion. There was talk of setting the trio up as a group when Pyro Pixie was knocked out of *Crew Selection*. Bruno Brookes, marriage on the rocks, made a play to get back with Alexandra Beach for career-boosting exposure. Whenever he came within a hundred yards of Weather Girl, angry clouds gathered – even indoors. If Bruno showed up on the programme, it would be as a soggy spectator, permanently beyond the Red Rope.

The break-out non-contestant of Episode One was Eric the Engineer from the Viper Strike maintenance crew. His catchphrase 'what idiot did that?' was already on badges and teapots. Comedians used it as a punchline. Peophole jokers cut together clips of collapsing buildings, exploding blancmange and Lovely Rita's dress falling off at Ascot with Eric exclaiming 'what idiot did that?' over and over.

Chrissie didn't need enlightened abilities to notice the mood changing.

Now the programme was running, everyone was *on* all the time.

Chrissie's confidence was shaky. The whole thing seemed soapier every day. She wasn't heiress of a cloak legacy. She was the next Boring Bosun. The Serious Channel, seething over Red-Tel's ratings, hosted a debate about whether it was appropriate to select a national hero by polling the 'Jonty to Jupiter' electorate. The verdict was heavily against. A 'Cloaks not Jokes' movement started. That was on merch too. Red-Tel got a tithe from doing down its own show.

The 'Cloaks not Jokes' johnnies had a point, Chrissie reckoned.

From Devil's Dyke, she knew how serious cloakery could get.

People died.

If the Sixths were ever all that stood between England and an invasion of dinosaur Nazis, London might well be crushed under scaly jackboots.

Episode Two would roll on.

LOULEE IN STUDIO 9

THE VERPETTE IN CHRISSIE'S ROOM HAD PICKED UP Eleanor's bogeyman terrors and believed a green ninja was working against Christine Chambers. Vile plans were afoot to undermine the client. Tish, trade-name Worried Winifred, openly suspected Loulee was the covert cutthroat behind an anti-Shade campaign.

Tish glared at Loulee whenever she came near.

Ghosts suggested Tish must have weapons in her big bag. It'd make sense to cripple her before she got so jittery she pre-emptively stabbed, shot or gassed Loulee. The ghosts were spoiling for a scrap.

It would be larfs to swap sleeveless jacket for green bodystocking and slide along the wall of the studio to freak out Worried Winifred. Via ghosts, Loulee could access a range of ninjutsu skills. Okiyo Kyuketsuki, assassin for the Tokugawa Shogunate, ate ninjas for breakfast. Mostly, she poisoned tea and served death in elaborate ceremonies which lasted days. She was a dab hand with the throwing star and once opened a rebel lord's throat with a razor fan during a formal dance. Okiyo wound up throttled, drowned and fed to crabs, so she had a lot of anger to work off.

As Loulee walked over to Chrissie's corner, Tish's hand went into her bag. A neck-pulse marked the spot Okiyo would strike in a killing chop. Loulee wiggled her fingers as if trying to get rid of writers' cramp. You couldn't do karate with wiggly fingers.

Other ghosts whispered that it was a bad idea to let Okiyo out often. Loulee agreed. The ninja nobbler itched to shave Loulee's eyebrows and stain her teeth black, as high-born ladies did during the Tokugawa Shogunate (1603–1868). That eerie visual would frighten the taxpayers. Not gear. Not aces. Not peach.

Presently, it wasn't Loulee's face under discussion but Chrissie's.

'Nina wants to spray fake tan on me,' Chrissie told Loulee.

'I did *not* say that,' said Nina Ninian.

'Highlight my natural liquid honey skin tone, then.'

'Less inaccurate.'

Nina showed her forearm, striped with samples of pancake from pale to purple.

'Should I pick one?' Chrissie asked.

Tish clicked with her Vone and sent a blurt.

'What are you doing, Laeticia?' said Loulee.

'Convening a focus group?' suggested Nina.

'Sharing with Christine's Room,' said Tish. 'The Loop this has to be kept in.'

'My skin is a sensitive subject, apparently,' said Chrissie.

'You've not done the temple-shave for a few days,' said Loulee.

'The wig covers your brilliant work,' said Chrissie.

Loulee thumb-pointed to a fly-eye.

'You're on this show with and without the wig.'

'Not sure I want to be seen shaving. I always nick myself.'

'"What idiot did that?"'

'Exactly.'

Chrissie put the wig on. Nina settled it. Tish suggested an adjustment and was ignored. Then Loulee put in the hairpins so it was done properly.

Tish couldn't say whether she liked it. She'd need to confer with the Room.

Loulee still resisted putting this kind of care into her own visual.

Maybe chalk-white face with smears of greasepaint in the middle of her forehead and jet-black teeth wasn't a *terrible* idea?

Her trade-name could be Yūrei Rantan No On'nanoko. Ghost Lantern Girl. No one would vote for that.

She had a secret way through the ordeal of *Crew Selection*.

She didn't want to win. It would, in fact, be a hassle if she did.

Of course, she had to beat Hereward. In all likelihood, she'd already knocked him out of the running with help from Eric the Engineer. Wherever Viper Strike struck, someone said 'what idiot did that?' An unintended consequence was that clever money shifted to Loulee. There was a risk that she might win without trying. Obviously not caring polled well with the tune-in-drunk-for-a-larf segment of the audience. Flaming Nora! She was courting the McDribblefart vote!

Withal, she had to watch out for Asmida binti Geoffrey Reynolds.

Okiyo Kyuketsuki could pin a snake to a dartboard with a throwing star at eighty paces. But Loulee's new nemesis was likely to slide up from behind.

'Don't look now, Louls but the fly-eyes are buzzing this waywards...'

Asmida was in the studio, modelling a fur coat hacked off something endangered and a Union Jack knit cap.

Garter Snake wanted a rematch with Girly Dervish.

As a cutthroat, Asmida was a toughie. It took Flat Cat to beat her. She'd won dozens of scraps but her loss to Loulee was all over Peophole.

Loulee had won every scrap she'd been in – all one of it.

She could let Okiyo, Yvyra or Oghulqaimish loose on Asmida and the odds wouldn't be bad – though not necessarily in her favour. Okiyo, for instance, got her best results by taking targets by surprise. She'd rather poison a formidable opponent than cross swords. Besides being illegal even under the loose rules of *Crew Selection*, it might not work. The toxic doxy was immune to her own venom.

Snake eyes flashed at Loulee.

Chrissie laid a hand on her shoulder.

'Say the word and I'll put the lights out.'

'Thanks but we might as well get it over with. She's not going to let up, is she?'

'She's not a pushover like Hereward,' said Chrissie.

'Newsflash – I know.'

Garter Snake had an entourage. Six young men in tight, scale-patterned t-shirts and headscarves. They might not always be the same six. Asmida had a pool of flunkies, fans and terrified tagalongs – rotating them so each remained anonymous. After Episode One, contestants cottoned on that they could be upstaged by their Rooms. Ftatatunno and Eric the Engineer polled better than Pyro Pixie and Wonky Strike. Eunice didn't mind. Hereward very much did. Worried Winifred, at least, was no threat to Chrissie. She was comedy relief in a show which was farcical enough as it was.

'Oh, Arssssse,' hissed Asmida.

'My dance card is full,' Loulee said. 'But I'll make room for you. Just you, me, the music... and something with a bit of an *edge* to it...'

She unpinned a Sheriff star – grappled from a machine in a Skegness arcade last bank holiday – from her lapel and gave it the proper Okiyo flick. It whizzed past Asmida's face and bounced off the scarved head of one of her young men. If Loulee had sharpened the tin toy, it'd have stuck in.

Memo to self: get real *shuriken* and fix them to her jacket. Cutthroats would mistake them for flair until it was too late.

With a shrug which rippled down her whole body, Asmida shucked her fur. It fell like shed skin. Two of her young men bumped heads trying to pick up the coat.

Whenever Garter Snake did the stripper shoulders move, fly-eyes focused on her shiny pale green belly, corded with muscle and glistening with product (snake oil?). Each time, her football shorts were cut higher on the hip. The Union Jack bustier shrank too. By Episode Six, *Crew Selection* would have to go out after the watershed.

Asmida's body wavered from side to side while her head stayed in place.

Oghulqaimish identified seven objects within reach usable as edged weapons.

Chrissie spoke up and got in the way.

'Louls, Asmida, park this,' she said.

Fly-eyes focused on Lady Shade.

'We need to learn not to scrap with each other,' she said.

'Plenty out there have problems with us. Can we not get on for five minutes without blood on the floor?'

Honestly, Loulee thought, *no*.

Asmida shrugged and held up her hands as if she hadn't started it...

The moment held. Chrissie was aces on camera, earning brownie points. Mediation, leadership, focus. The Shadow Cabinet was getting into Chrissie's mind.

Loulee's hackles raised. Ghosts did not approve of her backing down.

Ghosts did not understand being on television. They were invisible to anyone who hadn't found the Lantern in their cupboard... or, at most, flickered across the corner of the eye of folk enlightened enough to be attuned to the spirit. Eleanor Wynter, hardly anyone's idea of sensitive, for instance. Sometimes, Nelly's eye was drawn to an empty space where a ghost was standing. It could be how she came by her ninja fixation.

The doors of Studio 9 opened as if they'd been kicked in. A stubble-headed, barrel-chested, beef-faced middle-aged man barged in. Across the front of his white t-shirt was written 'Geoff Reynolds Goods Yard' in Union Jack lettering. A white domino made his face look even redder. If the mask was a disguise, he probably shouldn't advertise his name and business on his chest.

'Who's pickin' on my girl?' he bellowed.

He had a new tattoo of a coiled cobra on his meaty upper arm, covered in glistening gel.

Asmida's dad.

Garter Snake almost curled up into a ball. Taller than Loulee or Chrissie, she shrank to smaller than a short arse. Loulee hadn't known reptiles could blush. Liverish lines burned on her face, grouting between her usually seamless scales.

'*Perseten dengen ayah!*' muttered Asmida.

Thanks to the ghost of explorer Bryndis Minervudóttir – fluent in forty-six languages with a working knowledge of about a hundred others including dialects, argots and slangs – Loulee knew exactly what Asmida binti Geoffrey Reynolds said to Geoffrey Reynolds bappa Asmida. She trusted the compliance team at Red-Tel included a Malay linguist who'd know to bleep it out for broadcast.

Loulee, Chrissie and everyone else found pressing matters which needed seeing to – wardrobe adjustments to make, Peophole Purviews to dial, letters to stick stamps on.

The Reynolds reunion was captured on video from half a dozen angles.

Unless Hereward flew into the Post Office Tower, this was going to be the standout clip of *Crew Selection: The Splendid Sixth* Episode Two.

ASMIDA BINTI GEOFFREY REYNOLDS – GARTER SNAKE

'GIVEN A CHOICE, I WOULDN'T GO AROUND WITH "daughter of Geoffrey Reynolds" as a surname. But it's on my birth certificate, vaccination records and the register of every school, prison or secure unit I've been in. For most of my life, I could pass Geoff Reynolds in the street and not recognise him. Which was all right by me.

'When he brought Mum over from Borneo – after writing off for a wife in a magazine offer – he congratulated himself for not being colour-prejudiced. In his Goods Yard, he had all sorts under him from all over the place. His best mate was "Chocky Brown". He never noticed how much Renard Breton – trade-name Samedi Nuit – hated being called "Chocky Brown". Still, he loves a goat curry does Geoffrey Reynolds, provided it comes with chips. When I came out green he found there were limits to tolerance. I was born in a transparent, dissolving egg-sac – with brothers and sisters who didn't survive. I ate them in the womb.

'The last time I saw Dad before this week was my first court appearance. I was twelve and had set fire to the Yard. My venom sacs hadn't matured. I wasn't lucky like Eunice Uglow. I couldn't just think up a firestorm. So I spilled half a dozen bottles of butane. Someone had absent-mindedly parked a lorry-load of lighter fluid in the Yard while the price went up. It was raining so the stuff didn't burn well. A shed caught fire but that was the extent of it. I'd have got off with a belting, only some dozer was dossing in the shed. He wasn't even burned much but... Well, it was taken seriously. Dad sat at the back of the court with a face like a broken toe. His brief said he'd taken more safety precautions than his insurance company could ask for. There was no accounting for the mischief in me. A *naga* is a wicked serpent spirit and that's how I was born. They summonsed a hoodoo expert – Magic Bloody Iona – to explain it. The way it was put, I was lucky not to be sent to a zoo or put down like a sheep-worrying dog.

'After Aylesbury – Borstal for Girls – everything else was a Pontins Holiday Camp... including the Wavy Lines corridor at Devil's Dyke. The Aylesbury uniform is pinafores and mob caps, like an old-time servant girl. They use disciplinary devices like the scold's bridle and the stand-up-straight corset. I do not naturally stand up straight. I bend.

'Mum visited me in prison and kept me up to date on Dad. Then she went home. I don't blame her. With the money from *Crew Selection,* I'll go to Borneo too. I've never been east of Amsterdam and I only went there to nick a painting for Lord Adder, who you shouldn't get me started on or we'll be here all day and I'm *peckissssh.*

'Suddenly, it's turned out I'm British after all. God Save Her Maj QV2... Jam and Jerusalem and muffins for tea with the crusts cut off. If I'd known that all it took was a flag halter I'd have run up the Union Jack years ago. The cloak bit. I quite fancy being a Splendid. Though there are drawbacks. It turns out I'm related to many, many people I'd never heard from previously. Most of 'em are temporarily short of funds and reckon I'm the soft touch to help out with a postal order. Do me a favour. Where were they all those visitors' days at Aylesbury and Devil's Dyke?

'You know, I tell a lie about Dad.

'I did see him between then and now. *Once.* And the bleeder saw me too. I was in a glass cage at Low Ceilings, Little Madam's club in Beak Street. Yes, the place where that bloke got topped that time and they never found the head. Which was well after I was gone so no need to reopen the file. Dad was in with some district councillors from the Forest of Birmingham... showing flash, buying rounds, laying on the goose-grease. It was some bit of business with the Yard. Protected trees cut down for timber. Not even worth calling a fiddle. Dad's not a cutthroat in that sense. He barely makes ha'pennies with his tickles. That night, he lays a wedge of tenners on the counter to buy booth dances for the Brummies. He looks down the line, clocks me straight off and whispers to Madam to keep me away from the punters. I allow that I might have hissed and flicked the tongue at him.

'He was bee-lucky not to get taken out the back and bent over the bins like Johnny Sans Bonce. Madam must have been feeling soft that evening. I got early cocoa while revels proceeded in the booths, presided over by Geoff Largesse Reynolds. A fine time was had by all. As were the blokes from Brum. Cashing up, Madam discovered Dad's wedge was tenners top and bottom with a stuffing of luncheon vouchers in the middle. He doesn't know it but I saved his Yard from a proper, professional torch job. Little Madam found me useful – and not just for the dancing, which I did mostly to get the kinks out of my spine. If you X-ray my legs and arms, you see what look like vertebrae instead of long bones. Lots of cartilage. I can get in and out through gaps the Red Rope think too small to bother putting alarmed grilles over.

'Mum told me I was never far from Dad's thoughts. When I was in the news with the Great British Snake-Off, he pitched telly channels on a fly-eye documentary about being the honest, hard-working father of a notorious cutthroat. He made a sample pilot, mostly him doing the round of pubs and clubs with a stand-up comic routine about... Well, about being the dad of a danger to society. He dubbed in laughter from dead people. Even then it didn't sell. It's on Peophole.

'So that was it for family ties. I had other fish to fondue – Lord Adder, the Scream Team. Then Flat Cat gave me a pasting, the wretch. I had a long stretch in Devil's Dyke to look forward to.

'When the Vision Controller said he could get me ticket-of-leave, I saw opportunities. Red-Tel came up with this Garter Snake rigmarole, which I took to from the first. I was fed up with Wavy Lines jammies. And there is, of course, the money. Talk about fiddles.

'But I knew who'd crawl out again...

'So here we are.

'I should have changed my name by deed poll to Asmida Pembunakapakbapa or Asmida Anakperempuantiadasiapa but didn't get round to it. So Geoffrey Reynolds is back. In the running for Father of the Fortnight.

'Honestly, I could spit.'

GEOFFREY REYNOLDS – WHITE VAN MAN

'LOOK, LOVE, IT'S NOT EVEN A CONTEST.

'My girl will win. No arguments. Asmi above all. Asmi all the way. I'll take any odds, any bet you like. Here, on the table. Know what those are? Only the keys to the *original* White Van. With "Geoff Reynolds Goods Yard" on the side. A Moskevitch 434, from Satra Motors of Byfleet. Laminated windscreen, two-speed wipers, radiator blind and reversing lamp included as standard features. Beauty, that van. Empire-builder. And I'm prepared to put the 434 up against whatever you like because I know how it'll turn out. Asmi is the Sixth. That's all they'll sing.

'She'll do Streatham proud. All the blokes and betties at the Yard back her all the way. To the bristles, they say. My girl will win... for Britain. Them others better watch their backs, is all I'm saying. It won't be pretty. It'll be brutal. She's always been on her way to the top, that one.'

ELEANOR AND THE SIXTHS

RED-TEL CONSIDERED RECREATING THE SPLENDIDS' Hallowed Hall in Studio 9 but a focus group decided the real thing was boring. Its visual was like any other boardroom. *Crew Selection* needed a more convincing Top Cloak Headquarters. In place of the Tri-Lion's ergonomic chairs and quietly costly landscapes, the Half-Hallowed Hall used leftovers from the space fiction variety series *Commander Weirdo's Rockin' Rocketship Revue*. Think Box cabinets decorated with dials and tape spools. Model rockets and solar system mobiles. If nothing was happening, Camera Clare played with distorting lenses and got low-angle shots of stuffed aliens.

One wall was draped with green fabric which gave Eleanor the abdabs. The cloth stood in for a panoramic window. When the programme went out, viewers saw a dramatic skyline of fog-shrouded London. In the studio, it was a curtain of evil emerald. She was in on some secret surprises but knew script pages were routinely withheld from her. GEIST had spies in the studio. She didn't trust anyone. Except Garnet Graill. His self-interest was so naked he was reliable. He'd always openly to do what was best for himself. Refreshing amid so much smiling duplicity.

Viper Strike was a production headache. The gargantuabot stood eighteen feet tall. If Clare included its face-screen in shot she couldn't miss showing the untidy mess of lighting rig and the top edge of the set walls. Giving the box kite a giant chair would look silly so it ape-crouched like a big, angry fridge. The repaired face-screen looped a clip of Jackson-Walker's audition tape. Eleanor doubted the contestant would be let near the controls again.

The original idea was that Jackson-Walker would sit at the table with the five women. He was in the competition. The contraption was classified as equipment. But bolus of the week was laying low since 'what idiot did this?' caught fire on the Personals. Ling must be proud of herself.

She was the oddest contestant – no visible Room, too many shadows. An agent of GEIST? One of the Sixths probably was.

Anjulie Glas, the Arse Prod, had orders from the Vision Controller to bring Jackson-Walker back into the fold. It was too early to lose him. He was supposed to be the mums' favourite and a sop to blokes uneasy with the idea of a woman – *any* woman – turning on the rain or beating up crocks. Right now, Jackson-Walker's seat was filled by Eric 'What Idiot Did This?' the Engineer.

Glas was meeting Jackson-Walker's parents to discuss the return of the authentic idiot to the programme. The issue had to be sorted before Red-Tel could make headway on Episode Two.

The five Sixths – the women – who'd turned up for work on time lounged around a mock-up of the Star Table. They straightened and smiled when Sixth Senses told them Garnet was aiming a camera their way. He snapped candids from shadows. He took more clicks of Chambers than the others, though the tabs were mad for Garter Snake glammies. So Eleanor knew where *his* vote was going.

Chambers hid behind Spex when the lights were on. She'd changed since Devil's Dyke. Sometimes, if looked at for a moment without focusing, Chambers was a column of black flame with violet crackles. Eleanor had told Garnet *and* Clare this but they'd not caught the effect on click or clip. It was only visible to the naked eye. And seemingly only her naked eye.

Alexandra Beach was in a different class. Her newly serious attitude went with established serious abilities. She didn't bang on about sponsorships any more, which sent profits up. The soft sell was keyed to a more monied demographic. Garter Snake was the biggest look-at-*meee* mary in an assortment of attention hogs. She was so upfront about her cutthroat record she couldn't be the GEIST mole. That didn't mean she wouldn't turn nasty if the wind changed.

The Draycott's drips – Chambers, Ling, Uglow – gossed and giggled together. A teacher would separate them but this wasn't a classroom. Jah was under orders to let the trio get comfortable as a girly gang before pitting them against each other. Ratings rose when friends fell out.

The production team had reviewed all the previous series of *Crew Selection – Royal Yacht, Eurovision, Mountain Rescue, Windmill Girls, Jupiter Mission*. Lessons were learned about what worked and what didn't. Don Loki Baird clued them in on the secret – 'it doesn't matter who wins, it matters who watches'.

Baird was never on camera. Jah and Glas might be glimpsed on B-roll. Some alfs and berts snuck in view if they could get away with it. But Eleanor was centre screen. Not a contestant but in the game. No one told her but she knew bonus points were awarded for doing her damage. Which was why she looked out for ninjas. If flan-flingers could get past the Red Rope, green garrotters had horrifyingly easy access.

If she got nobbled in Episode Four, then Episode Five would be about the Sixths avenging her. Eleanor might bravely appear with strategic bandages to host the big vote in Episode Six. Equally, she might not. Ivan Cornish was available. Garnet's smile might be viewer friendly. Glas could step in at a pinch – the jagged white streak in her black hair was a strong visual. Eleanor had seen Garnet and Glas in earnest huddles with higher-ups, which set her own Sixth Sense a-tingle. Dot Schilling might sign off on sidelining a banner client in a real coma. As a breathing prop on *VIP Ward* she'd be less trouble.

This was not how the story would go if Eleanor had anything to say about it. But now the programme was actually on the box, *Crew Selection* took on its own life.

In his post-mortem on Episode One, the Vision Controller flagged the bright sparks. So far, only two competitors registered as positives. Reynolds and Ling. Jackson-Walker registered but not in a way which did him favours. Weather Girl brought the ice but Ling felled the gargantuabot with a 'look behind you' trick – very televisual, unlike creeping frost on off-camera circuit boards. Reynolds was showy and got her kit semi-off at the drop of a hat. According to spotty researchers, she was a massive presence in the Smut Hutch. Clips from the Nipplesome Naga's booth-dancing days got endless redials. Clicks with superimposed modesty bars ran daily in the *Nova*.

Would Reynolds' ratings hold after Episode Two?

This week, viewers would meet her father, who stood up for his daughter by getting between her and the camera. Geoff Reynolds handed out business cards at all opportunities. Eleanor had thrown away three. She knew his type. He wanted to be on the telly. He told himself it was about supporting family or drumming up trade but the need was more basic – to be seen, to be on the show, to be a face not a face in the crowd. She'd had a touch of his madness before she learned what ought to have been obvious – the wheel *always* turned. Geoff was better at getting past security than Sandii Beach's shut-out-in-the-rain ex. The Red Rope had confidential instructions not to make it too difficult for the father of the freak to crash the set. His effect was instant and obvious. At some point, his daughter would whip off her patriotic bra and strangle him with it.

Conflict. Comeuppance.

Great telly.

The face-clip on the gargantuabot was disrupted. The screen showed static.

Hereward Jackson-Walker entered the Half-Hallowed Hall, escorted by a lawyer in a Savile Row three-piece and a scientist in British RoboDynamics overalls. Jackson-Walker's silver spacesuit was studded with mo-cap golfballs and slashed to the waist. That tall redhead who alfed and berted for Glas glided along several paces behind him. The (very rich) parents had been reminded of contractual obligations. The (very idiot) son was doing what he was told. He might even get sympathy votes.

'*Vy-purrr stry-yike*,' sounded – a new, less abrasive arrangement.

Eric scooted out of the chair and Jackson-Walker sat between his new best enemies, Ling and Beach. If he was uncomfortable, you couldn't tell. At the lawyer's nod, he arranged his mouth into an adorable half-smile, half-pout. The fuzz on the box kite screen cleared to show the same living expression, three times life size. His moist eyes might suggest a puppy. Or jab-tears.

Adrian Jah gave Eleanor a count to an entrance.

Time to spring the bad news on the Sixths.

She strode onto the set, followed by Camera Clare. With the heat of the lights on her face, Eleanor came to life. It was like hearing applause. The curtain was up. The show was on. She didn't need jabs.

Several contestants had brought circus flyers with them. They should all have received one. Special delivery.

UPSIDE-DOWN GONK'S CIRCUS
IS COMING FOR YOU!

See the PUNCH AND JUDY MAN! See the
BEE-YOU-TIFUL LADY!
Hear the MUSIC MACHINE! Feel the GRIP of the
STRONG MAN! Dice with SEVEN WAYS TO DEATH!

FUN for CHILDREN OF ALL AGES.
ROLL UP ROLL UP FOR THE MYSTERY FAIR.
***Being for the Benefit of* MAJOR WOOD.**

Uglow's poster had burned fingermarks.

'I love circuses,' she said to Ling and Chambers. 'We should dress as clowns and go.'

'I hate clowns,' said Garter Snake – who'd torn her flyer in half.

'Aren't circuses supposed to come *to* places rather than *for* people?' said Chambers. 'And look at the pictures.'

The flyer was illustrated with porcelain baby-doll faces – all cracked, most with missing eyes or noses, one upside-down.

'They aren't selling this to me as fun for children of my age,' said Chambers.

Eleanor sat. The Star Table was round – with a taller seat for the host. A constellation was etched on the surface. Clare did a full circle to get everyone's faces in.

'This is a trap,' said Ling, holding up her flyer.

'Yes,' said Eleanor, twiddling knobs which did nothing while the big screen warmed up to show a *Crew Selection* title card. Script scrolled across a screen in Eleanor's placemat. Anything important to the story was triple underlined in red. Otherwise, she could be herself.

Eleanor clicked her fingers and the title card was replaced by Inspector Hawkshaw. A third of the series budget was contributed by the Information Retrieval service on condition their mascot be a regular feature. In ad break bumpers, Inspector Hawkshaw – a trenchcoat with an eye in a magnifying glass for a head – was tagged 'the Splendid Seventh?' Martin Masters would only sign off on that if there was a question mark.

'Hi, Nelly,' said the Inspector.

That hadn't been in rehearsal!

'Glad to see you're keeping an eye out, Inspector,' she came back.

The magnifying glass winked. Jah did the voice by talking into a widget. The squawkprint was Sergeant Bert from early episodes of *Dosson of Dark Green*.

'You've all heard from Upside-Down Gonk's Circus,' Eleanor said.

The poster, enlarged, filled the big screen.

'Pay attention, Sixths,' said Eleanor. 'What do you see here?'

'A depressing night out,' said Ling.

'"Fun for children of all ages",' said Uglow.

'Dolls,' said Chambers. '*Broken* Dolls.'

Lady Shade was not slow.

'A familiar name in the annals of crime,' said Eleanor. 'Inspector, could you enlighten us...'

A text piece popped up on screen, illustrated by clicks and clips. The Broken Doll was a long-established brand in cutthroatery, adopted by individuals and groups over the years. A Regency highwayman... A Victorian adventurer... A Liverpool protection mob between the wars... At least two homicidal maniacs... The triple-jointed art critic-thief who set fire to all those L.S. Lowrys... A gangcult who staged smash-ins at the Stock Exchange and the Albert Hall. Always with variations on the visual: a porcelain face with a crack across it, sometimes with a missing glass eye, sometimes with Cupid's bow lips.

'Underworld sources tell us we're dealing with a cutthroat krewe,' said Jah through Hawkshaw. 'The New Broken Dolls. Here are faces and names to start you off...'

A clip of the crowds at the Tri-Lion last week. A thin, roofed tent of striped canvas – a framework costume on a wiry entertainer? Hand-puppets performed against a black velvet backdrop. A crocodile chewed a policeman's head. Eleanor shuddered, remembering this individual at Sweeney Todd's.

'Mr Swizzle...'

'The Punch and Judy Man,' said Uglow, pointing to the flyer.

Clips of Blackpool Tower collapsing like a condemned factory chimney... Co-ordinated explosions blowing out the windows of arcades... Screaming children fleeing across the beach.

'We all remember *that* bank holiday,' said Eleanor. 'Mr Swizzle is *still* wanted for questioning in connection with the tidal wave of terror. The council took away his performers' licence and – it seems – he took away their tourist trade.'

A click of a real doll. No, a real person with a face like a doll. A thin blonde in a police mug shot, beehive taller than the measuring scale on the wall.

A blurry clip, taken outside the Design Centre by a civilian with a Vone, of Poltergirl floating. Telekineticised rubbish bins emptied on the blonde, who was wearing a stripy jersey, eyemask and oversized black flat cap. An Up to No Good outfit if ever there was one.

'The Bee-you-tiful Lady,' said Uglow.

'She's no lady,' said Beach. 'That's Cyndi Doll.'

Garter Snake hissed. Asmida had worked with Cyndi in the Low Ceiling Club. They hadn't got on. When Little Madam found out Cyndi was skimming the take, she set the Nasty Naga on her. That bit of story so far had commended Cyndi to the Vision Controller as New Broken Doll material.

'Cynthia Deane Dolan,' said Hawkshaw. 'A dangerous woman. Holloway couldn't hold her.'

She hadn't been a fit for the Low Ceiling Club either.

A security-eyestalk clip from a post office. A lout in an ill-fitting drab olive uniform was weighed down with guns, grenades and knives. He sprayed the ceiling with a stutter of bullets, raining plaster on customers and clerks. He shot out the camera.

'Ah, Seven Ways to Death?' suggested Chambers.

'Johnnie Seven,' said Hawkshaw. 'The One Man Arsenal.'

'That leaves the Strong Man and the Music Machine,' said Uglow, who liked this game because she was aces at it.

'Ashton Dakin and Tarquin Tadcaster,' said Eleanor. 'Kung Fu Grip and Juke Box Jerry. Long criminal records but not exactly Scotland Yard's highest priority. Your basic heft. Fetch, carry, and hold the jewellery shop manager down while a nastier throat turns the thumbscrew to get the combination. The Ringmaster is more interesting.'

The next clip was a classic.

Upside-Down Gonk screeching as he leaped about an open-air playground – hanging from climbing frames, slipping down a blood-slick slide – while tossing sticky wads at police constables. The gum ate through blue serge and raised purple welts. The inverted smile in the felt face was a crescent of toothy malice. Production of *Floppit Funnies* paused when Boyd Waylo popped the clip on the *Cutting Commentator* Purview.

'Upside-Down Gonk,' said Hawkshaw. 'The Floppit who flipped.'

'I understand these New Broken Dolls are cutthroats,' said Chambers. 'But why is the circus coming for us? The threat is right there in the headline. I mean, we're freshers. We haven't had time to annoy anyone enough to have arch-nemeses.'

Several Sixths laughed at that.

'I mean, don't this shower have cloaks they'd prefer to pick scraps with? Poltergirl or Night Mist? Shouldn't they be sending "I'm coming for you" threats to the British Lions?'

'We're getting to that,' said Eleanor. 'Inspector...'

Fly-eye footage showed a building in Farringdon. Daytime. A busy street. People passing by. Businesses open. Bustle and chatter.

'This is surveillance of suspects Major Wood and Cyndi Dolan,' said Hawkshaw.

Red circles went round blurry heads. Hunching over an outside table at a Chauncey Chee, Cyndi was obvious by her extra height. Wood was out of focus on the other side of the street.

'Remember "Being for the Benefit of MAJOR WOOD"?' said Eleanor. 'This is him. Another career cutthroat. A toy soldier. As any of you who have brothers know, toy soldiers get broken.'

The little man with the moustached mask was talking with a woman in a trouser suit.

'That is Property Close, an unethical estate agent.'

'Is there any other kind?' asked Ling, getting smirks.

'Case specialises in renting out rookeries,' said Eleanor. 'You know what I mean. Cutthroat cottages. Derelict reptile house with facilities for a dropaway hatch over the crocodile pit. Replica Aztec step-pyramid with excellent parking and disabled access in Dalston. She's showing the New Broken Dolls the Human Figure Works in Cowcross Street. They're looking for a lair...'

'Isn't this a bit too afternoon home make-over programme for us?' ventured Beach.

'Wait for it,' said Eleanor.

Jackson-Walker knew what was coming. He looked at the table as if searching for a particular star in the etched constellation.

Smoke trails streaked into view and the Human Figure Works was blotted out in a flash which broke up the image. The blast knocked the fly-eye out of position.

The spinning picture froze...

There was Viper Strike, missile ports open, Jackson-Walker's blown-up face showing an aggressive grin.

The clip moved again. The building in flames... Major Wood flat on the pavement... injured civs crawling away... windows broken on both sides of the street ... sirens and sobbing and fire crackle... Cyndi looking up, taking off her shades to show eyes gleaming with an intent the techs hadn't needed to animate. She might as well have shook her fist and shouted 'we will be avenged!'

The Sixths understood a scrap had been picked.

With dangerous people. Real throats, not folk who got their slots by popular vote after capering on a game show. The Sixths didn't know their nemeses were pre-selected by the Vision Controller. The throats from Todd's were supposed to be softies, so far as crims went. Eleanor wondered whether wires were crossed. The more she learned about the New Broken Dolls, the less soft they seemed. The Vision Controller might be hoping for blood on the floor to boost ratings. How much bigger than *Jupiter Mission* would this series of *Crew Selection* be if a contestant or two got killed? If not a contestant, then someone else on the programme – Geoff Reynolds, that drip who alf and berted for Chambers, the podgy lad who mooned about Pyro Pixie?

Or the front woman?

Eleanor should make a separate deal with the Red Rope for a protection detail. Or go off-books and hire her own heft. She couldn't trust the Red Rope, Red-Tel or Dot Schilling. They'd stake her out as ninja bait in a heartbeat.

The screen showed the New Broken Doll line-up... arrest photos, blurry captures, charge sheets. Silent footage of the Human Figure Works on fire.

Everyone looked at Jackson-Walker, who'd started something they now had to finish before it finished them.

Someone had to say it.

Several of them did.

'What idiot did that?'

CHRISTINE AT THE STAR TABLE

HEREWARD DIDN'T RESPOND TO THE CLIP. HIS Marquiss Management handler had told him talking spoiled his trademark pout-smile (the schoolgirls' bedroom poster visual) so he should avoid verbals. Chrissie suspected this was a tactful way of delaying the moment when viewers caught on to his depthless dimness.

Sinclair Oakes, the lawyer, did his best to calm the situation. He wasn't smooth enough to stop Garter Snake from playing to the rear stalls.

'Cyndi *Doll*,' she said. 'Mr *Swizzle*! Even Johnnie Flamin' *Seven*! Do you have any *idea* what those throats are capable of? I vote we shove Wonder Wanker in the street in just his y-fronts and let him take his chances with the Revenge Squad.'

Hereward's lower lip wobbled.

'I'd advise against that,' said Oakes. 'Red-Tel has a duty of care.'

'Red-Tel didn't pick a scrap with lethal maniacs,' said Weather Girl. 'This idiot did.'

'Now you've opened that box,' said Oakes, 'let's address it.'

He handed out five identical envelopes. Loulee opened hers and laughed.

'We're enjoined to refrain from using the word "idiot" in

a derogatory fashion with regards to the client, Hereward Jackson-Walker trade-name Verp Strike...'

'"Viper Strike,"' said Hereward, glumly.

'... especially in the phrase "what idiot did that" or variations thereof.'

'Like "what idiot did *thisssssss*?"' hissed Asmida.

'I imagine so,' said Loulee. 'Synonyms for "idiot" like "moron", "clot", "cretin", "blockhead", "lackwit" – Shakespearean that – or "fool" are likewise discouraged, under pain of suit for libel for... Ah, get this... "Unfair and discriminatory practices with a tendency to undermine the business endeavours of the client". So, in essence, anyone who tries to win this contest is being mean to precious Hereward, who is labouring under the disadvantage of... What? Being an *idiot*!'

'Shut it, Looby-Loo,' said Hereward.

Garter Snake tore her envelope in half without opening it.

Oakes gave her a replacement. She tore that too.

'You've received the injunction as a blurt on your Vones,' said the lawyer. 'Copies have gone to your representation.'

Camera Clare was on set, getting close-ups. Hereward automatically reassembled the pout-smile when he saw the red light on the camera. You could teach a dog to do that.

There were important questions he'd never answer on camera. As the first contestant to do something colossally stupid – if that was a legally permissible description – he was wary of punching himself in the face again.

After Episode One went out, Chrissie's Dark Vone rang with blurts from Vidar, Chell, Symon, Monica Maude and the All-Powerful Jupiter Boy. Even Polly O squirted an enigmatic rune. The Coterie abandoned the Viper Strike express and tried to climb aboard her puff-puff train. Hereward was hurt. He didn't understand friendship bestowed at the dictat of paid-for Polly O was provisional. Chrissie knew that if she took a flan to the face or made an unguarded comment about some post-crock gangcult, Coterie support would evaporise like Double-Quick Milquik.

'Don't you need permission from the Lord Mayor to shoot off rockets in a built-up area?' asked Eunice, looking at Hereward's lawyer. 'No one's ever explained to me what I can and cannot set fire to. And I'd like to know.'

'Your pyrokinesis brain-bump and a box of matches are legally the same thing,' said Loulee, with a slight Hungarian accent. 'Don't burn anything with one you wouldn't with the other.'

Eunice tilted her head as if she'd never thought of it that way.

'I'd... ah... concur,' said Oakes.

A penny dropped about Sinclair Oakes. Chrissie had seen him before.

He wasn't a lawyer. He was an actor who played lawyers. A semi-regular on *Letsby Avenue* as brief for mug of the week. He vanished from the serial after his agent put a 'for your consideration' Best Supporting Actor BAFTA ad in the trades without consulting Red-Tel. Goss was he'd been shoved through the same exit as Sparkling Eyes. Now he'd found a new gig. Still playing lawyer.

'Is the other fellow a real scientist?' Chrissie asked, surprising Oakes.

The chubby chappie in British RoboDynamics overalls was polishing Viper Strike's nacelles with an oily rag. He looked more like a boffin than Eric the Actual Engineer so he must be an actor. Chrissie had a flash visual of him with a third eye and a fishbowl helmet. Commander Weirdo from the short-lived, critically derided *Rockin' Rocketship Revue*. Had the Jackson-Walkers bought up all the discontinued Red-Tel contracts? She was offended they hadn't hired Perky Purkiss to be Hereward's minder.

More shouting and haranguing. Envelopes were brandished. One caught fire.

Chrissie wondered whether Eleanor Wynter would step in, then thought better. Nelly was hostess, not in charge. A zoo keeper, not one of the chimps. If orders came from the Control Room, she'd call the class to order... but with a row in progress, her job was to let Clare get it in the can.

Last time there was a scrap, Chrissie had got in the middle and cooled it down... but that was looking out for Loulee the way Loulee looked out for her. It played well, though. Maybe she should be peacemaker again, even if it meant speaking up for Hereward.

She thought too slow.

'Calm, please,' said Weather Girl, getting in there first.

A slight wind blew across the set. Chrissie felt it in her hair and on her face. Not a threat but a reminder.

The shouting stopped. Alexandra Beach was old – maybe thirty-two. Brown Owl in this troupe. She wasn't used to being taken seriously but the others listened to her. They were all often dismissed as dunces and duffers. Hereward wasn't the only one who resented that to the back teeth. If Weather Girl could grow up and get respect, so could anyone.

'If the grass is wet, there's no point arguing with the sky,' said Sandii. 'We have to adjust to things as they are. And plan for things as they will be.'

That was majorly gear. Chrissie wanted to whistle.

Not Dr Robot inspiring or Moonlight Flit cool – but good enough for now.

Was this the beginning of Weather Woman? Most of the Sixths were here to become names. Sandii Beach already was a name. What she wanted was to be in a different league division. *Real News*, not *Fun News*.

'We're in a scrap,' she said. 'Make no mistake about that. People could – people *will* – get hurt. We should think about this circus coming for us... and be ready to bring down the big top.'

Chrissie felt something scraping her knee. Under the table, Weather Girl was shoving her legal letter at Chrissie's lap.

She understood. Some things had to be communicated privately – not on camera or via a Vone which copied blurts and squirts to Anju the AP.

Chrissie eased back in her chair as if stretching and looked down.

Printed in smuts in small capital letters were clear instructions. Chrissie passed the envelope to Eunice, who'd pass to Asmida, who'd pass to Loulee. Concentrating particulate matter into words on paper wasn't among Weather Girl's publicly listed abilities. A hidden talent. Like Urban Fox's mind control. And Aunt Jas's languages.

'Garter Snake,' said Sandii, 'you know most about who we're up against...'

'What do you mean by that?'

Asmida's neck cobra coiled. Bringing up her cutthroat career got an instant reaction.

Though this was a cover for reading her instructions.

'That you're a Wavy Lines witch,' said Eunice.

'A lot you know, Lime Loser,' said Asmida.

An old-fashioned Devil's Dyke corridor spat!

Garter Snake threw the balled-up legal letter with Weather Girl's instructions at Pyro Pixie. It caught fire and ash fell. Evidence destroyed. Neat and tidy.

Everyone pushed chairs back and moved away from the Star Table.

Clare panned between Asmida and Eunice, who were clearing space for a scrap. Someone must be worrying how much of the set was fireproof. Would Nelly stop the row escalating? Of course not. There was chance of a to-do with hair-pulling, scratching, venom spittle and spontaneous combustion. The highest-rated *Crew Selection* episode ever was the French Pub Windmill Girl punch-up.

Chrissie remembered Eunice overdoing it as Claggart when Draycott's did an all-girl *Billy Budd* as school play. She was a better actress now. Maybe they had drama classes at Devil's Dyke.

Heat haze wavered between the scrapping Sixths. Asmida's head bobbed from side to side. Nictitating membranes blinked across her snake-slit pupils. How weird was that? What did the world look like to her?

While fly-eyes were on Asmida and Eunice, Chrissie quietly slipped round the table. Loulee already had a grip on Hereward's upper arm. Weather Girl stood up to cover Chrissie sliding behind her to grab Hereward's other arm.

'Now, now,' said Alexandra, conjuring a cloud of water droplets which reacted with the heat to fill the studio with thick, harmless hot mist.

Hereward thought better of squealing as Chrissie and Loulee walked him off the set. They hustled him into the Ladies. If there were cameras and microphones here, Red-Tel knew better than to broadcast footage from them. Fury directed at peepers would outweigh the value of anything they got. Unless it was really juicy.

To be on the safe side, Chrissie made the room much, much darker. Mirrors went black.

LOULEE QUESTIONS HEREWARD

'SO WHAT ARE YOU GOING TO DO,' HE ASKED, LOWER lip stuck out. 'Duff me up?'

'"Not the face, not the face!"' said Loulee

'I do *not* sound like that.'

'Not in your head you don't.'

No one sounded quite right in the Ladies. Chrissie's shroud of darkness didn't only affect light. It did weird things to background noise. Even the pee-and-perfume pong was different. A whiff of brimstone.

Loulee would worry about that later.

Enyedi Boglárka had nineteenth century ideas about uncooperative witnesses. Hereward's brief would object to persuasions applied to his client involving candle flame and paprika.

'We're not going to hurt you,' said Chrissie. 'We need to talk.'

Hereward's panic was as one-sided as his smile. Was half his face frozen from work done on his eye-twitch? If so, the surgery didn't help. He blinked like a broken traffic light.

'I didn't do anything,' he said. 'Not anything wrong. We're cloaks. We fight crime. Viper Strike *strikes*.'

He looked at Loulee as if expecting to be slapped.

She stroked the frozen side of his face. He flinched.

'It wasn't my idea,' he insisted.

'Nothing ever is, is it?' said Loulee.

'That's not fair.'

'Maybe not,' said Chrissie, reasonably. 'Talk us through it, Hereward. From before *Crew Selection*. When did Viper Strike start?'

'When I was eight.'

Loulee and Chrissie looked at each other. They hoped Garter Snake and Pyro Pixie could keep up the mock scrap – which could turn into a real scrap if tempers got misplaced – long enough for them to get the whole story.

'It was Christmas...'

'*A Császár nevében*,' swore Boglárka... In the name of the Emperor!

The ghost lawyer recognised the start of a shaggy dog story.

'You know some Christmases a new toy is suddenly popular?' said Hereward. 'A playground craze or telly advert sets it off. All kids want the same present. But they've not made enough, so parents get into scraps in Hamley's or go to the black market for imitations made in Hong Kong.'

'Like the Floppit Flea Circus,' said Chrissie.

'Or the Double Deckers Bus,' said Loulee.

'Yes but not those. That Christmas, it was the Schloup. Remember the Schloup?'

Loulee did. Lamb Bear had a schloup phase.

Sunil and the Schloup was a cartoon about a lonely lad and his best friend, a silvery shapeshifting puddle. The theme was a grot pop song. A Christmas number one which got played well into January. It set Loulee's teeth on edge whenever she remembered it. Like now.

'Know who got the licence to make schloup toys? British RoboDynamics. Dad's company. So, after mentioning what I'd like for my big present every two days starting on November 23rd... Did I get a schloup on Christmas morning?'

'Is this your origin story?' asked Loulee. 'My guess is you were disappointed.'

Hereward's blinky eye went watery.

Loulee remembered Lamb Bear's schloup. A stretchy transparent membrane filled with iron filings. It changed shape thanks to an electro-magnet core which burned through batteries – not included, of course – and provided hours of fascination until it froze in a rude shape on Boxing Day. No amount of fresh batteries would bring back its full schloupness. Later there was a product recall and exchange programme but Lamb Bear never wanted to see a schloup again.

'The toy didn't work,' said Loulee. 'The line was a disaster.'

'I get that now but being an eight year old whose dad made schloups, it didn't seem reasonable that I didn't get one. Of course Dad knew BRD was cranking out duds. With seasonal orders to fill he couldn't go back on the deal. Substandard schloups kept exploding, poisoning pets with iron filings, getting frozen...'

'That's what happened to ours.'

'*You* got a schloup for Christmas?'

'No, my brother did. I got a Floppit Flea Circus.'

'Lucky moo,' mumbled Chrissie.

'Your household – your family – got a schloup?'

'Well, yes.'

'Mine didn't. My big present was the General, a robot war games system. Tanks came out of its tummy and planes launched from its epaulettes. Programmed with a thousand different scenarios.'

Loulee suspected the General cost more than her parents' car. Possibly their house.

'Did it have batteries included?'

'Its power source was static electricity sucked out of the environment. Viper Strike works on the same principle.'

'Is the subtext of this moving childhood memoir that Daddy's products are on the schloupy side?' asked Loulee.

'Not all of them. The General works perfectly. It was a prototype. Didn't come to the market for two years and was too pricey to be a Christmas craze. It was designed as a Think Box for military exercises but became an executive toy. Marius Stok has one.'

'Happy ending, then?' said Chrissie.

'No. I never played with the General. The instruction manual was the size of a telephone book and written in algebra. I took the boxes the General came in and sticky-taped them together into robot armour. I ran around the house and grounds shouting "Vy-perrr Stri-i-ike". I wouldn't take the robot boxes off for meals or baths or bedfordshire. Mum put in an emergency dial on New Year's Day to Dr Miranda. Everyone wanted to have their kids seen by Dr Miranda, she was ever so costly. She said they should let me play it out. I viper-struck all over the place until it was time to go back to school... where Viper Strike lasted about a minute before prefects threw me in a duck pond. Dr Miranda had expensive things to say about the school environment. I asked for a new General to be friends with the first one for my birthday in February. Mum knew I just wanted more boxes. They got me a schloup instead. The bugs were worked out but the craze was finished. I watched it change shape for an afternoon and it went in the toy room with the General and Horsey Dorsey and the Magic Ian Box of Tricks and hasn't been seen since.'

It was a wonder the Jackson-Walker toy room hadn't been squatted by cutthroats as a rookery. There must be broken dolls in it.

'I kept at Viper Strike on paper,' he went on. 'I filled exercise books with designs and diagrams. I got A-plus in technical drawing. I know everyone thinks I'm double thick but I'm whizz-o at technical drawing. Neat. Exact. I kept quiet about Viper Strike but still worked on it. I was sort of waiting to become enlightened. But that didn't happen.'

He looked at Chrissie and Loulee with envy.

'I'm not enlightened,' said Loulee.

Hereward didn't believe her.

'You glow with it,' he said.

'That's something else. I don't want to go into it at the mo.'

'She's enlightened, though,' he said, nodding at Chrissie.

'*Dark* enlightened,' said Loulee.

'That's a thing?'

'Why do you think it's so gloomy in here and the mirrors are black but still infinite pools of night?'

'I hadn't noticed.'

Chrissie got self-conscious. The mirrors turned a bit more normal.

'When you didn't wake up to find you could fly or seep through walls, what happened?' Loulee asked.

'I got out my exercise books. I put it to Dad that sponsoring a cloak would be good for BRD. A thing about Dad – he listens to me. More than Dr Miranda, even. He knows a bright idea when he hears one and doesn't dismiss it because it comes from the "what idiot" idiot. I showed him my gargantuabot design. He wanted to put a racing car driver inside but I said it had to be me. It's supposed to be a piloted vehicle. Engineers wanted a box kite to minimise operator risk. They never get that Viper Strike ought to be a suit not a widget.'

She wasn't forgetting the Worst Date of the Century – and Boglárka wanted to brand the Hapsburg seal on Hereward's forehead – but a spark of empathy made Loulee want to go back in time and hug little Hereward in his sticky-taped boxes and tell him that not getting a schloup for Christmas wasn't the worst thing in the world. That wasn't a Boglárka thought. One of the softer-hearted, more sentimental ghosts must be exerting a fluence. There weren't many of those. Maybe it was all her and she was becoming a better person. Yuck.

'Your father's company made the gargantuabot,' said Chrissie.

Hereward nodded.

'I saw clips of the demonstration at Woolwich Arsenal,' she went on. 'Blowing things up.'

'It was a real test. The programme which runs the General devised enemy strategy. Not easy gameplay. Especially in a room full of people shouting advice while I worked the controls.'

'How did you get from crushing obsolete tanks in a glorified air display to picking a scrap with the New Broken Dolls?'

'I was *fighting crime*.'

Loulee and Chrissie looked at each other.

'We're cloaks,' he said. 'It's what we do. Right?'

Chrissie obviously didn't think of it like that. Despite being a Sixth, Loulee wasn't even sure she was technically a cloak. Fighting crime was low on her to-do list.

'After Woolwich Arsenal, high-level chinwags went on between BRD and Red-Tel. Dad and the Vision Controller huddled with lawyers. *Crew Selection: The Splendid Sixth* has been on the cards for a while. They had to wait for a Splendid to quit or die and vacate a chair. Viper Strike was the first contestant pencilled in.'

Loulee bet the Vision Controller told that to all the Sixths.

Except her. She knew she was an add-on.

'Then that clip of you and the crocks was everywhere... And Devil's Dyke... Plus the time Bruno Brookes's wedding got rained on... That scary snake woman's dance-scraps are *all over* the Smut Hutch – so they tell me. You were all out of the gate and Viper Strike was stood still. We had to make an impression. We only had the Woolwich Arsenal clips. They look like, well, toy adverts. A Viper Strike figure is in the pipeline. You'll all get one. For promotional purposes.'

'Peach,' said Chrissie.

That empathy spark for eight-year-old Hereward was snuffed.

'I could do with a new voodoo doll with your face,' said Loulee. 'My old one's fallen to pieces from all the pins stuck in it.'

'You lot were fighting crime... Well, scrapping with crocks and cutthroats. I've seen the gen on Devil's Dyke. *Adam Tussaud,* Chrissie? Silent Terror? Scary Mary? That's More Than More Than. Viper Strike had to catch up. Targets were researched before the launch. We didn't just Hawkshaw "People Doing Crime Near Your Location". The Human Figure Works wasn't the only coup. Dial the *Viper Strikings* Purview. I did good, broke up cutthroat krewes...'

'Broke up a few things, from what we saw.'

'Yes, well, there were differences of opinion. I'm pilot, you understand. I work the box kite. At least I did at first. But the General suggests options. Dad was in the Room, with Eric and Oakes and too many others who got into rows. Mum had things to say. She's less keen on the project. It's hard to concentrate. Human Figure Works was supposed to be a surgical strike.'

'Not the biggest air raid on London since the Blitz,' said Loulee.

'That was, ah, excessive.'

'"Targets were researched",' quoted Boglárka. 'Get in with a follow-up question.'

'Ah, yes, Hereward, "targets were researched". How, exactly?'

'Why do you sometimes sound Hungarian?'

'Don't dodge the question. How, exactly?'

'Did you liaise with the police?' asked Chrissie.

'No. They aren't happy with Viper Strikings, actually. The

police are lower-paid Red Ropers, really. That's what Mum says. They don't make policy. We do. Top People. Cloaks. Better men. BRD Information Gathering made suggestions. The Red Rope scouted the ground to be sure the gen was up to date. The system worked twice. No complaints about those strikings. The video pirates and the mutilation games. Everyone was happy to see those krewes clobbered. With the Human Figure Works, the suggestion came from Red-Tel, I think. We didn't confirm with the Ropers because it was already cleared. I still reckon the gen was gear. These New Broken Dolls *are* a menace. Files came to Information Gathering along with a punch-card for the onboard Think Box. I think that's where the problem was. Extra holes in the punch-card. Or not enough. That's the difference between a good biffing and a street reduced to burning rubble.'

'Were you there when the file and the card were delivered?'

'Oh, yes. Despite what they say I'm in my own Room.'

'Who handed over the gen?'

'I don't know. She wore a mask.'

Loulee and Chrissie looked at each other again.

'What kind of mask?' said Loulee, trying not to sound Hungarian. 'Describe it.'

'All over the head, like the Reddleman or Poltergirl. Blackout Spex. And green. Very green. Like that stuff on the wall of Studio 9.'

'How did she move?'

'Sneaky, silently... like one of those Japanese stealth wallahs.'

'Scissors,' said Chrissie. 'Nelly's not a nutter.'

BOYD WAYLO, THE CUTTING COMMENTATOR – AGENT OF GEIST

'IT'S NOT LIKE GEIST CENTRAL IN VADUZ ISSUE YOU with a membership card, an enamel badge and an information pack. Once a satrapy is recognised, a stipend is paid into an offshore account in the Bahamas. I doubt if many above the level of heft join for the pay. You have to get past old ideas of how political, criminal or religious movements are organised. GEIST is something else. Motivations are all over the place. Think of it as a Fan Club for Evil... for what the commonality have decided should be called as Evil. No two satrapies are alike. The Octopiranha incident started with a techno satrapy scheme derailing a thaumaturge satrapy ritual.

'Our thing began with the Satrap. A man with a mask. Several masks, as it happens. He brought us all in. He was prime mover. It was his initial idea. But he didn't plot the plan. That was Modred Murda, the throat with no throat. No disguise can cover *his* secret identity. A slice of his upper body – the neck, one shoulder, a sliver of chin – is just *not there*. It's like looking into a starfield or a microscope. If he eats a fish supper, it ends up in his stomach – so in some sense his absentee gullet connects with the majority of his body. He's the man with the disembodied head and detached arm. It's down to a scrap he had with Lady Shade twenty years ago. He remains bitter. So he signed up for revenge. Big motive that, revenge.

'There's a lot of it about. Tit-for-tat vengeance one-upmanship keeps these cloak-and-throat feuds going forever. Look at Quackanapes and the Cartoonist. Modred started it – throats generally do, and cloaks react – but the Satrap wasn't about to tell him to his floating face that his condition was his own fault. He got heated on the subject. Strange steam came out of the void where his Adam's apple ought to be. The Satrap took him on as strategist. Modred fixated on the Shade, of course. That was key. An area of commonality.

'What Lady Shade did to him forged a permanent link between him and the Shade Legacy... A mystical shadiness, perhaps? He spotted Christine Chambers and knew her for what she could be... and what use she could be in the service of disruption. Whenever the girl flexed her abilities, something resonated in Modred's displaced larynx. No one liked to say it but every time that happened there was fractionally more nothing and fractionally less physical presence to Modred Murda.

'The Astro Ace and the Green Ninja were makeweights. The Satrap recruited them for specific parts of the plan. Actually, recruitment was my department. I was given a list of qualities and connections needed. With Yvonne Ayres, it was about personal resentment and connections inside Devil's Dyke. The plot needed someone well-placed to let people in or keep them out. And stake the vampire. We had a line to William Wax, who wasn't in the satrapy but was part of the plan. Modred even accounted for him going off-piste to kill Dr Chambers' pet patient. So long as Lady Shade – Modred's prime target – was still alive to suffer, casualties were fine by him. Despite his tradename, he never murdered anyone that anyone has found out about. But if incidental bodies fill morgue trays, he doesn't mind. Christine Chambers needed to be at Devil's Dyke. That was the first thing. There was clever-clever business about fortune cookie messages, which Modred chortled over for a week. Old-fashioned devious mastermind showing-off.

'After Devil's Dyke, the Green Ninja stepped up and I didn't need the details. The Green Ninja was embedded with *Crew*

Selection, which brought in a new supporting cast of idiots, operants, showoffs and expendable voids.

'The Satrap wasn't concerned with who got killed and who stayed alive. That wasn't the point he was making. For him, it was business. He was creating an opportunity. That was how I worked it out – saw through the mask.

'Our Satrap is Carter de Beers, boss of the Red Rope.

'By demonstrating security shortcomings at Devil's Dyke, he was soliciting for trade. Making an argument for privatisation. The stuff with Shady Lady Two was a sop to Modred. If the *Crew Selection* shambles makes the Splendid Six look frivolous, it's to the good from his point of view. High-profile cloaks being laughed at creates a climate in which he can convincingly bid for government contracts. The Satrap kicked the machine in motion but lost interest once he had his lobbying points. A satrap isn't necessarily in charge, any more than Queen Vee tells the Deputy Prime Minister what to do. In the end, de Beers was one of the less important members of the satrapy. You have to set aside notions of hierarchy, intent and outcome. Which isn't easy for placids and put-up-with-it wallahs.

'This is how GEIST works. People who don't necessarily share anything much club together. Individuals have specific objectives but will put up with collateral happenstances along the way. Or just don't care. The idea that a Modred Murda stratagem is worked out to the smallest detail like a train timetable is ridiculous. It's more like toss-a-banger-and-see-who-jumps. Modred didn't give a pickled herring for the Red Rope's share price or who stood with five other fools in the Tri-Lion. If I had a twelfth of my body transported to the beyond, I wouldn't either. The Astro Ace wasn't fussed about getting caught, which is why we were careful not to let her know secret identities. We gave her all sorts of false clues and trails – she was supposed to think the Satrap was Marius Stok – but she didn't squeal on us anyway, so that was wasted effort.

'De Beers and Modred thought they were in control. They were getting what they wanted, neat and tidy. A profit. Revenge. But that's not proper disruption. Doing to Europe what Lady Shade did to Modred Murda. That was about the size of it. No, I wasn't the secret fluencer, either. I spotted cracks where wedges could be hammered. I listened to Modred moan about what had been done to him and thought more deeply than he ever did about his connection to the Shade Legacy. I shared my conclusions knowing someone would pick up the big mallet. For a while, I thought it would be the Green Ninja. But she was just running errands and cocking a snook at useless bosses.

'No, the real hub of this wheel was the Mannikin...

'Look her up. William Wax's popsy. A made thing, puppeteered like his other toys. The Mannikin is a blank-faced armature. A vessel for a consciousness. A Ouija board with articulated limbs. She started out as Wax throwing his voice, telling himself he was fanciable and brilliant. Then, another mind – maybe minds – moved in, using the love doll as an operant. The clippings say she was stolen from Scotland Yard's Black Museum after Adam Tussaud was sent down. It was more like an escape. She crawled out of custody on her own stumps. Someone was driving.

'We brought her in as a way to communicate with Wax. Or that's what we thought. Now, I reckon she brought us in for... I don't know. Convenience. She made operants of us all. I saw through de Beers' mask before the end of our first confab. I could winkle out the secret identity of, say, Moonlight Flit, if I were bothered. But I don't really know who or what the Mannikin is. I only know this was their scheme. No one had a better idea so I went all in on it.

'I didn't recognise her squawkprint. I say "her" but I don't know. It could *be* Wax or some part of his broken mind. He imagined her in the first place so he could have given her life of sorts. Maybe it *is* Marius Stok – it's too easy to collect evidence which makes him out to be an Agent of GEIST. Or it could be a Think Box raised to self-awareness by a magic set of punch-cards. Or it could be Wax really did have a girlfriend. Some shut-in stay-at-home fan with a bump of long-range telekinesis. The Mannikin might have been some mad throat bird's box kite all along. You be the judge.

'Mostly, she sat in the corner when we were strategising. But a mind was inside, looking out. Chipping in with binding suggestions. A puppet exercising the fluence. If that doesn't scare you, you haven't paid attention. From the way the Mannikin ran things with whispers, I wouldn't put it past her to be the secret fluencer behind every dire disruption since the release of *Never Mind*. When all this enlightening got loose, an equal amount of endarkening seeped out. It's time the balance got tipped the other way. That's just me freewheeling.

'For larfs. To see the pretty flames. To look into a deeper, darker, stranger abyss. For... whatever. I don't have to explain.'

DAKIN AT THE DOGS

TO KEEP BUSY, DAKIN TOOK A TURN ROUND THE DOGS. He wore a peaked cap with a silver paper emblem. A civ would take him for a security guard.

It was July. Short-sleeve shirt and picnic in the park weather. But the stadium was cold, wet and smelly. A recent gale had torn away tarpaulins and soaked every building on the site. The east stand collapsed like a bad-tempered game of Pick-Up Sticks. Water puddled in the criss-cross tunnels under the greyhound track.

Everything was rotten. No one could get through a day without putting a foot through a floor. The loopy idea that abandoned industrial or entertainment structures made ideal rookeries often meant heft sustained more injuries from misadventure than scraps with cloaks. Try getting workman's comp out of the Lord Adder or Lady Godawful. Dakin would pick a seaside boarding house over a disused warehouse or bankrupt ghost train any day of the week. Such was not his lot. In Hackney Wick Stadium, asbestos fibre swelled through every crack. He kipped in a room with buckets under drips and scarfed Curry-in-a-Hurry every other meal. The Dogs still reeked of unhappy animals.

The New Broken Dolls had gone south double-time.

Dakin was the only one still visiting the Doll Hospital.

Major Wood was sitting up in bed with a Vook, reading a seven-volume *Life of Marlborough*. He'd be there long enough to finish it, out of harm's way. He had the best of it.

The Major always asked how the campaign was going.

Dakin didn't have the heart to tell him about Upside-Down Gonk's Circus. He hadn't wanted the NBDs to be a clown show but the rest of the krewe blindly stuck on red noses and slipped into floppy shoes. Cyndi suggested Dakin wear a leopard-skin jockstrap and call himself Metal Micklewhite. His shiny hand blew up into a cannonball at the thought. Cyndi liked the visual but the shift gave Dakin arthritic pain in his knuckles. Inside the steel bludgeon were overstressed and aching regular bones.

Chain of command was broken. Dakin wasn't in charge, if he ever had been. It was mostly Cyndi and UDG – with nudges from the Vison Controller's messenger girl, the Green Ninja.

He looked in on a bike garage where there was a lot of noise.

UDG dangled on a bungee from a steel beam, drilling a troupe of pasty-faced jugglers.

A wooden hand grenade rolled at Dakin's feet. He scooped it up and lobbed it back the way you'd throw an easy one to a four-year-old in pity. Butterfingers fumbled the catch. The pineapple plonked against corrugated iron. He trusted this shower would get in more practice before the Gonk dished out live bombs.

Dakin looked at greasy faces. Their make-up was running.

The clown cadets came from UDG's fan club. The ones who stuck with him after he flipped. Proper loonies. Sweaty herberts to boot. Welcome as dogshit in the Dolly Mixtures.

He turned away and continued his busywork patrol.

Fly-eyes overhead kept filming for *Crew Selection* – though the NBDs had mostly forgotten they were on telly.

At Todd's, he'd wondered whether Red-Tel were careless with background checks. Now he reckoned things were always planned to go sideways. The programme had their pick of nutters. This funfair was expected. The question was how Dakin got on the Sick in the Head List with Johnnie Shoot-the-Ceiling and Mr Bleeding Swizzle. He didn't think he'd like the answer.

Surroundings were insalubrious. Dakin kicked a cracked crash helmet across the pitted track. The skid-lid skittered into a trench. Something aquatic leaped out and darted towards the far stands. The site was infested with hybrids bred for the arena.

That day the gargantuabot struck, Regency Gates sent a minion rather than handle the viewing personally. That tinkled suspicious bells so they steered clear of the Estate Agent. They had to find a new rookery on their own.

Cyndi remembered the Hackney Wick Stadium from her French Poodle phase. More or less a legit arena until the Society for the Promotion of Cruel Sport took over. When Top Dog got sent down, all his businesses went kaput.

The CONDEMNED signs were so old locals thought the dump was actually called The Condemned Stadium. If the sodding Smudge didn't make the Dogs so bloody damp, it'd have burned down years ago.

Cyndi visited Rexwell Pitt and had him scratch a signature on a contract. A firm called 'the Fred Rope' was hired for three beads and a banana to provide security for the Dogs, giving the NBDs legitimate reason to move in.

On arrival, Johnnie Seven went on a 'dosser hunt' to scare off tramps. The Dogs was too rank even for the least picky down-and-outs. The lad came back in a mood. Juke Box Jerry got the lecky on but the stadium was wired like those displays of fairy lights where if one bulb blew the whole string went dark. Not a working kettle to be found. Only Upside-Down Gonk was comfortable with the accommodations. He hung from the underside of stands, making excited 'wheee-eeee-eeee' noises whenever he caused a collapse and bounced out of the way of certain death.

On his rounds, Dakin clocked all points of entry and exit. If the Dogs ever re-opened, he knew how to rob the takings with a three-man krewe. Of course, when Top Dog was Top of the Dogs, no throat dared to think of such a tickle.

He looked up at the glass frontage of the Managers' Box.

There were bloodstains across the window from the time Urban Fox tore through the Board of Directors of a waste-dumping firm on a jolly. They'd paid top dollar to watch the Girder Murderer scrap with a rhino kidnapped from Whipsnade Zoo.

Lorryloads of gear turned up regularly, packaged for the Fred Rope Concern. Dakin didn't want to know what was in the boxes marked 'party hats' or 'novelty straws'. So much stuff was piled under canvas in the car park, they had to take security patrols seriously. Very tempting to the tealeaf were mystery boxes. Chancers out for a tasty tickle might see the stadium as fair game now. If Johnnie shot some smash-and-grab merchant and hung him from a fence, the NBDs might earn respect from the criminal classes... but there'd be less welcome consequences. They'd already invited the *Crew Selection* batty betties to a scrap. He wasn't even sure they were the kiddiwinks the Vision Controller had sold them. Plus: too many murders and Poltergirl or the British Lions would be on their necks.

He was OMO in the NBDs, OMO and ODC. Odd Man Out/Ordinary Decent Criminal. Having a trick hand barely counted as enlightenment. If he was ever banged up in Devil's Dyke, he'd be on the Buff Corridor. Heft.

The rest of the gang were variety acts. Polka Dot Corridor cases. Suitable for the end of the pier – only Mr Swizzle had blown up the pier. Upside-Down Gonk was a teatime telly bright light gone criminally doolally. Juke Box Jerry was all about the Hit Parade. Cyndi Dolan and Johnnie Seven took their trade-names from toys. So did Dakin, come to that. 'Kung Fu Grip' was a feature of Action Man in the 1970s. He still wasn't getting measured for leopard y-fronts.

How had it come to this?

It was reactive. When cloaks – once your basic plods in masks – started poncing about like pop singers, strippers and novelty acts, throats followed suit. Made a party of it. Got more interested in being on the box and registered redials than proper crimes.

Who started it?

Ron and Reggie in their Sunday supplement sharkskins? Adam Tussaud and the Chamber of Horrors? Top Dog and his SPCS?

Dakin approached the Suspect Shed. Regency Gates might describe it as a Feature of Interest. The Shed was anchored in concrete and not covered in moss or mould. It must have been put up after Top Dog was collared. None of the NBDs could pick the lock and they'd all tried. Shooting at it didn't work either. The Shed looked like spackled cardboard but withstood a fusillade which would turn steel plate into string vest. Funny thing – Johnnie Nitwit swore it wasn't on site when he did his recce. He said it had shown up by magic. It was the Suspect Shed from there on.

The krewe were so idle they had time to spin Suspect Shed theories. A stash-house for some cloak's gear? Portal to another dimension where coppers rode on pandas instead of in panda cars? A puzzle box set by a contraptioneer, set to reward any clever dick who solved it by slicing their guts with a clockwork scimitar? The Broken Doll of the 1990s was a death trap specialist. Was he fuming in a retirement villa, narked that his legacy was being tarnished by a carnival cludge? One last death trap could be his lesson to identity usurpers.

Dakin walked round the Shed. No one hiding behind it.

Then he walked back again and the Green Ninja was there.

'Cribbins, girl... Put some bells on, why don't you? Nearly gave me a heart attack!'

Had she been inside the Suspect Shed? Or crept up craftily?

The Green Ninja angled her shapely head – the only way she could indicate wordless wry amusement what with her fizzog covered by featureless silk. She wore Bug Spex, a bomber jacket with emerald fur trim, green matador britches and country lady wellies. He supposed she was some sort of throat.

The NBDs had not seen hide nor hair of Don Loki Baird since Todd's.

Instead, Greenie popped in occasionally to hand over readies and other helpful items. She'd provided home addresses for all the Sixths so those bloody circus posters could be delivered.

Dakin didn't see why the baby cloaks had to be warned.

Half the throats doing serious porridge got nobbled because they couldn't resist popping cryptic clues on the Personals. Nine times out of ten, masked-up crims arrived at the Museum of Precious Plunder or Rattle-Yer-Jewels Belgravia Ball with intent to steal only to find a waiting cloak – or, worse, a cloak group – who had them in the back of a police van before you could say Robert Robinson.

Throating used to be all about the fiddles.

Now it was jokes lifted from Briteway Value Christmas crackers.

The ninjette wanted to see Cyndi. The messenger girl didn't want the neck-ache of looking at Upside-Down Gonk on the ceiling. So Cyndi – by any reasonable measure, two books of Green Shield stamps short of a Teasmade – became point of contact.

They all had theories about who was under the hood.

Johnnie swore it was Eleanor Wynter. Unless they made wellies with six-inch invisible lifts, Greenie was taller than the woman they'd met at Todd's.

Cyndi said – and Dakin was prepared to consider this – she was one of the so-called contestants, out to scupper the competition. The question then was: which one? The only Sixth they'd ruled out was Garter Snake, who was green of a different shade. Asmida binti Rag and Bone Geoff couldn't walk without her cobra-neck wiggle... and Greenie got about like a person with normal arms and legs.

Dakin had a ten bob note on Louise Ling, who he knew nothing about. She'd had something odd going on at the Tri-Lion. She didn't seem alone. Cyndi's pick was Little Match Girl. She wore loose, padded flame-retardant clothes which could easily cover ninja slinkiness. JBJ said it was Urban Fox, seeking vengeance for being replaced. UDG and Mr Swizzle didn't care. By them, they'd all pay and that was the way to do it!

'I love what you haven't done to the place,' said Greenie.

Her squawker was programmed to sound like the Blue Cat off *Magic Roundabout*.

A bit sexy and a bit scary.

Dakin might have considered he was in with a chance. It was a nagging possibility Greenie might be a puppet person worked by a bloke in a bunker.

'We wanted somewhere a gargantuabot attack couldn't make any worse.'

Greenie did a twirl turn, Spex glinting – they were recording all this, of course – and took in the dumpiness of the dump.

'Good for the telly,' she said. 'There are angles.'

Cyndi came down from the manager's box. Johnnie Seven and Juke Box Jerry joined the Shed party. UDG was busy with his fan club and Mr Swizzle kept his own company. Four feuding hand personalities were enough for a busy – if horribly abusive – social life without anyone else involved.

Cyndi was in her Kidnapped Fashion Model Takes Over the Terror Cell outfit: scarlet Stán evening frock raggedy-slashed to show off a yard of leg, sten gun with foldaway stock, spare clips taped to the thigh, jungle camo Alice band, ammunition boots, and a necklace of plastic severed doll heads. Just what bad little girls wanted for Christmas.

Johnnie saluted and JBJ tooty-fruited.

Whenever Cyndi showed up in a fresh outfit – ie: every bloody five minutes – there had to be a pause to admire and ooh-aah. Or else there'd be tears.

After that settled down, Greenie took something out of her inside pocket – Chubb key on a ring with a Lego Dr Robot fob.

'I understand you're wondering about the shed.'

Everyone looked at the Suspect Shed.

Greenie handed the key to Cyndi. She fit the key in the lock and pulled the Shed door open. Nothing inside but dark. No garden tools or death trap.

'We think you need an equaliser,' said Greenie. 'After the Viper Strike.'

Johnnie's face scrunched. He hated Hereward Jackson-Walker almost more than Her Majesty's Post Office. He didn't get an argument from the rest of the krewe. The box kite pilot wanted a belting.

'This shed is supposed to help?' Dakin asked.

'Step inside and see. You'll have to do it one by one. It's smaller inside than you think. It could look like a cathedral but that'd be ostentatious. Sheds always fit in. Men like sheds, haven't you noticed?'

'They've rabbited about little else this week,' said Cyndi.

Dakin wanted to say that wasn't true.

He also didn't want to step into the shed.

'Johnnie,' said Cyndi. 'Hop to it. In the shed, report back, on the double...'

'Yes, ma'am,' he said, and stepped smartly through the doorway.

He vanished as if he'd walked into a vertical fall of black ink. For half a tick, the back of his head, legs and jacket showed – then the dark closed over him.

Juke Box Jerry burst out an *uh-oh uh-oh* sample.

'Give it time,' said Greenie.

Dakin wanted to ask her whose side she was on – but he knew... The side of the programme. If feeding Johnnie Stupid to a ravenous shed meant a bump in viewing figures, her only concern would be whether her Spex got the best angle on the action.

The ink rippled and Johnnie came back – but different.

When he went into the Shed, he wore his usual seven guns, knives and baggy soldier suit. Now the accoutrements and weaponry were gone. His fatigues were tailored. His eyes were bright with something like intellect. He even had a better haircut.

'That took *ages,*' he said.

'You were gone less than a minute,' Dakin told him.

'If you say so, squire.'

'Where are your guns?' asked Cyndi.

Johnnie held up his hand as if doing a card trick. Instead of producing the ace you'd picked, he conjured an automatic with slim silencer. The gun bloomed into existence in his grip. A crosshairs gunsight manifested in his right eye. He spun, pointing at the air, making pew-pew sounds with his mouth. The automatic discharged noiselessly. Dakin smelled burnt matches.

'Nice,' said Cyndi, unconvinced.

'Wait for it,' said Johnnie. The gun wasn't there any more.

Pigeons fell out of the sky, one by one – some a few yards away, others all around the track. A Red-Tel fly-eye spiralled sparking into the stands.

'That one's free,' said Greenie. 'Any more come out of your wage packet.'

Dakin looked at a dead bird. It had a round red hole in its chest, neater than any bullet hit he'd ever seen.

'"That's all right, Mama,"' blared JBJ.

'You ain't seen nothin' yet,' said Johnnie.

He held up his hands and a rocket launcher appeared.

Everyone told him not to fire but he tugged the trigger. A missile streaked into the pile of broken wood and concrete where the east stand used to be. A silent explosion turned the mess of rubble into a cloud of ash.

'That's the non-lethal property damage setting,' explained Greenie.

'How do I turn on the indiscriminate killing?' asked Johnnie.

'We'll come to that. The rest of the krewe have to catch up.'

Johnnie kept a list of the kids who didn't come to his tenth birthday party. He'd turn their homes to brownfield sites unless talked out of it. Non-lethal setting or not, being in a third floor flat when a building was evaporised by a phantom rocket was liable to result in death or serious injury. Also, it was barse-ackwards. If he went after anyone, it should be Daddy Seven.

Or, more to the point, Viper Strike and the other Sixths.

'It's a condition of your employment that no one gets badly hurt,' the Vision Controller had said. That now seemed renegotiable. After all, Major Wood got badly hurt. Was indiscriminate killing on the table?

'Kung Fu Grip, you're next,' said Cyndi.

He didn't have time to protest. He was shoved into the Shed...

... a long time later, he stepped back, changed.

That tingle in his metal hand – sometimes shivery-pleasant, sometimes arthritic-stabby – was all over his body.

His Fred Rope cap and pea-coat were gone. He wore only swimming trunks.

Not leopard-pattern, thank Christmas. Navy blue, with a stripe.

He looked at his hand, shifting it from pinkskin to silvery and back. The effect ran up his arm and across his chest. His face prickled as it turned to tin. His bleary eyes cleared. He could see a mile in pin-sharp stereoscopy. He read the number plate on a council van parked in Waterden Road. He had an all-over thrill. His trunks got tight as he bulked up. He was eye-level with Cyndi, which was a first.

'All hail Mr Apollo,' chimed JBJ...

... who, at this rate, would be a whole Electric Light Orchestra after a turn in the Shed.

'Johnnie, shoot Kung Fu Grip. One in the chest, two in the head...'

The showoff pulled two cowboy Colts from behind his hips and pew-pewed – with a ping-neeoww ricochet. Nothing could stop the nit making gun noises with his mouth.

Dakin didn't even feel the hits.

'Bloody non-lethal rounds,' said Johnnie.

'Those weren't non-lethal,' said Greenie.

One of the ricochets dinged Juke Box Jerry in his lavalamp shoulder-pad. Glowing goo dribbled out of the wound.

'You better go next,' said Cyndi.

Gratefully, JBJ hopped to it.

'See you later, perpetrator,' he sang.

Dakin turned back to skin and wondered what the shed had done with his coat. He checked his scars. They were still there, though he didn't have to hold his gut in. Even as flesh and bone, he felt better, faster, fresher. Not the way you did with a jab or a quart of grog. This was an all-through-the-body tonic. He fancied doing fifty push-ups and beating the track record chasing the robot hare.

If this was what the Shed did to comparative normos like Dakin and Johnnie, what would happen when Upside-Down Gonk and Mr Swizzle went through? Was this how you spawned an octopus-piranha hybrid the size of Jodrell Bank?

JBJ came back in a coat of many colours, wearing all the Beatles' faces at once.

A chord – that opening THWANNNGGG! of *Never Mind* – shook the stadium.

'I'm the Young Generation,' he sang. 'I am the God of Hell Fire. I am the Antichrist. Freude, schöne Götterfunken. Ah-woo-ooo!'

'It's got a beat and you can dance to it,' sad Greenie. 'It's a hit.'

'Get the other two,' Cyndi told Johnnie. 'Knock 'em out and drag 'em here if you have to.'

He saluted and sped off.

Dakin looked into the Shed. He couldn't remember what it was like inside. Just a spell in the dark.

This was a turn-up for the books and no mistake.

Juke Box Jerry raised his arms. His sorcerer sleeves swished. He waved his hands like a conductor. Music came out of the defunct-till-this-moment PA system.

Circus music.

CHRISTINE AND WEATHER GIRL

ALEXANDRA BEACH STOOD BETWEEN ASMIDA AND Eunice and talked them out of their scrap with calm words. Weather Girl encouraged the battling belles to shake hands, which they did – gingerly. Pyro Pixie didn't burn Garter Snake's palm. Asmida didn't spit venom at Eunice's fringe. The windowless studio felt sun-warmed, stuffiness dispelled by gentle, scented breeze.

Weather Girl would get points for leadership, mediation and being the grown-up in the room. Sandii was the only Sixth Chrissie could imagine on the Splendids' podium, shoulder to shoulder with Dr Robot and the Green Knight. An adept with nothing left to prove.

Given that Sandii Beach came to *Crew Selection* as a lightweight, Chrissie was impressed with her. Next to Moonlight Flit or Flat Cat, she was a joke cloak. In person, she wasn't half the nitwit the tabs made her out to be. When she was relaxed, confident and cheerful, the sun came out. Chrissie had told Mimsy Weather Girl used a godgame ability for trivial purposes. Now she knew better. Sandii saved up for when it counted. The other stuff was goss. If it came to a scrap between Sunny Disposition and Shady Lady, Chrissie would lose.

Not optimal. That sort of thing turned cloaks to cutthroats.

Chrissie's abilities, her *dark* enlightenment, would suit cutthroatery. That gave her the queases. She had an inkling the point of the Shadow Cabinet was to keep Shades from going bad. None had, so far as she knew – not all the way bad. Some things she'd learned about the pre-Aunt Jasmine Shades shocked her. The Original Dr Shade was a terror. Sergeant Shade kneecapped spivs who forged ration books.

Reacting to the near-scrap, Eleanor Wynter had Pyro Pixie and Garter Snake perched under spotlights for an uncomfortable follow-up interview. Asmida twisted and turned on a stool not made for a person with anglepoise vertebrae. The scrappers couldn't explain why they'd kicked off at each other...

... because it wasn't real.

Though, of course, it was. They were always competing.

This was still a game show. Being a better co-operator than the next contestant was a well-established *Crew Selection* stratagem. The honeyed smile with a little acid. Being too obvious a schemer was a vote-loser. But being a gullible twit didn't win prizes either. If you didn't stoop to sabotaging the competition, you could out-*nice* them. Queen Mum Floella wasn't as nice as Bernard Saint, overall winner of *Crew Selection Mountain Rescue*.

Wearing so many masks was exhausting.

Loulee slipped Hereward back into a corner of the set and did a look-round to check whether anyone had clocked their absence. Keeping track of all the fly-eyes and pinpoint spy-cams was tricky.

There were scorch marks on the studio floor. Someone had used a fire extinguisher.

Replays of Asmida and Eunice dance-fighting were on several screens as a lesson to the hot-tempered and the cold-blooded... but also to give the viewers something to look at while the combatants were unforthcoming.

Chrissie needed to talk with Sandii to share what they'd got out of Hereward. The headline was that there really was a Green Ninja.

A Queen Mixer. Probbo in the pay of Red-Tel.

As if the series format didn't make contestants jumpy enough, the Vision Controller had an agent provocateur to keep things lively. Stockholders would be delighted. Ordinary people were liable to get hurt. Rule One – this wasn't about who'd win the contest, this was about who'd watch the show.

Nelly wasn't in on it. She was the wolf-crier shouting about ninjas from GEIST.

The bright light was as in the dark as the Sixths. Red-Tel didn't trust her to be that good an actress. She wasn't cleared for the full story because she had to be convincingly surprised when it got dicey. Or even deadly. Chrissie more than anyone knew Nelly had form for being paranoid but she really was at hazard here. Everyone on camera was fair game. Even Tish from Schilling, who was peeping nervously round a fake wall. Or Garter Snake's opportunist dad, who was doing local radio interviews as if Asmida were already a Splendid.

'Can either of you say what the problem is?' Eleanor asked.

Asmida and Eunice zipped lips.

'I can,' said Loulee, loudly, from a corner of the set – attracting a fly-eye cutaway and prompting a chair-swivel from Nelly. 'The problem is that they're violent voids. Isn't this show supposed to be about cloaks? People to look up to. So why the Devil's Dyke's cases? Actual cutthroats. With criminal records. People to lock up. Has everyone forgotten Eunice set fire to a school? I haven't because I was in it at the time. Asmida has had a go at me too. She was wearing Wavy Lines prison pyjamas then – not the flag. That was only six months ago. How do we know these menaces aren't here to nobble the Splendids? Infiltrate and subvert... you know, like the *Green Ninja*.'

Eleanor jumped at the mention of her personal bogeyman.

Was she surprised someone else took her seriously? Or pretended to.

Loulee *was* that good an actress. Better than Chrissie, which was irritating if she were being honest. Chrissie played leads in school plays but her friend got steal-the-show supporting roles – Madame Arcati, Mercutio, the Artful Dodger. Loulee didn't even want to act professionally – or model or whatever. She had other things to be getting on with.

Loulee continued her rant about cutthroats, creating a new character. She mimicked Polly O's drawl and Lovely Rita's chirrups. Maybe her ghosts helped, though Chrissie wasn't sure she believed in them. It could be that Loulee had a range of natural enlightened abilities. She'd given each of her talents their own name and personality.

Chrissie had never seen the Lantern.

Camera Clare was on Loulee now, with the fly-eyes getting cutaways of Nelly and the Devil's Dyke reprobates.

Eunice forgot this was a diversionary act and wiped hurt tears at being shamed on telly by a fellow Draycott's girl. Asmida remembered she was playing along and sneered sly defiance. For a woman with a bendy backbone, she had a considerable spine.

Rather than go back to the loo, Weather Girl led Chrissie out of a side fire exit which ought be alarmed. She must have frozen the klaxon while all eyes were on the scrap. Sandii Beach had a big, obvious talent all the better to hide the subtle things she could do with it. Chrissie had seen her cook a Vesta Chow Mein by looking at it cross-eyed.

They were on a narrow walkway at the back of the studio complex, overlooking the Thames. Regular dredging allowed access to the docks. The water roiled with brown silt. Across the river, the *Cutty Sark* was back in its berth after that pointless coup when the Cartoonist put it in a giant bottle.

There were fly-eyes about – miked for sound, of course.

At a gesture from Weather Girl, small, specific clouds formed around the doodads. One plopped into the river and sank.

'Do you want a go?' Sandii asked.

Chrissie still wasn't confident with her violet lightning. If she concentrated and tried aiming dark energy, she crackled like a breakfast cereal advert effect. Better results came from acting on instinct, though that was a risk. She worried – thank you, Mimsy Mountmain! – too much instinct would make permanent, black-rimmed holes in reality. For which she would be blamed.

Not to be completely out-enlightened, she pointed and thought.

A fly-eye buzzed into the electric billboard on top of the studio, briefly disrupting an image of Eleanor Wynter holding up a domino mask to promote *The Splendid Sixth*. 'Six will stand up – One will be invited' became 'Sxqwiffle wiffle stiffle ipple – one woffle offle boffle invi – fatal error code zorgblatt'. Then changed back again.

'Shot,' said Sandii, approving.

Chrissie told the woman what Hereward had told her and Loulee.

Not the childhood Christmas sob story. The Green Ninja.

'You think Eleanor's right?' said Chrissie. 'Someone's sabotaging the series?'

'Yes and no,' said Sandii. 'Someone sabotaged Viper Strike and got a cutthroat krewe angry with him – and, by extension, us. That's not *necessarily* bad for the show. It might be truly deeply bad for us.'

Weather Girl was thoughtful. Wind stroked her hair.

'Contestants have got hurt on *Crew Selection*,' she said. 'Windmill Girls wound up in hospital. The family of a Jupiter Mission wash-out are suing over irreversible nerve damage. That's been hushed up. This feels different. Not accidents or competition getting out of hand... but baked into the show from the off. I can't believe the risk is worth it. Red-Tel have a franchise and a charter. They could win a ratings war and still be off the air by autumn.'

'Nelly's half-way round the twist. I know. I'm one of the imaginary threats she's got rid of. But could she be right? A green ninja from GEIST.'

Weather Girl smiled.

'Are there really GEIST satrapies anymore? And isn't this too petty for them?'

'Getting their pick into the Splendids would be a coup.'

'Yes but even Garter Snake isn't GEIST material. Your friend Louise, though. At a stretch, she might... No, I can't believe it. You'd know. You're sharper than you think.'

Chrissie didn't give Sandii an argument.

'Red-Tel are sinister enough without bringing GEIST into it,' said Weather Girl. 'The Vision Controller needs this series of *Crew Selection* to be explosive. The brand is ageing. It could be Baird has a ninja on a leash. Deniable if caught. Promoted if they get away with it. Remember the channel can barely keep its top soap serial on track. The in-house Think Box guaranteed *Rockin' Rocketship Revue* would be a ratings sensation. We can't expect Red-Tel not to make a dog's dinner of any wicked plans they hatch. But we need to be wary of how far they'll go. We need to look out for each other.'

Suddenly, rain fell out of clear blue sky.

A bubble glowed around Weather Girl. Chrissie didn't have a protective aura but her uniform included a raincoat and a waterproof wig.

'I'm not doing this,' said Sandii.

The rain stopped. Chrissie's coat steamed as if a sun lamp were aimed at her.

'Also not me,' said Sandii, now concerned.

Multiple fly-eyes were on them. Whatever this was would be on the record and in the next episode.

The electric billboard was still acting up.

Eleanor Wynter's face blurred, pixellated and reformed as someone else's – an all-over-the-head hood like a big bruised thumb.

Chrissie didn't recognise the mask. A *new* New Broken Doll?

'Alexandra Beach... Weather Girl... you have committed crimes against the climate...'

The distorted voice came from a PA system. Loud enough to rattle windows and startle gulls.

'... and you will be chastised... You have the word of *Jack Pariah*.'

Sandii looked annoyed.

'Who the hell is Jack Pariah?' asked Chrissie.

Eleanor and Jack Pariah

Every light in the studio went out except the indicators on the cameras. Had Red-Tel forgotten to put a half-crown in the meter? Eleanor was sure someone was chameleoned against the green curtain, eyes disguised as dots. When the lights came back seconds later, the Ninja was nowhere to be seen.

Her earpiece shrilled.

The snake woman slid off her stool and assumed a coiled defensive pose.

'Jah... Glas?' Eleanor said, tapping her throat mike.

She was practiced in under-her-breath communication with the Control Booth. No one could listen in unless they were monitoring the frequency with high-level spy kit.

'Anju's out of her chair,' said an unfamiliar voice. 'There's a situation on the roof.'

'Who is this?'

'Lynne Lythgoe.'

Ah, the alf or bert. Tall, broad-shouldered, ginger. Blue jump-suit and more gadgets than a high-street electrical outlet. Three paces behind Glas, except in minefields when she was three paces ahead.

'We're lining up clips to roll... *now,*' said Lythgoe.

A fly-eye view – wobbly, with water on the lens – showed the electric hoarding on the studio roof. The silhouette of the Cardinal Wolsey Street complex was Noah's Ark turned upside-down. The sensual hull-curve was spoiled by the old-fashioned hard-sell sign stuck on top. An architect lost an award nomination for that client-imposed add-on.

Eleanor looked at her own face.

She wasn't happy with the visual. An old *Letsby Avenue* promo click. She preferred the portfolio shots Garnet Graill had taken for *Crew Selection*. They weren't printed before the deadline imposed by the alfs and berts who fed punchcards into the billboard's Think Box. Wonky pixellage made her eyes look shifty.

'This is a minute ago,' said Lythgoe.

There was a crash-flash and Eleanor was looking at someone else...

A liver-coloured hood with big eyes behind a Spex-strip.

'Alexandra Beach... Weather Girl... You have committed crimes against the climate... and you will be chastised... You have the word of *Jack Pariah*.'

This squawker obviously distorted the voice. How far down the widget menu from 'Sexy Kitten Purr' or 'Birthday Message from Queen Vee' was the 'Diabolical Mastermind Ultimatum' option? Eleanor was annoyed her image was tampered with but relieved she wasn't the stated target of this Jack Pariah. Liverface was hung up on the weather.

Where was Sandii Beach?

Slipped away for a seaside holiday? She'd been all smiles for the cameras and sweet saintliness when she got between the touchy tearaways...

... which seemed suspicious.

None of these people could be trusted.

'We're digging up background,' said the voice in her ear. 'Spin the wheels until we have firmer gen.'

Normally, Lythgoe would be on a Vook, desperately Hawkshawing 'Jack Pariah'. With her in Glas' chair, some other alf or bert would be fumbling that chore.

'I didn't see a Jack Pariah in Fleet Street,' Eleanor told Lythgoe.

'He's not one of ours. This isn't scripted – it's improv. Someone else's doing.'

'Splendid.'

'Word of the week, luv,' said Lythgoe – a little too familiar. 'Don't fret your jets. We're reacting. It's what we do. We're telly professionelles.'

Eleanor decided the Arse Prod's assistant would be gone by the Next Tuesday.

As a rule, she didn't like tall women. Lythgoe might catch fly-eyes with all that red hair. So, she could go...

Weather Girl strode across the set.

Where had she been? Her uniform could change with the seasons. It was light sky-blue at the moment. She could conceivably go green and invisible. Alexandra Beach was not acting as expected. If she really was Sandii. GEIST used spray-on masks which held up for two days before dissolving. Given a fakeface and the right squawkprint anyone could be anyone else.

Weather Girl went into a conspiratorial huddle with Chambers and Ling.

Interesting axis there. Three in – which meant three others out. Classic *Crew Selection*.

Garnet Graill got clicks of the trio. The goody goodies. Beach and Chambers smiled while Ling let her hair fall over her face. Eleanor could count on Ling to be who she said she was even if she had more shadows than there were light sources.

'Get quotes from Weather Girl,' said Lythgoe-in-her-ear.

Eleanor was irritated at being told to do what she was about to anyway. Of course she was going to quiz Sandii Beach.

Weather Girl settled on a stool, poised as a statue. She knew exactly how to toss her hair and arch her back to appear comfortable. She wore the kind of spike-heel boots which permanently altered your centre of gravity.

'Weather Girl,' said Eleanor. 'Do you have any comment on this statement from the cutthroat Jack Pariah?'

'Climate cranks come out of the woodwork sometimes,' said Beach. 'If Jack Pariah is one of them I'll be happy to set him straight.'

'... and if talk doesn't satisfy him?'

'Then I'll be happy to knock him flat.'

Ice in her eyes, for a moment. Then smiles again.

'We've found the face-card,' said Lythgoe-in-her-ear.

Clicks scrolled up on the screen. Fuzzy street-eye night-time encounters, all violent. Jack Pariah was identifiable by an earlier version of his hood as he kicked seven bells out of unrecognisable persons. His uniform was shabby silk bomber jacket, bovver boots, and a see-through mesh blouse showing rows of grenade-pin and beer-can ring-pull piercings. A chest tattoo read UNCLEAN. In one click, he was shoving Coffin Dodger's head into a water-butt... In another, he was passed out in his own widdle while kids with magic markers changed his tatt to read UNCLE IAN. A clip found him in the middle of a scrap between gas-masked plods and animal-masked protestors. It was hard to tell which side he was taking but his boot-toes were bloody.

'A loverly fellah all round,' said Lythgoe.

A whispered precis of his Hawkshaw write-up followed. Eleanor repeated Lythgoe's gen on a two-second delay as if she knew it by heart and was sharing with the viewers. If that wasn't an enlightened ability, she didn't know what was.

'There's confusion as to whether Jack Pariah is a cloak or a cutthroat,' she said. 'He debuted in the 1990s at the height of the grim 'n' grit wave. In those dark ages, a breed of cloak took to crippling cutthroats while bragging that they were mightier-fisted than Night Mist or more feral than Urban Fox. Most smoked or drank themselves out of the game double quick. It's possible the original Jack Pariah went that way and someone else has taken up the name. He used to paste manifestos on lavatory walls, using ransom note letters cut out of smut mags. We're not going to read any of his screeds because he uses language unacceptable on the box – also, because he goes on and on and on. Safe to say, he's not a jolly jeremy.'

'Is he enlightened?' asked Chambers.

Lythgoe paged through notes and Eleanor drew breath.

'No one knows. There might be something mystic or cyber about the big boots. He's been in scraps with formidable foes. George Cross, Mark Shark. Don't laugh – Mark Shark was a Splendid. From what Jack Pariah said about Weather Girl, he could be a fanatic with views about how other people should use enlightened abilities.'

Beach looked concerned. 'By "other people", he means...'

'You, obviously. He might have an issue with women in masks... or with, as you have yourself admitted, your goss column lifestyle.'

'Maybe he just doesn't like sunny days.'

'He's made a mistake,' said Chambers, leaning in to get on camera.

'How so?'

'Jack Pariah hasn't only picked a scrap with Weather Girl,' she said. 'If you come for one of us, you'd best be prepared to take us all on.'

Somehow, the Sixths formed a posed group around Sandii Beach – Uglow and binti Geoff crouched in front, Chambers and Ling either side. Even Jackson-Walker at the back. Camera Clare moved in to get the visual.

Garnet took the click that would be on the next hoarding.

That new 'Viper Strike' chime sounded.

'Come and have a go,' said Ling...

'... if you think you're hard enough,' said Beach.

'The Vision Controller is happy,' said Lythgoe-in-her-ear.

Eleanor didn't much love these pink pages. Improv made her nervous.

LOULEE AND THE DETECTIVES

LOULEE PINCHED CHRISSIE'S LAPEL. IT WAS ALL WET.

'Argument with the river?' she ventured

'Sudden shower,' said Chrissie.

Chrissie's coat and hat were soaked. Something had happened.

Ghosts chimed in with deductions. Quite a few were Little Hawkshaws. Besides their other talents, they'd solved mysteries, exposed murderers, thwarted plots – and got little thanks for it. Now they were eager to chip in. Loulee was irritated when they pre-empted her line of thought. It didn't take three pipes and a magnifying glass to notice a wet raincoat on a dry day.

'Before Pariah spoke through the sign, it rained,' Chrissie said. 'Like a big bucket of water emptied from on high. Came and went in seconds.'

'Like a Weather Girl special?'

'I'm not the only reason there's a climate,' said Sandii. 'This is England. It rains. Often. Naturally.'

'Was this natural?' asked Loulee, nudged by Ercolina.

Sandii paused. 'No,' she admitted. 'This was something else.'

'It was *aimed,*' said Chrissie. 'Flung like a flan.'

Loulee realised Camera Clare was covering this huddle. Eleanor horned in, too – ready to pounce with comment or accusation. Loulee hoped Nelly wouldn't ask what Chrissie and Weather Girl were doing outside the studio.

The other Sixths let Loulee have the conch for the moment – so at least she didn't have them shouting in her lugholes too.

'Ask the witch how she makes water,' insisted Ni Tien.

'She means how she makes it rain,' said Ercolina, 'not how she goes to the lavatory.'

Loulee knew that.

'Can anyone else do what this woman does?' asked Boglárka.

'Then you'll have suspects,' said Ni Tien. 'Apprehend and torture each of them until one confesses.'

The Lady Ni Tien (1634–1662), greatest calligrapher of her day, was scribe to Judge Wan, renowned for the arrest and execution of seventeen murderers, thirty-six thieves and eighty-one treasonable conspirators. The Judge's career was built upon the acuity of his unacknowledged advisor. He eventually had Ni Tien arrested and executed for theft from the court treasury – a substitute for the real embezzler, a nephew of his. Two years later Wan was poisoned for an inheritance by another of his many nephews. Generation after generation of the Wan family were rotters.

'Everyone confesses under torture,' said Ercolina. 'It's of limited use.'

'Only if you're clumsy,' said Boglárka. 'You must force the suspect to volunteer details known only to investigator and criminal. It is vital not to give prompts, even unintentionally. Within those restrictions, torture is your friend.'

Many ghosts failed to understand things had changed since their day.

Still, it was worth asking...

'Sandii,' said Loulee. 'Are there other people who can make it rain?'

'Not like I do. The Met Office ran tests. My enlightenment is attuned to pressure, moisture and temperature. It's as if there are knobs, which I can twiddle. Hot/cold. Wet/dry. Still/windy. I thought of taking a meteorology degree but the course was filled with swots. It's not that interesting a subject. Too many charts and tables. The Met Office had scientists working on a machine to reproduce my abilities. A weather gun.'

'Did it get off the drawing board?'

Sandii was reluctant. 'Yes, but the government abandoned the project when the prototype proved too expensive to run. They were talking half a million pounds for thirty seconds of rainfall over a limited area. No use for farming or... Well, there were budget cuts and the Ministry of Defence put it in mothballs.'

'But someone with money and resources could make it work?'

'A *lot* of money. I imagine they'd need money and resources to take over the electric billboard too.'

Boglárka, Ercolina and Ni Tien started accusing suspects and arguing cases. With effort Loulee tuned them out.

'I know someone with money and resources,' said Chrissie.

Everyone looked at Hereward.

'Not this again,' he said.

Asmida took hold of two of Hereward's mo-cap bobbles and twisted him backwards over a table, slithering over him as if she were giving a scary booth dance. Ni Tien approved. The gargantuabot they'd been treating as furniture creaked. Hereward made a fist and Viper Strike raised an arm.

'Off him, Garter Snake,' snapped Weather Girl.

Asmida listened. Sandii was being Head Girl again.

Hereward relaxed as the *naga* let go of him. Asmida backed away sinuously. The gargantuafist opened.

'What reason would he have to single me out?' asked Weather Girl.

'You're winning this competition,' said Chrissie.

'I am *not*.'

'You absolutely are. You're the only one of us anyone's heard of...'

'... not in a good way.'

'You have respect,' said Chrissie. 'Even Asmida just did what you told her and she's pretty much a snake... No offence.'

Asmida hissed.

'You understand your abilities and can control them. I wish I could twiddle imaginary knobs. I'll be lucky to get through the series without cracking the space-time continuum and spoiling everyone's nice day out.'

Loulee suspected Chrissie would regret letting that slip.

'So you all have motive to get at me?' said Weather Girl, looking at five Sixths.

No one contradicted her. Ni Tien and Boglárka suggested individual tortures suited to particular contestants.

'This gives me something to think about,' said Weather Girl.

A cold wind blew through the studio.

'The Sixths are wondering whether Jack Pariah is using an artificial device to control the rain,' said Eleanor, for the viewers' benefit. 'That's a change from his boot-to-the-bonce street tactics but the days of grim 'n' grit were a long time ago. This is a new era of...'

Suddenly the fire escape door was pushed in. A section of the wall came with it.

Sparks fell from ruptured wires. Plaster dust made Loulee cough.

Ni Tien shrieked, terrified that a dragon was attacking the studio. She had a fear of dragons. Being dead hadn't helped her get over it. She got it into her head that dragons ate ghosts.

Someone stood in the breach – wearing a brown hood and bloody big boots. A backpack trailed wires and tubes which connected to upper-body exo-skeletal splints and braces.

Jack Pariah.

'I've come to kick bums and suck Opal Fruits,' he squawked in machine-mockney, 'and I've finished the last strawberry one.'

CHRISTINE AND THE SIXTHS VS JACK PARIAH

STUDIO LIGHTS WERE A NUISANCE. CHRISSIE NEEDED darkness to be at her best and there was too little of it. She felt lightning crackles around her fists.

This new clod had made an entrance to intimidate.

If Jack Pariah could batter down a chunk of wall, he could as easily open a not-very-secure door and walk into the studio.

Chrissie gathered a thin shroud of shadow and tried winding it around the Opal Fruit fancier.

Before she could get a grip, Hereward punched the air.

Viper Strike punched at Jack Pariah. The metal fist was checked in mid-thrust. Hereward strained uselessly.

The 'Viper Strike' sting choked off.

Chrissie lost concentration and had to start again.

Jack Pariah wasn't tall. The mechanical harness worn over his greatcoat was an add-on to his 1990s visual. Pipes ran down his arms to funnel arrangements. He held Viper Strike's fist back with a raised funnel.

It wasn't a force field but a blast of arctic wind.

Weather Girl walked across the studio to meet her new nemesis.

'What's your problem, pal?' she asked.

Jack Pariah aimed his other funnel at her. A dribble came out, as if it were a leaky tap. Eunice tittered.

'Alexandra Beach... Weather Girl...' he said, less amplified, 'you have committed crimes against the climate...'

The squawk widget was switching on and off. The ominous Jack Pariah voice was interrupted by words in a weedier Northern accent.

Chrissie knew him from somewhere. The widget broke. Jack Pariah continued with confidence, as if reading out football results.

'... and you will be chastise... You have the word of...'

Weather Girl laughed.

'Bruno?' she said, in astonishment. 'I know it's you.'

The funnel fired concentrated hail at Alexandra Beach, knocking her into a display of foam rubber alien heads. A firehose gush followed the hail, washing Weather Girl across the floor. Water and TV studios do not go well together. Cables discharged whiplash arcs. Tish screamed and hid behind Viper Strike. Asmida climbed a wall above an electrified puddle.

Jack Pariah was Weather Girl's ex.

He couldn't be the original Jack Pariah, who was breaking bonces in Balham when Bruno Brookes was primary school tiddlywinks champ in Bingley. The backpack dragged on Brookes' shoulders and he struggled with the rain-and-wind blasters. They weren't from the previous Pariah's arsenal. Alexandra Beach had mentioned a prototype weather gun which was too expensive to use.

'Sandii,' said Brookes, in a higher pitch, 'are you all right? I didn't mean to...'

Weather Girl was flat out, battered and unconscious – but breathing. The hail had hit her like a thousand shotgun pellets.

Brookes hadn't thought it through. He was suddenly terrified.

He tried to run to Sandii – probbo out of concern, rather than to finish the job of killing her. No one wanted to take a chance on that, though.

Chrissie – on instinct, as Sandii had suggested – conjured a noose of dark matter and tossed Brookes back at the hole he'd puffed through the wall. No knobs involved. She conducted an arc of black material as if twirling a banner. She looped the dark rope and whipped Brookes's ankles, flipping him over.

The Jack Pariah helmet cracked against the wet floor.

Brookes was ringed with pale fire (thanks, Eunice). The headpiece popped off entirely. Bruno 'Back of the Net' Brookes was unshaven and red-eyed.

Eunice set light to his combat trousers. Asmida slashed his chest with barb-tipped fingers.

And Viper Strike struck.

Hereward ouched as he put his shoulder out miming a big punch.

The gargantuabot fist connected. Bruno Pariah's backpack crumpled under him. The expensive equipment was scrap now.

'It's no use,' Brookes said. 'I'm broke.'

Chrissie drew back her dark lariat. It disappeared up her sleeve like roll-out tape pulled back on its reel.

Loulee nipped in to check Brookes for fractures. She'd done the Red-Tel first aid course. And could be semi-possessed by Florence Nightingale.

'You're just beaten,' she told him. 'A few bruises are all.'

'Not broken,' he said. 'Broke. Every time I used the Weather Weapon, it cost half a million quid. On top of the hire fee and the security deposit that's forfeit. I could only afford five charges – two rain, two wind, one hail. That's the houses, the cars, the record collection... all of it. Gone. Peed away.'

'What on Earth were you thinking?' Loulee asked.

Brookes scrunched up his eyes, sorry for himself.

'I wanted back in,' he said.

Shadow slipped into Chrissie's hand, hardened and honed to a dagger-point. Solid rage turned into a weapon. She had to hum to herself to evaporise the dark blade. Bruno Brookes wanted stabbing. He'd even asked for it. That didn't mean she had to oblige him. The Guide Pledge about using her abilities wisely covered not acting on angry impulse.

Security and medical people swarmed around and dragged Brookes away.

More concern was shown for the woman he'd shot at.

Eleanor, who'd managed not to get drenched, tried to get Sandii to respond to simple questions. Weather Girl was moaning. Dr Keane, the on-set medic, performed a thorough examination. He had a doodad which measured vital signs. It pinged and dinged alarmingly.

Adrian Jah and Lynne Lythgoe were down from the Control Booth, assessing damage to the set and the equipment.

There were health and safety concerns.

Weather Girl tried to sit up. Her hair and make-up were for obvious reasons water- and windproof. Her visual stayed perfect even after a right battering. She groaned. Swirls of fog coalesced around her – a soft, semi-opaque cocoon.

'This woman is off the programme,' announced Dr Keane.

Lynne Lythgoe – Former Assistant to the Assistant Producer

'The Vizh Con and Martin Masters had an unholy dust-up about video of the Jack Pariah scrap. Masters wanted the footage wiped. The clip gave the impression any farquhar with a blow-your-house-in gun could huff 'n' puff through cardboard and invade the Hallowed Hall. Viewers might think it was easy to catch the Splendid Six napping. If Bruno Brookes had approached the real Hallowed Hall with his Weather Weapon, he'd have been nabbed before he got within aiming distance. Cardinal Wolsey Street isn't as secure. Autograph hunters pop get-past-the-Red-Rope tips on the Personals. It's a flan-flingers' paradise on the Personals.

'Bruno knew about the hush-hush Climate Cannon because he was Weather Girl's cuddlebunny when the Met Office and the MoD splurged dosh to imitate her enlightened abilities through science and black magic. He had a number for a dodgy boffin who was willing to look the other way as he borrowed the prototype. Moreover, he could get grubby paws on the bag of cash it took to fire up the system. The Climate Cannon burns money like nobody's business. It runs on ground sapphires, unicorn ivory and impossibly rare postage stamps. Every time it's used, something unique and irreplaceable has to be shoved into a slot to be converted from matter to energy.

'Being a weather warrior for eight minutes cost Bruno nine and a quarter million quid. He could barely cover half that by liquidating his assets. Red-Tel waived damages on the condition he sign over rights to his Jack Pariah persona, clearing usage on his blink-and-you'll-miss-it reign of terror. I've heard drum solos last longer than Bruno's cutthroat career. Weather Girl didn't bring charges, though Bruno's missis did. Many of the valuables he evaporised were jointly owned. He's not a real throat, is he? He won't get Devil's Dyke. He begged for protective custody. Not from Weather Girl, when and if she gets better... or even from Illona and her vampire brief. No, he's worried about Jack Pariah. The real one. Seems he didn't buy the franchise. Anju said it was worth assigning a fly-eye to Bruno. Footage of a punishment beating might be too rough for broadcast but would make a tasty deleted scene on the box set.

'You'd ask "what was he thinking?" but everybody knows...

'Bruno Brookes saw his ex in a peak viewing series while he was shifted from League Division One on *Fun News* to late-night bowls highlights. He wanted to write himself into Weather Girl's comeback. He pitched to *Crew Selection* and Adrian Jah ghost passed. That's when the telly fellahs listen to the idea, agree it's fabulous and can't miss, sign off with "great meeting" and never talk to the supplicant again. It's brutal. The name is flagged at reception and the phone exchange, so they can't get through. They stay home and wither away. It's not personal. The Vizh Con liked Geoff Reynolds more for the "estranged family member tries to get back with the contestant" sub-plot. The Pariah gambit got Bruno on the programme – but for one episode only as throat of the week. He can't be the voice of *Lawn Bowls* after assaulting a national treasure. So that's that for him. He's Gone. Well past Next Tuesday. Wednesday's chip paper.

'The immediate issue was Weather Girl.

'No one was unhappy a Sixth was down. By Episode Three, someone needed to go. Sandii Beach was likely to get the black spot anyway, despite her name recognition factor. Internal memos listed her as "the Known Quantity". Being enlightened and lovely didn't help when someone threw a hundred gallons of rain in her face. She was seven years older – officially, even – than the next oldest contestant. If Weather Girl won, it'd be boring. She was never the bookies' favourite. She was so clearly a cut above that, upset was inevitable. The front-runner stumbles. Crocodile tears and sniggers. Everyone liked her and she played clever by assuming leadership. Viewers preferred her as mentor than player. So off to hospital she went. Everyone sent flowers. Anjulie had me order a hamper from Fortnum's from the production team.

'Anju missed the excitement on Pariah Day. Which got me noticed.

'I did panic a bit but didn't get drowned. I fed Nelly lines. I got release forms signed before anyone could think of dialling their agents. I arranged for tapes to be copied and strategically misfiled before Masters could show up with an electro-magnet. I sat with Illona and recorded a tell-all which fed the *Scurrilous Rag*. Adrian Jah told me I'd earned gold stars and would be remembered when promotions were decided.

'I shouldn't have been surprised two days later when I turned up at the studio door at the usual five forty-five in the morning to discover my key-fob on the fritz. The doodad was confiscated by the Red Rope. A security heft gave me a Dear Jane letter along with a pay-off packet and an injunction compelling me not to attempt contact with the *Crew Selection* production staff. Guess what – my name is flagged at reception and the phone exchange. I tossed my ID lanyard in the river and cycled home against the commuter tide. I was back in bed before most people had breakfast.

'I'm early evening front desk at Sunny Gym in Seven Sisters Road now. Same money, less stress, no prospects.'

DAKIN AND THE COTERIE

HE STOOD TO ATTENTION BY THE STRETCH ROLLER, passed off as a chauffeur in his Fred Rope cap and gunmetal skin sheath. The disguise wouldn't pass with pobs who had half a brain, but this mob weren't the sort to pay attention to a driver.

Cyndi wore her Bubbly Recruiter for an Aquarian Sex Cult outfit – white spray-on trews, gold chainmail brassiere, calfskin tailcoat two sizes too small for her, cyber tiara with peacock plumes, silver slippers with retracted toeblades. Her wardrobe was in the ether now, materialising as required like Johnnie's armoury. Sometimes, she shuffled through visuals in a blur. Dakin wasn't sure it was a good thing. Cyndi was barmy enough before she went into the Shed.

This was the last of the pick-ups.

The Green Ninja had given the New Broken Dolls names and locations, along with face-cards to prevent mistakes. Some pick-ups meant journeys beyond the smoke. A few involved enlightened individuals. Which meant persuasive measures like Juke Box Jerry's Pied Piper hypno-flute. Others were shooter-in-the-ribs, bag-over-the-bonce jobs. Always a risk of something kicking off. Especially with this mob and their connections.

Nabbing Bruno Brookes meant waiting outside Manchester Road nick for him to be let loose with a stern warning after being held without charge for forty-eight hours. He'd got into a bit of bother with his ex. The Green Ninja showed clips of the plonker's frontal assault on the Sixths as an example of what not to do. Brookes wasn't talkative in his pen at the Dogs – unlike other pick-ups, who raised a racket until JBJ played them a medley of fluty mesmerotunes.

This shower – the so-called Coterie – were pushovers.

Netting them was a simple matter of turning up at their gaffs in a top motor and Cyndi handing out all-areas passes like the Fairy Liquid Godmother. Planted rumours on Peophole, Whispers and the Personals bigged up an imminent flash bash – the Scarlet Spectre's Surprise Shenanigans. Queen Vee had cancelled all public engagements to be free and was about the only person important enough to be guaranteed an invite. This or that pop star was down to do a turn. As with every other command performance, solstice festival or protest march, it was rumoured that the Beatles would make this their last live gig before ascending permanently to a higher plane. Marius Stok had commissioned a one-off tuxedo from Stán which would be burned after the evening. Cyndi had a giggle making this stuff up. She was especially amused when nobs dropped hints or outright claimed they'd had invites to the fictional party. No one asked who the Scarlet Spectre was. The trade-name was made up for the occasion.

So far, they'd collected Vidar Tieck and Michelle Lemnnos from Chelsea, Symon Allott from St John's Wood, Marcus Milner from Shad Thames, Martyn Susal (trade-name, if you can believe it, the All-Powerful Jupiter Boy) from Sloane Square, and Monica Maude from a bijou basement in Barnsbury. The route zig-zagged across post-codes, not for convenience but in order of precedence within this gaggle of jab-eyed butterfly people.

Milner's face-card needed updating. He no longer went by 'Dr Crockery' and was kitted up in nineteenth century funeral clobber. Tieck explained that Milner's new lifestyle visual was 'vicky boy', which combined outward respectability with underlying decadence – lacy corsets peeping through rips in his too-tight frock coat, no arse to his trousers to show off frilly crimson knickers. Dakin stopped feeling even slightly sorry for what was going to happen to the pobs later in the evening.

Last address on the list was in Duchess Mews, off Duchess Street, lair of Coterie queenpin Polly Opal. The daughter of someone who owned Lincolnshire but hung on to Rutland as a spare room. An uncle had married beneath himself into the Norwegian Royal Family. She was evidently adored and feared by her krewe in equal measure. Everyone secretly hoped Polly O hadn't been invited to the Surprise Shenanigans so they could have one over on her. From the build-up her pals gave her, Dakin reckoned she must be a right piece of work.

Cyndi kept bubbling and encouraged liberal sampling from the Roller's drinks cabinet. Fizzle and grog went down well. Monica Maude – the only coterite with even a quantum of nous – asked Cyndi about the venue for the Surprise Shenanigans and was told it was part of the surprise. Her friends told her to pipe down and enjoy the ride. Allott said he got car sick but no one paid him any attention.

They had to wait in Duchess Street while Polly O let anticipation build for fifteen minutes. Above the mews, a fly-eye was getting footage. This would be part of the show.

A special seat was reserved for Miss Opal. A squid ink daiquiri was ready in a gimbal-balanced armrest holder.

Finally, Polly O deigned to join the tour. Her outfit cost four times as much as the next most expensive but was bereft of frippery, frill and fancy. The silk shroud in blue-white matched her nose ring and chin stud. Some heathen temple got looted by an ancestor to furnish those sparklers. There was probably a curse on the jewels but demons were too afraid of their wearer to enact it.

The others wore their laminates proudly. Polly O took hers from Cyndi as if it were a bus ticket and shoved it into a handbag which seemed too small to hold an After Eight mint.

Everyone had something rehearsed to say to Polly O and said it at the same time. She Who Must Be Paid Obeisance To sipped her drink and winced like a judge about to award four out of ten.

Dakin remembered the Inner Voice, who ran the mind-slaved Silent Terror gangcult before he got banged up in Devil's Dyke. He was an enlightened hypnotist who could bend weaker minds' wills to his own. Polly O had the fluence without even magical mind sauce. The Coterie was a cludge of her operants.

Admirable, in a way. She'd make a half-decent throat – only she was too rich to need to thieve anything. If she wanted to be a cloak, she could have her uncle dial an unlisted number and bump the winner of *Crew Selection* to take the Splendid Sixth spot for herself. He'd trade bulletproof skin for her chequebook any day of the week.

'Before we move off, your host asks you put these on,' said Cyndi, passing out ghost-masks. 'To preserve the surprise, we're keeping our route secret.'

The masks had no eyeholes.

Everyone slipped the masks on with only a few larky comments. Except Polly O.

'I have contracts which limit what I may wear. This dress is a Vautrill.'

'So is the mask,' said Cyndi, pointing to a tiny logo.

That told her. Polly O settled the ghost-thing on.

'I don't like blindfolds,' said Monica Maude, again showing she was the least dim of the krewe.

Cyndi checked that all the others had their masks fitted and couldn't see a thing. Then she lightning-poked knock-out points in Monica Maude's neck and forehead, putting her to sleep. The girl's startled eyes remained open as she slumped against her safety belt.

'These are lovely and cool,' said one of the passengers.

The insides of the masks were treated with goodnight fluid.

Within seconds, the Coterie were all in dreamland. No drinks were spilled. Those armrest gimbals really worked.

'Right,' said Cyndi, in a deeper, less bubbly voice. 'To the Dogs.'

CHRISTINE AND THE FAST-BREAKING STORY

'HAVE YOU SEEN YOUR BOYFRIEND THIS MORNING?' asked Loulee.

Chrissie took a long moment to realise she meant Garn.

What with everything else, it was easy to forget she had a boyfriend. Garn was always around but it was ages since they'd had time off together. Their last date was a teatime at the Chauncey Chee in Mellish Street. She scarfed everything from the cakes and fancies side of the menu and went through Garn's contact sheets to approve clicks for publicity use. Eleanor had already got at the folder and crossed out pics which made Chrissie – or other contestants, including verit Beauty Queen Alexandra Beach – look like anything. Garn was glum about the process. Ninety per cent of his work was scotched on the whims of ninnies. He kept the best rejects for his portfolio.

Chrissie looked around the rebuilt (and reinforced) set.

Something had bothered her. She only now realised what it was. Garn wasn't slipping in and out of shadows, aiming and clicking. She missed the tick-tick shutter sound.

'I waited half an hour for my shoot,' said Loulee. 'He didn't turn up.'

The Sixths had private photo-sessions scheduled. Red-Tel needed solo pics Eleanor didn't get a nay on. In a *Crew Selection* subplot, design teams were competing to create an Arsinoë uniform. Today, Loulee was supposed to be clicked in three costumes. Viewers would vote on the visual. If the mood took them, they'd pick the silliest gear Loulee could be forced to wear. What larfs.

At the mo, Loulee was dressed like Arsinoë's more famous sister Cleo... or at least like Lovely Rita in that Elstree musical *Asp!* Pharaonic head-dress, swimming costume, diaphanous cloak. Scabbarded swords hung from her belt. They made walking or sitting a problem.

'What *do* you look like?' said Chrissie.

Loulee was too piqued to be embarrassed.

'Have you ever heard ghosts laugh?' she said. 'Take it from me, you don't want to.'

Without Weather Girl, *Crew Selection* was drifting. A mid-series slump was likely. Quibbles kept cropping up. The production team was in a right old state. Anju's assistant was discontinued for no reason anyone understood. The Arse Prod had to assist herself while also doing most of Adrian Jah's job. Captain Not-So-Floppy was 'in meetings', which was code for the show being in trouble with higher-ups and it being a priority to find elves to blame and sack. Anju's white streak now spread over most of her hair. Camera Clare was working with her arm in a cast. Part of the set had fallen on her when Bruno Pariah barged in. Worn-out runners were replaced by yet-to-be-traumatised new bugs as if this were a combat platoon at the arrowtip of an expeditionary force into well-held enemy territory.

Sandii getting hurt brought home to the other Sixths that they were at risk.

Hereward's mo-cap suit now had enough armourplate to make him a miniature of the Viper Strike mecha. Loulee suggested it might not even be him inside.

'Has anyone seen Nelly's boyfriend?' asked Eunice. 'He's just stood me up.'

Eunice sported a new Pyro Pixie visual – red principle boy tunic and tights with swirly flame motif, shiny fireman's helmet, asbestos ClodHoppers. She was down for the session after Loulee's.

'If you mean Garnet Graill, he's not Nelly's boyfriend,' said Loulee.

'He's clicking her all the time. And he was with her at Devil's Dyke.'

Chrissie saw how Eunice got the idea. She wasn't the first to make the assumption. She'd thought she was too busy to get jealous. Maybe she could fit a snit into her schedule. How much more could she take from Eleanor Wynter?

'Garn didn't turn up for work this morning,' Loulee said. 'I had two other outfits as bad as this one to model for him.'

'What *do* you look like?' said Eunice.

'That seems to be question of the day,' said Loulee.

'No,' said Chrissie, 'question of the day is "where is Garn?" He's usually first in the studio every day and last to leave. He's getting a better deal out of this programme than any of us. If he's not here, something's wrong.'

'Ftatateeta and Tunno aren't here either,' said Eunice. 'No squirts or blurts and their Vones don't pong when I ping.'

Who else was missing?

The three Draycott's girls looked around. Hereward was with Eric the Engineer getting his sparkplugs tuned up. Asmida was chatting with Seumas, her recently acquired agent. She might be thinking of swallowing him whole then digesting him over the next three weeks. Tish from Schilling was in a corner with a Green Penguin. She'd learned the first rule of show business: there will be endless hours of not much happening so always have a book to read.

Of course, Sandii Beach wasn't here.

A siren sounded. A new feature. They only knew what it was because it had been tested several times last week. After Bruno Brookes/Jack Pariah, Red-Tel installed an early warning system. It also served as a general call for attention.

The big screen showed Eleanor sat at a desk in a new Stán LaserBlazer. You could have someone's eye out with the upturned collar points. She was live. Nelly had taken to being beamed in from her own studio rather than mingle with the hoi polloi. It wasn't just her ninja phobia. She liked being a big head.

'Attention all Sixths,' she said. 'We've news of developing situations. Rediffusion-Televersion disavows all knowledge of any criminal actions which might be in progress and cautions participants in *Crew Selection* that they are at risk of injury to their persons and reputations. Reasonable measures have been taken to ensure the safety of contestants but a guarantee cannot be made to cover every outcome.'

Most of that was written by Red-Tel lawyers. Variations on the announcement had been sprung on them regularly since the Weather Weapon incident.

A fly-eye view of a building complex on fire filled the screen. Explosions went off like phosphor flares, blanking the image for seconds. Aeromechas were deployed to fight the blaze. They flew into flak and pranged, tumbling to earth in a rain of bolts and sparks.

'This is the British RoboDynamics Factory at Mucking Marshes...'

Hereward paid attention.

'What idiot did that?' said Eric, still milking last week's slogan.

He didn't get laughs.

'We understand the facility came under attack shortly after dawn,' said Eleanor in voice-over.

The screen cut to clips taken inside the factory.

Doors exploded inwards. A man-shaped figure strode through flame, packing heavy weapons. It fired from hands, shoulders and helmet. Machinery blew up. Personnel got out of the way. The camera lens cracked. The footage was silent, which made it eerier.

Who was that with all the guns? Not *another* Jack Pariah?

More outside views. Three silver silos wreathed in fire, collapsing one by one, puffing flame across surrounding scrubland. Staff fleeing on foot or in runabout milk floats. A company charabanc ploughed into sticky mud. Someone in a blimped mecha suit bounded blob-like through a fence gap and fell into long grass.

'A warning, authenticated by the use of a code-word, was received from the New Broken Dolls as the attack began,' said Eleanor. 'They claim this is a reprisal for the Viper Striking in Farringdon.'

'Hang on a mo,' said Loulee. 'Red-Tel have an open channel of natter with our arch-nemeses?'

Hereward sat down. Viper Strike didn't. Safety measures

were now installed, along with punch-cards which overrode the operator's trigger finger if litigable property damage was likely.

'We understand there have been no fatalities,' said Eleanor.

That was some relief, though Chrissie thought it might be too early to make such a definitive statement.

'It was the first incident today.'

Chrissie, Loulee and Eunice looked at each other.

Chrissie was worried now. She called Tish over and was given her Dark Vone. She sent a squirt to Garn's number and got a 'not available' blurt.

Another fly-eye view. An urban industrial area. Car parks, business estates. Acres of tarpaulin-covered loads on wooden pallets. Sorting sheds and a prefab site office.

Asmida hissed.

Reynolds Goods Yard. Proprietor – Garter Snake's dad.

He wasn't at the studio either. His absence was too much of a mercy – especially for his *binti* – for anyone to complain about. They'd feel a tiny bit guilty about that some time in the future. When they got back from their holidays in 2058.

'This was a few minutes after the first attack,' said Eleanor.

The fly-eye swooped for a view of a fellow in a coat of many colours striding towards the chained gates. He had a floppy felt hat, banana boots and a musical suit. Squeeze-box with piano keyboard. Brass euphonium over the right shoulder. Cymbals on knees. Hi-hat on his head. Mouth organ on a frame. Lennon Spex with black and white hypno swirls.

Asmida looked up at the screen.

Again, the footage was silent. The one-man band played. Small items rolled out of his way. It must be magic music. Fence chains melted. Geoff Reynolds pitched up in a Garter Snake t-shirt and pyjama bottoms, holding an I'M BACKING BRITAIN mug. Chee boiled over and scalded his fingers. The mug flew into fragments. Geoff staggered, ripples of force playing on his jowls. He was not best pleased. What hair he had rose like a dandelion clock.

Asmida smiled, enjoying the show. Chrissie had almost forgotten to be afraid of the ex-cutthroat. Her golden eyes fixed on the screen. Happy to see her father suffer. Chrissie felt a chill at her want of feeling... but also a little sad. Asmida had been born a *naga* but she was like this because of how she'd been treated afterwards.

The euphonium bell pulsed like a big-lipped mouth, oompahing something Joshua-like. Fences crumpled. Covers tore off crates of surplus, contraband or just-plain stolen goods. Geoff levitated and was bent backwards in the air... and the fly-eye cut out.

'The New Broken Dolls inform us they hold hostages,' said Eleanor.

Clicks came up on screen.

Geoffrey Reynolds, Union Jack gag plastered over his mouth.

Asmida shrugged.

Garn, clutching a camera like a blood donor clutching a crucifix when caught after dark in Highgate Village.

Chrissie felt as if she'd been walloped.

Ftatateeta and Tunno, mummified in masking tape, faces covered by ability-damping muzzles.

Eunice made and put out fires.

Bruno Brookes, unshaven and glum.

No one was here to care either way.

Loulee with a different hairstyle in a zoo-keeper's uniform. No, of course...

'Lamb Bear,' Loulee exclaimed.

Chrissie's thoughts were racing. It'd be Hereward's verps next...

Video panned across the hostages in dingy captivity. Grubby whitewashed walls. Sawdust on an earth floor. Playroom furniture in primary colours – restraints were painted to match. Lamb Bear looked least worried under the circumstances... Geoff Reynolds was the angriest, bare arms purple because he'd been tied tightly... Ftatateeta kept trying to be swift but movement set off her muzzle's electro-shocks and frizzed her already frizzy hair.

At the end of the pan wasn't Mr and Mrs Jackson-Walker but a familiar bedraggle of folk – Vidar, Chell, Symon, the ex-Dr Crockery, Monica Maude, the APJB and Polly O. The Coterie, chain ganged together by chi-chi anklets of party lanyards.

Hereward said things which would be bleeped on broadcast.

'The New Broken Dolls have your loved ones,' said Eleanor.

'Your task for today, Sixths, is to rescue them. Time may be running out.'

Chrissie realised the studio was lit only by the screen. Techs fiddled, presuming the fault was theirs.

It wasn't.

She had dispelled light to summon dark.

She unclenched and the lights came back up.

So this was a pickle.

ROUND TABLE, RE: LOVED ONES

LOULEE LING: I want some real clothes. Then I want some real answers.

ELEANOR WYNTER: So far as we can tell, the New Broken Dolls have seized people close to all of you... loved ones.

ASMIDA BINTI GEOFFREY REYNOLDS: Asss far asss I'm concerned, they can keep Geoff.

EUNICE UGLOW: You don't mean that, Asmida.

ASMIDA: Don't I? Let me think. Yesss, no. On reflection, I don't think they should keep him. They should bury him.

CHRISTINE CHAMBERS: They've taken Bruno – why?

LOULEE: I imagine their list is out of date.

EUNICE: Sad, really. Sandii's so bright and confident and lively...

ASMIDA: ... wasss...

EUNICE: You'd think she'd have other loved ones beside her ex. Do you think they were still seeing each other?

HEREWARD JACKSON-WALKER: Why have they taken your boyfriend, Eleanor? Are you a Sixth too now, replacing Weather Girl?

CHRISTINE: Garn isn't...

ELEANOR: ... my boyfriend!

CHRISTINE: He's mine, sorry.

EUNICE: You never said. How groovy. How long have...

ELEANOR: To the point... Loved ones in danger.

LOULEE: Hereward, you seem to have more loved ones than the rest of us put together... and Eunice has two.

HEREWARD: I wouldn't expect you to understand...

LOULEE: Your parents - who are safely unkidnapped, even if their factory burned down - pay Polly O to have you in her cludge.

HEREWARD: Who told you that?

CHRISTINE: Let's not get distracted.

HEREWARD: Christine! You cow.

ELEANOR: Any observations?

EUNICE: Striped poles... sawdust. This is that circus. Upside-Down Gonk's Circus.

LOULEE: Remember I said it was a trap.

CHRISTINE: It has cheese in it now, Louls.

LOULEE: Tell me about it. We can't go barging

in like... like Jack Pariah. But we've got to do something. It's not fair these people should suffer.

ASMIDA: Is that you in the zoo-keeper hat?

LOULEE: My brother. Twin brother. Lamb Bear.

ASMIDA: You but not a woman - tasssty. I'd be more interessted in ressscuing him than, sssay...

CHRISTINE: Yes, we know. Your dad. Pardon the rest of us for actually caring about people.

LOULEE: Lamb Bear looks after snakes. You might be in with a chance. He could get you a spot at the zoo.

EUNICE: Ftatateeta and Tunno will be working out how to escape.

ASMIDA: How long were you all on the Lime Corridor? That's the sssoftest in Devil's Dyke - and none of you essscaped from there.

HEREWARD: Chell has a sawdust allergy. She'll get weeping blemishes. And the All-Powerful Jupiter Boy has anxiety in unplanned situations.

LOULEE: Why am I not surprised?

HEREWARD: You've never got over not being in the Coterie, have you, Arsinoë?

LOULEE: What can I say? My parents aren't rich enough to buy me friends. I'm forced to resort to, I don't know, being nice to people.

CHRISTINE: Do you know what I think Weather Girl would say?

EUNICE: I miss her.

CHRISTINE: Me too. I think she'd tell us to

stop squabbling and embarrassing ourselves. So far, most of what we've done has been posing and showing off. Now, we have a crisis – a mission. We can't just wear cloaks, we have to *be* cloaks. As Loulee says, it's a trap. They'll be expecting us to rush in and trip up. That they could do what they've done demonstrates the New Broken Dolls aren't just voids. So we have to surprise them. There's talent around this table. Let's please put it to some use.

JASMINE AT THE SAFE HOUSE

JASMINE CHAMBERS, FORMER MISTRESS OF SHADOWS, lay on a lilo. She looked up at cloudless morning sky. Her pale skin would never tan but she wouldn't shrivel to dust either. She used to avoid direct sunlight. Having left the night-game, she could lounge away a morning in the open. Her retreat robe wasn't black but mint green. Her visual wasn't dark enlightened. Just on holiday.

She was post-Lady Shade... Post-cloakery... Post-Richard...

The loss would never be tolerable but bereavement no longer shrieked in her mind every waking moment then haunted her dreams. She wasn't moving on. If pushed, she was still angry. But she wasn't catatonic. She could consider other things. Progress.

The Safe House was an experimental community of the future. A miniature monorail wound between domes composed of hexagonal facets. A hydroponic seaweed farm was staffed by cuddlebots. Buildings nestled in the landscape's natural contours. Tomorrow Town, built in 1965 in anticipation of the Year 2000, became obsolete when the future arrived early and in a form H.G. Wells, Dan Dare or Patrick Moore wouldn't recognise. The Think Box was dismantled and its copper punch-cards used in a mosaic. The machine's cathedral-sized housing now held a zero-gravity pool – an alarming sphere of clear water with strange tides and unfriendly fish.

A localised miracle conjured by Magic Iona minimised the wind, rain and midges which bothered the rest of the Yorkshire Dales. The futurists who founded Tomorrow Town never cracked climate control. Some were peeved that a witch finally did the job for them. To many strivers of the '60s, enlightenment seemed like cheating.

In a joint venture, the Shadow Cabinet and Martin Masters bought Tomorrow Town and turned it into a retreat for cloaks who needed a break. Jasmine had been here before, as resident head-shrinker. She was back in her old plastigloo – a translucent dome with a spongy floor and a stash of Moorcock paperbacks.

The Safe House was run by Dr Lark and the Hard Bard.

Dr Lark was a proponent of the benefits of not doing anything in particular. The Hard Bard prescribed hikes up mountains while chanting poetry in a dead local language. He was slightly put out that omnilingual Jasmine could understand Brigantian.

Aside from Mark Shark, a permanent retreatee on the books as a swimming teacher so he could pretend to be on staff, Jasmine was the only cloak currently recuperating at the Safe House. When she arrived, there was a wobble as the Hard Bard, Wet Mark and other underemployed primpers and pamperers competed to offer strenuous comfort when she wanted to hide under duvet covers. Dr Lark called them off and let her be.

There were things to worry about. The Devil's Dyke debacle wasn't satisfactorily explained. An official board of inquiry and a covert investigation were looking into the incident. She'd given her testimony. Findings would probably be sealed for ninety-nine years. The Red Rope was overhauling security at the secure hospital. Carter de Beers had wrestled a fat contract from HMG. The White Corridor was installing unheard-of levels of lockdown. All the prize pupils wanted was for Christine not to come back. Terrifying in itself.

Jasmine cared less about her old workplace than her newly enlightened niece.

Her own recovery – from shock, not physical harm – meant absenting herself when she ought to be supporting Christine. Letting Poulton-Jones, the Shadow Cabinet, Mimsy Mountmain or Dot Schilling take up the slack gave her guilt pangs. It could be all too much for the girl.

Dr Lark limited contact with the outside world. Jasmine could write and receive letters. No Vone or Vook. No wireless, television or newspapers. Telepaths said voices in their head fell silent inside the Safe Zone. Mark Shark no longer heard the Call of the Deep. There weren't even ghosts. Magic Iona saw those off when she sorted out the midges.

A 'get well soon' card had come from Mimsy, with a message in Morse pricked out with a pin inside the brush of a cartoon fox. Christine was making a television programme rather than scrapping with crocks and cutthroats. Good. Telly was only pretend. For the most part.

Jasmine felt a slight disturbance in the fresh air.

She also heard a distinctive huffing. The Hard Bard jogged up the hill towards her.

'This isn't allowed,' he said, holding out a small black box.

She sat up and took the present. Cool to the touch, it was not metal, wood or ceramic. She recognised blackstuff, dark matter.

'So why are you giving it to me?'

'This isn't *usually* allowed,' he clarified. 'Dr Lark argued against it but it's from your lot – the Shadows – and they pay the gas bill.'

Jasmine was surprised the Safe House had gas. She had imagined the place ran on karma and kelp.

'It's urgent,' he said and huffed off.

Jasmine put the box on the ground, settling it in the grass. It expanded into a square about six feet across, encompassing the lilo. Then grew into a cube, encompassing her.

The inside was infinitely dark in all directions. She stood on darkness and in darkness. She saw herself but nothing else.

Figures coalesced at an indeterminate distance from her. Six persons in robes. Black hoods with eyeholes, voluminous black sleeves, latex surgeon's gloves.

The Shadow Cabinet.

She was used to them, if anyone ever could get used to them.

'What is it this time?' she asked.

It took long seconds to get an answer.

'It's Christine, of course,' she said. 'What now?'

ANJULIE GLAS, THE GREEN NINJA

'CHRISTINE CHAMBERS WAS A GRENADE. THE CIRCUS stratagem was to pull her pin.

'No, we didn't know the likely blast radius.

'I was arrested, if you remember, on Gibraltar. We weren't sure if that was far enough away.'

CHRISTINE IN CHARGE

'I'M GOING TO BE THE ONE TO SAY IT, CHRISSIE,' Loulee began. 'Last time you rounded us up for a mission, you instantly changed your mind then hared off on your own. What's different?'

Chrissie didn't have an answer.

Except now they were on television. She'd had months to realise how bloody stupid she'd been at Devil's Dyke. She'd been a danger to herself and others. It was a miracle they came through alive and relatively not insane.

'We did all right then,' said Eunice. 'And that was real. This is a... game.'

Chrissie and Loulee bit their lips.

Eunice hadn't worked it out and it verit wasn't fair to tell her.

They were past games, even the rigged, dirty games of *Crew Selection*. Chrissie reckoned safeguards were removed to make the show more real. More dangerous. BARB gold.

Eleanor Wynter didn't give away more than the Control Room wanted the Sixths to know but Chrissie reckoned the kidnappers were out for blood and victory. She'd blame Hereward the Waste but probbo this was always the plan. The Vision Controller was a pricier, legalised Inner Voice. He saw players as operants who gave up free will when they signed contracts.

But Loulee had a point. She had to address it.

'Louls, I'm sorry about what happened at Devil's Dyke. We had a lot to take on board quickly and I didn't handle it in the best way.'

... though she'd scythed through the White Corridor. Surely Aunt Jasmine's prize pupils were worse than these New Broken Dollies? Top of the bill cutthroats, not also-ran nuisances. Music hall turns like Mr Swizzle and Juke Box Jerry – even with added kit and clobber – were closer to crocks or suchlike voids. Troublemakers not lifetakers. One was a flipped-out Floppit, for heaving's sake.

Dark confidence bloomed.

She remembered night and fury. A sense of being inhabited rather than enlightened – channelling something shared with Shades of yore... Less coherent than Loulee's ghosts... A black thundercloud spitting violet bolts... An ocean of ergs pouring through her eyes to wash away everything in sight.

She didn't want that again. She contained her confidence.

If this was a game, it was a different one. New rules.

On the big screen was a fly-eye view of Upside-Down Gonk's Circus. A castle of orange-and-black striped tents beside a ruined stadium.

Fairground attractions filled the grounds. Punters tested their strength with a hammer-bell or shied hoops over wood-blocks to win goldfish in plastic bags. Civs. Candidates for the 'among the incidental casualties were...' list.

'That'ss the Dogss,' said Asmida. 'In Hackney Wick.'

'You know this how?' asked Hereward.

'Top Dog'ss old rookery. Famousss for Animal Fun Nightss. Urban Foxxss sshut it down. Don't you keep up, Wiper Trike?'

'Viper Strike.'

'Sssilly me. I was forgetting. How are you reptile-related?'

Asmida hissed. She had a hostility problem. But she'd been helpful.

'Thanks for the gen,' said Chrissie.

'The addresss was on the circusss flyer,' said Asmida. 'Like Arsssie said, it'ss a trap. All the hossstages – they're tethered goatsss. I'm not biting.'

It'd be easiest to leave Garter Snake behind. Who knew when

she'd switch sides or backstab a rival? Asmida was hell-bent on winning. It was the one thing she agreed with her dad about. But Chrissie knew they all had to be in this.

'It'd be good telly,' said Chrissie. 'A redemption arc, Asmida. Viewers love a family reconciliation.'

'You can win big take-home prizes,' whispered Loulee. 'And give the visual that we can't get by without you.'

'Which we can't,' said Eunice.

Asmida flicked her tongue out of her lipless mouth. She didn't know how that looked to warm-blooded people. She snake-blinked and nodded.

'All righty. Redemption I'm up for. Reconsssiliation not a hope.'

Chrissie was aware of Nelly watching her. And the cameras. She made an effort not to fuss with her wig.

Loulee wore her sleeveless jacket over a navy-blue boiler suit donated by Practical Effects Pete. Not sexy but not inhibiting. She'd lose votes for that. But whichever ghosts she let in on this caper wouldn't trip over veils and swords.

'Do we just take the Tube and pitch up at the circus?' asked Eunice. 'We've got invitations.'

'I can fly there,' said Hereward.

'Watch out Moonlight Flit,' sniped Loulee.

'You can fly Viper Strike there and stay here you mean,' said Chrissie.

'Yes, about that...'

Eric the Engineer, the 'what idiot' man, perked up at Hereward's signal. He put on a flying helmet stamped with the British RoboDynamics logo.

'I've arranged us a lift,' said Hereward.

Jasmine and the Shadow Cabinet

'Jasmine Chambers,' said the shadow with the tallest hood-point, raising a finger of accusal at her.

Christine should be dealing with the Shadow Cabinet now, not her.

'Marius, I know it's you,' she said.

Outside of the shadows, she'd met Marius Stok a handful of times. He'd toured the White Corridor with two Home Secretaries. He was often on television. Lowering his voice an octave didn't disguise it.

'I know who most of you are,' she went on. 'Fred, really? Keeping quiet doesn't make you any less you. Lady Leaves, of course. A retired Blackfist – your right hand is twice the size of the left. And... I think... Joshua Unwin. You represent business, right? The only one I'm not sure of is the new boy. I could make an educated guess. Most people don't think you exist so maybe you're a mask under a hood.'

None of them took off their silly bugger balaclavas.

Before the *Never Mind* moment, cloaks needed funding. For those without private fortunes, that involved sponsorship. Which meant answering to someone. Cutthroats had it easier. They could steal.

Dr Shade had the Shadow Cabinet. The circle renewed over

the decades, recruiting replacements through means no Shade needed to be told about. Jasmine admitted she'd relied on them. Natural abilities were well and good but a Shade needed Poulton-Joneses, lock-ups, toys and transport. With Christine taking on the mantle, she'd hoped she'd heard the last of the black hoods.

'Yes, it's Chrissie,' said Fred Regent – Richard's best friend, retired from Scotland Yard after service as Deputy Commissioner – 'and I'm afraid it's GEIST.'

She might have known.

'It's *always* GEIST.'

'Technically,' said Joshua Unwin with that giveaway 'yes but...' drawl, 'it's a rogue GEIST satrapy.'

'Aren't they all?' said Lady Leaves – glamour model cloak ('Lucy in the Sky'), married into a title, retired to respectability and good causes. It must have been a toss-up between the Shadow Cabinet and the Society for the Fen Frog.

'A plan has been in motion for months,' said Stok.

Jasmine was half-certain Marius Stok was a GEIST Satrap himself.

Maybe from a non-rogue satrapy with stronger ties to GEIST Central. So much large-scale trouble boiled down to scraps between pompous men in silly hats.

'Tell me about it,' Jasmine said. 'Messages in fortune cookies... Ultimate secure doors opening and closing at whim... Adam Bloody Tussaud waking up and playing the dickens... All at the same time as my niece goes dark. Of course it's a plan. We plan too, don't we?'

'Measures are in place,' said Stok.

'But we're still having this cosy chat. Did anyone order chee?'

'You're one of the measures, Jasmine,' said Fred.

'Won't Urban Fox do instead?'

'She's not a Shade and she's retired,' said Lady Leaves.

'Lucky her. She doesn't have a Foxy Cabinet to answer to, does she?'

She sighed. Even in this limbo, she heard her own breath whistling.

'I'm paying attention. Now, give me the bad news...'

LOULEE IN THE AIR

'IT WAS SUPPOSED TO BE A SURPRISE,' SAID HEREWARD.

The British RoboDynamics Boadicea Class helicopter took up ten spaces in the Cardinal Wolsey Street car park. Eric peeled off black plastic to show a fresh dayglo design. VIPER STRIKE AND THE SPLENDID SIXTHS was written on the side door. 'Viper Strike' was three times bigger than the rest of the billing. If Martin Masters had signed off on that, she would eat Chrissie's wig.

'It was my idea,' Hereward went on. 'A rapid response option.'

Loulee admitted this situation needed responding to rapidly. So long as Hereward wasn't piloting. And 'rapid response' wasn't just verpspeak for rushing headlong into an almighty balls-up.

Contessa Erco perked and flexed Loulee's fingers.

The ghost hadn't only driven cars, she'd piloted planes. She set a speed record for giving a lift to Mussolini from Rome to Kafiristan for a secret conference with someone evil who lived in a cave up a mountain. The Contessa's only experience with helicopters was watching a prototype contraption spin to pieces twenty feet in the air in 1921. That didn't stop her wanting to play with this twenty-first century whirlybeast.

So she wasn't much help.

To everyone's relief, Eric the Engineer turned out to be also Eric the Pilot. Basically a Poulton-Jones. Hereward couldn't fit in the pilot's seat anyway. His new cyber suit was too bulky. It trailed connector cables which plugged into armour and robo-doodads. Meet the new improved Viper Strike.

The Sixths clambered aboard the chopper. Inside, it looked like a coach only less comfortable and with more straps.

Yvyra was worried they were being swallowed and digested by the Big Sky God.

Oghulqaimish wanted to know where the swords were.

Dolly Filch remembered going up in a hot air balloon over London. She'd picked pockets as nobs craned to see their big houses below.

Loulee concentrated. If Dolly fully manifested, she was liable to snaffle items – coins, handkerchiefs, vital lug-nuts. Her effects department overalls had many swag pockets. She felt less a clot dressed like this beside contestants in gaudy, revealing get-ups.

There were six passenger seats.

BRD had forgotten this was a television show. Or hoped to deliver pre-edited flattering-to-Hereward footage to Crew Selection. But, of course, Weather Girl's seat was free. Camera Clare could sit in and get close-ups of the Sixths as they sped to the rescue. She asked for smiles all round. Only Eunice delivered.

'"If it's not on tape, it didn't happen",' said Clare, repeating an often-heard note.

Eleanor Wynter had her own transport and support staff. A convoy of armoured vans with a motorcycle escort.

There was milling and indecision. Anju the AP was absent again. That tickled Ni Tien's bump of suspicion, especially so soon after the discontinuation of her helper elf. General Floppy was forced to do several on-the-floor jobs on top of his director duties. Jah was sorely in need of a clipboard.

The helicopter could be in Hackney Marshes in a trice.

But the Wynter parade had to get there first, to film the arrival. Crew Selection would want to soundtrack the approach with the 'Dambusters March' or 'Legend of Xanadu'. Jah insisted Eleanor have a head start. Her semi-legit Scotland Yard ID – which obliged traffic policemen to clear roads for her – was getting a lot of wear.

In the studio, Chrissie had taken charge. Hereward's surprise backfooted her. She was too often in the habit of deferring to louder, stupider people.

'Don't let him take over,' Loulee told her friend. 'He's still an idiot.'

Chrissie nodded. Eunice leaned over, eager to take instruction.

'Let him crasssh and burn,' hissed Asmida. 'Then sstep up.'

Several ghosts thought that sound advice. Many had had men like Hereward in their lives – especially near the end of their lives.

Eric got the go-ahead and flicked switches.

The rotors creaked alarmingly as they began to turn. Loulee gripped armrests and grit her teeth. She was not a happy flyer.

For once, a modern gadget alarmed Loulee more than it did the ghosts.

She hoped British RoboDynamics put more effort into the Boadicea than, say, the Schloup. Or the defence system of their factory. Or failsafes on Viper Strike Mk 1. Or those electric fondue sets which exploded if you used Gruyère. Or...

Loulee decided not to remember more BRD consumer disasters.

Contessa Erco rose again, insisting Loulee shove Eric out of the pilot's seat and take the controls. She came close to shoving Loulee out of her own head.

Not for the first time, the ghosts felt more a liability than an advantage.

There were stakes. People were in danger. And she'd rather take a bus.

Chrissie put a hand over hers and squeezed.

'He'll be all right,' said Chrissie. 'Lamb Bear. We won't let the voids hurt him.'

Trust Chrissie to worry more about Loulee's loved one than her own.

MONICA MAUDE – HOSTAGE

'WE WOKE UP IN CAGES WHICH PONGED OF DOG.

'The silver chauffeur and the tall hostess weren't around. Three tubby chums were left to see we didn't escape. We were in an underground animal enclosure. Straw on the floor. The guards wore lederhosen and whiteface with red circles on their cheeks. They turned out to be a renegade Floppit fan club. They were more interested in a wall of closed-circuit televisions than tormenting hostages with pain prods or throwing slop into feeding bowls. On the screens was a circus. Jugglers, contortionists, stilt-walkers. Sunday night granny telly. Urgh.

'Vidar and Chell still thought this was the Surprise Shenanigans and reckoned the Scarlet Whosoever was being radical. To get to the verit party, we had to escape from the dog pens. They tried to unlock their cages using laminates like keycards. It wasn't worth arguing with them.

'The All-Powerful Jupiter Boy threw a wobbly but calmed after a pain prodding.

'We weren't the only prisoners. I recognised the brewery heir Garn Graill and that beef-faced geezer from *Crew Selection* – the one with the cobra woman daughter.

'Polly O talked in French to a pretty, long-haired fella who showed her he'd already picked his cage-lock with a bent nail.

He was waiting for his moment.

'Another captive had piled straw over his head and was moaning. "That's Bruno," said Garn, "don't mind him. He's been taken as a hold over someone he put in hospital, so he's liable to be rescued last."

'I worked it out. "This is about the Sixths. We're leverage over them. That's the lizard stripper's dad."

'"That's right," said Garn. "The kids with muzzles are friends with the Little Match Girl."

'They were in a reinforced cage. When they nodded, their muzzles shocked them. Which was excessive. They rated extra precautions because they had extra resources. They were enlightened. I remembered them from *Crew Selection* too – I don't watch it, just skim the highlights on Peophole, to be part of the conversation – the very quick girl and the boy who could flatten a piano. Not exactly Great Britannia or Moonlight Flit.

'"We're here because of Chrissie," exclaimed Vidar. "Lady Shade!"

'"No, that's me,' said Garn. "You're here because of..."

'It hung in the air before anyone said the name.

'"Perishing Hereward," swore Chell. "Can we talk to someone in charge? This is a mistake. None of us care about *Perishing Hereward*. He's not Coterie Verit. He's an add-on.'

'"It doesn't work like that,' said Garn.

'I don't see the point of Hereward. Or get how he got glued to us. He was just there one day. No one liked to come straight out and say he was the Archbolus of Voidbury. I think he turned up with Symon. Or maybe he latched onto Chrissie when she was on one of her outs with Garn. We should have thrown him back in the pond.

'The screens showed a helicopter in flight. It had "Viper Strike" on the side.

'Polly O summoned one of the fan club voids to her exclusive cage and whispered in his ear.

'He snapped to attention like a head waiter finding a prime table for her in a fully booked restaurant. His pals hustled to the pretty fella's cage and took away his bent nail. Then they triple-locked him in with extra chains.

'Polly O was freed and escorted out of the pens. She didn't look back.

'The lock-picker said some things about her. None of us agreed. He should have known what to expect. Polly O is so far up on the Wheel it's a wonder she can breathe.

'Garn got clicks of Polly leaving. They'll never be cleared for publication.

'Marcus tried to talk to the head lederhosen lout too. He claimed he was the arch-nemesis of Lady Shade. He wanted to call himself Dr Victoriola. If there was to be a scrap with the Sixths, he volunteered to be on a roof with a sniper rifle. He was sure the circus folk would lend him a sniper rifle. For a moment, it looked like he'd get his shot. Guards opened his cage. Then they laughed. The biggest clown gave Marcus a thorough pain prodding. After he came round, he told us he'd been attempting a ruse to escape and would have got help to rescue us. No one believed him.

'Garn was surprisingly not that fussed about Marcus offering to kill his girlfriend from a distance. Fair enough – Dr Crockery as was wouldn't know which end of a rifle to hold if instructions were written on the stock. However, the shock-muzzled kids were livid. They'd been in captivity before and had strong views on snitches. When we got out of this, Marcus would have to look over his shoulder for them. He'd be in for a pasting. A thousand fingerflicks delivered in less than a second will leave a whacking great bruise. And he could get out of casualty to find his parents' house flattened like a flapjack.

'The All-Powerful Jupiter Boy screamed for Viper Strike to save us.

'Usually, Symon calmed APJB down. But – and it was funny none of us had noticed – Symon wasn't with us. He didn't have Polly O's pull, so we knew he was for it. The circus needed to hang a maimed hostage from a fence to show they weren't pretending. Symon got picked.

'He wouldn't have been my first choice. Losing Marcus or Jupe would have been a relief or at least kept the noise down. Symon had an invisible talent. Or a talent for being invisible. He was never anyone's first choice for anything. Good or bad. Unlike Chell or Hereward, he didn't stand out as useless either. He was one of the ones in the middle. Until now. Poor thing.'

DAKIN AND VIPER STRIKE II

THE SIXTHS WERE COMING!

A fleet of beetle-black minivans found parking spots outside the Dogs. Crew piled out with camera gear.

Eleanor Wynter was on the scene, spieling as fly-eyes fanned out to get views of the circus.

Johnnie wanted to lob mortars at the media. Dakin cooled him off.

'Save it for the Sixths,' he said.

Some of Upside-Down Gonk's operants wore big papier mâché heads – flap-eared elephants, long-necked giraffes, angry tigers. The Flipped Floppit wanted to parade his fan club through the Shed to create a verit humanimal menagerie. Everyone else felt that could get out of hand and not in a good way.

Now they all had vitality plus, fathead ideas were fizzing ten a penny.

'Look,' said Cyndi, 'up in the sky...'

Afternoon clouds whipped apart as if a lawn strimmer were dipped in a bowl of egg white. Dakin's improved eyes focused on a black shape.

'That's them,' said Dakin. 'In a bleedin' chopper.'

Johnnie whipped up a shoulder-launched anti-aircraft cannon.

It wouldn't go off. An override was built in to prevent Johnnie bringing down seven varieties of hell. One big aerial fireball and a rain of body parts and twisted metal wouldn't be much of a show.

This scrap had to be a spectacle. Anything else was a contract violation.

Besides, no one knew which of the Sixths could survive a mid-air detonation with enough juice – and a serious grudge – to be a major nutache. That Pyro Pixie person was friends with fire.

A welcoming party was stationed at the main gate. Johnny with his soldier suit and hey presto armoury. Dakin in his Silver Adonis posing pouch and machine oil. Cyndi modelling her Dungeon-Mistress Hired by Insane Information Retrieval Tycoon Who Thinks He's Emperor Heliogabolus visual: silk hat, scarlet tailcoat, Miss Whiplash corset, fishnet stockings, spike-heel boots, and blood-speckled fissure of cleavage.

They were the first line.

The real freaks – Mr Swizzle, Upside-Down Gonk, Juke Box Jerry – ran sideshows. Know-nothings milled about as set dressing. Some bakewells who thought they were auditioning for a booth dancing attraction, ex-Top Dog hefts who heard the commotion and pitched up for old times' sake, and random mugs drawn by JBJ's hurdy-gurdy selections who took this for a nice family day out and were happily stuffing their gobs with candyfloss and waiting for the fun to start.

Which would be just about now...

The helicopter hovered. Litter gusted in whirlpools. Those with hats held on to them. Minions bent double while Eleanor Wynter stood straight and kept up the rabbit. Cameras turned skywards.

Doors in the floor of the helicopter opened.

Were they going to drop bombs? Not sporting, if so.

Big boots lowered through the hatch. Then tin legs, a metal torso, outstretched arms and a robot head.

It wasn't the gargantuabot which totalled Cowcross Street but was obviously in the same line. Viper Bloody Strike.

Johnnie's override clicked off.

This target he was allowed to take a shot at.

Dakin put metal fingers in his metal lugholes – scraping steel on steel – before Johnnie pulled the trigger.

A plume of flame spurted out the back of the rocket-launcher and melted a patch of asphalt.

The missile sped towards Viper Strike II's chest.

The mecha zipped to one side faster than expected. The old model was clunky. This one was designed for nippiness.

The rocket was now someone else's problem. Not a good day to be working on the allotment, perhaps.

A diamond of dark appeared in the sky, rimmed with purple.

Dakin had seen it before, on a smaller scale.

The rocket popped into the rip in reality. The diamond zipped up after it.

'Wha... ?' said Johnnie.

'Christine Chambers,' said Cyndi. 'Lady Shade. Whatever.'

She was the Sixth who most prickled Dakin's chrome-finish hide. Her party piece gave him the fear. He didn't even like to think about those holes she made. Or what he saw inside them if he squinted.

Johnnie had another rocket – a bigger one, with a cluster of warheads – loaded and ready to fire. Cyndi gripped his shoulder, indicating he should hold off.

'There's something different about that box kite,' she said.

The gargantuabot touched down gently, without even going into an impact crouch. Slimmer-hipped than the last version, it moved more like a person than a machine. That wasn't due to an improved interface.

'That's not a box kite,' he said. 'There's someone inside it.'

'Peregrine Plonker,' said Cyndi. 'The merchant banker with the friends who hate him.'

The gargantuabot walked towards them. An automated ticket taker – the straw-hatted fibreglass upper half of a jolly showman perched on a box of bolts, levers and circuitry – bent backwards.

This Viper Strike had no telescreen face. Just a metal mask with camera-lens eyes.

'Lay down your weapons,' came an amplified squawk. 'Release the hostages. In the name of the law.'

Johnnie whisked his rocket launcher into a cloud of whirling parts which reassembled as a set of knife-grenades. He chucked them at Viper Strike. They flew towards the mecha like mad starlings but detonated in harmless puffs of flame. The gloss on the bucket-head carapace wasn't even scratched.

Viper Strike raised its arms, aiming...

... an all-too familiar sight.

Cyndi pushed Johnnie aside and walked up to their visitor.

On her heels, she was almost eye to eye with the robot mask. She did not look like someone who was about to surrender.

But she also can't have looked too dangerous.

The thick soft lad inside the ironmongery probably saw a tall fit bird more likely to ask him for his autograph than take a can-opener to his crotch.

A grievous mistake.

As she got near Viper Strike, Cyndi took hold of her lapels. Which deepened her cleavage. Dakin saw gleams in those camera eyes and guessed where they were focusing. Hyphen Herbert was hot and bothered inside his cyber undies.

'My face is up here,' she told him.

From under her lapels, she took a length of shimmering scarf – the grippable end of a cheesewire monofilament.

Cyndi looped the scarf around the robot neck – the camera eyes bugged like a cartoon – and pulled the noose tight.

The gargantuahead popped off like a champagne cork.

Viper Strike buckled at the knees, red fluid spurting out of its neck aperture, and collapsed in a sparking, twitching heap.

Cyndi poked the fallen mecha mug with the shiny toe of her spiked boot.

She looked up at the hovering chopper and tipped her hat to the survivors.

Johnnie, of course, had to ruin the moment by picking up the severed head and waving it at the cluster of cameras.

Still, that was back at the Sixths for Major Wood!

CHRISTINE IN COMMAND

THE HELICOPTER TOUCHED DOWN AND THE DUCK'S-arse end opened up.

The soldier doll still held up Viper Strike's noggin.

'That red stuff is coolant, not blood,' said Loulee. 'Hereward's head wasn't in the headpiece. He's scrunched up in a control capsule inside the torso. His arms and legs aren't in the mecha arms and legs either.'

The tall woman sliced off one of the gargantuabot's arms with her trick scarf. She held it like a trophy and flapped its hand.

'You know this how?' Chrissie asked.

Loulee rolled her eyes, as if indicating an invisible person standing next to her.

'A ghost engineer?' Chrissie whispered.

'The Contessa. She thinks in technical diagrams.'

'Hereward isn't dead,' Chrissie told Eunice and Asmida.

Eunice was happy. Asmida was not fussed.

'Yet,' said Loulee. 'He could drown in coolant. Or be electrocuted by the suit's insides. Or they could prise him out of its chest and kick him to fishpaste.'

'His head isn't in the headpiece,' shouted Eric – who'd not heard the chat thanks to his big cans.

Chrissie looked at the entrance arch.

The tall woman – Cyndi Doll – was playing with the arm. The soldier – Johnnie Seven – produced a series of small-arms and pinged shots off Hereward's chest-plate. The bullets made dents. The armour wouldn't hold up forever.

A little buzzing of distress came over the chopper's intercom.

'Viper Strike down... Request evac... Cover fire...'

'Ignore that,' said Asmida.

'Would that we could,' said Loulee.

This was going to be a scrap and a half. The visual had to be good because they were on telly. They also had to win, not just for viewer votes. Loved ones and innocent parties – and even voids like Marcus Milner – had to be saved. That was the brief.

A shame this was happening in August. A long light evening. Chrissie would have liked velvet night to give her added vim and cover inelegant pratfalls.

She scoffed a Kendal Mint Cake, angling herself away from Camera Clare so she wouldn't look like a pig on television. Tish, who was safe back in Cardinal Wolsey Street, had issued emergency sweet rations. Ideally, Chrissie would fuel up before a scrap with a heap of bangers and mash followed by a whole rice pudding – but there wasn't time for a proper nosh. She hoped she had the ergs she needed.

Asmida was salivating.

'You'll want Cyndi, I suppose,' said Chrissie.

That lipless mouth wide-smiled and the forked tongue flicked.

'SSSertainly...'

'Eunice, do you reckon you can sort out the soldier doll? We talked about what you can do with your enlightenment.'

Eunice gave Chrissie a thumbs-up. Her thumb flicked flame like a Ronson.

'I'll take the metal minder. Louls, you're on crowd safety. Sorry it's boring but it has to be done. Too many surplus civs on site. If you shift them out of line of fire, it'd be a help. We can't afford incidental casualties.'

Loulee was quiet a moment. Chrissie now knew what that was about. Ghosts were arguing. Some bloodthirsty spooks felt pampering bystanders was beneath them. Being dead, they put less value on other peoples' lives. Loulee needed to overrule them and stay in command.

Loulee was the only Sixth Chrissie could trust to look after supporting artists instead of playing up to the camera or going berserk.

Eunice didn't have enough experience of life outside institutions. She didn't get that burning down a school because of one annoying rule was a poor choice. That she meant no harm was no comfort to flammable folk or their insurers.

Asmida didn't care who got hurt – including herself. She was a match for Cyndi, another name in the nutter file. They had personal enmity too. A useful subplot .

'Let's not charge in like Hereward,' said Chrissie. 'We'll walk over there reasonably...'

'... and set them off like fireworks,' shouted Eunice.

A burning path streaked towards the circus entrance. Johnnie Seven looked up from the wreck of Viper Strike, blaze reflected in his goggles. Bunting smouldered and burst into flame.

Asmida bounded out of the helicopter.

'Wait for me,' said Eunice and ran after the *naga*.

Chrissie gave a 'what did I say' look to Loulee, who gave a 'what did you expect' shrug back at her.

'Come on Glamour Girl,' said Loulee.

Chrissie stepped onto solid ground. She cast an evening shadow before her. It flowed like a river of night.

ELEANOR IN THE THICK OF IT

SHE WAS ANNOYED THAT THE NEW BROKEN DOLLS HAD kidnapped her pet snapper. It had been explained that Garnet Graill was involved with one of the contestants. Eleanor didn't bother to learn which hussy had claws in him. Any Sixth would pawn a nana to get flattering close-ups.

Crew Selection had a policy against backstage entanglements unless plotted and scripted. Writers pitched ships – Worried Winifred/Handsome Hereward or Blackfist/Pretty Chrissie – but so much else was on the boil that no pairings were anywhere near screen-ready.

Graill was good. He made Eleanor look good. He had bright ideas. Also, he was her discovery – not provided by the programme. They'd made the most of a breaking news opportunity at Devil's Dyke. She needed the snapper slaved to her. Schilling would fix that.

The Sixths should be in competition with each other, not her.

But because of an unwise liaison, Graill was a hostage. In a cage where he was no use to Eleanor.

She made do with fly-eyes until Camera Clare slid out of the helicopter.

The director was in her earpiece again, telling her things she already knew or didn't need to know. Adrian Jah was covering too many jobs and doing none of them well. Anjulie Glas was another irksome absence. She didn't have the excuse of being abducted.

At this rate, Eleanor would end up presenting, directing and producing *Crew Selection* on her own.

She'd want to renegotiate fees and billing.

Being outside the studio was always a risk. Considering what happened to Sandii Beach, being in the studio was chancy enough. It had been on the table that Weather Girl might dispel rain or fog if climate got in the way of filming. That went out the window when Sandii got hospitalised by bolus Bruno.

So this was Hackney Wick Stadium. Light breeze and the smell of roadworks.

Things on fire. Clowns in oversize shoes.

Today's scheduled set-piece was a scrap between the Sixths and the NBDs – a proper cloak-and-cutthroat barney. Not on the scale of the Battle of Battersea but plenty of biffing and thumping. Tragic losses. Daring rescues. Someone having their silly face pushed in. Foulness foiled and virtue rewarded. Points and prizes. Eliminations to be determined. Not too many loiterers or production staff putting in injury claims. Alfs and berts kept to the safety of the fleet of Red-Tel vans.

Eleanor glimpsed an emerald flash. Mingling with animal-head performers.

Her own deadly foe was here – the Green Ninja!

Was this a subplot she'd not been looped into or had she acquired an enlightened, deadly flan-flinger? She had a notion the Green Ninja had been about all along. She kept telling people who wouldn't listen that sinister slyboots were out to get her. If she got got they'd feel stupid but she'd be in no position to rub it in.

She suppressed an impulse to run and hide.

Clare got a shot of her walking into a trouble zone. Eleanor worked her shoulders to project confidence.

She would show them all.

Garter Snake was dancing around Cyndi Doll. They ought to be evenly matched but Cyndi was nippier on spike-heels than her record suggested. The cutthroat had tricks up her ever-changing sleeves. Asmida hissed and darted but her slashing didn't connect. She spat venom.

Then Cyndi slapped the snake girl across the face.

... and knuckled her again with the backhand.

That surprised Asmida. Cyndi shouldn't be quicker than her.

The NBD face-cards were out of date. That's what happens when researchers go missing or get Next Tuesdayed.

From somewhere, Cyndi produced a leather handbag with metal knobbles. She fetched Garter Snake a clout on the side of her head.

Asmida was unsteady on rubbery legs. She wavered from side to side, not sinuous but dazed. The *naga* would lose votes with this poor showing. She was supposed to be the tough nut.

Meanwhile, Johnnie Seven conjured bludgeons, axes, blowtorches and pistols to use on the fallen hulk of Viper Strike. Like Cyndi's glad rags and battering bag, the weapons came from nowhere and got sent back there after use. The *wrongness* of that was like silver foil on new fillings.

Viper Strike was in a sorry state but its chest-hatch was unbreached. So far.

Somewhere inside, Hereward Jackson-Walker was in foetal position. Blubbing, probably. It'd be hard to justify keeping him in competition after this, even if his verps made a fuss. Viper Strike was going out.

The show would miss him. Every crew needed an obvious idiot to take it out on.

Frustrated, Johnnie started booting the robot's tin ribs.

Eunice Uglow watched from a safe distance. It was like one of those routines where comedians politely let each other do their worst with fruit flans and canned cream before responding with desserts of their own.

No... It was cleverer than that.

Too cunning for the Little Match Girl to think up by herself. Someone was giving her ideas.

Eleanor felt the heat from a dozen yards off. The thermometer was rising. Johnnie's khakis smouldered. His skin blistered. Usually, the Uglow effect was full burn. This was Pyro Pixie on simmer.

Christine Chambers also stood back and let the cutthroats get on with it. She summoned ghastly black stuff from the atmosphere... Or did she leak it from her pores? Dark tendrils extended from her fingers. Blacklight burned behind her Spex.

Her veins were traceries of graphite. Eleanor hoped Clare was getting the spooky effect. If her visual went weirder, Chambers could win a scrap but lose the audience. Eleanor could happily scratch Chambers too. She'd never trusted Christine. The kitten had come back from the canal once. This time, the bag needed to be tied up with stronger string.

'Watch your backs,' Dakin told Cyndi and Johnny.

The metal mauler eyed Chambers but at least paid attention to the other NBDs. Eleanor had pegged him as 'the sensible one' at the initial meeting. Every crew needed one of those too. He also had a made-over visual. Shinier, bulkier, less clothed.

Johnnie spun and saw Eunice standing there.

The void looked past her – even though she was wearing a fireman's helmet and a flame-pattern leotard – because this small person couldn't possibly be turning a heat ray on him. She was only a girl. Hadn't the tin soldier stayed awake in briefings? Or watched the flipping programme? They were three episodes in. Everyone should know the contestants by now.

Johnnie looked back at Dakin, for clarification...

Eunice stepped closer.

The pips on Johnnie's epaulettes popped. Realisation finally dawned.

'You little...'

Johnnie's hands were full. Two pistols with tommy gun clips. Dum-dum bullets. Little explosives to turn small wounds into gaping injuries.

Not a clever choice, considering...

The gun barrels went soft and drooped embarrassingly. Eleanor could imagine the unkind remarks on Whispers...

Then the magazines exploded, ruining Johnnie's hands and the front of his shirt.

His face burned. He fell backwards, screaming.

Eunice looked pleased with herself. But also more like a cutthroat than a cloak.

Viewers could turn against her too. They'd seen a lad set on fire and squeal like a ninny. That would get sympathy from some of the mums.

What would Pyro Pixie do next? Boil goldfish? Burn down a circus?

Eunice turned to Cyndi...

'That's quite enough of that,' said the tall troublemaker, sloshing Little Match Girl with her goodnight handbag.

With Eunice insensible, the temperature dropped.

Asmida crawled out of range, probably reassessing her career choices.

Eleanor had expected the Sixths to perform better. At this rate, they'd have to rework the programme as *Crew Selection: Cutthroat Krewe*. Vote for the vilest villain. The Scream Team had vacancies whenever members got sent down. Truro Daine, their mad manager, would probably be less ruthless at the contracts stage than Martin Masters.

Meanwhile, it was dusky. True sunset wasn't for ages so Eleanor knew who to blame.

With Viper Strike, Garter Snake and Pyro Pixie kissing canvas, it was Shadow Drip's turn to mix it with the baddies.

Cyndi and Dakin looked smug.

'You join us at a tense moment in Hackney Marshes,' Eleanor said as Clare got a good angle. 'Despite valiant efforts, the Sixths have *not* prevailed over the New Broken Dolls. The cutthroat crew still hold hostage an assortment of plus ones, relatives and pets. Could this be a turning point? Is it possible None of the Above will prevail and the Splendids will be one short of Six at the end of the series? It has to be said hotly tipped competitors like Viper Strike, Garter Snake and the Little Match Girl have not covered themselves in glory. Arsinicola has apparently fled the field in shame...'

'She's shepherding people to safety,' said Jah in her ear. 'We have film of her saving a family from crock clowns.'

'... in shame, saving her own hide – doubtless a big no-no with the voters at home,' Eleanor ploughed on.

Christine Chambers gave Eleanor the side-eye.

Evidently, she could hear all this.

'At this juncture, only one Sixth stands...'

Asmida tried to get up. Her unusually bendy anatomy defeated her. She couldn't straighten her neck, back or legs. Her backbone disconnected from her hipbone... Her hipbone disconnected from her leg-bone...

Christine eyelocked the NBDs.

'Lady Shady,' Eleanor continued. 'The most mysterious, least touted of the six Sixths. Pitted against Cyndi Doll and Kung Fu Grip, formidable cutthroats who've put her competition out of the running. It's almost as if Her Shadiness were in on a dubious deal. Has she fully embraced the raging dark core of her being? Many – including respected commentators Boyd Waylo and Dr Victoriola – suggest this makes her more a menace than many an outright wrong 'un. Could we be about to see the verit cutthroat who has masked herself as a cloak all along?'

'Keep talking, Nelly,' said Chambers. 'There's a ninja behind you.'

Unable to resist, Eleanor turned and saw multiple camera crews, grateful innocents recently shepherded to safety by Louise Ling, some carnival performers with big heads and a stack of unconscious clowns.

No Green Ninja.

'Made you look,' said Chambers.

The chit was begging for discontinuance. She could join that Lythgoe person in the labour exchange! Or take Jill di Ferrante's bed in *VIP Ward*.

'Now, you two,' said Chambers. 'Cynthia Dolan and Ashton Dakin – yes, I did the homework – I don't suppose you'd like to give up now and let me have my boyfriend back. Oh, and the others.'

The harpie and the heft looked at one another, then Christine.

'Didn't think so,' said the Sixth.

Black material poured out of the palms of her hands like fast-blossoming negative explosions.

DAKIN IN THE DARK

IT WASN'T WHAT HE EXPECTED.

It wasn't what *anyone* would have expected.

There was no impact, no tidal wave of night overwhelming him, no roaring tornado of dark matter.

He was Somewhere Else.

Somewhere cold and dry.

He was out in the open, on uneven terrain. No man-made structures in sight. No sun, moon or stars. A faint purple tinge to the blackness outlined a horizon. He couldn't tell how far or near it was.

He wasn't alone in the dark.

He was grasped – though he was supposed to be the one who did the gripping – by a giant fist of terror. It wasn't something he could toughen up and get over. No way round it. He was bottling.

He had made his last bad decision.

Red eyes opened close to his face.

CHRISTINE AND THE CUTTHROATS

SHE HELD DAKIN AND DOLAN BY THEIR THROATS.

Dark ribbons wound round their heads, knitting into mummy-wrappings.

Chrissie wanted to *send them away*.

She pushed them through slits in reality. They disappeared. Her hands dipped into black vertical pools.

She silently counted to ten. She had an idea that the count was much, much slower in the *away*... the Purple Place.

Then she brought the cutthroats back. Apertures sealed behind them. Darkstuff leaked and evaporised.

Dakin, the man with the kung fu grip, wasn't steely any more... just a shivering, old-ish bloke in a Tarzan nappy. Chrissie tasted his terror, which disturbed her. She felt what he felt, saw herself as he saw her... and didn't like it much. Aunt Jasmine and Urban Fox had talked about the flipside of her gifts. She understood the temptation to go fully dark. It was an easy win. Too easy. She'd have to live with consequences. Drat! Had Nelly made the right shout? 'Verit cutthroat'. She really didn't want to live down to that.

She let Dakin go.

He backed away, calmly at first, bloodshot eyes on her... then broke into a run and fled. He didn't stop to give a post-scrap interview to the mop-up crew. He was dropping out of the New Broken Dolls.

Chrissie supposed she'd won something.

A scrap, or a kind of scrap.

But she didn't understand *how*. Aunt Jas might be able to tell her what she'd done – or, more importantly, whether it was a justified use of her talents or deeply, dangerously unwise.

She still had Dolan to deal with.

The tall woman wasn't as frightened as Dakin. Which meant she was too crackers to have even a partial understanding of her dip into dark. Or had a different reaction to being *sent away*. Maybe she liked the Purple.

Nelly was in close, commentating. Camera Clare captured footage of this cloak-on-cutthroat action.

Chrissie held Cyndi's neck with both hands.

The woman was too tall to be lifted off her feet. Chrissie's elbows ached.

Ribbons of darkness fluttered. Little black holes opened and closed like the mouths of fish. Peep-portals to the beyond. Easy to mistake for after-images – spots before her eyes. Did they register on film?

Cyndi changed her outfit.

She went through...

... suit of armour with Mayan engravings, snouty mask sporting exaggerated curly eyelashes. Quetzalcutie.

... crimson bodystocking feathered with detachable darts, head-dress with deely boppers. Red Nightingale.

... bowler hat, umbrella, black Burtons suit, jewelled knuckle dusters. City Girl.

Chrissie took blows to her side from that handbag mace.

What was in it? Concrete blocks?

It would make so much sense to let go and send her away. *Further away.* Giving Dakin a taste of the dark made him run away. Cyndi Doll wasn't as easily persuaded.

She was strong – capable of bending Chrissie like a hairpin.

She couldn't be talked to.

This wasn't anything to do with being on television. If Cyndi was supposed to lose this scrap, she hadn't got the pink pages. She wasn't the simple throat they'd been told about. She'd changed. All the New Broken Dolls were levels up from where they'd been before. The bells and whistles proved this wasn't just a game show any more. If it ever had been.

Lady Shade II was as liable to be knocked down as Perky Purkiss.

... tributes are coming in... After the news, there'll be a memorial special... The Girl Guides issued condolences to...

Chrissie's internal worrying was drowned by Nelly's hushed, excited commentary.

'... it looks like it's curtains for this outclassed contestant. Black curtains.'

Eleanor Wynter would be the last person to get the memo. The safety buttons on the ends of the foils were removed. This was not a fix for the fans like afternoon wrestling. But a scrap to the death.

Another slam to the side. A knee in the stomach.

Chrissie was losing her grip... mind... consciousness. The pain was going away. A bad sign, like the last stages of hypothermia – when the cold felt like a warm bath.

Spit. She'd like to have known how it all turned out.

A ray of light cut through whirling shadows.

A man floated down from the sky. A cloak wearing a proper cloak – plush black dotted with mini-moons of reflective stuff like cats' eyes. Off-white gym kit showed off lithe limbs. Longish blonde hair in a Beatle cut. Handsome in a bland, fuzzy way which was hard to describe. Even features. Blue eyes. Ultrabrite smile.

Moonlight Flit.

Even Cyndi was impressed enough to lay off the handbagging.

'Ladies,' said the cloak, with a slight hum in his voice.

Chrissie's dark ribbons reeled in. She calmed. It was something in the cloak's aura, perhaps in the aura of his cloak.

'... in a surprise development, Moonlight Flit has appeared on the scene,' said Nelly, needlessly. 'Perhaps the mystery man will give us a few words...'

The cloak just looked at Eleanor and she shut up.

That was as impressive an ability as bending steel bars or disintegrating granite.

Asmida, who had slithered close, gazed at the flying man. His boot-soles hovered six inches above the ground, giving the impression that he was tall enough to look eye-to-eye with Cynthia Dolan.

A squeak came from the mangled squawkbox of Viper Strike. Hereward wasn't fishpaste yet.

Inside the light cast by the newcomer, everyone relaxed. No one wanted to scrap. A mental thing, like Urban Fox's secret ability. Chrissie resented it but was in too good a mood to complain. It was vibes. Lunar vibes. The hum of the spheres. Relax and float.

She wasn't dying any more. Neither was she scrapping.

Cyndi was too angry to be completely calmed.

She wanted to rip off Chrissie's fingers, stamp through Viper Strike's chest.

She wore an Astronette Gladiatrix Up for a Scrap With a Venusian Scorpion-Shark outfit – midriff-baring leotard with crustacean shoulderpads, heavy gravity bubble helmet, moon boots, gauntlets studded with diamond drill-bits.

She screeched and reached for Chrissie. Her gauntlets extended grabbles.

Moonlight Flit hugged Cyndi from behind – pinning her arms to her side, whispering something soothing into her ear. Then they were both gone.

Chrissie saw Clare angling higher and higher, wincing as she cricked her neck. Her arm was still in a cast so this must be agony. Possibly worth it for the shot.

Moonlight Flit rose fast – the speed of light? – and was for an instant only a spark in the evening sky.

When the cloak was gone, his aura of calm went away too.

Chrissie was bruised, trembling and knotted inside. She leaked darkness from under her fingernails. Not something she wanted shown on television.

'Moonlight Flit is not, of course, a contestant on *Crew Selection*,' said Eleanor. 'It seems the cloak was on one of his regular aerial patrols and took the trouble to come gallantly to the aid of damsels in disarray. How this affects the competition is a question for the Adjudication Board...'

... of whom Chrissie hadn't heard until just now.

'... and, most of all, the voting viewership. Should this intervention by an above-the-fold cloak be considered disqualifying for any Sixth who might have benefited? Or are there things which need explaining about the relationship of light and dark… Shadow and the moon… Lady Shady and Moonlight Flit.'

'Give it a rest, Nelly,' said Chrissie.

'You what?' exclaimed Eleanor, instantly furious. The lit-up piping of her LaserBlazer rippled.

Chrissie thought she'd been scrapping with the wrong voids. She only had one arch-nemesis on this show.

How many points would she get for breaking Nelly's nose?

Then she was calm again, beyond grudge diaries and knuckly punches.

Moonlight Flit was back from his sky trip. Cyndi Doll was limp in his arms, asleep. Her floating, filmy raiment changed colour as she dreamed.

'She passed out in the upper atmosphere,' he explained.

Something about his voice was familiar.

Moonlight Flit presumptuously handed the unconscious – and heavy – cutthroat to Chrissie. Her knees buckled.

Could someone qualified take the NBD off her hands? A policeman, perhaps?

Chrissie lay the dozing Doll on the ground.

Asmida crawled over to Cyndi and flicked her face with her tongue. She touched Cyndi's throat. Her fingernails were shiny tortoiseshell, like guitar plectrums.

'Perhaps best not,' said Chrissie.

Eunice was also up and about. She focused heat and melted bolts on the Viper Strike torso. A panel fell off. Hereward, sweaty and snotty, sprung out like a Jack-in-a-box… and instantly gave up on trying to follow the story so far.

'Moonlight Flit,' said Nelly, 'can you comment…'

He was gone again. He obviously liked doing that.

It was in his name. His obvious enlightenment was that he could fly. He got by in the upper atmosphere without breathing equipment. But he was also quick. He could *flit*. Like Ftatateeta, only in mid-air. How did he get up speed with no ground to push against? Hummingbirds and dragonflies were fast – but they had wings.

Perhaps the cloak was made of strange matter. Light in the

way Chrissie's ribbons were dark?

What would happen if they kissed?

For a start, she'd be in all kinds of trouble with all kinds of people – and, for a finish, it might set off another *Never Mind* moment and yin-yang the world into a different plane of existence... Possibly best not to be attempted in her first months as a cloak. Aunt Jas might have choice things to say.

Moonlight Flit wasn't a cloak she'd thought much of before this evening.

In this moment she found it hard to think of anyone else.

She hoped that would pass.

That *voice*. She'd make a connection in a sec. No. She didn't have it.

'That Moonlit Fellow really is annoying,' exclaimed Eleanor.

Clare waved her unbroken hand under her chin to indicate Nelly was on-mike and might not want the sentiment all over Whispers. She'd be beset by Flithead flan-flingers. Moon Worshippers made Nelly's Nutters seem reasonable.

A piece of luminescent paper floated down.

Chrissie caught it, looked it over and passed it to Eleanor.

The release form was authenticated with a signet ring impression of a full moon in butter-yellow wax. The cameo appearance of Moonlight Flit was licensed to *Crew Selection* on condition that a token fee went to a children's charity administered by the Variety Club of Great Britain. That's what professionalism looked like.

Eleanor rolled up the form and tucked it away.

Moonlight Flit was gone and his vibes with him.

Chrissie could concentrate on other pressing matters.

She had a boyfriend. Who was a hostage in a cage somewhere nearby. He needed rescuing – preferably by her, without help from a passing top of the range cloak. She needed to take care of her own personal business. And, thinking of how the story was supposed to go, to be *seen* to take care of it.

Dazzled as she'd been by light, she'd also sensed darker dark than before.

The shadow she'd thrown on Ashton Dakin had seriously spooked Mr Kung Fu Grip. She doubted they'd see him again in a hurry.

But using her abilities like that rattled her too.
She was playing with dark forces.
This was all getting a bit much.
She could really do with a plate of chips.

Loulee and the Green Ninja

SHE WAS HAPPY TO BE OUT OF THE BIG SCRAP. BUT crowd control was a drag.

At first, people she tried to warn didn't take her seriously. They reckoned they were at a funfair and in no mood to be told not to enjoy themselves. A couple of dim vicky boys were certain they'd scored invitations to something called the Surprise Shenanigans and would not be told otherwise. However, when crock clowns started spraying boiling water from their spouts, civs changed their minds about Loulee being a spoilsport and ran pell-mell hither and yon. Explosions and rains of bullet casings were even more persuasive. Now she was ignored by panicking people she was trying to direct to safe exits.

One gate was run by Red Rope utter gits in body armour. They turned people away, ordering them to leave by other routes. A young woman in a blue-white evening gown – Polly Opal – was escorted through the gate. It turns out you could have an exclusive exit. A Red Roper held an armoured parasol to shield Her Oneness from shrapnel. Loulee presumed the other hostages were still held captive. Polly O had multi-purpose 'get out of jail free' cards for all occasions and wasn't sharing the wealth.

The Queen of the Coterie was assisted into an Arctic White

armoured car. Under-chassis rotors whirred. The wheels tucked in as the air-car rose and flew away from this unfashionable postcode. Flightpaths over the city would be disrupted. Opal whims overruled anyone else's schedules.

More explosions. Some gunfire.

Screams. Clown cackles and 'that's the way to *dooo* it' gloating.

A few Vone-clutching diehards popped clips on Peophole as if they were war correspondents. Spoilers for the next episode or valued viral promotion? Red-Tel lawyers would decide. Not anything Loulee needed to care about.

A persistent fly-eye followed her. She was cutaway footage at best.

The crock clowns were easily sorted. Using Yvyra's skills, she bopped their soft heads with the knotted end of a length of rope. She tied the voids together. Small children pelted punchy punchinellos with unwanted sweets. Which would learn them.

This carnival was seriously grot. Worse than grot. Worse Than Worse Than.

A whole orchestra of barrel organs struck up an out-of-tune meld of 'A Mouse Lived in a Windmill in Old Amsterdam' and 'Helter Skelter'. A poorly erected big top, tethered to a central pole, flapped like a giant striped starfish. Hook-ended guylines lashed about in the wind. Food frazzled on braziers, scenting the evening air. Chestnut, jellied eel and pie stalls were unmanned. Foolish scoffers were tempted to loot snacks.

Loulee decided to name her remote camera tagalong.

Eye-Eye the Fly-Eye. Someone was piloting it from a minivan in the car park. She didn't know who, what with all the comings and goings. By now, Canteen Cathy might have been reassigned to the mixing desk.

So far as Loulee was concerned, Chrissie had already won *Crew Selection*. Lady Shade II would be on the podium with the Splendid Six. That didn't mean Arsinoë couldn't come out of this bizarre interlude with *some* credibility.

She was getting better at using ghost talents without letting ghosts take charge.

She ringmastered the hubbub like a professional. She'd done work experience as a primary school teacher. This was a lot like that – though less dangerous emotionally. Like kids, ghosts irritated, charmed, surprised, endangered and delighted her in exhausting rapid succession. But she didn't have the stabs of love and terror which went with supervising a class of Year Twos. A month of that had nearly broken her.

She was never having children. Her heart couldn't cope. But she was going to be an *amazing aunt* like Jasmine Chambers.

Which meant Lamb Bear was obliged to have multiple children.

Which meant Lamb Bear had to be rescued. Before this hurly-burly hullabaloo got even more out of hand.

Several ghosts who knew firearms intimately told her the New Broken Dolls were using real bullets. Sandii Beach got hurt more or less by accident because Bruno Brookes was a clot. Being a clot was possibly worse than being evil. A clot who got carried away did unintended damage. Proper cutthroats were habitually more focused.

What happened when proper cutthroats got carried away?

Her guess was that was this.

The stadium had once been a dog track. The arena was surrounded by dilapidated stands.

There were no civs here. Apparently.

She had to make sure no one was hiding. Okiyo Kyuketsuki, the nearest thing to a ninja in the hubbub, sensed danger. In this game, that was like expecting rain on Bank Holiday Monday. Of course there was danger.

Loulee needed more specific warnings.

A properly tethered tent was set up in the centre of the track.

Ghosts shouted at her.

'Yes, I know it's a trap,' she said out loud. 'This whole evening is a trap.'

She remembered Eye-Eye the Fly-Eye had an Air-Ear and hoped the man (or other) in the minivan would think she was talking to him and, thus, the audience.

She was still keeping the Ghost Lantern under wraps.

She'd quite like to put it away for a spell after this.

Being semi-possessed by a speed-crazed fascist diva every time she looked at a nice motor was becoming a grind. And the Filcher's kleptomania would eventually land her in hot water.

Loulee stood to lose friends, employment opportunities and the welcome extended in any number of corner shops.

Lantern ghosts were all good at something. Which didn't mean they were good.

A few of them unironically spooked Loulee. Being good at climbing trees or having nice handwriting was hard to argue with. But Okiyo was basically good at *murder*. Not a party piece Loulee had much use for. Not so far...

She walked across long grass which grew where the racing track had been to the sideshow tent. The entrance was unmanned, though there was a kiosk.

What was this? Freak Show? Ghost Train?

She had to explain what a ghost train was to ghosts who had lived well before there were trains.

When she got close, she saw the faded sign.

Wibberly Wallaby's Hall of Mirrors. 'As seen on TV'... in *Floppit Funnies,* until Red-Tel paid attention to complaints. The Aussie Floppit's smirk gave some children bad dreams. A Whispers natter insisted Wibberly Wallaby kept Kev Koala's cut-off head behind the tubes of Four-X in his portable fridge.

Ni Tien deduced this was the concealed entrance to the underground cages where the hostages were being kept.

'Hats off to Hawkshaw,' said Loulee.

The Ear-Ear and the ghost were equally fazed by that.

'I mean "excellent deduction, my lady",' Loulee thought, addressing the ghost detective.

Loulee should dial Chrissie. And the other Sixths. This couldn't be as simple as walking into the pens and freeing Lamb Bear and the rest. There would be guards. And traps.

The Sixths should go in mob handed. From several directions.

But Loulee was *already* mob handed.

Yvyra was an expert in traps, pitfalls and hidden dart-pipes. Oghulqaimish ached to wield the sabre Loulee had kept from the second-worst Arsinoë costume. Okiyo Kyuketsuki was sly and without ruth. Dolly was nippy and stealthy. If a clown car was parked nearby, Contessa Erco could handle the getaway drive. There'd be room for all rescuees in the back seat.

Loulee was aware of Eye-Eye hovering, expectantly.

Freeing the hostages would be a good thing, of course. She'd get points and votes she didn't need or want. She wasn't just resigned to losing this game. She was determined not to come top of the form. She hadn't wanted to play in the first place and had no interest in the prize. If she were sent off in disgrace, she'd be happy... so long as Viper Strike and Garter Snake lost worse than she did.

Seeing Lamb Bear in a cage had shocked and upset her.

Not the ghosts – *her*. The ghosts tended not to feel too fondly about brothers and uncles or boyfriends and husbands. Hostages were expendable voids. It was their own fault for getting captured. They should have looked over their shoulders.

It wasn't only her brother. Ftatateeta and Tunno were charter members of Loulee and the Luvvers, shortest-lived cloak krewe of all time. She liked them, even if Gerald went red whenever she talked to him and unconsciously squashed cups and saucers while failing to meet her eye. She only slightly distrusted Garnet Graill, though she worried that he was overattentive to Nelly the Peril. Even the Coterie didn't deserve this – though she knew better than to expect any thanks from the All-Powerful Jupiter Bolus, Dr Whatevery and the rest. Vidar Tieck would ask her what took so long.

She'd go into the Hall of Mirrors and take a look.

If it was promising, she'd dial Chrissie. And the others.

Everyone deserved a shot at rescuing their loved ones.

Mostly.

Asmida wasn't fussed about her dad, of course. And Weather Girl wasn't here, which was Bruno Brookes' own fool fault.

So – a couple of bonus loved ones were going spare.

Someone was by the ticket kiosk now. Someone dressed in green.

Another challenge which needed to be met? Unmask the Green Ninja.

Ni Tien and Enyedi Boglárka told her the Ninja's secret identity was Anjulie Glas.

They had different workings-out but made a convincing consensus. Splendidery had a Hawkshaw element. Finding out, tracking down, spotting clues. Most cloaks had to be sort of detectives. The hubbub had that covered while Loulee's competition were stuck on the first chapter of the Green Penguin.

The solution fit the facts. Anjulie had been not about at times coincidental with verit Green Ninja sightings. Her motivation for mischief was obscure but could be drawn out in an interrogation provided candlewax and paprika were kept out of reach so a confession would be admissible in court.

The Green Ninja stepped into the open.

And obviously wasn't Anjulie Glas. A figure-hugging body-sheath hung on a bonier person than the curvy Arse Prod.

Ni Tien and Enyedi Boglárka argued.

Okiyo told Loulee this was a *different* Green Ninja.

It could be a whole sect. Or a cult.

The ninja took two steps back, into the tent.

From those two steps, Okiyo gauged that this was not someone she was confident of besting in a scrap. Or murdering from the next room.

Oh peach. Not news Loulee wanted to hear.

Other ghosts – Yvyra and Oghulqaimish – were confident they'd win... but Loulee remembered they'd been confident before and got killed. They also knew less about ninja-type scrapping than Okiyo Kyuketsuki, who was back in the Lantern and not coming out until a new hapless twit opened a cupboard and became the next Ghost Lantern Girl.

So who was this mystery woman?

Loulee really should dial Chrissie now. And the verit Splendids.

Chrissie had put down Adam Tussaud and the other grade-one cutthroats on the White Corridor. She could eat Green Ninjas for breakfast and have room for three Shredded Wheat.

Under the music, Loulee heard engines revving.

She checked that Eye-Eye was still with her and clocked that there were people in the stands now. Not a good crowd but thirty or forty scattered around the arena. Some wore big Floppit heads. An usherette was selling those 'an hour from now you'll regret eating one' hot dogs.

Canvas tore and a giant electric hare – relic of the dog track – roared out of the tent. An animalbot stretched over a Norton motorcycle...

... Loulee felt for the Contessa but she wasn't there.

Things were so dire the ghosts were deserting her.

The Green Ninja straddled the hare. As she revved the Norton, metal teeth champed. It looked like they could inflict a nasty nipping.

Loulee wasn't even sure the Green Ninja was a person.

The hare-bike seemed more alive than she did. Her costume hung empty between ribcage and hips and bunched around her thin neck like a schoolgirl's socks.

The mask was tight against a noseless, mouthless face. Just cheek curves and eye depressions.

Best to put on a show.

From her top pocket, Loulee took a shuriken twisted out of scrap metal – melding ideas from Yvyra and Okiyo – and sharpened on a whetstone. She flicked it at the Green Ninja's face.

It stuck there, with a satisfying thunk.

For an instant, she was clutched by that have-I-gone-too-far spasm she had when a Year Two she'd told off was on the point of tears. Then a rip in the mask grew. The Ninja reached up and tore off her silk hood.

Underneath was a polished wooden blank.

No wonder she'd been reminded of Adam Tussaud.

This was that cutthroat's popsy – the Mannikin.

Unless she had ghost help immediately, Loulee was dead. The Mannikin wasn't competing in a game show. She was a chilly killer. Patsy Kensit got a BAFTA for playing her in that Gary Oldman *Chamber of Horrors* film.

The bendy armature was an operant. Like a box kite, a fly-eye or – under certain circumstances – a Ghost Lantern Girl, the Mannikin was a piloted thing. Someone else was throwing their mind into it.

The hare-bike leaped...

... and Loulee was in the Lantern, watching as if through a distorting lens, as her body was knocked over. The Mannikin spilled off the saddle, loose-limbed and unoperated. The rolling bike crushed its legs. White woodpulp showed through shredded green tights. The hare-bike's onboard Think Box shorted out with a pulse which knocked Eye-Eye out of the sky-sky. The remote camera was a paperweight now. And whatever happened next was off the record.

Was Loulee dead? Dying was not a winning strategy.

Hold on. Her body was moving, though she wasn't in it.

Okiyo was in the Lantern with her. And Bryndis. And Ninurmahmeš – quiet lately since there'd been little call for tanning expertise. And others.

But some were missing... Some who might have helped.

'You're too trusting,' Boglárka told Loulee.

It could never be said that Boglárka was too trusting. Nevertheless, she'd died from not expecting a proven schemer to be treacherous when it came to matters of honour with pistols.

Loulee was not used to the wrapped-in-cotton-wool feel of being in the Lantern. This was what being a ghost was.

She had a fly-eye view of her former body.

There was life in her yet. She heaved the broken bike off her legs and stood, using the sword as a cane. She shook her shoulders and uncricked her neck as if loosening up before a gymnastics display.

Loulee ought to be relieved. Getting up was a win.

Only she wasn't driving her body.

Yes, she thought – too bloody trusting by half.

Eleanor Follows the Story

THE TWITTERING IN HER EAR TOLD ELEANOR TO concentrate on the big top.

The remaining New Broken Dolls – Upside-Down Gonk, Mr Swizzle, Juke Box Jerry – put on a show by the castellated tent. Circus music jangled. Jugglers, conjurers and come-on merchants did warm-up acts. The fun for all the family display was an invitation to argy-bargy.

Lady Shady, Pyro Pixie and Garter Snake were up for the scrap.

Jackson-Walker, out of his secure dustbin, was pissed off enough to pitch in without his gadgets. He might get votes for that. Brave, angry and stupid was a winning combination… if seen from far enough away to blur the blood and bruises. Say, on a settee in the front room.

Eleanor brought the audience up to date.

'… though some of the deadliest Dolls have been defeated, those deadlier still remain a threat…'

'How can there be deadlier than deadliest?' carped Jah in her ear.

Eleanor would not be thrown. She must demand an off switch for her earpiece. Or at least a volume knob.

A red-and-yellow-striped cannon rolled out of the tent,

hauled by sweating Floppits. It was the calibre of big gun funfairs used to shoot ladies over an ahhhhing crowd into a net. Cyndi Doll must have a pointy shell bathing cap and full metal tights in her wardrobe. But she was off the bill.

Drum-roll laid it on thick. A curlywurly fuse burned like a sparkler.

The cannon went off. Five times.

It didn't roar so much as *splurge*, squirting lumps of grey goo the size of beachballs. The soft missiles squelched onto grass, well short of the Sixths. Asmida flicked the Vs with both hands and shouted 'pathetic'.

Then the goo gobbets rolled together and reared up en masse.

Eyes appeared in the puddingy heap.

'Stick a fork in it,' exclaimed Jackson-Walker, 'it's the Schloup!'

The haystack-sized globbering mass rolled aggressively forwards, extending wicked tentacles. Eunice Uglow made a conjuring gesture which possibly dislocated her shoulder. A fence of flame rose. Tentacles withdrew like salted slugs. Malevolent hissing came from the sludge cludge.

Jackson-Walker was even angrier than he had been.

He was taking the Schloup personally. But without his gargantuabot or robodynamic armour, he was practically a civ.

The scion of science and industry pulled what looked like a household battery torch. It was a laser pointer with a slicer-dicer setting. He twisted a dial. A thousand-foot scimitar of refined light cut through the Schloup. Left to right. Up and down. Back and forth. Over and again.

'Take that!' he shouted. 'That's for ruining Christmas! And that's for the bloody "Schloup Schloup Song"! Viper Strike Rules, OK!'

The Schloup segmented like a watermelon used in a demonstration by a samurai sword salesman. Individual cross-sections stuck together again... until a central core was halved. With dying eyes in separate slices, the motor was done for. Schloup slop spread on the ground like a hundredweight of blancmange.

Emboldened, Jackson-Walker – in bare feet and cyber-undies – leaped over the flame barrier and charged into the big top, waving his laser with abandon. Curtains of canvas fell. The top of a (mercifully) unmanned observation tower was sheared off.

'He's already had a warning about collateral damage,' said Jah.

Someone in Jackson-Walker's Room reacted. His laser was remotely de-activated to avoid court cases. And loss of life, of course. The idiot could easily lop a wing off Concorde.

'Come on,' said Pyro Pixie

She made a gate in the flame and walked through it.

Berserk Floppits barrelled at her. Unavoidable fireballs formed in front of their faces. They went down screeching. Animal masks caught light.

Garter Snake, limber again, bounded after the Little Match Girl. She would not be outdone in violence. She punched, kicked, scratched and headlocked circus acts in a display of dirty sexy scrapping. She kneecapped stilt-walkers and tossed greased dwarf wrestlers into gunge pits. She dodged acid-squirting soda-siphons with impossible sideways bends. She tore red noses and pom-pom buttons off clowns.

Something huge shifted inside the big top.

A star attraction.

A fanfare sounded, then merry music poured forth. The tattered tent fell apart like a cack-handed fan dancer's feathers. A bouncy gargantuabot stood in the centre of crossed spotlights. It jogged floppily, like a boxer warming up.

This was Upside-Down Swizzle.

An answer to the question of what do you get if you cross a four-armed living Punch and Judy Show with a demented children's programme presenter then blow the result up to the size of the Royal Festival Hall.

Camera Clare had to run back to get the whole thing in the picture.

'Viper Strike, Viper Strike,' parped Jackson-Walker – voice cracking and lost in the roar of the one-man band's 'Entry of the Gladiators'.

'Look up,' said Jah.

'I am,' murmured Eleanor to her throat-mike.

'No, upper up.'

She did. A man stood in mid-air, arms crossed, cloak flapping. Moonlight Flit again. He looked down on the giant cutthroat.

As evening shaded into dusk, the flying man shone. A

spotlight played across his cloak. Moons flashed like polished pebbles in a running stream.

'Can we get rid of the party-crasher?' Eleanor asked.

'He gave us a release form, so we're fine with him.'

'But the competition...'

'Come on, Nelly, you know better than that.'

Upside-Down Swizzle flipped. What had seemed to be its feet stuck up like extra heads. It turned slowly, gibbetted puppets hanging from yard arms spaced around its middle.

The policeman puppet caught fire. Flames spread to the crocodile.

Garter Snake found Juke Box Jerry. She wrapped long arms and legs around the one-man band. Constricting like four pythons, she squeezed till his cracking ribs sounded like a breaking xylophone. She headbutted his mouth organ into his gullet.

Uglow's fires spread around the particoloured girth of Upside-Down Swizzle.

Moonlight Flit shone beams from all directions at once.

The scrap filled the sky. Fireworks went off. Minions fled, no longer committed to the cause of cutthroatery. Freed operants scurried, suddenly keen on saving their skins. They could be vox-popped in the car park.

Jah kept directing Eleanor to look this way and that...

She also heard his instructions to Clare and other ground staff. Fly-eyes were marshalled.

'Don't catch fire,' he said.

A *wrongness* prickled, though.

This was what *Crew Selection* needed at this stage in the series. Spectacle worth switching over for. Item One of next day's chee urn natter. Grandstand footage of the most mahoosive monumenace since the Octopiranha. Cloaks on deck, abilities a-blazing. New Improved. More Than More Than. Super Gear.

Something was missing. Someone or someones had gone astray.

The Vision Controller trusted Eleanor with this project. She was included in the process from the beginning. She answered to Don Loki Baird, not Captain Floppy or any Arse Prod. Her job was to seek the verit, the bigger story playing out in shadow while distracting lights flashed in time with the orchestra.

This scrap was *showing off*. No one was being rescued.

Where was Christine Chambers? The sly one.

Eleanor turned away from the blazing battle. She made out a trail of darkness, leading to the abandoned stadium.

That was where the verit was.

She tried to get Clare's attention. Jah told her to let the professional do her job. She was swatted away like a pest. Jah would rue that.

This was when she could have done with Garnet Graill.

Instead, she used the backdoor code she'd talked Graill into implanting in the Red-Tel fleet of fly-eyes and slaved a single eye to herself. Clare and the other crews were on the big scrap, getting comprehensive coverage. Eleanor had a gut feeling their footage would be B-roll. Only she was on the real story.

Which was happening somewhere else.

She walked along the dark path. Her fly-eye followed close above, like a toy balloon won in the coconut shy.

CHRISTINE IN THE HALL OF MIRRORS

AS THE SCHLOUP CAME TO PIECES, HER DARK VONE pirriped.

Chrissie knew it'd be important but being seen to answer a dial in the middle of an epic scrap wouldn't go down well with the viewers at home.

She slipped away, shrouded in shadow. As the sun set, she grew sharper. Buzzy with dark ergs. She had to concentrate.

Om Om Om Om. Keep it together, Chrissie.

A blurt came from Anju the AP. So she was still on the programme.

A three-dimensional map of Hackney Wick Stadium opened on Chrissie's Vone. A pulsing you-are-here hat represented her. Arrows led to the dog track. One level below was a cludge of cartoon rabbits.

Anju also squirted 'hint hint – this way to hostages'.

Chrissie looked at the big top battle. Moonlight Flit had pitched in – again. Asmida had Juke Box Jerry on the mat and was giving him a horror hug. Eunice conjured fire dragons to dive-bomb a candy-striped juggernaut. Even Hereward was busy somewhere.

Was only Chrissie getting the map and the hint?

Had some high-up meeting decided to give her a crib sheet

for this week's mission? She knew to be wary of nudges and pitfalls. Everything might be a trap.

She could share the gen with the others...

She was the only one who remembered they were supposed to be as much a team as competitors. Hereward hared off with his thousand-foot laser lash at the first sight of his childhood bugbear. Asmida and Eunice charged right after him. They weren't in concert with each other – or her. The other Sixths weren't fussed whether Lady Shade threw herself into the scrap with the fe-fi-fo-fumming grotbot.

She'd be worried about them – except for Moonlight Flit.

If a verit first division cloak held their hands, they couldn't get in too much trouble.

Could they?

Garn and the others needed rescuing.

Too many cutthroats thought leaving hostages dangling over pits of burning coals or tethered to work-benches with automatic saws was funny.

Chrissie walked quickly, her shadow flowing around her, straining to break free and forge ahead. Her hat ate arrows on the Vone map. The rabbits hopped.

She copied Anju's blurt to Loulee, who wasn't otherwise engaged with the Big Top Bogey. Roping her in on the rescue made sense. Loulee would want to get Lamb Bear out of his cage. Her ghosts might be useful.

One might know something about defusing booby traps, for a start.

There would, of course, be booby traps.

She got a received ping from Loulee. And a response pong.

Peach. Stalwart Sparky on the case.

A Loulee hat popped up onscreen. She was on the lower level, where the hostages were caged.

In the centre of the stadium was a sideshow tent. The arrows aimed at it.

Wibberly Wallaby's Hall of Mirrors. Peach, Aces and Gear. No one's favourite Floppit. 'As Seen on TV'.

A cardboard Wibberly had been vandalised with lime green paint. A mangled machine lay in a strew of wires. Its torn-off metal head had long bunny ears and razor-edged bunny choppers.

Not ominous at all.

She was being shown the quickest way. Not necessarily the safest. It was nearly night. She brimmed with black oomph.

Shadier than ever. With purple flashes.

She stepped into the tent and came face to face with herself.

She didn't much like the dark visual. And this was an ordinary mirror. Inside would be a maze of distorting glass. She had an urge to blot reflections out with extradimensional ink.

She looked down at her Vone and moved her hat along the arrows by putting one foot in front of the other. She wasn't distracted by the hunched or elongated mirror-Chrissies keeping pace with her.

Someone else was in the Hall – hiding multiple images behind infinite Chrissies. She stopped dead and turned round – slowly, then swiftly. The other matched her moves.

Who was it? Not Loulee, who was one floor down. Someone crafty and silent.

All the advertised New Broken Dolls were accounted for.

Major Wood was on the sick list. Cyndi Doll was asleep and handcuffed. Kung Fu Grip had the wind up. Mr Swizzle, Upside-Down Gonk and Juke Box Jerry were in the big scrap with Moonlight Flit and the other Sixths. Were unadvertised guest cutthroats held back for surprise appearances? That would be typical *Crew Selection*.

If her secret arch-nemesis turned out to be Wibberly Wallaby she was going to complain to the manufacturers.

Still and all, who could bother her now?

At Devil's Dyke, she'd nobbled prize pupils. The Jibbenainosay, Scary Mary, Guy the Gorilla, *Adam Tussaud*. Compared to those arch-fiends, the New Broken Dolls were boli and voids. After that scrap, this was a gentle downhill slope. She didn't even need to work the pedals.

Overconfidence, Chrissie, beware! The Aunt Jasmine/Urban Fox cautionary voice pirriped in her head.

She was getting tired of being told not to get too excited, take on too much, go too far...

She was a Shade. No sneak hiding behind glass could best her.

She snapped her fingers and violet chain-lightning cracked

through the tent. All the mirrors to her right cobwebbed like safety windscreens... then fell apart. Dark diamonds sparkled on sawdust. She did the same to all the looking glasses on her left and was alone in a Hall Without Mirrors...

No, not *alone*.

Someone sat in a deckchair, unmoving.

She walked carefully towards the nap-taker.

She found what looked like the aftermath of a disastrous ventriloquist act.

A man in a dinner jacket and bow-tie was slack in the chair. A mask covered the lower half of his face. Cradled in his lap was a verit broken doll. A life-sized dressmaker's dummy, legs smashed to splinters. Shreds of a green costume hung from its frame. Its face was a featureless oval with a throwing star stuck into it.

Chrissie had seen stars like that before. Loulee made them for a ghosts to practise with. A ninja knick-knack.

Was the sleeping vent as much a dummy as the dummy?

His mask was odd. Why would a ventriloquist cover his mouth? Surely the point was to *show* the straight man's lips didn't move when the funny fellow talked?

The *greenness* of the ragged threads nagged. It wasn't the emerald of the Green Knight. Or the grass-green of Green Shield stamps. Or the near turquoise of a Green Penguin cover.

It was the green of the CSR screen. Nelly's nightmare green.

Watch out, there's a ninja about!

The ventriloquist stood up and the dummy came unstrung.

Chrissie stepped back, alert. She looked into the vent's face.

The black wasn't a mask. It was an abyssal void.

She had the face-card.

Modred Murda.

Aunt Jasmine's old arch-nemesis. Malcolm Sandys, one-time Soho nightclub tout. He escalated his crookery and adopted the trade-name Modred Murda when he set out to cop the Most Wanted spot vacated after Adam Tussaud was sent to Devil's Dyke. Murda was a master of stratagems and schemes. He plotted plans which took much mental and physical effort to undo.

Of course, the mannequin was *the* Mannikin. Adam Tussaud's popsy – or puppet – or favourite prop. The sinister shag doll. Murda stole the armature from the Black Museum and incorporated her into his routines. Modred Murda and the Mannikin. You didn't get one without the other.

Murda was a tribute act which got out of hand.

Until Aunt Jas wiped part of him out of this reality. She hadn't meant to go so far but Adam Tussaud impressions got on her wick. Especially when Murda took up William Wax's feud with Lady Shade. After many scraps and skirmishes, Aunt Jas got very annoyed with Murda and partially *sent him away*.

As Chrissie understood it, Murda was missing his neck and a shoulder-joint. That part of his body was shifted to a separate plane of existence. The Purple.

His profile needed an update for the evening edition.

Black absence gaped between Murda's forehead and wishbone. His disembodied arm was now his disembodied forearm. He wore a ducky-white wine waiter glove. Looking into the emptiness where most of his face used to be, she saw glints like distant stars.

Was this an 'ah-hah, gotcha!' moment?

Revenge by proxy?

The successor to Adam Tussaud versus the successor to Lady Shade.

Murda stepped courteously aside, dropping the remnants of the Mannikin. He kicked the deckchair, which folded flat with a snap.

They stood over a trapdoor.

The arrows on the Vone map went down a level. Underground was a complex of rooms. The cartoon rabbits were in a hopping, begging, save-us-o-shady-one frenzy. Loulee's hat was down there too.

Murda lifted the trapdoor, with a mime's mocking politeness.

What expression would he have showed?

Genuine sweet concern – in atonement for former misdeeds.

Sneery contempt – as if ushering an enemy into a pit of tarantulas.

Box B seemed most likely to get the tick.

Looking at what was left of Malcolm Sandys gave Chrissie the queases cubed. She had serious pause about pressing on with Shady cloakery. If this was the sort of damage she could inflict – even on a not-nice, not-kind person – she didn't know if she wanted any of it. When she sent Dakin and Cyndi away, she felt part of herself going too... and that had only been for a few seconds.

Murda had been like this for *years.*

But Garn needed rescuing.

Think of the sad rabbits.

Chrissie would get this mission accomplished – and maybe resign from the contest. Have a good long think about the Shade Legacy. Look at uni applications, change her agent. Not winning *Crew Selection* could be a decent career move. The Boring Bosun was better liked than Jonty McDribblefart.

Where did Modred Murda fit into this?

She'd have to talk with Aunt Jas.

Immediately, coals were burning and saws were buzzing.

She heard cries for help from below. Not cartoon bunnies but verit people in verit distress. Opening the trapdoor announced rescue was near.

Still, she hesitated.

It's not called a trap*door for nothing.*

Her aunt's arch-nemesis, an evil-doer of the direst stripe, stood back so she could climb down into a basement of doom. Silvery mirror shards somewhere in his abyssal gob shone like exposed teeth. If he slapped on a Wibberly Wallaby mask, he couldn't be more disturbing.

It's not too late to send up a flare to summon Moonlight Flit. Or a troupe of aerial guides armed with principles and catapults.

'Christine,' hissed a voice from below.

She looked through the trapdoor.

Loulee was at the foot of the steps, beckoning her. She had one of her Egyptian swords.

Chrissie went downstairs into the level beneath the arena.

A single white glove waved her off.

BOYD WAYLO, THE CUTTING COMMENTATOR – AGENT OF GEIST

'INEVITABLY, THE SATRAPY CAME APART AT THE seams.

'I was the only one the Satrap could reach when he lost his nerve. The penalties of being in the phone book. De Beers got what he wanted after Devil's Dyke and didn't keep his eye on the ball as *Crew Selection* went up in flames. He had his government contract. So far as he was concerned, everything else was a mop-up op. Tickertape came in about the circus at the Dogs and he shat out his spine. Scared he'd lose all he'd gained. He was *incensed* that Murda and the Mannikin – an old cutthroat team – were indulging in pointless, destructive revenge.

'I didn't break it to him gently. I explained that pointless, destructive revenge was *all* they wanted. Astro Ace was the same and he had no complaints about her. Murda and the Mannikin were off on their own. De Beers had paid no attention to the delivery from GEIST Central of the one hundred million franc Shed of Transformation. Someone pulled strings to get that out of the weapons bunker and dropped off in Hackney Marshes. I reckon the Big Thinkers wanted to test the item before using an even bigger shed in an even more damaging context. Or else they were as terrified of the Mannikin as everyone normal and pulled a top-secret project out of mothballs so she'd stop showing up at their absolutely untraceable home addresses posing as a bomb delivery girl. The idea of a worked-out, calculated Modred Murda stratagem was a nonsensical sham De Beers had bought into – and initially financed – for his own reasons. After that, downhill momentum took over.

'De Beers forgot that a satrap wasn't really in charge.

'GEIST isn't about anyone having orders obeyed. Or getting wishes granted. Members of a satrapy aren't operants.

'For GEIST, it's about rolling, exponentially spreading chaos. The fun stuff.

'That was the Shade Legacy too... or what Murda and the Green Ninja saw could be made of it. Murda was there at the end, thinking whatever bang he set off couldn't do worse to him than the creeping nothing he was already afflicted with. Greenie hopped it to Gib, as far off as she thought might be safe. I stayed put to watch pretty flames. On television, like everyone else. I'm a dedicated telly addict.

'De Beers was going to dial. He had unlisted numbers for the Deputy Prime Minister, Martin Masters, the Queen Mum, Marius Stok, Sir John of Scotland Yard and the British Lions. He'd have sounded like a loon but someone would have been curious enough to look into it and initiate countermeasures.

'So muggins himself had to step in and shut him up.

'How do you get through the Red Rope?

'A big pair of scissors does the job. Him being found dead in his inner office wasn't much of an advert for his security protocols. His heirs will lose clients over that.

'Funny thing about GEIST satraps – more of them get carked by their comrades than nicked by cloaks or other arms of the law. Every satrapy has to have someone like me, ready to call it a day...

'That was me finished, though. All the rest of it was Murda and the Mannikin.'

CHRISTINE AND LOULEE IN THE DARK

'THIS WAY,' SAID LOULEE.

'To the rabbits?'

Loulee nodded, impatient. Which wasn't like her.

This was the first time her brother got kidnapped so she was excused.

Was this their lives now? Cloakworld.

Chrissie was relieved her parents were at an Anarcho-Buddhist Happening on Pitcairn Island, far from all this grief. Garn could look after himself – or at least turn captivity to his advantage by taking pics. She knew he wasn't a fan of being part of the story. It was why he kept stepping back to get clicks of her – or, annoyingly, Nelly – in the thick of saleable action. But he'd recognise an opportunity. Inside scoops from the dungeon of despair. Heart-rending personal messages from hostages would be worth more if a rescue went wrong. Asmida's dad would yell the address of his burning junk yard while playing the lead in a beheading clip.

This underground level smelled more of animals than clowns. Lightbulbs burned in little cages every ten feet. The floor was cracked tile and beaten dirt.

Urban Fox had been down here when she was scrapping with Top Dog. The same old sites kept cropping up, like on *Letsby*

Avenue when they didn't want to pay for a new set so a new culprit took over an old culprit's digs. There was a factual basis for that.

'There will be traps,' said Chrissie.

Loulee hopped impatiently.

Surely she wasn't jittery? She was the hold-back-and-be-cautious one. Chrissie was the run-into-untold-peril person.

'I've scouted,' said her friend. 'There aren't. Except a small one I tripped with the sabre.'

'We were led this far...'

Anju's blurted map. Modred Murda's Hall of Mirrors.

'... there must be *something*.'

The cartoon rabbits were in a big hexagonal room just down this corridor. Chrissie presumed she trusted the map.

'*Vigliacca*,' said Loulee.

'Pardon?'

'It's something... a ghost says...'

Chrissie looked at Loulee. She held her sword oddly. Her eyes were off model.

She saw what was up.

'Is the ghost with us now?' she asked.

'*Si*, yes...'

'A *Spanish* ghost?'

'*Italiano, idiota...*'

Chrissie dodged the clumsy sabre-slash.

Loulee was an operant. Someone was pulling her strings and tooting the whistle.

Contessa Ercolina!

Chrissie put the lights out in the passage. The bulbs turned black. She could see in the dark. The ghost piloting Loulee couldn't.

Chrissie flattened against a wall and watched Loulee dance awkwardly, not like herself, sword-prodding where she thought Chrissie might be. Loulee hunched and kept leaning to one side. A tic. Usually, when channelling ghost expertise, she was confident. She executed tasks with enviable skill – whether making an omelette with whatever was left over in the fridge or climbing a brick wall with minimal finger- and toe-holds. Now, she was blundering.

The Contessa might be a demon driver but her fencing was rubbish.

Chrissie knew about the hubbub. One ghost was trying to be boss of all the others. It wasn't as easy as she'd thought it would be when she decided to stage a coup. Erco was in the saddle but had a devil of a time holding on to the reins.

It would have helped if Aunt Jas, Urban Fox or someone had given Chrissie tips on performing exorcisms on the fly. Chrissie hadn't reached that chapter in the Book of Shades.

She knew how to keep it dark – and felt herself getting stronger, lither and sharper in the shadow. But that was it.

All Chrissie could think of was giving the possessee a sound wallop and hope Loulee woke up in her right mind with a lump on the bonce. She wasn't confident. A sound wallop was a tricky prospect. Too sound and a skull got cracked. Not sound enough and a sabre-wielding ghost got angry enough to cut her open. An inexpert, inelegant slash might still sever an artery.

'I hear you breathing,' said the Contessa. Her accent was only slight. But sneery.

'... and I see you coming,' said Chrissie.

She made a fist and punched Loulee on the chin. As hard as she could, which wasn't very hard. She still felt she was punching her friend – which, really, she was. If the Contessa got knocked back into the Lantern, Loulee would have the bruise.

An in-built circuit-breaker meant she couldn't rely on the scrapping skills she'd used against those crocks under that bridge, let alone the storm of purple lightning she'd let loose on the White Corridor or in the Hall of Mirrors. She might have to find a workaround. Or else get used to being a kebab.

The Contessa stuck her sword into the wall. It jammed fast.

Chrissie whirled out of the way. She trod on spongy air steps rather than the floor. She bumped against the ceiling before she tumbled that in true dark she wasn't bound by gravity. Up, up and...

Call me Darklight Flit.

Dot Schilling would not love this. Chrissie could fly in the dark. A banner client had top of the bill enlightened abilities but only in conditions where she couldn't be clicked or clipped. Chrissie was a living 'no publicity' clause.

The Contessa spat and swore.

Outside of their talents, Loulee hadn't said much about her ghosts as people. She gave the impression many were a handful. One or two really weren't who you'd want round for chee. The Contessa was obviously one of those. An angry spirit.

Ercolina must have been in hiding. A secret arch-nemesis.

It struck Chrissie she knew where the Contessa hung out when she wasn't in the Lantern or Loulee. She'd been the Mannikin!

For how long? Had she been William Wax's cutthroat companion and Modred Murda's malevolent muse? Or was she a new entrant in the Let's-Get-Chrissie stakes, moving into the abandoned armature the way the New Broken Dolls squatted Top Dog's old rookery?

This anti-Shade stratagem must have been brewing a while.

Mum and Dad's world tour gift horse. Fortune cookie messages. The Devil's Dyke security system wobbles. The Green Ninja. Hereward starting a war with the NBDs. Free passes to the circus. Arrows on a Vone map. Chrissie was close to joining the dots and seeing the picture.

For what it was worth – which was little.

The Contessa patted the many pockets of Loulee's boiler suit. She found tools and widgets too small to be weapons and flung them away. A packet of wine gums bounced off Chrissie's arm.

Chrissie knew what the ghost was looking for.

'Loulee doesn't smoke, Erco,' Chrissie said.

The Contessa spat a word beginning with p. Either Ercolina had married into a title after being raised by uncouth brigands or uppercrust Italian convent schools in her day didn't teach the Girl Guide Pledges.

'Hah,' said the Contessa. 'Shows how much you know.'

She'd found a flip-top Ronson.

Chrissie remembered Loulee getting the lighter as a Christmas present. Her French gran assumed any girl turning fourteen would be on two packets of Gauloises a day. Over the years, Loulee must have used it five or six times to burn things which weren't cigarettes. She carried the sturdy, clunky gadget out of affection for her *mémére*.

Drat.

A flame appeared in the dark, underlighting Loulee's face.

Spooky fire-shadowing made her look different. Her expression wasn't hers. Her eyebrows did something they weren't naturally inclined to.

The Contessa spotted Chrissie – who was not where she expected her to be.

'You float,' she said.

'I fly,' said Chrissie, puffing as if she could blow out the flame.

She rushed at her possessed friend and – wincing at the thought – fetched her a clout on the side of the head. An approximation of a sound wallop.

The lighter dropped and the fire disappeared. The return of darkness was like a Fizzle boost to Chrissie. A delicious little hit of ergs.

That trick was *tasty.*

In the dark, Chrissie pushed herself off two walls and the ceiling and fell on Loulee, tugging hair and slapping and shouting.

'Leave her alone, *spettro*... Get out of her this instant...'

'Try and make me,' snarled the Contessa.

'Don't think I *won't*...'

The circuit-breaker remained a nuisance. With Loulee at hazard, Chrissie was no better at wrestling than boxing. The ghost held her friend's body hostage.

All the thought Chrissie had put into using her enlightenment judiciously went by the wayside.

She'd not revised for this exam. It was a cleft stick rather than a conundrum. No solution written upside-down under the illustration.

The dark in the passage grew darker still, with that purple tinge which made Chrissie feel profoundly cold. Maybe she needed the extra shadow to get through this.

Or maybe it came with a final curtain.

LOULEE IN THE LANTERN

CHRISSIE HAD SPRUNG SOME SURPRISES.

But was making a Chrissie-hash of it.

Loulee could only watch the Contessa using her body like a dodgem car.

The other ghosts were distracted by their own wispy obsessions. They lost interest in what went on outside the Lantern.

Eupraxia did mental arithmetic.

Ninurmahmeš had tanning ideas.

Sybil was sobbing. Faintly. Her little wick was almost burned down.

Chrissie could fly now – at least indoors, where there was no risk of going up and up until breath ran out. Darkness didn't just pour out of her sleeves but manifested as a cloud of fog only she could see through. Her own Smudge.

But she wasn't winning this scrap.

Enyedi Boglárka deigned to peep.

'I see five ways your friend could kill Ercolina with simple application of pressure.'

Loulee tried to explain that Ercolina was already dead. Those simple applications would do for someone else. Someone whose brother needed rescuing.

Boglárka didn't see a difference.

Loulee was fed up with ghosts. They had a poor attitude.

When Chrissie bashed Ercolina in the real world, Loulee felt it in the Lantern.

Ghosts didn't feel anything.

Loulee did. So she wasn't dead.

'Come on, Chrissie, give it some wellie,' she tried to shout. 'Lamp me proper. Black my eyes and stick me one in the breadbasket.'

Chrissie couldn't hear her. But the Contessa could.

Ercolina gabbled in Italian, constantly.

The Contessa was like this when she drove. She talked to herself in one long abusive sentence full of swears. It was her way of blotting out the funk.

It was a thing Loulee didn't get about the ghost.

When Loulee drove her Lambretta at speed, it was a thrill. She wanted more. She even recognised the craving as slightly dangerous. Which didn't prevent her from testing her limits.

The Contessa's need was different.

Yes, she was transported by physical sensation. Ercolina Medici d'Olivola had been to bed with men who'd taught Rudolf Valentino a thing or two about the Latin lover racket. She preferred going full throttle in a car or a plane or on a motorbike. She went cross-eyed with pleasure when a needle juddered against the upper limit of a speedometer. She'd lived her life desperate for inventors to make more powerful rockets to put under her seat. But along with the thrill was *terror*. The rush frightened her into joy.

She needed to be *afraid* to feel alive.

Chrissie was giving Ercolina what she wanted.

Loulee didn't feel sorry for the ghost who'd evicted her from her own body. Especially since she was convinced the Contessa knew all about kidnapping Lamb Bear. That was not even considering her being friends with Mussolini. But Loulee had a trickle of pity. Ercolina had been wired very wrong in life and being dead hadn't done her any favours.

She saw Chrissie take the Contessa by her throat and lift her off the floor.

As Chrissie clutched, Loulee felt it.

There was dark all around. With violet electric arcs.

Loulee was back in her body. Ercolina was gone – not to the Lantern but some other hidey-hole. There was always what was left of the Mannikin.

Loulee kicked pointlessly, feet off the floor.

The grip on her neck meant she couldn't tell Chrissie to lay off.

She lifted her hand to Chrissie's face and displaced her Spex. Her friend's eyes were black ball bearings with violet veins.

Chrissie slammed Loulee against one wall, then the other.

Not optimal. Un-gear. Worse Than Worse Than.

ELEANOR AT THE TRAPDOOR

IT WASN'T A HALL OF MIRRORS ANY MORE.

Inside the tent was a carpet of broken glass.

'We're following Lady Shade, darkest horse of the contest,' Eleanor addressed the fly-eye. 'Perhaps we're close to the pen where the New Broken Dolls have the Sixths' loved ones, possibly subjecting them to unimaginable torture...'

She didn't believe that but the audience needed to be geed up. Each challenge had to have higher stakes than the last.

Her platform Bulls crunched smashed mirror. The rest of her ensemble was Stán but she insisted on practical, comfy boots. Her feet were seldom on camera. She knew better than to wear fashion shoes while hustling over uneven ground. The way *Crew Selection* was going, being able to run for her life was up there with smiling through disasters and always having something to say as a qualification for the gig.

By an open hatch was a folded deckchair and a smashed life-size puppet.

Someone was taking this broken doll theme too far. The puppet wore what was left of a green singlet which gave Eleanor a momentary abdab.

Was this what she'd been afraid of?

The Green Ninja couldn't hurt her now.

She saw one of its arms wasn't broken and stamped on it. The fresh break made a satisfying *snap*!

The puppet flopped up, as if trying to stand on shattered legs.

Its face was a wooden oval with a star stuck in it.

But the blank managed a fuming expression – as if all the more furious to find it had no mouth to scream out of.

A human face was imposed on the blank. Waves of stiff ringlets and pencilled-on eyebrows. The woman was very angry. And very insane. Her see-through body shrouded the shattered wire-and-wood skeleton. She wore the ghosts of old-fashioned clothes. A fur-trim jacket, jodhpurs and jackboots.

Eleanor was vindicated. She was not paranoid. There really was a Green Ninja.

She had proof!

The ruin stiffened and collapsed, more broken than before. Inanimate. The woman with the lacquered hairdo was evaporised. Discontinued. Gone.

Eleanor stuck a toecap at the remains. Nothing.

Problem solved. She trusted her pet fly-eye caught that.

She hadn't given out a foolish ninny yelp when the dummy came to life. She had stared the Green Ninja down as it gave up the ghost.

With the proper voice-over, it would be a victory.

Now what?

A man-sized shadow gathered nearby. Not a shadow cast on the glittery floor or the tent canvas. A freestanding shadow, like the silhouette in a CSO screen. The Green Ninja's Master? Eleanor didn't like to look at it for fear of being driven mad by its depths of dark but also didn't like to look away in case it pounced.

At the end of one shadow-arm was a white glove.

Not the classy kind but a big silly cartoon hand. Three lines on the back. Fingertips like spoons.

The glove pointed down at the hatch.

Eleanor wondered whether she should try to interview the shadowman (she supposed it was a man – it was a male dress glove). She'd ask who he was and what he was doing here but got the impression he was predisposed to being mysterious. She didn't see any mouth. The idea of a voice coming from the swirling absence gave her an extra helping of the horrors.

The glove bobbed, pointing more insistently.

The hatch led to steps. She heard a to-do of some sort going on under the arena.

Possibly a daring rescue she ought to be present at.

Maybe she'd even find Graill and his camera.

Not announcing herself, she went down the stairs.

MONICA MAUDE – HOSTAGE

'AFTER THE GUARDS RAN OFF, IT WAS BORING BEING A kidnap victim.

'Vidar suggested playing I Spy. He got no takers.

'The pretty fella wanted an explanation of Polly O's behaviour. He used words like "traitor" and "sneak". Which showed he wasn't Coterie. It's not done to ask for an explanation of Polly O. He was angry. We all were but it gets tiring. Only Mr Reynolds had the wind to stay furious for hours. He was gagged so we didn't have to pay attention to him.

'Garn Graill kept clicking. Artistic studies of us in cages.

'From where we were, we saw the wall of screens at awkward angles. No way of telling verit news from special effects. Moonlight Flit was in a scrap with a giant funfair freak. We supposed that was actually happening. Chell and Vidar bleated about how much they fancied the shining cloak. They were both Moon Worshippers but had never mentioned it to each other.

'I asked if anyone had seen Symon. No one had. The point of maiming a hostage was to show a cutthroat krewe meant business. Where was the visual of Symon hanging on a fence? Maybe he'd escaped or been let out. None of us could imagine how or why. Chell and Vidar said disappearing was typical Symon. No one minded when he was there or missed him when he wasn't.

'The pretty fella had another bent nail but couldn't reach the new padlock on his cage. Instead, he had the little girl with the frizzy hair back up against her bars and fiddled with the catch on her muzzle.

'That was legit clever.

'I asked him who he was and he said "Lamb Bear" which I suppose is "Lambert" with garlic. It gets complicated but he's the brother of that stuck-up friend of Chrissie's. The sword girl on that talent programme. The All-Powerful Jupiter Boy said "yuck" about the sister. Marcus bragged he'd voted for her over Chrissie to be the Splendid Sixth because of... reasons. Not wanting Chrissie to win, he meant. Also not wanting to vote for Hereward.

'The other muzzled brat was interested in Lambert's progress. His cage wasn't adjacent so he was left out. If tampered with wrongly, the muzzle shocked the girl. Fajajita or somesuch, though I don't think she's Mexican. Lambert said sorry and kept fiddling.

'Mr Reynolds shook his bars, forehead veins throbbing. The door of the next cage creaked open because the voids guarding us didn't check its lock wasn't rusted. However, Bruno Brookes was in that cage and he didn't feel like coming out. He piled more straw over his head.

'There was a sudden flare from the screens and the giant was on fire.

'"That was a moonburst," said Chell. "A finishing move Moonlight Flit saves till last."

'Then the rubbery double doors – like the hospital corridor ones you ram stretchers through – were pushed in. A couple of scrappers flew into the cage area.

'Yes, I said "flew". It was Chrissie – a transformed, cloud-of-darkness Chrissie. She was flying without a broomstick. She had hold of Lambert's sister. Maybe they weren't friends any more. It happens. They were in what looked like a tussle to the death. In a dark flash which left smoky stains on the floor tiles, Chrissie took the girl *somewhere else*. We still saw them, spinning inside a fishbowl of black water, but they weren't here. They were pictures on a screen. Or seen through distorting glass. Grot stuff. Horrible to look at.

'The All-Powerful Jupiter Boy screamed and wet himself.

'We knew Chrissie was dark enlightened. It wasn't until we saw her with blackness pouring out of her eyes that any of us understood what that meant.

'She wasn't a cloak – she was a monster, something else, a *whatever*.'

CHRISTINE IN THE PURPLE

THIS MUST BE WHAT IT WAS LIKE IN LOULEE'S Lantern.

Chrissie saw herself – a fury in black tatters – floating off the floor without the benefit of wings. Her fingers gripped Loulee's neck. A violet-fringed diamond doorway opened in mid-air and she pushed Loulee through it.

From the cages, people shouted.

Chrissie wanted to shout at herself.

Was she possessed by the Shade the way Loulee had been possessed by the Contessa? No, she was still here. But she was somewhere else too. Her essence was divided between the verit and the Purple.

She was *sending Loulee away*. The Purple pulled her too.

It was as if she'd tossed an anchor over the side without noticing her ankle was caught in the unrolling chain.

She had a lot of second thoughts.

Contessa Erco was out of it – she'd already fled Loulee's body, gone to where bad ghosts go. But Chrissie couldn't call a halt to the violent exorcism. The Purple was no place for a Ghost Lantern Girl.

Chrissie had got rid of the ghost but was losing the girl too. All she'd have left was the Lantern.

This was what had happened with Aunt Jasmine and Modred Murda.

This was what Modred Murda wanted to happen with her and Loulee.

She was to send her best friend away and be packed off after her… to wander wastelands forever, in silence and shadow. Dimly aware of what transpired – triple word score! – on the non-astral plane. But unable to do anything about it. Not optimal.

She loosened her grip on Loulee – still holding her but not throttling.

It might not be so bad here.

Except the diamond doorway didn't close behind them like a zip-up tent. The rip was a wound. Darkstuff leaked through like poison blood.

Murda wanted that.

Ruination in two realms.

Double grot. Rats!

ELEANOR ON THE SCENE

HOSTAGES SHRANK AGAINST THE FAR WALLS OF cages. Television screens *popped* like bursting eardrums. A tornado of black nothing whirled in the middle of the room. Hands or faces pushed out of the angry cloud then were sucked in again.

Chambers and Ling. The troublemakers. Making trouble.

Eleanor was here for that. Her fly-eye flew too near the maelstrom and fritzed.

But Garnet Graill had a camera. He was the one hostage not cowering.

'Get this on film,' she told him.

Her instinct was to shout as if over a thunderstorm but the whirlwind was silent. Her voice was too loud.

'Where are you?' asked Adrian Jah. 'You're missing the climax.'

'No I'm not,' she said into her throat mike. 'The action is here, while you're looking somewhere else. You can thank me later.'

Graill extended a long lens between the bars of his cage.

'I'll get this on film,' he said.

'Good idea,' she admitted.

That wasn't quite what she meant but there was no time to chew it over.

Others showed some curiosity. Ling's twin brother. Garter Snake's annoying father. The Whisk Kid, freed of restraints. That Ton o' Bricks bolus. Empty-eyed Bruno Brookes. Some translucent wraith in a Stán original. A furious vicky bloke. A shower of bedraggled voids in their glad rags. An audience.

'It's come to this,' Eleanor said. 'Christine Chambers and Louise Ling, best of friends, worst of enemies... Lady Shade and Arsinoë, scrapping for a prize neither might win... Which is cloak, which is cutthroat? Here, so close to rescue, what will befall the horrified hostages...'

'No one says "befall",' said Jah – who must at least be following this from his van.

'... have we come so far, only to...'

A hand – no, a *glove* – fell on her shoulder, fingertips icy.

Eleanor was shoved towards the shadow frenzy.

Don't become part of the story, she thought.

She saw the reflecting eye of Graill's lens, getting footage of her falling into a dark fissure...

CHRISTINE CHAMBERS – GIRL GUIDE

A THIRD PERSON ARRIVED IN THE PURPLE.

Where up was sideways and down was derry-derry...

Where darkness and decay and despair and doom held illimitable dominion over all and all and all...

Hello, Nelly!

Eleanor Wynter was scooped through the portal by the palm of a Kong-sized white glove. From inside the Purple, Modred Murda looked different. What had been absent was present but not in the shape he had started with.

He wasn't a tribute act any more. He was a headliner. Most of him was head. With arrow-tip quills of hair. Haunted tunnelmouth eyes. A maw with teeth like grinding rocks. All molars and no fangs.

Being partially *sent away* did this to him.

Being wholly sent away was liable to do worse to the new visitors.

Beyond the diamond wedge window, Ftatateeta moved very very slowly to release statue-still hostages from their cages.

The Whisk Kid was faster than the human eye.

From the Purple – where time was a stuck record stuttering 'yeh yeh yeh' for ever after – Ftatateeta's quickness registered as extreme slowth.

Check the dictionary. You're not getting a triple word score for slowth.

Chrissie wasn't holding Loulee any more. They were hearing each other's thoughts.

And both heard Nelly's wordless panic.

She didn't see Purple. She saw Green. Her nightmare green.

It was an out of this world thing. Overlapping minds. Another blooming hubbub.

So this was what Chrissie had done with her enlightened gifts.

Stuck them here on a different plane or planet. A how-low-can-you-go limbo.

Saying sorry wasn't going to be any comfort.

Now, the diamond portal was slimmer – more like a slit...

Ftatateeta took an age to break a lock by tapping it a thousand times between a tick and a tock... Or, from the Purple point of view, once every quarter of an hour.

Lamb Bear, the boy with Loulee's face, wore a mask of encouragement.

Chrissie, look at Nelly...

Eleanor Wynter wasn't taking to the Purple.

Around her were jagged cracks, vivid green. Her blazer piping burned like dull neon. Her fear infected this place. Made it Worse Than.

Chrissie knew why Modred Murda wanted Nelly here.

A new Lady Shade needed a new Nemesis.

There had always been something about Eleanor Wynter. She half-saw but didn't understand. Not quite enlightened, not quite dark. But different.

She saw the ghosts, thought Loulee.

That made her paranoid.

No, more paranoid.

Being a name and a face made her paranoid. Elevated enough to feel the Wheel turning under her. Not elevated enough for security.

Every Carlotta knows there's a Christine coming for her to take away everything she's scrapped and scrimped for.

Eh what?

She means the Christine in Phantom of the Opera, *not you... the chorus girl who replaces the bright light.*

Thank you, Encyclopaedia Loulitannica.

Modred Murda and the Mannikin and the Green Ninja had made Eleanor Wynter into the perfect Nemesis of Shade.

The Anti-Shade. Eleanor Edahs.

Nelly had been nudged, tormented and manipulated as much as Chrissie.

Though she'd still been a *năiniú* about it.

In the Purple, the scrap would go on till a' the seas gang dry. Cloak and cutthroat, dark and light, fine and dandy, Perky and Pinky, world without end, end without world...

Stop it, you're getting Rhymered.

This place did that. Look at Modred Murda.

What if they *didn't* scrap? Chrissie and Nelly? Christine and Carlotta?

What if they stopped competing like ants locking horns over crumbs scattered on the table by a boy with a magnifying glass who'd incinerate the winner anyway?

Modred Murda and the Mannikin were horrors. But what about the Vision Controller? Garn and his camera? The Shadow Cabinet? The viewers at home?

They would never have enough of Chrissie until she was not there at all. A slower, sneakier way of making her vanish. Maybe being *sent away* to the Purple gave her a perspective.

She knew what she wanted to be.

A Guide is honest, reliable and can be trusted.

A Guide is helpful and uses her time and abilities wisely.

A Guide faces challenges and learns from her experiences.

A Guide is a good friend and sister to all Guides.

A Guide is polite and considerate.

A Guide respects all living things and takes care of the world around her.

Pretty heavy from you, Chrissie. Normally, you can barely make it through the Floppit Hop...

A good friend and sister to all, Louls.

Hitting Nelly in the face over and over and over won't solve any problems...

... but might be fun.

Not helpful, Loulee.

Sorry, couldn't resist.

'Christine,' said Aunt Jasmine in her head, if clear as she had a great Vone signal. 'Stop being self-indulgent and bring your friends home this minute. You're a Shade. If you can reach the Purple you can come back.'

She looked around. No Aunt Jas.

'I'm still in the Safe House. I can see the Purple from here. Inside it's a continent. From here, it's a Christmas tree ornament. A bauble.'

The sand underfoot was what you got when black rain became snow.

They were close to an almost-buried sphinx.

Anyone you know? asked Loulee.

Modred Murda, revenge complete. Part of the landscape.

A screaming face outcrop in a desert of particulate gunpowder without a match to set it off. The end result of picking on someone who could pick back, long ago. At least he was all in the same place now.

'This isn't your fault,' Chrissie told her aunt.

'I know. It isn't anyone's. Except Malcolm's.'

Malcolm Sandys. The secret identity. The bitter, pitiful civ. No one special.

We still have the Eleanor Issue, thought Loulee.

According to the plan jotted down in Malcolm's Grudge Diary, Eleanor Wynter would become Nelly the Nemesis, arch-enemy of Lady Shade... Top Dog to her Urban Fox... The Cartoonist to her Quackanapes... Captain Hook to her Peter Pan... A flung flan to her face, over and over and over. A lifetime of this...

Which she could avoid by leaving Eleanor here.

All of Eleanor, not just a slice.

Do that and it'll be someone else. Lady Shade's original nemesis was Adam Tussaud... Modred Murda picked up the baton. There are a lot of Nelly's Nutters out there. Imagine what any of them would be like as a cutthroat.

'Thanks for the fortune cookie, Sparky.'

She'd have come round to that way of thinking on her own but Loulee thought of it first. That was Loulee.

The portal was only a crack, now.

Chrissie and Loulee each took one of Eleanor Wynter's arms and dragged their worst enemy through the slit back to...

... A room full of squabbling hostages.

Eleanor at a Loss for Words

What just happened?

Something green. Ghastly green.

Her earpiece was gabbling again.

Adrian Jah congratulated her on being where she was for the non-event of Lady Shade and Arsinoë arriving to rescue hostages who had already freed themselves... while missing the spectacular scrap in which Moonlight Flit and the other Sixths defeated the last of the New Broken Dolls.

She knew something more had happened.

Graill must have it on film.

A white glove was discarded on the floor, dusty and trampled. She thought about picking it up and putting it on.

Uck. No. Triple grot.

But...

She wasn't frightened any more. She was angry.

Chambers and Ling smiled smugly, relieved about something obscure, weirdly elated and weepy. They looked at her as if they expected thanks...

... which was an *insane* idea.

... or to be interviewed about their recent victory over... Who knows what they thought they'd beaten. The odds? She didn't think so.

She signalled Graill to get a two-shot of her and that quick pickpocket. The girl had got her muzzle off and used her swift fingers to break the cage locks. Intelligent application of an enlightenment.

'We're fortunate to have secured a few moments with the heroine of the hour... ah?...'

'Ftatateeta Sha'arawi,' said Adrian Jah, reading off a sheet.

'Whisk Kid.'

The little girl with the hair explosion couldn't stop fidgeting, which made her hands disappear to the naked eye.

'ThnkyvrymchNllyIcldnthvdntwthtLmbrtnGrld...'

Chambers and Ling laughed.

At her. At *Eleanor Wynter.*

This would not end well for them.

Loulee and the Hostages

Now she'd been to the Purple and inside the Lantern she appreciated having her feet back on the ground in the real world.

Nelly's face was a picture. The subtitling elves at Red-Tel might sort out Ftatateeta's fastspeak for broadcast but Eleanor Wynter was at a loss.

Who knew what she thought had just happened?

Or whether being *away* had changed her mind at all.

Subjectively, they'd been in the Purple for an extended afternoon... between taps of Ftatateeta's callused forefinger.

To everyone else, they were gone and back in a blink.

It would take major explaining. Which she'd do her best to get out of. Unless anyone asked, her policy going forward was to keep mum.

Lamb Bear was the last to be let out.

'Does this change your mind about animals in cages?' she asked.

'Our reptiles are kept in appropriate environments. As you well know.'

She thought of needling him more – it was fun...

... but hugged him instead.

One of the Coterites – Monica Maude – looked at them weirdly.

'Yes, we look alike, get over it...'

'His hair is long and your hair is short, but...' Monica said.

'... it comes out the same,' said Loulee and Lamb Bear at once.

That happened sometimes. Monica was spooked by it.

Weird. The silly bit had been held hostage by desperate cutthroats and shrugged it off as a typical night on the town but a twinny verbal tic set off her tingles. Oh well, they'd had a grot evening. She'd let the Coterie off a bollocking this once.

Everyone had to cope the best they could.

Tunno Bricks hid behind Asmida's dad. Both red-faced, for different reasons.

'Well done for being brave, Gerald,' Loulee said.

Straw flattened in cages. Only Loulee noticed.

Ftatateeta was bored with being interviewed and wanted to run off and see what was happening in the big top.

No one wanted to take off Geoff Reynolds' gag.

Loulee did anyway. She got few thanks.

Asmida's dad stalked off, rumbling that he expected considerable compensation for damage to his business and person.

Loulee looked at Chrissie, who shrugged.

She knew, she knew – what did she expect?

It had to be done. Besides, if Geoff wanted to give his daughter a piece of his fuming mind it was all right with Loulee. Garter Snake remained a menace who needed slapping.

Loulee wasn't a better person for all she'd been through.

Pity. Oh well.

But she had thoughts about her lantern and the ghosts. Being fully possessed by the Contessa gave her fresh perspective. She was going to make changes and set hard and fast rules.

The ghosts were on notice.

Everyone left the room with the cages. There was considerable mopping up activity in the fairground. The Coterie invented rumours of an After-Party.

'Sorry, Louls,' said Chrissie – who'd sent her to look after innocent bystanders just before the big scrap. 'I reckon we've missed the Circus.'

'I'm not fussed, really.'

'Thought not.'

She and Chrissie leant against each other, tired.

Garnet Graill leant in to get a click of the visual.

CARNABY STOKE – THE CLOAK BLOKE

'SO, WHO SAW THAT COMING?

'The winner is...

'Someone not really in the competition.

'Wait a minute – what?

'The public – bless 'em – was overwhelmingly for Moonlight Flit. There he was on telly, performing deeds of selfless heroism, enlightened chivalry and mighty bottom-kicking. Who wouldn't vote for that? Before Red-Tel could disqualify the established cloak, Martin Masters had a shining moon-seal on a contract. He'll be the Sixth Splendid and a credit to the side. You can't complain. In abilities, achievements and visual, the Flit is Fit. He makes the line-up stronger. If it comes to it, the Splendid Six can take on the Major League and not worry about Phoebe Rays. In a moon vs sun scrap, they cancel each other out. Rather a verit national hero than – sorry to say it – a *competition winner.*

'But who *is* Moonlight Flit?

'Most secret identities are a sham. A certain society milksop always runs off in a flap five minutes before the Green Knight rides in to the rescue... but we're all too flippin' polite to mention *cough cough* that the Hon. Anthony Herrald might *not* be a spineless jelly after all. Moonlight Flit, though, is a mystery.

We're compiling a list of colourless nobodies no one notices leaving the room just before the moon comes out.

'Meanwhile, *jai guru deva om* then... Glory to the Shining Remover of Darkness.

'With the rising of the moon, *Crew Selection* is stuck with a dud final episode. A long way second in the public vote comes Eunice Uglow, who still hasn't decided on a grown-up tradename. Pyro Pixie or the Little Match Girl won't do. If her management, the recently floated Lough-Luff & Associates, seal a promo deal, she could make her debut as Rosa Ronson. You heard it first on *Secret Identity,* cloaktailers. The Splendids magnanimously invented a Junior Side for Eunice. Her krewe includes her old chums the Whisk Kid – another non-runner who scraped more votes, it should be noted, than several official entrants – and the Flattener. I imagine Masters is having Dr Robot childproof a wing of the Tri-Lion for the Junior Side Clubhouse. Lough-Luff & Assocs have snapped up Ftatateeta Sha'arawi and Gerald Bone too.

'Asmida Reynolds earns more from her Peophole Purview and Personals Presence than any other Sixth. Garter Snake is this year's Boring Bosun. She'll be bright light of a steamy X-certificate revue at Soho's famous Windmill Theatre. *Secret Identity* has copped a front row comp at the premiere of *Slitherdance*. You'll find revealing clicks on this Purview you won't even see on the Smut Hutch. That's before the censors make us take them down, so dial early and dial often. We accept all forms of digi doughnut. Asmida tells us she has no plans for crime – committing or preventing – and will concentrate on the saucier side of the entertainment industry. Still, snakes shed skins all the time. She'll bear watching as much as she's watched bare.

'You can pick up Viper Strike merchandise at knock-down prices in flea markets and car-boots all over the country. Especially since British RoboDynamics recalled those action figures whose batteries explode if you yank both arms at the same time. Hereward Whatsis-Poshname hasn't been seen or heard from much since that last episode went out, though he made a public statement about volunteering for the Jupiter Mission. The statement being that he wasn't volunteering for the

Jupiter Mission. Whispers has it that Hereward is the '& Assocs' in Lough-Luff & Assocs. Which means he's fetching Milquik and mopping up spills as an unpaid intern. So long as his dad's firm doesn't provide Rosa Ronson with their patented deadly dodgy widgets...

'Weather Girl is out of hospital. Have you noticed it's rained less since she got better. We'll provide updates about the barrage of private prosecutions she is bringing. She could end up owning Rediffusion-Televersion.

'The other two – the makeweights – Christine Chambers and Louise Ling... who knows what's happened to them and who cares? Not I, sirrahs, not I...'

CHRISTINE AT THE SAFE HOUSE

'PLEASE TELL ME YOU'RE NOT GOING TO WEAR A GIRL Guide uniform and take a trade-name like Brown Owl Woman.'

Aunt Jasmine was trying to be understanding about Chrissie's New Direction.

But not quite managing it.

'Wilma Woggle,' suggested Loulee, who wasn't helping either.

At the mo, Chrissie wanted to take a gap year from her gap years.

She was still with the Schilling Agency, but not as a banner client. Dot blamed her for Tish's defection. Chrissie was a slightly tainted proposition. Red-Tel had expected her to do better than fourth or fifth (depending on whether you counted Moonlight Flipping Flit) in *Crew Selection*.

So there was that.

Loulee came third or fourth, after Eunice and Asmida. At least Chrissie beat Hereward, though it was close. Stupidly haring into that big scrap without armour turned out well for him. He looked better to viewers when he wasn't Viper Strike – though he only avoided being trampled by Upside-Down Swizzle because Garter Snake had a moment of telly-friendly altruism. Otherwise, a clown shoe the size of a bread van would have fish-pasted him. Weather Girl was left off the final tally. If a stack of last-minute votes from one post code in Devon were counted, she'd have taken second place. Alexandra Beach had devoted fans in the Met Office.

The Powers That Be at Red-Tel were in no hurry to find Chrissie anything to do. There might be a fill-in spot as Bin Brenda on *The Rubbish Quiz*. And a guest stint as an injured cloak – essentially, Weather Girl but younger and not infringing a trade-name – on *VIP Ward*.

She still needed industrial quantities of chocolate and chips.

This rest and recuperation spell at the cloaks' spa – arranged by the Shadow Cabinet – was a pause for reflection. They let Garn tag along. He agreed to leave his cameras behind – a massive positive for their relationship, though she suspected he'd sneaked something past Dr Lark. She'd never known him to wear cufflinks. The stones – garnets, of course – on this set occasionally clicked.

Loulee wasn't over the fact that their favourite Splendid was on staff. She was learning to swim in Mark Shark's zero-gee pool. Not a skill she'd bothered to pick up in London, despite there being a river running through the city and often finding herself mucking about near canals or docks. She'd designed her own costume and bathing cap. Mark Shark was more hilarious than expected. It took a while to realise what was so funny about him being funny. He was dry. As in droll.

Loulee didn't summon a channel-swimming ghost to crib from. She wanted to learn something on her own. 'I'd like to be good at something for more than a week,' she said. Chrissie could tell the ghosts weren't with Loulee as often – though they hadn't gone away altogether. The Lantern was in a cupboard nearby. Chrissie still hadn't seen it but was more convinced that it existed.

Aunt Jas reported to the Shadow Cabinet and came back with news about the GEIST satrapy behind the recent trouble. The Red Rope and the Cutting Commentator were in it. Plus that guard at Devil's Dyke who let William Wax out and – of all people – Anju the AD. With above the fold cutthroatery from Modred Murda and the Contessa as the Mannikin... Or was that the Mannikin as the Contessa? A bad lot. Either rounded up or disappeared or – in some cases – dead.

Chrissie still didn't see why Modred Murda picked on her.

'You don't see why anyone picks on anyone,' said Loulee. 'You're soft, you are.'

Possibly. She wouldn't change that, though.

The New Broken Dolls were in legal limbo, theoretically protected by their deal with *Crew Selection* but obviously guilty of much mischief not covered by any it's-just-a-game get-out clause. They were in Devil's Dyke or Wormwood Scrubs, except Ashton Dakin. Kung Fu Grip had signed with Red-Tel as bright light of *On the Run,* a series in which he evaded plods and vigilante cloaks. Viewers were invited to send in sighting reports or win prizes by assisting in his apprehension. Chrissie sort of hoped the programme ran for several series and Dakin never got caught. She had guilt twinges about traumatising the not-very-wicked throat. A reformation arc tugged the heartstrings. In the first episode, Dakin hid out in the ruins of Reynolds Goods Yard and bought a getaway motor from Asmida's dad. He detected and disabled the tracking device Geoff hid in the boot, beating the double-dealer out of a prize. Hosting *On the Run* was Lynne Lythgoe, who scored highly in audience research on the episodes of *Crew Selection* she'd popped in and out of. Another Christine for Carlottas everywhere to worry about.

Eleanor Wynter was back on *Letsby Avenue*. Jill di Ferrante was out of her coma with a new personality. Possessed by an entity intent on picking apart DI di's life piece by piece. Only Canteen Cathy knew someone else was driving Jill's body. Chrissie didn't think she'd enjoy the storyline. She was 75% convinced dismantling her life piece by piece was what New Nelly wanted to do to her.

Eleanor might no longer see green ninjas in every coal hole but her experiences at the Dogs and in the Purple hadn't been good for her mental health. She wasn't the same person she'd been before she *went away,* but she was no better.

Even if Nelly didn't become Chrissie's arch-nemesis, there were other candidates to worry about. Marcus Milner called himself Dr Something Else now. Not as in she couldn't remember his trade-name but as in the phone book listed him as 'Else, Dr Something'. If he had a gangcult, they'd be 'the Elsies'. Yes, it was stupid. But also sinister. Heaven only knew what Marcus had against her. Loulee said he was just an envious, spiteful little shit. Harsh, but fair.

Without a Vone, she didn't know whether she was in or out of the Coterie. They hadn't loved being kidnapped but clips of them in fetching distress set a trend. As soon as it got out that Polly O was (briefly) in a cage, every club in town put bars in their bars and straw on the floor. Hot Hostage kicked vicky boys and crocks out of the lifestyle columns. Natters sprung up about where to obtain quality handcuffs and gags. Lovely Rita recorded a themed covers album – 'Chains', 'Please Release Me', 'Help'. If Hot Hostage was what there was to go back to, Chrissie was chilly about a return to the Circuit.

Symon, of all people, sent her a nice letter (not a squirt or a blurt so it got delivered) thanking her for trying to rescue him and the others – which was odd since a) Ftatateeta did the technical work of freeing and b) she couldn't remember Symon being in the cage room after she came back from the Purple. Hey, she was befuddled and on a virtue high. Symon didn't stand out in any circumstances.

The same day, she got a note on shiny paper from Moonlight Flit. He invited her to a midnight feast at Derry & Toms Roof Garden. She told Garn to make him jealous. He got excited about the exclusive, saleable clicks he could get of Lady Shade and Mr Moon sharing a yin-and-yang black-and-white cocktail. She'd throw flashback sulks about that for a while yet.

Loulee magnanimously said Garn *might* have been joking.

He sold a lot of clicks of the Hackney Big Top Flip Flop to *Spectrum*. He had offers from Sunday supplements. *Real News* was dialling him too. He was going up on the Wheel.

Good for him. Provisionally.

Should she go for that midnight feast? She asked Loulee, who threw the question back to her. If she wanted to be in an eternal triangle, it was up to her and – by the way – was she absolutely sure Garnet Graill *wasn't* the secret identity of Moonlight Flit? That sort of thing had happened before.

It was a ridiculous idea, of course – Garn would have had to slip unnoticed out of a cage to fly Cyndi Doll into orbit then back again then out again to vanquish Upside-Down Swizzle then back again to be rescued. Could Moonlight Flit do that? He might be able to bilocate.

No, it wasn't worth thinking like that. On those grounds, anyone could be anyone. It was cheating.

Chrissie had another driving test booked for when she got back to London.

She was getting in miles of practice on the Dales, with Garn in the passenger seat of Aunt Jasmine's Mini Cooper not being too judgemental. He didn't make her calm, though – compelling evidence that he wasn't Moonlight Flit. She didn't know whether she was disappointed or not. It made her head spin and caused violet crackles. Sometimes she took lessons with the Hard Bard, who said things in an ancient language when Chrissie misused the clutch. Aunt Jas said Chrissie didn't want to know what they meant. Chrissie told her she was starting to understand anyway. Another instance of creeping Shadiness.

Whatever she did next, she was still enlightened.

She didn't fancy more scraps with cutthroats but the Shadow Cabinet wittered on about her responsibilities as a Shade. She kept thinking about the Guide Code.

A Guide is helpful and uses her time and abilities wisely.

A Guide is a good friend and sister to all Guides.

A Guide respects all living things and takes care of the world around her.

Nothing wrong with that. Enlightenment put her in a position to take all sorts of diabolical liberties. It was down to her to, well, be helpful and a good friend. That it was simple didn't make it easy. Which was the point, she supposed – drat it.

She was becoming more comfortable with Shadiness and all it entailed. Aunt Jas and Loulee noticed. Even Garn was getting the picture.

She was improving at what she could do.

When the sun went down, Chrissie felt the dark rise.

She heard music. Unreleased extra *Never Mind* tracks.

The sounds *transported* her. *Changed* her.

She hadn't told Loulee yet but she was flying outdoors now. Up in the sky. With the birds but avoiding the planes. It was Better Than Better Than.

Jyid. Gear. Aces. Peach.

She still didn't have a settled trade-name. It deffo wasn't going to be Glamour Girl.

Maybe she could get away with simple verit.
Call herself Christine.
Christine™. ©hristine.
Look... Up in the sky... It's a crow... It's Concorde... No, it's...
Christine. Just Christine. Whatever.

CODA: MISS KILL

'...THIS IS OUR NEW DIRECTOR OF THERAPY.'

As usual when she dropped in, Miss Kill had to catch up. A lecture was in progress.

The man talking was Sewell Head. She remembered him. Little bureaucrat.

'With Dr Chambers choosing not to return and Dr Dew on medical leave, Dr LaDacru has joined us. I've asked him to review treatment of all White Corridor patients.'

A partial explanation. Of things she had missed.

There would be more. There always were.

Head brought someone into her room. A man in black.

Long coat with high collar. Crimson cravat. Ebony winkle-picker shoes. Patent leather hair. Widow's peak. Fu Manchu stache. Piercing eyes. Visible cheekbones. Lips parted to show razor-teeth.

So, another one. Blood-drinker. Nosferatu. Vampyre.

That didn't bother her. She had another concern.

She had to seem like the woman people took her for. She did not want to give away her presence. She was at a disadvantage. She'd never met, seen or heard the person she must pretend to be. She only had clues to go on. Even keeping quiet and being watchful, a wise course when trying not to give herself away, could be a tell. This Persephone might be a chatterbox.

The first few times she'd snapped awake in this reality, she'd given herself away at once. People knew she wasn't their Persephone at once. Murdering witnesses didn't cover up her presence in a body which was her own but also not. In fact, it raised a fuss – brought attention. Landed her on the White Corridor.

Even when she didn't murder the first persons she saw, she was *known*.

The others on the White Corridor recognised her. They thought they had a lot in common with her. Though they'd murder her too. Scary Mary was keen not to cede her position as Most Dangerous Woman in Britain (*This* Britain) to an extra-continual trespasser. Staff were easier to gull – though the nightshade and the nosferatu knew her tells. The time they spent with Persephone gave them advantages. That they were absent was good news. An opening and an opportunity.

She'd spent more time here lately. Getting sharper. Fitting in. She could witter on about *The Archers* or *Horse & Hound*. She did well. Impersonating this Persephone. Staff always saw through her after a while. She knew she was rumbled when guards became very, very wary – eyes on her, hands on pain prods, within reach of panic buttons. She'd learn, though. Eventually, she'd be able to gull them all.

Maybe she'd be Miss Kill primarily – with only occasional, inconvenient visits from the other. There'd been a shift. Vibrations in the Purple. A cosmic wind blowing the other way.

'You can leave me with the patient, Dr Head,' said Dr LaDacru.

'I'll leave you with Persephone,' said the Director, mimicking LaDacru's intonation.

A spell of persuasion. Interesting.

The bureaucrat left, humming to himself. 'We Can Work It Out'. A hit here and her place. There were overlaps. Sometimes only little things – the face on a ten-shilling note, a little blue sachet of salt in a bag of plain crisps – gave away that she was far from where she started.

Miss Kill and Dr LaDacru were alone in Persephone's room. Cell.

Persephone had been – and Miss Kill still was – sitting at a table, looking down at a jigsaw of 'The Hay Wain'. Persephone had been filling in the sky. Miss Kill picked up a piece from a little group of cloudy pieces.

'She's left-handed,' said Dr LaDacru. 'You're not.'

That was news. It was how she'd been giving herself away.

She tried to put in a bit of cloud with her left hand and couldn't do it smoothly. Her wrist wouldn't work.

She could use knives ambidextrously. But not do a jigsaw.

'No need to pretend. You're who I've come to see.'

Nothing within reach could be used as a weapon. Unbreakable furniture was bolted to the floor. White Corridor inmates weren't allowed even plastic scissors or cutlery. This Persephone ate her semolina with a cardboard spoon. But Devil's Dyke couldn't – or at least hadn't – taken away her hands.

If Dr LaDacru was here to finish her, she'd finish him first.

She knew the lore. A stake through the heart.

If she punched his hankie pocket, she'd break ribs. Two more precise jabs and his own broken bones would pierce his heart.

In moments, he'd be dust on the floor.

Then she'd snort the red powder. Which would temporarily juice her up. As a semi-vamp, she could rip open locked doors. She could murder her way out of jail.

'Do not trouble yourself,' said Dr LaDacru. 'I'm not a turnkey or a policeman or a – what do they call it? – cloak. I'm picking up a side. I have need of certain specialisms. You are eminently qualified. I am a great fan of your work. Not just your achievements here on your appearances so far, but the great things you have done in your home continuum. I'm not from here, either. Or there, come to that. Where I'm from, those who wear black cloaks aren't admired. They're feared.'

She decided not to murder LaDacru.

'A terrible name, by the way,' she said. 'Do people not work it out in their heads? Or aren't you famous here?'

He clacked long, hard nails like castanets.

'It's a mental tic, like being right-handed,' he admitted. 'You – or the you who you were – do jigsaws. I – like many of my kind – do crosswords. Anagrams, cryptic clues, fill-in-the-blanks. An advance on counting sunflower seeds.'

He was distracted by the groups of jigsaw pieces this Persephone had made. Sky/clouds, water, trees/greenery. The cottage and the horse-drawn cart – the easy bits – were complete. And all the edges. LaDacru's scarlet tongue poked between his teeth. Some Nosferatu compulsion came over him. His hands flew like swift little bats. Bending over the table while looking upside-down at the picture, he pressed all the remaining pieces into place within seconds. That gave him satisfaction. He bit his lip slightly, giving himself a girlish red mouth.

'I've met a you before,' she told him. 'You – *he* – owe me money, for... Well, for services rendered.'

'I will assume my kinsman's debt.'

He put a leather pouch on the table. She undid a drawstring. It was full of gold teeth. Gleaming – licked clean.

'No pockets in these pyjamas,' she said. 'And they search. Daily.'

He took the pouch back. It disappeared under his black coat-skirts.

'I shall look after it for you. Persephone Gill shouldn't be here with the – as they call them – prize pupils. I have recommended a transfer. To the Lime Corridor. You understand?'

She did. It was like leaving the door open and keys in a car parked outside.

'We shall meet three nights from now. In a pub called Todd's, in Fleet Street. Do you know it?'

'I can find it.'

'Of course. In the meantime, consider these...'

He laid cards on the table, on top of the jigsaw. They were like king-size cigarette cards. Pictures of football players or pop singers, with names, statistics and biographical details on the back. But not football players or pop singers. Some faces she knew. Some she didn't. She memorised them all.

Louise Ling – Ghost Lantern Girl.

Symon Allott – Moonlight Flit.

Susan Rodway – Poltergirl.

Brixton Braden – Blackfist IV.

Harold Takahashi – Jun Zero.

Christine Chambers – 'Just Christine'.

Dr LaDacru took back the cards. Like a conjurer, he made

them disappear. He was showing full fang now. His eyes went the colour of his cravat.

'Your kill list?' she asked.

'Not at all,' he said, without conviction. 'Just individuals – enlightened individuals – of whom we must be wary. Your specialism may be necessary. Or uncalled for. It is as well to consider options. I'm remembered for my mastery of strategy.'

That wasn't what the LaDacru she knew was remembered for.

'So, what is your next stratagem... Count?'

'No need for that, Miss Kill. Call me Satrap. Welcome to GEIST.'

ABOUT THE AUTHOR

KIM NEWMAN is an award-winning writer, critic, journalist and broadcaster who lives in London. He is a contributing editor to the UK film magazine *Empire*, and writes its popular monthly segment, 'The Cult of Kim Newman'. He also writes for assorted publications including *Sight & Sound*, *The Dark Side* and *The Guardian*. He makes frequent appearances on radio and TV, and is the chief writer of the BBC TV series *Mark Kermode's Secrets of Cinema*.

He has won many awards, including the Bram Stoker®, International Horror Guild, Prix Ozone, British Fantasy and British Science Fiction Awards, and been nominated for the Hugo, World Fantasy, and James Herbert Awards. Kim also writes non-fiction books focused on popular culture, film, and television, including a comprehensive overview of the horror film industry, *Nightmare Movies* (Bloomsbury).

You can keep up to date with Kim's events and writing via his website johnnyalucard.com. Find him on Bluesky @annodracula.bsky.social.

ACKNOWLEDGEMENTS

Thanks, as always, to Cath Trechman, who uses her powers for good. Also: Alf and Bert (phantom editors of Power Comics), Dan Berlinka, Prano Bailey-Bond, David Barraclough, Robert Chandler, Simret Cheema-Innis, Kabriya Coghlan, Paul Cornell, Fenton Coulthurst, Andy Ryan, Paul Simpson, Natasha MacKenzie, Richard Mason, Meg Davis, Barry Forshaw, Antony Harwood, Sean Hogan, Rod Jones, Stephen Jones, Grace Ker, Nick and Vivian Landau, Paul McAuley, Paul McCaffrey (look for his *MAW* artwork online), Maura McHugh, Helen Mullane, Jerome Newman, Sasha Newman, Robert Shearman, Emily Smith, Tom Tunney, Matthew Turner. Oh, and the Beatles. Special thanks to Nahrein Mirza and Larry Wilson.

Praise for

MODEL ACTRESS WHATEVER

"Anarchic, exuberant and endlessly inventive.
This may be the best superhero movie I've ever read."
M.R. CAREY, internationally bestselling author of *Infinity Gate*

"Kim Newman's florid fantasies can't be pitched as a cross between this and that, they're an explosion of genre TNT in pop-art baubles of verbal delight that fizz on the page."
STEPHEN VOLK, writer of *Ghostwatch* and *The Good Unknown*

"Newman's trademarks are razor-sharp prose, a biting wit and big finishes you never see coming but always feel inevitably perfect – all of which are fully on display in *Model Actress Whatever.* This is a spectacular, alt-reality superhero story, almost operatic in its scale, and splendidly Newmanesque. Highly recommended."
ANGELA "A.G." SLATTER, award-winning author of *The Cold House*

"What if Austin Powers (only filmed by Brits) had a baby with *EastEnders* (also filmed by Brits), and it grew up to be a (British) version of the Adam West era Batman, driving a Jensen Interceptor?"
CHARLES STROSS, author of The Laundry Files series

"Set in an alternate history Enlightened by a magically mysterious Beatles' chord, *Model Actress Whatever* brings Newman's Diogenes Club series bang up to date and dives deep into the superhero mythos. Fast and furiously funny, exuberantly imaginative and achingly hip, this is Newman at the top of his game."
PAUL MCAULEY, author of *Loss Protocol*

"Somehow manages to be futuristic and nostalgic at the same time."
M.A. BENNETT, author of *No Escape*

"When it comes to the dazzling creation of a fantasy world which is both like and unlike our own, Kim Newman has no peers. This sardonically funny vision of empty celebrity and quirky superheroes set in an alternative London has all the untrammelled wordplay and inventiveness of his masterpiece *Anno Dracula.*"
BARRY FORSHAW, *Financial Times*

"With *Model Actress Whatever,* the always-transgressive Kim Newman subverts the superhero genre with all the aplomb that he brought to vampires in *Anno Dracula.*"
STEPHEN JONES, award-winning editor and writer

"The powerline connection between Michael Moorcock and the spangly multiverse lunacy of the present moment, this is an exciting, literary, urgent venture into what happens to super heroes as they cross the Atlantic, and why. Newman transcends pastiche and ends up telling the truth very loudly. Unmissable."
PAUL CORNELL, author of the Witches of Lychford series

Also by Kim Newman
and available from Titan Books:

Anno Dracula
Anno Dracula: The Bloody Red Baron
Anno Dracula: Dracula Cha Cha Cha
Anno Dracula: Johnny Alucard
Anno Dracula: One Thousand Monsters
Anno Dracula: Seven Days in Mayhem (graphic novel)
Anno Dracula 1899 and Other Stories
Anno Dracula 1999: Daikaiju

The Night Mayor
Bad Dreams
Jago
The Quorum
Life's Lottery
The Man From the Diogenes Club
Professor Moriarty: Hound of the D'Urbervilles
An English Ghost Story
A Christmas Ghost Story
Angels of Music
The Secrets of Drearcliff Grange School
The Haunting of Drearcliff Grange School
Something More Than Night

Video Dungeon (non-fiction)